THE BEST BRITISH SHORT STORIES OF 1922

EDITED BY

EDWARD J. O'BRIEN AND JOHN COURNOS

1st WORLD
LIBRARY
Literary Society

The Best British Short Stories of 1922

Edited By

EDWARD J. O'BRIEN AND JOHN COURNOS

© 1st World Library – Literary Society, 2004
PO Box 2211
Fairfield, IA 52556
www.1stworldlibrary.org
First Edition

LCCN: 2004195295

Softcover ISBN: 1-4218-0122-1
Hardcover ISBN: 1-4218-0022-5
eBook ISBN: 1-4218-0222-8

Purchase *"The Best British Short Stories of 1922"*
as a traditional bound book at:
www.1stWorldLibrary.org/purchase.asp?ISBN=1-4218-0122-1

1st World Library Literary Society is a nonprofit
organization dedicated to promoting literacy by:

- Creating a free internet library accessible from any computer worldwide.
- Hosting writing competitions and offering book publishing scholarships.

Readers interested in supporting literacy
through sponsorship, donations or
membership please contact:
literacy@1stworldlibrary.org
Check us out at: www.1stworldlibrary.ORG
and start downloading free ebooks today.

The Best British Short Stories of 1922
contributed by Tim, Ed & Rodney
in support of
1st World Library Literary Society

TO STACY AUMONIER

BY WAY OF ACKNOWLEDGEMENT

Grateful acknowledgement for permission to include the stories and other material in this volume is made to the following authors, editors, literary agents, and publishers:

To the Editor of *The Saturday Evening Post*, the Editor of *The Dial*, the Editor of *The Freeman*, the Editor of *The English Review*, the Editor of *The Century Magazine*, the Editor of *Harpers' Bazar*, the Editor of *The Ladies' Home Journal*, the Editor of *The Chicago Tribune* Syndicate Service, Alfred A. Knopf, The Golden Cockerel Press, B.W. Huebsch, The Talbot Press, Dodd, Mead and Co., Stacy Aumonier, J.D. Beresford, Algernon Blackwood, Harold Brighouse, William Caine, A.E. Coppard, Miss R.C. Lamburn, Walter de la Mare, Miss Dorothy Easton, Miss May Edginton, John Galsworthy, Alan Graham, Holloway Horn, Rowland Kenney, Miss Rosamond Langbridge, Mrs. Mary St. Leger Harrison, Mrs. J. Middleton Murry, Mrs. Elinor Mordaunt, Max Pemberton, Roland Pertwee, Miss May Sinclair, Sidney Southgate, Mrs. Geoffrey Holdsworth, Mrs. Basil Hargrave, and Hugh Walpole; to Curtis Brown, Ltd., as agent for Stacy Aumonier, May Edginton, Elinor Mordaunt, Roland Pertwee, and May Sinclair; to J.B. Pinker as agent for J.D. Beresford, Walter de la Mare, John Galsworthy, G.B. Stern, and Hugh Walpole; to A.P. Watt and Son as agent for Algernon Blackwood and Lucas Malet; to Andrew H. Dakers as agent for A.E. Coppard; to Cotterill and Cromb as agent for Alan Graham; and to Christy and Moore, Ltd., as agent for Holloway Horn.

Acknowledgements are specially due to *The Boston Evening Transcript* for permission to reprint the large body of material previously published in its pages. We ask pardon of any one whose rights we may have accidentally overlooked.

We shall be grateful to our readers for corrections, and particularly for suggestions leading to the wider usefulness of this annual volume. We shall particularly welcome the receipt from authors, editors, agents, and publishers, of stories printed during the year beginning July 1, 1922, which have qualities of distinction but yet are not published in periodicals falling under our regular notice. Such communications may be addressed to *Edward J. O'Brien, Forest Hill, Oxfordshire.*

E.J.O.

J.C.

CONTENTS

INTRODUCTION

When Edward J. O'Brien asked me to cooperate with him in choosing each year's best English short stories, to be published as a companion volume to his annual selection of the best American short stories, I had not realized that at the end of my arduous task, which has involved the reading of many hundreds of stories in the English magazines of an entire year, I should find myself asking the simple question: What is a short story?

I do not suppose that a hundred years ago such a question could have occurred to any one. Then all that a story was and could be was implied in the simple phrase: "Tell me a story...." We all know what that means. How many stories published today would stand this simple if final test of being told by word of mouth? I doubt whether fifty per cent would. Surely the universality of the printing press and the linotype machine have done something to alter the character of literature, just as the train and the telephone have done not a little to abolish polite correspondence. Most stories of today are to be read, not told. Hence great importance must be attached to the manner of writing; in some instances, the whole effect of a modern tale is dependent on the manner of presentation. Henry James is, possibly, an extreme example. Has any one ever attempted to tell a tale in the Henry James manner by word of mouth, even when the manner pretends to be conversational? I, for one, have yet to experience this pleasure, though I have listened to a good many able and experienced tale-tellers in my time.

Now, there is a great connection between the manner or method of a writer and the matter upon which he works his manner or method. Henry James was not an accident. Life, as he found it, was full of trivialities and polite surfaces; and a great deal of manner - style, if you like - is needful to give life and meaning to trivial things.

And James was, by no means, an isolated phenomenon. In Russia Chekhov was creating an artistic significance out of the uneventful lives of the petty bourgeoisie, whose hitherto small numbers had vastly increased with the advent of machinery and the industrialization of the country; as the villages became towns, the last vestiges of the "romantic" and "heroic" elements seemed to have departed from contemporary Russian literature. As widely divergent as the two writers were in their choice of materials and methods of expression, they yet met on common ground in their devotion to form, their painstaking perfecting of their expressions; and this tense effort alone was often enough the very life and soul of their adventure. They were like magicians creating marvels with the flimsiest of materials; they did not complain of the poverty of life, but as often as not created bricks without straw. Not for them Herman Melville's dictum, to be found in *Moby Dick*: "To produce a mighty book you must choose a mighty theme."

Roughly, then, there are two schools of creative literature, and round them there have grown up two schools of criticism. The one maintains that form is everything, that not only is perfect form essential, and interesting material non-essential, but that actually interesting material is a deterrent to perfect expression, inasmuch as material from life, inherently imaginative, fantastic or romantic, is likely to make an author lazy and negligent and cause him to throw his whole dependence on objective facts rather than on his ingenuity in creating an individual atmosphere and vibrant patterns of his own making. The other school maintains with equal emphasis that form is not enough, that it wants a real and exciting story, that where a man's materials are rich and "big" the necessity for perfection is obviated; indeed, "rough edges" are a virtue. As one English novelist tersely put it to me: "I don't care for the carving of orange pips. All I ask of a writer is that his stuff should be big." Undoubtedly, some people prefer a cultivated garden, others nature in all her wildness. Nature, it is true, may exercise no selection; unfortunately it is too often forgotten that she is all art in the wealth and minuteness of her detail.

It seems to me that both theories are equally fallacious. I do not see how either can be wholly satisfying. There is no reason at all why a story should not contain both form and matter, a form, I should say, suited to the matter. Among the painters Vermeer is admittedly perfect; has then Rembrandt no art? Among the writers Turgenev is perfect. George Moore has compared his perfection to that of the Greeks; is it then justifiable to call Dostoevsky journalese, as some have called him? Indeed, it takes a great artist to write about great things, though, it is true, a great artist is often pardoned for lapses in style, where a minor artist can afford no such lapses. It was in such a light, with the true honesty and humility of a fine artist, that Flaubert, than whom none sought greater perfection, regarded himself before the towering Shakespeare.

This preamble is no digression, but is quite pertinent to any consideration of the contemporary short story, for I must admit that however fallacious is either of the prevalent theories which I have outlined, in practice both work out with an appalling accuracy. Of the hundreds of stories which I have had to read the number possessing a sense of form is relatively small, and of these only a few are rich in content; strictly speaking, most of them stick to the facts of everyday life, to the intimate realities of urban and suburban existence. Other stories, and these are more numerous, possibly as a reaction and in response to the human craving for the fairy tale, are concerned with the most impossible adventure and fantastic unreality, Romance with the capital R. They are often attractive in plot, able in construction, happy in invention, and their general tendency may be to fall within the definition of "life's little ironies"; yet, in spite of these admirable qualifications, the majority of these stories are unconvincing, lacking in balance, in plausibility, in that virtue which may be defined as "the writer's imagination," whose lack is something more than careless writing. How often one puts down a story with the feeling that it would take little to make it a "rattling good tale," but alas, that little is everything. A story-teller's craft depends not only on a sense of style, that is, form and good writing, but also on the creation of an atmosphere, shall we say hypnotic in effect, and capable of persuading the reader that he is a temporary inhabitant of the world the writer is describing, however remote in time or space that world may be from the world of the reader's own experience. And the more enlightened and culturally emotional the reader, the greater the power of seduction is a writer called upon to exercise. For it is obvious that all these hundreds of crude Arabian Nights tales and jungle tales and all sorts of tales of impossible adventure appearing in the pages of our periodicals would not be written if they were not in demand by the large public.

The question arises: Why is it that authors who deal with the intimate realities of our dull, everyday life are, on the whole, so much better as writers than those who attempt to portray the more glamorous existence of the East, of the jungle, of, so to speak, other worlds? I have a theory of my own to offer in explanation, and it is this:

A, let us say, is a writer who has stayed at home. Let us suppose that his experience has been largely limited to London, or still more precisely, to the East End of London. He has either lived or spent a great deal of time here, and without having actively participated in the lives of the natives and denizens of the district has observed them to good purpose and saturated himself with their atmosphere. He has, in an intimate sense, secured not only his scene, but also, either actually or potentially, his characters. English - of a sort - is the language of his community; and the temper of this community, except in petty externals, is, after all, but little different from his own. He has lost no time in either travelling or in learning another's language, he has had a great deal of time for developing his technique. He has, indeed, spent the greater part of his time in working out his form. He is, as you may guess, anything but a superlative genius; certainly, we may venture to assume that he is, at all events, a fine talent, a careful observer, a painstaking worker, possessed of inventive powers within limitations. He knows his genre and his milieu, and he knows his job. He observes his people with an artistic sympathy. He is an etcher, loving his line, rather than a photographer. Vast mural decorations are beyond him.

Then there is *B*. *B* is a traveller, something of an adventurer too. His *wanderlust*, or possibly his occupation as a minor government official, journalist, or representative for some commercial firm, has taken him East. He has spent some time in Shanghai or Hong Kong, in Calcutta or Rangoon, in Tokyo or Nagasaki. He has lived chiefly in the foreign quarter and occasionally sallied out to seek adventure in the native habitat. He has secured a smattering of the native tongue, and has even taken unto himself a temporary native wife. A bold man, he has, in his way, lived dangerously and intensely. He has besides heard men of his own race living in the quarter tell weird tales of romantic nature, perhaps of a white girl who came out East, or of a native girl who had won the heart of an Englishman to his undoing. At last *B* has had enough of it, and has come home to the old country, his England, and sits down to his new job, the exploitation of his knowledge and experience of the East. Possibly a few friends who had listened to his tales urged him to set them down on paper, and *B*, who had not thought of it before, thinks it is not such a bad idea, and getting a supply of paper and a typewriter launches forth on a career as a writer. He is intent on turning out a good tale, and does remarkably well for a novice, but his inexperience as a writer, his lack of form and technique and deliberateness will hinder his progress, though now and then he will turn out a tolerable tale by sheer accident. The really great man will, of course, break through the double barrier, and then you have a

Conrad: that is to say, you have a man who has lived abundantly and has been able to apply an abundance of art to his abundance of material. But that is, indeed, rare nowadays, and the whole moral of the little parable of *A* and *B* is that in our own time it is given but to few men to do both. The one has specialized in writing, the other in living. And the comparison may be applied, of course, to the two writers who have stayed at home, even in the same district. *A* hasn't much to say, but what he says he says well, because writing means to him something as a thing in itself; he finds compensation in the quality of his writings for his lack of rich material; the whole content of his art is in his form, and that, if not wholly satisfying, is surely no mean achievement. *B*, on the other hand, may have a great deal to say, and says it badly. He thinks his material will carry him through. He does not understand that the function of art is to crystallize; synthesize the materials at hand, to distil the essences of life, to formalize natural shapes. There should be no confusing of nature and art. A mountain is nature, a pyramid is art. We have no man in the short story today who has synthesized his age, who has thrown a light on the peculiar many-sided adventure of modernity, who has achieved a sense of universality. Maupassant came near to it in his own time. Never before have men had such opportunities for knowing the world, never before has it been so easy to cover space, our means of communication have never been so rapid; yet there is an almost maddening contradiction in the fact that every man who writes is content in describing but a single facet of the great adventure of life. Our age is an age of specialization, and many a man spends a life in trying to visualize for us a fragment of existence in multitudinous variations. An Empire may be said to stand for a universalizing tendency, yet the extraordinary fact about the mass of English stories today is that, far from being expressive of any tendency to unity, they are mostly concerned with presenting the specialized atmospheres of so many individual localities and vocations. We have writers who do not go beyond Dartmoor, or Park Lane, or the East End of London; we have writers of sea stories, jungle stories, detective stories, lost jewel stories, slum stories, and we have writers who seldom stray from the cricket field or the prize ring, or Freudian complexes.

Yet, in putting on record these individual tendencies of the short story, I should be overdrawing the picture if I did not call attention to what general tendencies are in the ascendent. The supernatural element is prominent among these. Stories of ghosts, spiritualism and reincarnation are becoming increasingly popular with authors, especially with the type I have described as *A*. This is interesting, since it evinces a healthy desire to get away from the banal facts of one's standardized atmosphere, the atmosphere of suburbia. It may be both a reaction and an escape, and may express a desire for a more spiritual life than is vouchsafed us. The love of adventure and the love of love will, of course, remain with us as long as men live and love a tale, and nine tenths of the stories still deal with the favored hero and the inevitable girl.

This book is to be an annual venture and its object is the same as that of Mr. O'Brien's annual selection of American stories. It is to gather and save from obscurity every year those tales by English authors which are published in English and American periodicals and are worth preserving in permanent form. It is well known that short-story writers in

Edward J. O'Brien and John Cournos

Anglo-Saxon countries have not the same chance of publishing their wares in book form as their more fortunate colleagues, the novelists. This prejudice against the publication of short stories in book form is not to be justified, and it does not exist on the Continent. Most of the fine fiction, for example, published in Russia since Chekhov made the form popular, took precisely the form of the short story. It is a good form and should be encouraged. It is also the object of this volume to call attention to new writers who show promise and to help to create a demand for their work by publishing their efforts side by side with those already accepted and established.

It has been the custom to dedicate Mr. O'Brien's annual selection of American stories to some author who has distinguished himself in the particular year by his valuable contribution to the art of the short story. We propose to adopt it with regard to our English selections. We are glad of the opportunity to associate this year's collection with the name of Stacy Aumonier. As for the stories selected for this volume, that is to some degree a matter of personal judgement; it is quite possible that other editors would, in some instances, have made a different choice.

JOHN COURNOS.

An additional word may be added on the principles which have governed our choice. We have set ourselves the task of disengaging the essential human qualities in our contemporary fiction which, when chronicled conscientiously by our literary artists, may fairly be called a criticism of life. We are not at all interested in formulae, and organised criticism at its best would be nothing more than dead criticism, as all dogmatic interpretation of life is always dead. What has interested us, to the exclusion of other things, is the fresh living current which flows through the best British and Irish work, and the psychological and imaginative reality which writers have conferred upon it.

No substance is of importance in fiction, unless it is organic substance, that is to say, substance in which the pulse of life is beating. Inorganic fiction has been our curse in the past, and bids fair to remain so, unless we exercise much greater artistic discrimination than we display at present.

The present record covers the period from July, 1921, to June, 1922, inclusive. During this period we have sought to select from the stories published in British and American periodicals those stories by British and Irish authors which have rendered life imaginatively in organic substance and artistic form. Substance is something achieved by the artist in every act of creation, rather than something already present, and accordingly a fact or a group of facts in a story only attain substantial embodiment when the artist's power of compelling imaginative persuasion transforms them into a living truth. The first test of a short story, therefore, in any qualitative analysis is to report upon how vitally compelling the writer makes his selected facts or incidents. This test may be conveniently called the test of substance.

But a second test is necessary if the story is to take rank above other stories. The true artist will seek to shape this living substance into the most beautiful and satisfying form, by skillful selection and arrangement of his materials, and by the most direct and appealing presentation of it in portrayal and characterization.

The short stories which we have examined in this study have fallen naturally into three groups. The first consists of those stories which fail, in our opinion, to survive both the test of substance and the test of form. These we have not chronicled.

The second group includes such narratives as may lay convincing claim to further consideration, because each of them has survived in a measure both tests, the test of substance and the test of form. Stories included in this group are chronicled in the list which immediately follows the "Roll of Honour."

Finally we have recorded the names of a smaller group of stories which possess, we believe, the distinction of uniting genuine substance and artistic form in a closely woven pattern with such sincerity that they are worthy of being reprinted. If all of these stories were republished, they would not occupy more space than six or seven novels of average length. Our selection of them does not imply the critical belief that they are great stories. A year which produced one great story would be an exceptional one. It is simply to be taken as meaning that we have found the equivalent of six or seven volumes worthy of republication among all the stories published during the period under consideration. These stories are listed in the special "Roll of Honour." In compiling these lists we have permitted no personal preference or prejudice to consciously influence our judgement. The general and particular results of our study will be found explained and carefully detailed in the supplementary part of the volume. Mr. Cournos has read the English periodicals, and I have read the American periodicals. We have then compared our judgements.

EDWARD J. O'BRIEN.

WHERE WAS WYCH STREET?

By STACY AUMONIER

(From *The Strand Magazine* and
The Saturday Evening Post) 1921, 1922

In the public bar of the Wagtail, in Wapping, four men and a woman were drinking beer and discussing diseases. It was not a pretty subject, and the company was certainly not a handsome one. It was a dark November evening, and the dingy lighting of the bar seemed but to emphasize the bleak exterior. Drifts of fog and damp from without mingled with the smoke of shag. The sanded floor was kicked into a muddy morass not unlike the surface of the pavement. An old lady down the street had died from pneumonia the previous evening, and the event supplied a fruitful topic of conversation. The things that one could get! Everywhere were germs eager to destroy one. At any minute the symptoms might break out. And so - one foregathered in a cheerful spot amidst friends, and drank forgetfulness.

Prominent in this little group was Baldwin Meadows, a sallow-faced villain with battered features and prominent cheek-bones, his face cut and scarred by a hundred fights. Ex-seaman, ex-boxer, ex-fish-porter - indeed, to every one's knowledge, ex-everything. No one knew how he lived. By his side lurched an enormous coloured man who went by the name of Harry Jones. Grinning above a tankard sat a pimply-faced young man who was known as The Agent. Silver rings adorned his fingers. He had no other name, and most emphatically no address, but he "arranged things" for people, and appeared to thrive upon it in a scrambling, fugitive manner. The other two people were Mr. and Mrs. Dawes. Mr. Dawes was an entirely negative person, but Mrs. Dawes shone by virtue of a high, whining, insistent voice, keyed to within half a note of hysteria.

Then, at one point, the conversation suddenly took a peculiar turn. It came about through Mrs. Dawes mentioning that her aunt, who died from eating tinned lobster, used to work in a corset shop in Wych Street. When she said that, The Agent, whose right eye appeared to survey the ceiling, whilst his left eye looked over the other side of his tankard, remarked:

"Where was Wych Street, ma?"

"Lord!" exclaimed Mrs. Dawes. "Don't you know, dearie? You must be a young 'un, you must. Why, when I was a gal every one knew Wych Street. It was just down there where they built the Kingsway, like."

Baldwin Meadows cleared his throat, and said:

"Wych Street used to be a turnin' runnin' from Long Acre into Wellington Street."

"Oh, no, old boy," chipped in Mr. Dawes, who always treated the ex-man with great deference. "If you'll excuse me, Wych Street was a narrow lane at the back of the old Globe Theatre, that used to pass by the church."

"I know what I'm talkin' about," growled Meadows. Mrs. Dawes's high nasal whine broke in:

"Hi, Mr. Booth, you used ter know yer wye abaht. Where was Wych Street?"

Mr. Booth, the proprietor, was polishing a tap. He looked up.

"Wych Street? Yus, of course I knoo Wych Street. Used to go there with some of the boys - when I was Covent Garden way. It was at right angles to the Strand, just east of Wellington Street."

"No, it warn't. It were alongside the Strand, befcre yer come to Wellington Street."

The coloured man took no part in the discussion, one street and one city being alike to him, provided he could obtain the material comforts dear to his heart; but the others carried it on with a certain amount of acerbity.

Before any agreement had been arrived at three other men entered the bar. The quick eye of Meadows recognized them at once as three of what was known at that time as "The Gallows Ring." Every member of "The Gallows Ring" had done time, but they still carried on a lucrative industry devoted to blackmail, intimidation, shoplifting, and some of the clumsier recreations. Their leader, Ben Orming, had served seven years for bashing a Chinaman down at Rotherhithe.

"The Gallows Ring" was not popular in Wapping, for the reason that many of their depredations had been inflicted upon their own class. When Meadows and Harry Jones took it into their heads to do a little wild prancing they took the trouble to go up into the West-end. They considered "The Gallows Ring" an ungentle-manly set; nevertheless, they always treated them with a certain external deference - an unpleasant crowd to quarrel with.

Ben Orming ordered beer for the three of them, and they leant against the bar and whispered in sullen accents. Something had evidently miscarried with the Ring. Mrs. Dawes continued to whine above the general drone of the bar. Suddenly she said:

"Ben, you're a hot old devil, you are. We was just 'aving a discussion like. Where was Wych Street?"

Ben scowled at her, and she continued:

"Some sez it was one place, some sez it was another. I *know* where it was, 'cors my aunt what died from blood p'ison, after eatin' tinned lobster, used to work at a corset shop -"

"Yus," barked Ben, emphatically. "I know where Wych Street was - it was just sarth of the river, afore yer come to Waterloo Station."

It was then that the coloured man, who up to that point had taken no part in the discussion, thought fit to intervene.

"Nope. You's all wrong, cap'n. Wych Street were alongside de church, way over where the Strand takes a side-line up west."

Ben turned on him fiercely.

"What the blazes does a blanketty nigger know abaht it? I've told yer where Wych Street was."

"Yus, and I know where it was," interposed Meadows.

"Yer both wrong. Wych Street was a turning running from Long Acre into Wellington Street."

"I didn't ask yer what *you* thought," growled Ben.

"Well, I suppose I've a right to an opinion?"

"You always think you know everything, you do."

"You can just keep yer mouth shut."

"It 'ud take more'n you to shut it."

Mr. Booth thought it advisable at this juncture to bawl across the bar:

"Now, gentlemen, no quarrelling - please."

The affair might have been subsided at that point, but for Mrs. Dawes. Her emotions over the death of the old lady in the street had been so stirred that she had been, almost unconsciously, drinking too much gin. She suddenly screamed out:

"Don't you take no lip from 'im, Mr. Medders. The dirty, thieving devil, 'e always thinks 'e's goin' to come it over every one."

She stood up threateningly, and one of Ben's supporters gave her a gentle push backwards. In three minutes the bar was in a complete state of pandemonium. The three members of "The Gallows Ring" fought two men and a woman, for Mr. Dawes merely stood in a corner and screamed out:

"Don't! Don't!"

Mrs. Dawes stabbed the man who had pushed her through the wrist with a hatpin. Meadows and Ben Orming closed on each other and fought savagely with the naked fists. A lucky blow early in the encounter sent Meadows reeling against the wall, with blood streaming down his temple. Then the coloured man hurled a pewter tankard straight at Ben and it hit him on the knuckles. The pain maddened him to a frenzy. His other supporter had immediately got to grips with Harry Jones, and picked up one of the high stools and, seizing an opportunity, brought it down crash on to the coloured man's skull.

The whole affair was a matter of minutes. Mr. Booth was bawling out in the street. A whistle sounded. People were running in all directions.

"Beat it! Beat it for God's sake!" called the man who had been stabbed through the wrist. His face was very white, and he was obviously about to faint.

Ben and the other man, whose name was Toller, dashed to the door. On the pavement there was a confused scramble. Blows were struck indiscriminately. Two policemen appeared. One was laid *hors de combat* by a kick on the knee-cap from Toller. The two men fled into the darkness, followed by a hue-and-cry.

Born and bred in the locality, they took every advantage of their knowledge. They tacked through alleys and raced down dark mews, and clambered over walls. Fortunately for them, the people they passed, who might have tripped them up or aided in the pursuit, merely fled indoors. The people in Wapping are not always on the side of the pursuer. But the police held on. At last Ben and Toller slipped through the door of an empty house in Aztec Street barely ten yards ahead of their nearest pursuer. Blows rained on the door, but they slipped the bolts, and then fell panting to the floor. When Ben could speak, he said:

"If they cop us, it means swinging."

"Was the nigger done in?"

"I think so. But even if 'e wasn't, there was that other affair the night before last. The game's up."

The ground-floor rooms were shuttered and bolted, but they knew that the police would probably force the front door. At the back there was no escape, only a narrow stable yard, where lanterns were already flashing. The roof only extended thirty yards either way and the police would probably take possession of it. They made a round of the house, which was sketchily furnished. There was a loaf, a small piece of mutton, and a bottle of pickles, and - the most precious possession - three bottles of whisky. Each man drank half a glass of neat whisky; then Ben said: "We'll be able to keep 'em quiet for a bit, anyway," and he went and fetched an old twelve-bore gun and a case of cartridges. Toller was opposed to this last desperate resort, but Ben continued to murmur, "It means swinging, anyway."

And thus began the notorious siege of Aztec Street. It lasted three days and four nights. You may remember that, on forcing a panel of the front door, Sub-Inspector Wraithe, of the V Division, was shot through the chest. The police then tried other methods. A hose was brought into play without effect. Two policemen were killed and four wounded. The military was requisitioned. The street was picketed. Snipers occupied windows of the houses opposite. A distinguished member of the Cabinet drove down in a motor-car, and directed operations in a top-hat. It was the introduction of poison-gas which was the ultimate cause of the downfall of the citadel. The body of Ben Orming was never found, but that of Toller was discovered near the front door with a bullet through his heart. The medical officer to the Court pronounced that the man had been dead three days, but whether killed by a chance bullet from a sniper or whether killed deliberately by his fellow-criminal was never revealed. For when the end came Orming had apparently planned a final act of venom. It was known that in the basement a considerable quantity of petrol had been stored. The contents had probably been carefully distributed over the most inflammable materials in the top rooms. The fire broke out, as one witness described it, "almost like an explosion." Orming must have perished in this. The roof blazed up, and the sparks carried across the yard and started a stack of light timber in the annexe of Messrs. Morrel's piano-factory. The factory and two blocks of tenement buildings were burnt to the ground. The estimated cost of the destruction was one hundred and eighty thousand pounds. The casualties amounted to seven killed and fifteen wounded.

At the inquiry held under Chief Justice Pengammon various odd interesting facts were revealed. Mr.

Lowes-Parlby, the brilliant young K.C., distinguished himself by his searching cross-examination of many witnesses. At one point a certain Mrs. Dawes was put in the box.

"Now," said Mr. Lowes-Parlby, "I understand that on the evening in question, Mrs. Dawes, you, and the victims, and these other people who have been mentioned, were all seated in the public bar of the Wagtail, enjoying its no doubt excellent hospitality and indulging in a friendly discussion. Is that so?"

"Yes, sir."

"Now, will you tell his lordship what you were discussing?"

"Diseases, sir."

"Diseases! And did the argument become acrimonious?"

"Pardon?"

"Was there a serious dispute about diseases?"

"No, sir."

"Well, what was the subject of the dispute?"

"We was arguin' as to where Wych Street was, sir."

"What's that?" said his lordship.

"The witness states, my lord, that they were arguing as to where Wych Street was."

"Wych Street? Do you mean W-Y-C-H?"

"Yes, sir."

"You mean the narrow old street that used to run across the site of what is now the Gaiety Theatre?"

Mr. Lowes-Parlby smiled in his most charming manner.

"Yes, my lord, I believe the witness refers to the same street you mention, though, if I may be allowed to qualify your lordship's description of the locality, may I suggest that it was a little further east - at the side of the old Globe Theatre, which was adjacent to St. Martin's in the Strand? That is the street you were all arguing about, isn't it, Mrs. Dawes?"

"Well, sir, my aunt who died from eating tinned lobster used to work at a corset-shop. I ought to know."

His lordship ignored the witness. He turned to the counsel rather peevishly.

"Mr. Lowes-Parlby, when I was your age I used to pass through Wych Street every day of my life. I did so for nearly twelve years. I think it hardly necessary for you to contradict me."

The counsel bowed. It was not his place to dispute with a chief justice, although that chief justice be a hopeless old fool; but another eminent K.C., an elderly man with a tawny beard, rose in the body of the court, and said:

"If I may be allowed to interpose, your lordship, I also

spent a great deal of my youth passing through Wych Street. I have gone into the matter, comparing past and present ordnance survey maps. If I am not mistaken, the street the witness was referring to began near the hoarding at the entrance to Kingsway and ended at the back of what is now the Aldwych Theatre."

"Oh, no, Mr. Backer!" exclaimed Lowes-Parlby.

His lordship removed his glasses and snapped out:

"The matter is entirely irrelevant to the case."

It certainly was, but the brief passage-of-arms left an unpleasant tang of bitterness behind. It was observed that Mr. Lowes-Parlby never again quite got the prehensile grip upon his cross-examination that he had shown in his treatment of the earlier witnesses. The coloured man, Harry Jones, had died in hospital, but Mr. Booth, the proprietor of the Wagtail, Baldwin Meadows, Mr. Dawes, and the man who was stabbed in the wrist, all gave evidence of a rather nugatory character. Lowes-Parlby could do nothing with it. The findings of this Special Inquiry do not concern us. It is sufficient to say that the witnesses already mentioned all returned to Wapping. The man who had received the thrust of a hatpin through his wrist did not think it advisable to take any action against Mrs. Dawes. He was pleasantly relieved to find that he was only required as a witness of an abortive discussion.

*   *   *   *   *

In a few weeks' time the great Aztec Street siege remained only a romantic memory to the majority of Londoners. To Lowes-Parlby the little dispute with

Chief Justice Pengammon rankled unreasonably. It is annoying to be publicly snubbed for making a statement which you know to be absolutely true, and which you have even taken pains to verify. And Lowes-Parlby was a young man accustomed to score. He made a point of looking everything up, of being prepared for an adversary thoroughly. He liked to give the appearance of knowing everything. The brilliant career just ahead of him at times dazzled him. He was one of the darlings of the gods. Everything came to Lowes-Parlby. His father had distinguished himself at the bar before him, and had amassed a modest fortune. He was an only son. At Oxford he had carried off every possible degree. He was already being spoken of for very high political honours. But the most sparkling jewel in the crown of his successes was Lady Adela Charters, the daughter of Lord Vermeer, the Minister for Foreign Affairs. She was his *fiancée*, and it was considered the most brilliant match of the season. She was young and almost pretty, and Lord Vermeer was immensely wealthy and one of the most influential men in Great Britain. Such a combination was irresistible. There seemed to be nothing missing in the life of Francis Lowes-Parlby, K.C.

One of the most regular and absorbed spectators at the Aztec Street inquiry was old Stephen Garrit. Stephen Garrit held a unique but quite inconspicuous position in the legal world at that time. He was a friend of judges, a specialist at various abstruse legal rulings, a man of remarkable memory, and yet - an amateur. He had never taken sick, never eaten the requisite dinners, never passed an examination in his life; but the law of evidence was meat and drink to him. He passed his life in the Temple, where he had chambers. Some of the most eminent counsel in the world would take his opinion, or come to him for advice. He was very old, very silent, and very absorbed. He attended every meeting of the Aztec Street inquiry, but from beginning to end he never volunteered an opinion.

After the inquiry was over he went and visited an old friend at the London Survey Office. He spent two mornings examining maps. After that he spent two mornings pottering about the Strand, Kingsway, and Aldwych; then he worked out some careful calculations on a ruled chart. He entered the particulars in a little book which he kept for purposes of that kind, and then retired to his chambers to study other matters. But before doing so, he entered a little apophthegm in another book. It was apparently a book in which he intended to compile a summary of his legal experiences. The sentence ran:

"The basic trouble is that people make statements without sufficient data."

Old Stephen need not have appeared in this story at all, except for the fact that he was present at the dinner at Lord Vermeer's, where a rather deplorable incident occurred. And you must acknowledge that in the circumstances it is useful to have such a valuable and efficient witness.

Lord Vermeer was a competent, forceful man, a little quick-tempered and autocratic. He came from Lancashire, and before entering politics had made an enormous fortune out of borax, artificial manure, and starch.

It was a small dinner-party, with a motive behind it. His principal guest was Mr. Sandeman, the London agent of the Ameer of Bakkan. Lord Vermeer was very anxious to impress Mr. Sandeman and to be very friendly with him: the reasons will appear later. Mr. Sandeman was a self-confessed cosmopolitan. He spoke seven languages and professed to be equally at home in any capital in Europe. London had been his headquarters for over twenty years. Lord Vermeer also invited Mr. Arthur Toombs, a colleague in the Cabinet, his prospective son-in-law, Lowes-Parlby, K.C., James Trolley, a very tame Socialist M.P., and Sir Henry and Lady Breyd, the two latter being invited, not because Sir Henry was of any use, but because Lady Breyd was a pretty and brilliant woman who might amuse his principal guest. The sixth guest was Stephen Garrit.

The dinner was a great success. When the succession of courses eventually came to a stop, and the ladies had retired, Lord Vermeer conducted his male guests into another room for a ten minutes' smoke before rejoining them. It was then that the unfortunate incident occurred. There was no love lost between Lowes-Parlby and Mr. Sandeman. It is difficult to ascribe the real reason of their mutual animosity, but on the several occasions when they had met there had invariably passed a certain sardonic by-play. They were both clever, both comparatively young, each a little suspect and jealous of the other; moreover, it was said in some quarters that Mr. Sandeman had had intentions himself with regard to Lord Vermeer's daughter, that he had been on the point of a proposal when Lowes-Parlby had butted in and forestalled him. Mr. Sandeman had dined well, and he was in the mood to dazzle with a display of his varied knowledge and experiences. The conversation drifted from a discussion of the rival claims of great cities to the slow, inevitable removal of old landmarks. There had been a slightly acrimonious disagreement between Lowes-Parlby and Mr. Sandeman as to the claims of Budapest and Lisbon, and Mr. Sandeman had scored because he extracted from his rival a confession that, though he had spent two months in Budapest, he had only spent two days in Lisbon. Mr. Sandeman had lived for four years in either city. Lowes-Parlby changed the subject abruptly.

"Talking of landmarks," he said, "we had a queer point arise in that Aztec Street inquiry. The original dispute arose owing to a discussion between a crowd of people in a pub as to where Wych Street was."

"I remember," said Lord Vermeer. "A perfectly absurd discussion. Why, I should have thought that any man over forty would remember exactly where it was."

"Where would you say it was, sir?" asked Lowes-Parlby.

"Why to be sure, it ran from the corner of Chancery Lane and ended at the second turning after the Law Courts, going west."

Lowes-Parlby was about to reply, when Mr. Sandeman cleared his throat and said, in his supercilious, oily voice:

"Excuse me, my lord. I know my Paris, and Vienna, and Lisbon, every brick and stone, but I look upon London as my home. I know my London even better. I have a perfectly clear recollection of Wych Street. When I was a student I used to visit there to buy books. It ran parallel to New Oxford Street on the south side, just between it and Lincoln's Inn Fields."

There was something about this assertion that infuriated Lowes-Parlby. In the first place, it was so hopelessly wrong and so insufferably asserted. In the second place, he was already smarting under the indignity of being shown up about Lisbon. And then there suddenly flashed through his mind the wretched incident when he had been publicly snubbed by Justice Pengammon about the very same point; and he knew that he was right each time. Damn Wych Street! He turned on Mr. Sandeman.

"Oh, nonsense! You may know something about these - eastern cities; you certainly know nothing about London if you make a statement like that. Wych Street was a little further east of what is now the Gaiety Theatre. It used to run by the side of the old Globe Theatre, parallel to the Strand."

The dark moustache of Mr. Sandeman shot upwards, revealing a narrow line of yellow teeth. He uttered a sound that was a mingling of contempt and derision; then he drawled out:

"Really? How wonderful - to have such comprehensive knowledge!"

He laughed, and his small eyes fixed his rival. Lowes-Parlby flushed a deep red. He gulped down half a glass of port and muttered just above a whisper: "Damned impudence!" Then, in the rudest manner he could display, he turned his back deliberately on Sandeman and walked out of the room.

*   *   *   *   *

In the company of Adela he tried to forget the little

contretemps. The whole thing was so absurd - so utterly undignified. As though *he* didn't know! It was the little accumulation of pin-pricks all arising out of that one argument. The result had suddenly goaded him to - well, being rude, to say the least of it. It wasn't that Sandeman mattered. To the devil with Sandeman! But what would his future father-in-law think? He had never before given way to any show of ill-temper before him. He forced himself into a mood of rather fatuous jocularity. Adela was at her best in those moods. They would have lots of fun together in the days to come. Her almost pretty, not too clever face was dimpled with kittenish glee. Life was a tremendous rag to her. They were expecting Toccata, the famous opera-singer. She had been engaged at a very high fee to come on from Covent Garden. Mr. Sandeman was very fond of music. Adela was laughing, and discussing which was the most honourable position for the great Sandeman to occupy. There came to Lowes-Parlby a sudden abrupt misgiving. What sort of wife would this be to him when they were not just fooling? He immediately dismissed the curious, furtive little stab of doubt. The splendid proportions of the room calmed his senses. A huge bowl of dark red roses quickened his perceptions. His career.... The door opened. But it was not La Toccata. It was one of the household flunkies. Lowes-Parlby turned again to his inamorata.

"Excuse me, sir. His lordship says will you kindly go and see him in the library?"

Lowes-Parlby regarded the messenger, and his heart beat quickly. An uncontrollable presage of evil racked his nerve-centres. Something had gone wrong; and yet the whole thing was so absurd, trivial. In a crisis - well, he could always apologize. He smiled confidently at Adela, and said:

"Why, of course; with pleasure. Please excuse me, dear." He followed the impressive servant out of the room. His foot had barely touched the carpet of the library when he realized that his worst apprehensions were to be plumbed to the depths. For a moment he thought Lord Vermeer was alone, then he observed old Stephen Garrit, lying in an easy-chair in the corner like a piece of crumpled parchment. Lord Vermeer did not beat about the bush. When the door was closed, he bawled out, savagely:

"What the devil have you done?"

"Excuse me, sir. I'm afraid I don't understand. Is it Sandeman -?"

"Sandeman has gone."

"Oh, I'm sorry."

"Sorry! By God, I should think you might be sorry! You insulted him. My prospective son-in-law insulted him in my own house!"

"I'm awfully sorry. I didn't realize -"

"Realize! Sit down, and don't assume for one moment that you continue to be my prospective son-in-law. Your insult was a most intolerable piece of effrontery, not only to him, but to me."

"But I -"

"Listen to me. Do you know that the government were on the verge of concluding a most far-reaching treaty with that man? Do you know that the position was just touch-and-go? The concessions we were prepared to make would have cost the State thirty million pounds, and it would have been cheap. Do you hear that? It would have been cheap! Bakkan is one of the most vulnerable outposts of the Empire. It is a terrible danger-zone. If certain powers can usurp our authority - and, mark you, the whole blamed place is already riddled with this new pernicious doctrine - you know what I mean - before we know where we are the whole East will be in a blaze. India! My God! This contract we were negotiating would have countered this outward thrust. And you, you blockhead, you come here and insult the man upon whose word the whole thing depends."

"I really can't see, sir, how I should know all this."

"You can't see it! But, you fool, you seemed to go out of your way. You insulted him about the merest quibble - in my house!"

"He said he knew where Wych Street was. He was quite wrong. I corrected him."

"Wych Street! Wych Street be damned! If he said Wych Street was in the moon, you should have agreed with him. There was no call to act in the way you did. And you - you think of going into politics!"

The somewhat cynical inference of this remark went unnoticed. Lowes-Parlby was too unnerved. He mumbled:

"I'm very sorry."

"I don't want your sorrow. I want something more practical."

"What's that, sir?"

"You will drive straight to Mr. Sandeman's, find him, and apologize. Tell him you find that he was right about Wych Street after all. If you can't find him to-night, you must find him to-morrow morning. I give you till midday to-morrow. If by that time you have not offered a handsome apology to Mr. Sandeman, you do not enter this house again, you do not see my daughter again. Moreover, all the power I possess will be devoted to hounding you out of that profession you have dishonoured. Now you can go."

Dazed and shaken, Lowes-Parlby drove back to his flat at Knightsbridge. Before acting he must have time to think. Lord Vermeer had given him till to-morrow midday. Any apologizing that was done should be done after a night's reflection. The fundamental purposes of his being were to be tested. He knew that. He was at a great crossing. Some deep instinct within him was grossly outraged. Is it that a point comes when success demands that a man shall sell his soul? It was all so absurdly trivial - a mere argument about the position of a street that had ceased to exist. As Lord Vermeer said, what did it matter about Wych Street?

Of course he should apologize. It would hurt horribly to do so, but would a man sacrifice everything on account of some footling argument about a street?

In his own rooms, Lowes-Parlby put on a dressing-gown, and, lighting a pipe, he sat before the fire. He would have given anything for companionship at such a moment - the right companionship. How lovely it would be to have - a woman, just the right woman, to talk this all over with; some one who understood and sympathized. A sudden vision came to him of Adela's face grinning about the prospective visit of La Toccata, and again the low voice of misgiving whispered in his ears. Would Adela be - just the right woman? In very truth, did he really love Adela? Or was it all - a rag? Was life a rag - a game played by lawyers, politicians, and people?

The fire burned low, but still he continued to sit thinking, his mind principally occupied with the dazzling visions of the future. It was past midnight when he suddenly muttered a low "Damn!" and walked to the bureau. He took up a pen and wrote:

"*Dear Mr. Sandeman,* - I must apologize for acting so rudely to you last night. It was quite unpardonable of me, especially as I since find, on going into the matter, that you were quite right about the position of Wych Street. I can't think how I made the mistake. Please forgive me.

"Yours cordially,

"FRANCIS LOWES-PARLBY."

Having written this, he sighed and went to bed. One might have imagined at that point that the matter was finished. But there are certain little greedy demons of conscience that require a lot of stilling, and they kept Lowes-Parlby awake more than half the night. He kept on repeating to himself, "It's all positively absurd!" But the little greedy demons pranced around the bed, and they began to group things into two definite issues. On the one side, the great appearances; on the other, something at the back of it all, something deep, fundamental, something that could only be expressed by one word - truth. If he had *really* loved Adela - if he weren't so absolutely certain that Sandeman was wrong and he was right - why should he have to say that Wych Street was where it wasn't? "Isn't there, after all," said one of the little demons, "something which makes for greater happiness than success? Confess this, and we'll let you sleep."

Perhaps that is one of the most potent weapons the little demons possess. However full our lives may be, we ever long for moments of tranquillity. And conscience holds before our eyes some mirror of an ultimate tranquillity. Lowes-Parlby was certainly not himself. The gay, debonair, and brilliant egoist was tortured, and tortured almost beyond control; and it had all apparently risen through the ridiculous discussion about a street. At a quarter past three in the morning he arose from his bed with a groan, and, going into the other room, he tore the letter to Mr. Sandeman to pieces.

Three weeks later old Stephen Garrit was lunching with the Lord Chief Justice. They were old friends, and they never found it incumbent to be very conversational. The lunch was an excellent, but frugal, meal. They both ate slowly and thoughtfully, and their drink was water. It was not till they reached the dessert stage that his lordship indulged in any very informative comment, and then he recounted to Stephen the details of a recent case in which he considered that the presiding judge had, by an unprecedented paralogy, misinterpreted the law of evidence. Stephen listened with absorbed attention. He took two cob-nuts from the silver dish, and turned them over meditatively, without cracking them. When his lordship had completely stated his opinion and peeled a pear, Stephen mumbled:

"I have been impressed, very impressed indeed. Even in my own field of - limited observation - the opinion of an outsider, you may say - so often it happens - the trouble caused by an affirmation without sufficiently established data. I have seen lives lost, ruin brought about, endless suffering. Only last week, a young man - a brilliant career - almost shattered. People make statements without -"

He put the nuts back on the dish, and then, in an apparently irrelevant manner, he said abruptly:

"Do you remember Wych Street, my lord?"

The Lord Chief justice grunted.

"Wych Street! Of course I do."

"Where would you say it was, my lord?"

"Why, here, of course."

His lordship took a pencil from his pocket and sketched a plan on the tablecloth.

"It used to run from there to here."

Stephen adjusted his glasses and carefully examined

the plan. He took a long time to do this, and when he had finished his hand instinctively went towards a breast pocket where he kept a note-book with little squared pages. Then he stopped and sighed. After all, why argue with the law? The law was like that - an excellent thing, not infallible, of course (even the plan of the Lord Chief justice was a quarter of a mile out), but still an excellent, a wonderful thing. He examined the bony knuckles of his hands and yawned slightly.

"Do you remember it?" said the Lord Chief justice.

Stephen nodded sagely, and his voice seemed to come from a long way off:

"Yes, I remember it, my lord. It was a melancholy little street."

THE LOOKING GLASS

By J.D. BERESFORD

(From *The Cornhill Magazine*) 1921, 1922

This was the first communication that had come from her aunt in Rachel's lifetime.

"I think your aunt has forgiven me, at last," her father said as he passed the letter across the table.

Rachel looked first at the signature. It seemed strange to see her own name there. It was as if her individuality, her very identity, was impugned by the fact that there should be two Rachel Deanes. Moreover there was a likeness between her aunt's autograph and her own, a characteristic turn in the looping of the letters, a hint of the same decisiveness and precision. If Rachel had been educated fifty years earlier, she might have written her name in just that manner.

"You're very like her in some ways," her father said, as she still stared at the signature.

Rachel's eyelids drooped and her expression indicated a faint, suppressed intolerance of her father's remark. He said the same things so often, and in so precisely the same tone, that she had formed a habit of automatically rejecting the truth of certain of his statements. He had always appeared to her as senile. He had been over fifty when she was born, and ever since she could remember she had doubted the correctness of his information. She was, she had often told herself, "a born sceptic; an ultra-modern." She had a certain veneration for the more distant past, but none for her father's period. "Victorianism" was to her a term of abuse. She had long since condemned alike the ethic and the aesthetic of the nineteenth century as represented by her father's opinions; so, that, even now, when his familiar comment coincided so queerly with her own thought, she instinctively disbelieved him. Yet, as always, she was gentle in her answer. She condescended from the heights of her youth and vigour to pity him.

"I should think you must almost have forgotten what Aunt Rachel was like, dear," she said. "How many years is it since you've seen her?"

"More than forty; more than forty," her father said, ruminating profoundly. "We disagreed, we invariably disagreed. Rachel always prided herself on being so modern. She read Huxley and Darwin and things like that. Altogether beyond me, I admit. Still, it seems to me that the old truths have endured, and will - in spite of all - in spite of all."

Rachel straightened her shoulders and lifted her head; there was disdain in her face, but none in her voice as she replied:

"And so it seems that she wants to see me."

She was excited at the thought of meeting this

traditional, this almost mythical aunt whom she had so often heard about. Sometimes she had wondered if the personality of this remarkable relative had not been a figment of her father's imagination, long pondered, and reconstructed out of half-forgotten material. But this letter of hers that now lay on the breakfast table was admirable in character. There was something of condescension and intolerance expressed in the very restraint of its tone. She had written a kindly letter, but the kindliness had an air of pity. It was all consistent enough with what her father had told her.

Mr. Deane came out of his reminiscences with a sigh.

"Yes, yes; she wants to see you, my dear," he said. "I think you had better accept this invitation to stay with her. She - she is rich, almost wealthy; and I, as you know, have practically nothing to leave you - practically nothing. If she took a fancy to you...."

He sighed again, and Rachel knew that for the hundredth time he was regretting his own past weakness. He had been so foolish in money matters, frittering away his once considerable capital in aimless speculations. He and his sister had shared equally under their father's will, but while he had been at last compelled to sink the greater part of what was left to him in an annuity, she had probably increased her original inheritance.

"I'll certainly go, if you can spare me for a whole fortnight," Rachel said. "I'm all curiosity to see this remarkable aunt. By the way, how old is she?"

"There were only fifteen months between us," Mr. Deane said, "so she must be, - dear me, yes; - she must be seventy-three. Dear, dear. Fancy Rachel being seventy-three! I always think of her as being about your age. It seems so absurd to think of her as *old*...."

He continued his reflections, but Rachel was not listening. He was asking for the understanding of the young; quite unaware of his senility, reaching out over half a century to try to touch the comprehension and sympathy of his daughter. But she was already bent on her own adventure, looking forward eagerly to a visit to London that promised delights other than the inspection of the mysterious, traditional aunt whom she had so long known by report.

For this invitation had come very aptly. Rachel pondered that, later in the morning, with a glow of ecstatic resignation to her charming fate. She found the guiding hand of a romantic inevitability in the fact that she and Adrian Flemming were to meet so soon. It had seemed so unlikely that they would see each other again for many months. They had only met three times; but they *knew*, although their friendship had been too green for either of them to admit the knowledge before he had gone back to town. He had, indeed, hinted far more in his two letters than he had ever dared to say. He was sensitive, he lacked self-confidence; but Rachel adored him for just those failings she criticised so hardly in her father. She took out her letters and re-read them, thrilling with the realisation that in her answer she would have such a perfectly amazing surprise for him. She would refer to it quite casually, somewhere near the end. She would write: "By the way, it's just possible that we may meet again before long as I am going to stay with my aunt, Miss Deane, in Tavistock Square." He would understand all that lay behind such an apparently careless reference, for she had told him that she "never went to London," had only once in her life ever been there.

She was in her own room, and she stood, now, before the cheval glass and studied herself; raising her chin and slightly pursing her lips, staring superciliously at her own image under half-lowered eyelids. Candidly, she admired herself; but she could not help that assumption of a disdainful criticism. It seemed to give her confidence in her own integrity; hiding that annoying shadow of doubt which sometimes fell upon her when she caught sight of her reflection by chance and unexpectedly.

But no thought of doubt flawed her satisfaction this morning. A sense of power came to her, a tranquil realisation that she could charm Adrian as she would. With a graceful, habitual gesture she put up her hand and lightly touched her cheek with a soft, caressing movement of her finger-tips.

II

The elderly parlour-maid showed Rachel straight to her bedroom when she arrived at Tavistock Square, indicating on the way the extensive-looking first-floor drawing-room, in which tea and her first sight of the wonderful aunt would await Rachel in half an hour. She had been eager and excited. The air and promise of London had thrilled her, but she found some influence in the atmosphere of the big house that was vaguely repellent, almost sinister.

Her bedroom was expensively furnished and beautifully kept; some of the pieces were, she supposed, genuine antiques, perhaps immensely valuable. But how could she ever feel at home there? She was hampered by the necessity for moving circumspectly among this aged delicate stuff; so wonderfully preserved and yet surely fragile and decrepit at the heart. That spindling escritoire, for instance, and that mincing Louis Quinze settee, ought to be taking their well-earned leisure in some museum. It would be indecent to write at the one or sit on the other. They were relics of the past, foolishly pretending an ability for service when their life had been sapped by dry-rot and their original functions outlived.

"Well, if ever I have a house of my own," Rachel thought regarding these ancient splendours, "I'll furnish it with something I shan't be afraid of."

With a gesture of dismissal she turned and looked out of the window. From the square came the sounds of a motor drawing up at a neighbouring house; she heard the throbbing of the engine, the slam of the door, and

Edward J. O'Brien and John Cournos

then the strong, sonorous tones of a man's voice. That was her proper *milieu*, she reflected, among the strong vital things. Even after twenty minutes in that bedroom she had begun to feel enervated, as if she herself were also beginning to suffer from dry-rot....

She was anxious and uneasy as she went slowly downstairs to the drawing-room. Her anticipations of this meeting with her intimidating, wealthy aunt had changed within the last half-hour. Her first idea of Miss Deane had been of a robust, stout woman, frank in her speech and inclined to be very critical of the newly found niece whom she had chosen to inspect. Now, she was prepared rather to expect a fragile, rather querulous old lady, older even than her years; an aunt to be talked to in a lowered voice and treated with the same delicate care that must be extended to her furniture.

Rachel paused with her hand on the drawing-room door, and sighed at the thought of all the repressions and nervous strains that this visit might have in store for her.

She entered the room almost on tiptoe, and then stood stock-still, suddenly shocked and bewildered with surprise. Whatever she had expected, it was not this. For a moment she was unable to believe that the sprightly, painted and bedizened figure before her could possibly be that of her aunt. Her head was crowned with an exuberant brown wig, her heavy eyebrows were grotesquely blackened, her hollow cheeks stiff with powder, her lips brightened to a fantastic scarlet. And she was posed there, standing before the tea-table with her head a little back, looking at her niece with a tolerant condescension, with the air of a superb young beauty, self-conscious and proud of her charms.

"Hm! So you're my semi-mythical niece," she said, putting up her lorgnette. "I'm glad at any rate to find that you're not, after all, a fabulous creature." She spoke in a high, rather thin voice that produced an effect of effort, as if she were playing on the top octave of a flute.

Rachel had never in her life felt so gauche and awkward.

"Yes - I - you know, aunt, I had begun to wonder if you were not fabulous, too," she tried, desperately anxious to seem at ease. She was afraid to look at that, to her, grotesque figure, afraid to show by some unconscious reflex her dislike for its ugliness. As she took the bony, ring-bedecked hand that was held out to her, she kept her eyes away from her aunt's face.

Miss Deane, however, would not permit that evasion.

"Hold your head up, my dear, I want to look at you," she said, and when Rachel reluctantly obeyed, continued, "Yes, you're more like my father than your own, which means that you're like me, for I took after him, too, so every one said."

Rachel drew in her breath with a little gasp. Was it possible that her aunt could imagine for one instant that there was any likeness between them?

"Our - our names are the same," she said nervously.

Miss Deane nodded. "There's more in it than that," she

said with a touch of complacence; "and there's no reason why there shouldn't be. It's good Mendelism that you should take after an aunt rather than either of your parents."

"And you really think that we are alike?" Rachel asked feebly, looking in vain for any sign of a quizzical humour in her aunt's face.

Miss Deane looked down under her half-lowered eyelids with a proud air of tolerance. "Ah, well, a little without doubt," she said, as though the advantages of the difference were on her own side. "Now sit down and have your tea, my dear."

Rachel obeyed with a vague wonder in her mind as to why that look of tolerance should be so familiar. It seemed to her as if it was something she had felt rather than seen; and as tea progressed she found herself half furtively studying the raddled ugliness of her aunt's face in the search for possible relics of a beautiful youth.

"Ah, I think you're beginning to see it, too," Miss Deane said, marking her niece's scrutiny. "It grows on one, doesn't it?"

Rachel shivered slightly. "Yes, it does," she said experimentally, watching her aunt's face for some indication of a malicious teasing humour. It seemed to her so incredible that this hideous parody of her own youth could honestly believe that any physical likeness *still* existed.

Miss Deane, however, was faintly simpering. "I have been told that I've changed very little," she said; and

Rachel suppressed a sigh of impatience at the reflection that she was expected to play up to this absurd fantasy.

"Of course, I can't judge of that," she said, "as we met for the first time five minutes ago."

"No, no, you can't judge of *that*," her aunt replied, with the half-bashful emphasis of one who awaits a compliment.

Rachel decided to plunge. "But you do look extraordinarily young for your age still," she lied desperately.

Miss Deane straightened her back and toyed with a teaspoon. "I have always taken great care of myself," she said.

Unquestionably she believed it, Rachel decided. This was no pose, but a horrible piece of self-deception. This raddled, repulsive creature had actually persuaded herself into the delusion that she still had the appearance of a young girl. Heaven help her if that delusion were ever shattered!

Yet outside this one obsession Miss Deane, as Rachel soon discovered, had a clear and well-balanced mind. For, now that she had received her desired assurance from this new quarter, she began to talk of other things. Her boasted "modernism," it is true, had a smack of the stiff, broadcloth savour of the eighties, but she had a point of view that coincided far more nearly with Rachel's own than did that of her father. Her aunt, at least, had outlived the worst superstitions and inanities of the mid-Victorians.

Indeed, by the time tea was finished Rachel's spirits were beginning to revive. She would have to be very careful in her treatment of her aunt, but on the whole it would not perhaps be so bad; and presently she would see Adrian again. She would almost certainly get a letter from him by the last post, making some appointment to meet her, and after that she would introduce him to Miss Deane. She had a feeling that Miss Deane would not raise any objection; that she might even welcome the visit of a young man to her house.

The time was passing so easily that Rachel was surprised when she heard the gong sound.

"Does that mean it's time to dress already?" she asked.

Miss Deane nodded. "You've an hour before dinner," she said, "but I'll go up now. I like to be leisurely over my toilet."

She rose as she spoke, but as she crossed the room, she paused with what seemed to be a little jerk of surprise as she caught sight of her own reflection in a tall mirror above one of the gilt-legged console tables against the wall. Then she deliberately stopped, turned and surveyed herself, half contemptuously, under lowered eyelids, with a set of her head and back that belied plainly enough the pout of her critical lips. And having admired that haggard image, she lifted her wasted hand and delicately touched her whitened, hollow cheeks with the tips of her heavily jewelled fingers.

Rachel stared in horror. It seemed to her just then as if the reflection of her aunt in the mirror was indeed that of herself grown instantly and mysteriously old. For now, whether because the reversal of the image by the mirror or because of that perfect duplication of her own characteristic pose and gesture, the likeness had flashed out clear and unmistakable. She saw that her father had been right. Once, incalculable ages ago, this repulsive old woman might have been very like herself.

She slipped quickly out of the room and ran upstairs. She felt that she must instantly put that question to the test; search herself for the signs of coming age as she had so recently searched her aunt's face for the indications of her former youth.

But when, with an effect of challenge, she scrutinised her reflection in the tall cheval glass, the likeness appeared to have vanished. She saw her head thrust a little forward, her arms stiff, and in her whole pose an air of vigorous defiance. She was prepared to admit that she was ugly at that moment, if the ugliness was of another kind than that she had seen downstairs. No! She drew herself up, more than a little relieved by the result of her test. The likeness was all a fancy, the result of suggestions, first by her father and then by Miss Deane herself. And she need at least have no fear that she was ugly. Why....

She paused suddenly, and the light died out of her face. Her image was looking back at her stiffly, superciliously, with, so it seemed to her, the contemptible simper of one who still fatuously admires the thing that has long since lost its charm. She caught her breath and clenched her hands, drawing down her rather heavy eyebrows in an expression of angry scorn. "Oh! never, never, never again, will I look at myself like that,"

Rachel vowed fiercely.

She was to find, however, before this first evening was over, that the mere avoidance of that one pose before the mirror would not suffice to lay the ghost of the suspicion that was beginning to haunt her.

At the very outset a new version of the likeness was presented to her when, during the first course of dinner, Miss Deane, with a lowering frown of her blackened eyebrows, found occasion to reprimand the elderly parlour-maid. For a moment Rachel was again puzzled by the intriguing sense of the familiar, before she remembered her own scowl at the looking-glass an hour before. "Do I really frown like that?" she thought. And on the instant found herself *feeling* like her aunt.

That, indeed, was the horror that, despite every effort of resistance, deepened steadily as the evening wore on. Miss Deane had, without question, lost every trace of her beauty; but her character, her spirit was unchanged, and it was, so Rachel increasingly believed, the very spit and replica of her own.

They had the same characteristic gestures and expressions; the look of kindly tolerance with which her aunt regarded Rachel was precisely the same as that with which Rachel regarded her father. When her aunt's voice dropped in speaking from the rather shrill, strained tone that was obviously not natural to her, Rachel heard the inflexions of her own voice. And as her knowledge of Miss Deane grew, so, also, did that haunting unpleasant feeling of looking and speaking in precisely the same manner. It seemed to her as if she were being invaded by an alien personality; as if the character she had known and cherished all her life were no longer her own, but merely a casual inheritance from some unknown ancestor. Her very integrity was threatened by her consciousness of that likeness, her pride of individuality. She was not, after all, a unique personality, but merely another version – if she were even that? - of a Miss Rachel Deane born in the middle of the previous century.

Moreover, with that growing recognition of likeness in character, there came the thought that she in time might look even as her aunt looked at this present moment. She also would lose her beauty, until no facial resemblance could be traced between the hag she was and the beauty she had once been. For, through all her torment, Rachel proudly clung to the certainty that, physically at least, there was no sort of likeness between her aunt and herself.

Miss Deane's belief in that matter, however, was soon proved to be otherwise; for when they were alone together in the drawing-room after dinner, and the topic so inevitably present to both their minds came to the surface of conversation, she unexpectedly said: "But we're evidently the poles apart in character and manner, my dear."

"Oh! do you think so?" Rachel exclaimed. "I - it's a queer thing to say perhaps - but I curiously feel like you, aunt; when you speak sometimes and - and when I watch the way you do things."

Miss Deane shook her head. "I admit the physical resemblance," she said; "otherwise, my dear, we are utterly different."

Did she too, Rachel wondered, resent the aspersion of

her integrity?

By the last post Rachel received her expected letter from Adrian Flemming. Her aunt separated it from the others brought in by her maid and passed it across to her niece with a slight hint of displeasure in her face. "Miss Rachel Deane, *junior*," she said. "Really, it hadn't occurred to me how difficult it will be to distinguish our letters. I hope my friends won't take to addressing me as Miss Deane, *senior*. Properly, of course, I am Miss Deane, and you Miss Rachel, but I'll admit there's sure to be some confusion. Now, my dear, I expect you're tired. You'd better run up to bed."

Rachel was willing enough to go. She was glad to have an opportunity to read her letter in solitude; she was even more glad to get away from the company of this living echo of herself. "I believe I should go mad if I had to live with her," she reflected. "I should get into the way of copying her. I should begin to grow old before my time."

When she reached her bedroom, she put down her letter unopened on the toilet-table and once more stared searchingly at her own reflection in the mirror. Was there any least trace of a physical likeness, she asked herself; and began in imagination to follow the possible stages of the change that time would inevitably work upon her. She shrugged her shoulders. If there were indeed any sort of facial resemblance between herself and her aunt, no one would ever see it except in Miss Deane, and she was obsessed with a senile vanity. Yet was it, after all, Rachel began to wonder, an unnatural obsession? Might she not in time suffer from it herself? The change would be so slow, so infinitely gradual; and always one would be cherishing the old, loved image of youth and beauty, falling in love with it, like a deluded Hyacinth, and coming to be deceived by the fantasy of an unchanging appearance of youth. Looking always for the desired thing, she would suffer from the hallucination that the thing existed in fact, and imagine that the only artifice needed to perfect the illusion was a touch of paint and powder. No doubt her aunt - perhaps searching her own image in the mirror at this moment - saw not herself but a picture of her niece. She was hypnotised by the suggestion of a pose and the desire of her own mind. In time, Rachel herself might also become the victim of a similar illusion!

Oh! it was horrible! With a shudder, she picked up her letter and turned away from the looking-glass. She would forget that ghastly warning in the thought of the joys proper to her youth. She would think of Adrian and of her next meeting with him. She opened her letter to find that he had, rather timorously, suggested that she should meet him the next afternoon - at the Marble Arch at three o'clock, if he heard nothing from her in the meantime.

For a few minutes she lost herself in delighted anticipation, and then slowly, insidiously, a new speculation crept into her mind. What would be the effect upon Adrian if he saw her and her aunt together? Would he recognise the likeness and, anticipating the movement of more than half a century, see her in one amazing moment as she would presently become? And, in any case, what a terrible train of suggestion might not be started in his mind by the impression left upon him by the old woman? Once he had seen Miss Deane, Rachel's every gesture would serve to remind him of that repulsive image of raddled, deluded age. It might well be that, in time, he would come to see Rachel as she would presently be rather than as she was. It would be a hideous reversal of the old romance; instead of seeing the girl in the old woman, he would foresee the harridan in the girl!

That picture presented itself to Rachel with a quite appalling effect of conviction. She suddenly remembered a case she had known that had remarkable points of resemblance - the case of a rather pretty girl with an unpleasant younger brother who, so she had heard it said, "put men off his sister" because of the facial likeness between them. She was pretty and he was ugly, but they were unmistakably brother and sister.

Oh! it would be nothing less than folly to let Adrian and her aunt meet, Rachel decided. In imagination, she could follow the process of his growing dismay; she could see his puzzled stare as he watched Miss Deane, and struggled to fix that tantalising suggestion of likeness to some one he knew; his flash of illumination as he solved the puzzle and turned with that gentle, winning smile of his to herself; and then the progress of his disillusionment as, day by day, he realised more plainly the intriguing similarities of expression and gesture, until he felt that he was making love to the spirit of an aged spinster temporarily disguised behind the appearance of beauty.

III

Rachel had believed on the first night of her arrival in Tavistock Square that, so far as her love affair was concerned, she would be able to avoid all danger by keeping her lover and her aunt unknown to each other. She very soon found, however, that the spell Miss Deane seemed to have put upon her was not to be laid by any effect of mere distance.

She and Adrian met rather shyly at their first appointment. Both of them were a little conscious of having been overbold, one for having suggested, and the other for having agreed to so significant an assignation. And for the first few minutes their talk was nothing but a quick, nervous reminiscence of their earlier meetings. They had to recover the lost ground on which they had parted before they could go on to any more intimate knowledge of each other. But for some reason she had not yet realised, Rachel found it very difficult to recover that lost ground. She knew that she was being unnecessarily distant and cold, and though she inwardly accused herself of "putting on absurd airs," her manner, as she was uncomfortably aware, remained at once stilted and detached.

"I suppose it's because I'm self-conscious before all these people," she thought, and, indeed, Hyde Park was very full that afternoon.

And it was Adrian who first, a little desperately, tried to reach across the barrier that was dividing them.

"You're different, rather, in town," he began shyly. "Is it the effect of your aunt's grandeurs?"

"Am I different? I feel exactly the same," Rachel replied mechanically.

"You didn't think it was rather impudent of me to ask you to meet me here, did you?" he went on anxiously.

She shook her head emphatically. "Oh! no, it wasn't that," she said.

"But then you admit that it was - something?" he pleaded.

"The people, perhaps," she admitted. "I - I feel so exposed to the public view."

"We might walk across the Park if you preferred it," he suggested; "and have tea at that place in Kensington Gardens? It would be quieter there."

She agreed to that willingly. She wanted to be alone with him. The crowd made her nervous and self-conscious this afternoon. Always before, she had delighted in moving among a crowd, appreciating and enjoying the casual glances of admiration she received. Today she was afraid of being noticed. She had a queer feeling that these smart, clever people in the Park might see through her, if they stared too closely. Just what they would discover she did not know; but she suffered a disquieting qualm of uneasiness whenever she saw any one observing her with attention.

They cut across the grass and, leaving the Serpentine on their left, found two chairs in a quiet spot under the trees. Here, at least, they were quite unwatched, but still Rachel found it impossible to regain the relations that had existed between her and Adrian when they had parted a month earlier. And Adrian, too, it seemed, was staring at her with a new, inquisitive scrutiny.

"Why do you look at me like that?" she broke out at last. "Do you notice any difference in me, or what? You - you've been staring so!"

"Difference!" he repeated. "Well, I told you just now, didn't I, that you were different this afternoon?"

"Yes, but in what way?" she asked. "Do I - do I look different?"

He paused a little judiciously over his answer. "N - no," he hesitated. "There's something, though. Don't be offended, will you, if I say that you don't seem to be quite yourself to-day; not quite natural. I miss a rather characteristic expression of yours. You've never once looked at me with that rather tolerating air you used to put on."

"It was a horrid air," she said sharply. "I've made up my mind to cure myself of it."

"Oh! no, don't," he protested. "It wasn't at all horrid. It was - don't think I'm trying to pay you a compliment - it was, well, charming. I've missed it dreadfully."

She turned and looked at him, determined to try an experiment. "This sort of air, do you mean?" she asked, and with a sickening sensation of presenting the very gestures and appearance of her aunt, she regarded him under lowered eyelids with an expression of faintly supercilious approval.

His smile at once thanked and answered her.

"But it's an abominable look," she exclaimed. "The look of an old, old, painted woman, vain, ridiculous."

He stared at her in amazement. "How absurd!" he protested. "Why, it's *you*; and you're certainly not old or painted nor unduly vain, and no one could say you were ridiculous."

"And you want me to look like that?" she asked.

"It's - it's so *you*," he said shyly.

"But, just suppose," she cried, "that I went on looking like that after I'd grown old and ugly. Think how hateful it would be to see a hideous old woman posturing and pretending and making eyes. And, you see, if one gets a habit, it's so hard to get rid of it. Think of me at seventy, all painted and powdered, trying to seem as if I hadn't altered and really believing that I hadn't."

He laughed that pleasant, kind laugh of his which had been one of the first things in him that had so attracted her.

"Oh! I'll chance the future," he said. "Besides if - if it could ever happen that - that your growing old came to me gradually, that I should be seeing you every day, I mean, I shouldn't notice it. I should be old too; and *I* should think you hadn't altered either." He was afraid, as yet, to be too plain spoken, but his tone made it quite clear that he asked for no greater happiness than that of seeing her grow old beside him.

She did not pretend to misunderstand him. "Would you? Perhaps you would," she said. "But, all the same,

I don't think you need insist on that particular - pose."

He passed that by, too eager at the moment to claim the concession she had offered him. "Is there any hope that I may be allowed to - to watch you growing old?" he asked.

"Perhaps - if you'll let me do it in my own way," Rachel said.

Adrian shyly took her hand. "You mean that you will - that you don't mind?" He put the question as if he had no doubt of its intelligibility - to her.

She nodded.

"When did you begin to know?" he asked, awed by the wonder of this stupendous thing that had happened to him.

"From the beginning, I think," Rachel murmured.

"So did I, from the very beginning - " he agreed, and from that they dropped into sacred reminiscences and comparisons concerning the innumerable things they had adoringly seen in each other and had had as yet no opportunity to glory in.

And in the midst of all these new and bewildering, embarrassing, delightful revelations and discoveries, Rachel completely forgot the shadow that was haunting her, forgot how she looked or felt or acted, forgot that there was or had ever been a terrible old woman who lived in Tavistock Square and whose hold on life was maintained by her horrible mimicry of youth. And then, in a moment, she was lifted out of her dream and cruelly set down on the hard, unsympathetic earth by the sound of her lover's voice.

"I suppose I'll have to meet your aunt?" he was saying. "Shall we go back there now, and tell her?"

Rachel flushed, as if he had suggested some startling invasion of her secret life. "Oh! no," she ejaculated impulsively.

Adrian looked his surprise. "But why not?" he asked. "I'm - I'm a perfectly respectable, eligible party."

"I wasn't thinking of that," Rachel said.

"Is she a terrible dragon?' he inquired with a smile.

Rachel shook her head, rejecting the excuse offered in favour of a more probable modification. "She's odd rather. She might prefer my giving her some kind of notice," she said.

He accepted that without hesitation. "Will you warn her then?" he replied. "And I'll come and do my duty to-morrow. I understand she's a lady to be propitiated."

"Not to-morrow," Rachel said.

The irk and disgust of it all had returned to her with renewed force at the first mention of her aunt's name. The thought of Miss Deane had revived the repulsive sense of acting, speaking, looking like that aged caricature of herself. Yet she wanted strangely enough, to get back to Tavistock Square; for only there, it seemed to her, was she safe from the examination of an inquisitive stare that might at any moment penetrate her secret and reveal her as a posturing hag masquerading in the alluring freshness of a young girl.

"I ought to be going back to her now," she said.

"But you promised that we should have tea together," Adrian remonstrated.

"Yes, I know; but please don't pester me. I'll see you again to-morrow," Rachel returned with a touch of elderly hauteur. And, despite all his entreaties, she would not be persuaded to change her mind. Already he was looking at her with a touch of suspicion, she thought; and as she checked his remonstrances, she was aware of doing it with the air, the tone, the very look that were her inheritance from endless generations of precisely similar ancestors.

IV

If she could but have lived a double life, Rachel thought, her present position might have been endurable, and then, in a few months or even weeks, the problem would be solved for ever by her marriage with Adrian and the final obliteration of Miss Deane from her memory. But she could not live a double life. Day by day, as her intimacy with her aunt increased, Rachel found it more difficult to forget her when she was away from Tavistock Square. In the deepest and most beautiful moments of her intercourse with Adrian, she was aware now of practising upon him a subtle deception, of pretending that she was other than she was in reality - an awareness that was constantly pricked and stimulated by the continually growing consciousness of her likeness to Miss Deane.

Miss Deane on her part evidently took a great pleasure in her niece's society. The fortnight of her original invitation had already been exceeded, but she would not hear of Rachel's return to Devonshire.

"Why should you go back?" she demanded scornfully. "Your father doesn't want you - Richard is one of those slip-shod people who prefer to live alone. I used to try to stir him up, and he ran away from me. He'll run away from you, my dear, in a few years' time. He hasn't the courage to stand up to women like us."

Miss Deane unquestionably wanted her niece to stay with her. She was even beginning to hint at the desirability of making the present arrangement a permanent one.

Rachel, however, was not flattered by this display of pleasure in her society. She knew that it was due to no individual charm of her own, but to the fact that she had become her aunt's mirror. For Miss Deane no longer, in Rachel's presence at least, gazed at herself in the looking-glass; she gazed at her niece instead. And as Rachel endured the posings and simperings, the alternate adoration and fond contempt with which her aunt regarded her, she was unable to resist the impulse to reflect them. Every day she fell a little lower in that weakness, and however slight the likeness had once been, she knew that now it must be patent to every observer. She copied her aunt, mimicked, duplicated her. It was easier to do that than fight the resemblance, against her aunt's determination; and so, by unnoticed degrees, she had permitted herself to become a lay figure upon which was dressed the image of Miss Deane's youth. She had even come to desire the look of almost sensual gratification on her aunt's face when she saw her niece so perfectly reflecting her own well-remembered airs.

And Rachel, too, had come to avoid the looking-glass, dreading to see there the poses and gesticulations of the old, repulsive woman whose every feature and expression had become so sickeningly familiar.

And, in all that time, Adrian had not once been to the house in Tavistock Square. Rachel had kept him away by what she felt had become all too transparent excuses. That terror, at least, she felt must be kept at bay. For she could not conceive it possible that, once he had seen her and her aunt together, he could retain one spark of his admiration. He would, he must, see her then as she was, see that her contemptible vanity was the essential enduring thing, all that would remain when time had stripped her of youth's allurement.

Nevertheless, the day came when Rachel could no longer endure to deceive him. He had challenged her, at last, with hiding something from him. Inevitably, he had become increasingly curious about her strange reticences concerning the Miss Deane whom he, in turn, had grown to regard as almost mythical; and all his suppressed suspicions had suddenly found expression in a question.

"What are you hiding? Do you really live with your aunt in Tavistock Square?" he had asked that day, with all the fierce intensity of a jealous lover.

Rachel had been stirred to a quick response. "Oh, if you don't believe me, you'd better come and see for yourself," she had said. "Come this afternoon - to tea." And afterwards, even when Adrian had humbly sought to make amends for his unwarrantable jealousy, she had stuck to that invitation. The moment that she had issued it, she had had a sense of relief, a sense of having gratefully confessed her weakness. Adrian's visit would consummate that confession, and thereafter she would have no further secrets from him. And if he found that he could no longer love her after he had seen her as she was, well, it would be better in the end than that he should marry a simulacrum and make the discovery by slow degrees.

"Yes, come this afternoon. We'll expect you about four" had been her last words to him. And, now, she had to tell her aunt, who was still unaware that such a person as Adrian Flemming existed. Rachel postponed the telling until after lunch. Her knowledge of Miss Deane, though in some respects it equalled her knowledge of her own mind, did not tell her how her aunt would take this particular piece of news. She might possibly, Rachel thought, be annoyed, fearful lest her beloved looking-glass should be stolen from her. But she could wait no longer. In half an hour Miss Deane would go upstairs to rest, and Adrian himself would be in the house before she appeared again.

"I've something to tell you, aunt," Rachel began abruptly.

Miss Deane put up her lorgnette and surveyed her lovely portrait with an interested air.

"Aunt - I've never told you and I know I ought to have," Rachel blurted out. "But I'm - I'm engaged to a Mr. Adrian Flemming, and he's coming here to call on you - to call on us, this afternoon at four o'clock."

Miss Deane closed her eyes and gave a little sigh.

"You might have given me *rather* longer notice, dear," she said.

"It isn't two yet," Rachel replied. "There are more than two hours to get ready for him."

Miss Deane bridled slightly. "I must have my rest before he comes," she said, and added: "I suppose you've told him about us, dear?"

"About *you*?" Rachel asked.

Miss Deane nodded, complacently.

"Well, not very much," Rachel admitted.

Miss Dean's look, as she playfully threatened Rachel with her long-handled lorgnette, was distinctly sly.

"Then he doesn't know yet that there are two of us?" she simpered. "Won't it be just a little bit of a shock to him, my dear?"

Rachel drew a long breath and leaned back in her chair. "Yes," she said curtly, "I expect it will."

Never before had the realisation of that strange likeness seemed so intolerable as at that moment. Even now her aunt was looking at her with the very air and gesture which had once charmed her in her own reflection, and that she knew still charmed and fascinated her lover. It was an air and gesture of which she could never break herself. It was natural to her, a true expression of something ineradicable in her being. Indeed, one of the worst penalties imposed upon her during the past month had been the omission of those pleasant ceremonies before the mirror. She had somehow missed herself, lost the sweetest and most adorable of companions!

Miss Deane got up, and holding herself very erect, moved with a little mincing step towards the tall mirror over the console table. Rachel held her breath. She saw that her aunt, suddenly aroused by this thought of the coming lover, was returning mechanically to her old habit of self-admiration. Was it possible, Rachel wondered, that the sight of the image she would see in the looking-glass, contrasted now with the memories of the living reflection she had so intimately studied for the past four weeks, might shock her into a realisation of the starkly hideous truth?

But it seemed that the aged woman must be blind. She gave no start of surprise as she paused before the glass; she showed no sign of anxiety concerning the vision she saw there. Her left hand, in which she held her lorgnette, had fallen to her side, and with the finger-tips of her right she daintily caressed the hollows of her sunken cheeks. She stayed there until Rachel, unable to endure the sight any longer, and with some vague purpose of defiance in her mind, jumped to her feet, crossed the room and stood shoulder by shoulder with her aunt staring into the glass.

For a moment Miss Deane did not move; then, with a queer hesitation, she dropped her right hand and slowly lifted her lorgnette.

Rachel felt a cold chill of horror invading her. Something fearful and terrible was happening before her eyes; her aunt was shrinking, withering, growing old in a moment. The stiffness had gone out of her pose, her head had begun to droop; the proud contempt in her face was giving way to the moping, resentful reminiscence of the aged. She still held up her lorgnette, still stared half fearfully at the glaring contrast that was presented to her, but her hand and arm had begun to tremble under the strain, and, instant by, instant, all life and vigour seemed to be draining away from her.

Then, suddenly, with a fierce effort she turned away her head, straightened herself, and walked over to the door, passing out with a high, thin cackle of laughter that had in it the suggestion of a vehement, petulant derision; of a bitterness outmastering control.

Rachel shivered, but held her ground before the mirror.

She had nothing to fear from that contemplation. As for her aunt, she had had her day. It was time she knew the truth.

"She *had* to know," Rachel repeated, addressing the dear likeness that so proudly reflected her.

V

She found consolation in that thought. Her aunt *had* to know and Rachel herself was only the chance instrument of the revelation. She had not *meant*, so she persisted, to do more than vindicate her own integrity.

Nevertheless, her own passionate problem was not yet solved. Her aunt would not, so Rachel believed, give way without a struggle. Had she not made a gallant effort at recovery even as she left the room, and would she not make a still greater effort while Adrian was there; assert her rivalry if only in revenge?

She must meet that, Rachel decided, by presenting a contrast. She would be meek and humble in her aunt's presence. Adrian might recognise the admired airs and gestures in those of the old woman, but he should at least have no opportunity to compare them....

And it was with this thought and intention in her mind that Rachel received him, when he arrived with a lover's promptness a little before four o'clock.

"Are you so dreadfully nervous?" he asked her, when they were alone together in the drawing-room. "You're like you were the first day we met in town - different from your usual self."

"Oh! What a memory you have for my looks and behaviour," she replied pettishly. "Of course, I'm nervous."

He tried to argue with her, questioning her as to Miss Deane's probable reception of him, but she refused to answer. "You'll see for yourself in a few minutes," she said; but the minutes passed and still Miss Deane did not come.

At a quarter to five the elderly parlour-maid brought in tea. "Miss Deane said you were not to wait for her, Miss Rachel," was the message she delivered. "She'll be down presently, I was to say."

Rachel could not suppress a scornful twist of her mouth. She had no doubt that her aunt was taking very special pains with her toilet; trying to obliterate, perhaps, her recent vision before the console glass. Rachel saw her entrance in imagination, stiff-necked and proud, defying the criticisms of youth and the suggestions of age.

"Oh! why doesn't she come and let me get it over?" she passionately demanded, and even as she spoke she heard the sounds of some one coming down the stairs, not the accustomed sounds of her aunt's finicking, high-heeled steps, but a shuffling and creaking, accompanied by the murmurs of a weak, protesting voice.

Rachel jumped to her feet. She knew everything then - before the door opened, and she saw first of all the shocked, scared face of the elderly parlour-maid who supported the crumpled, palsied figure of the old, old woman who, three hours before, had been so miraculously young, magically upheld and supported then by the omnipotent strength of an idea.

She only stayed in the drawing-room for five minutes; a querulous, resentful old lady, malignantly jealous, so it seemed, of their vigour and impatient of their sympathy.

When the parlour-maid had been sent for and Miss Deane had gone, Rachel stood up and looked down at Adrian with all her old hauteur.

"Can you realise," she asked, "that once my aunt was supposed to be very, very like me?"

He smiled and shook his head, as if the possibility was too absurd to contemplate.

Rachel turned and looked at herself in the glass, raising her chin and slightly pursing her lips, staring superciliously at her own image under half-lowered eyelids.

"Some day I may be as she is now," she said, with the superb contemptuous arrogance of youth.

Adrian was watching her with adoration. "You will never grow old," he said.

"So long as one does not get the idea of growing old into one's head," Rachel began speculatively....

* * * * *

But Miss Deane had got the idea so strongly now that she died that night.

Rachel was with her at the last.

The old woman was trying to mouth a text from the Bible.

"What did you say, dear?" Rachel murmured, bending over her, and caught enough of the answer to guess that Miss Deane was mumbling again and again: "Now we see through a glass darkly, but then face to face."

THE OLIVE

By ALGERNON BLACKWOOD

(From *Pearson's Magazine*, London) 1922

He laughed involuntarily as the olive rolled towards his chair across the shiny parquet floor of the hotel dining-room.

His table in the cavernous *salle à manger* was apart: he sat alone, a solitary guest; the table from which the olive fell and rolled towards him was some distance away. The angle, however, made him an unlikely objective. Yet the lob-sided, juicy thing, after hesitating once or twice *en route* as it plopped along, came to rest finally against his feet.

It settled with an inviting, almost an aggressive air. And he stooped and picked it up, putting it rather self-consciously, because of the girl from whose table it had come, on the white tablecloth beside his plate.

Then, looking up, he caught her eye, and saw that she too was laughing, though not a bit self-consciously. As she helped herself to the *hors d'oeuvres* a false move had sent it flying. She watched him pick the olive up and set it beside his plate. Her eyes then suddenly looked away again - at her mother - questioningly.

The incident was closed. But the little oblong, succulent olive lay beside his plate, so that his fingers played with it. He fingered it automatically from time to time until his lonely meal was finished.

When no one was looking he slipped it into his pocket, as though, having taken the trouble to pick it up, this was the very least he could do with it. Heaven alone knows why, but he then took it upstairs with him, setting it on the marble mantelpiece among his field glasses, tobacco tins, ink-bottles, pipes and candlestick. At any rate, he kept it - the moist, shiny, lobsided, juicy little oblong olive. The hotel lounge wearied him; he came to his room after dinner to smoke at his ease, his coat off and his feet on a chair; to read another chapter of Freud, to write a letter or two he didn't in the least want to write, and then go to bed at ten o'clock. But this evening the olive kept rolling between him and the thing he read; it rolled between the paragraphs, between the lines; the olive was more vital than the interest of these eternal "complexes" and "suppressed desires."

The truth was that he kept seeing the eyes of the laughing girl beyond the bouncing olive. She had smiled at him in such a natural, spontaneous, friendly way before her mother's glance had checked her - a smile, he felt, that might lead to acquaintance on the morrow.

He wondered! A thrill of possible adventure ran through him.

She was a merry-looking sort of girl, with a happy, half-roguish face that seemed on the lookout for somebody to play with. Her mother, like most of the people in the big hotel, was an invalid; the girl, a dutiful and patient daughter. They had arrived that very day apparently. A laugh is a revealing thing, he thought as he fell asleep to dream of a lob-sided olive rolling consciously towards him, and of a girl's eyes that watched its awkward movements, then looked up into his own and laughed. In his dream the olive had been deliberately and cleverly dispatched upon its uncertain journey. It was a message.

He did not know, of course, that the mother, chiding her daughter's awkwardness, had muttered:

"There you are again, child! True to your name, you never see an olive without doing something queer and odd with it!"

A youngish man, whose knowledge of chemistry, including invisible inks and such-like mysteries, had proved so valuable to the Censor's Department that for five years he had overworked without a holiday, the Italian Riviera had attracted him, and he had come out for a two months' rest. It was his first visit. Sun, mimosa, blue seas and brilliant skies had tempted him; exchange made a pound worth forty, fifty, sixty and seventy shillings. He found the place lovely, but somewhat untenanted.

Having chosen at random, he had come to a spot where the companionship he hoped to find did not exist. The place languished after the war, slow to recover; the colony of resident English was scattered still; travellers preferred the coast of France with Mentone and Monte Carlo to enliven them. The country, moreover, was distracted by strikes. The electric light failed one week, letters the next, and as soon as the electricians and postal-workers resumed, the railways stopped running. Few visitors came, and the few who came soon left.

He stayed on, however, caught by the sunshine and the good exchange, also without the physical energy to discover a better, livelier place. He went for walks among the olive groves, he sat beside the sea and palms, he visited shops and bought things he did not want because the exchange made them seem cheap, he paid immense "extras" in his weekly bill, then chuckled as he reduced them to shillings and found that a few pence covered them; he lay with a book for hours among the olive groves.

The olive groves! His daily life could not escape the olive groves; to olive groves, sooner or later, his walks, his expeditions, his meanderings by the sea, his shopping - all led him to these ubiquitous olive groves.

If he bought a picture postcard to send home, there was sure to be an olive grove in one corner of it. The whole place was smothered with olive groves, the people owed their incomes and existence to these irrepressible trees. The villages among the hills swam roof-deep in them. They swarmed even in the hotel gardens.

The guide books praised them as persistently as the residents brought them, sooner or later, into every conversation. They grew lyrical over them:

"And how do you like our olive trees? Ah, you think them pretty. At first, most people are disappointed. They grow on one."

"They do," he agreed.

"I'm glad you appreciate them. I find them the embodiment of grace. And when the wind lifts the under-leaves across a whole mountain slope - why, it's wonderful, isn't it? One realises the meaning of 'olive-green'."

"One does," he sighed. "But all the same I should like to get one to eat - an olive, I mean."

"Ah, to eat, yes. That's not so easy. You see, the crop is -"

"Exactly," he interrupted impatiently, weary of the habitual and evasive explanations. "But I should like to taste the *fruit*. I should like to enjoy one."

For, after a stay of six weeks, he had never once seen an olive on the table, in the shops, nor even on the street barrows at the market place. He had never tasted one. No one sold olives, though olive trees were a drug in the place; no one bought them, no one asked for them; it seemed that no one wanted them. The trees, when he looked closely, were thick with a dark little berry that seemed more like a sour sloe than the succulent, delicious spicy fruit associated with its name.

Men climbed the trunks, everywhere shaking the laden branches and hitting them with long bamboo poles to knock the fruit off, while women and children, squatting on their haunches, spent laborious hours filling baskets underneath, then loading mules and donkeys with their daily "catch." But an olive to eat was unobtainable. He had never cared for olives, but now he craved with all his soul to feel his teeth in one.

"Ach! But it is the Spanish olive that you *eat*," explained the head waiter, a German "from Basel." "These are for oil only." After which he disliked the olive more than ever - until that night when he saw the first eatable specimen rolling across the shiny parquet floor, propelled towards him by the careless hand of a pretty girl, who then looked up into his eyes and smiled.

He was convinced that Eve, similarly, had rolled the apple towards Adam across the emerald sward of the first garden in the world.

He slept usually like the dead. It must have been something very real that made him open his eyes and sit up in bed alertly. There was a noise against his door. He listened. The room was still quite dark. It was early morning. The noise was not repeated.

"Who's there?" he asked in a sleepy whisper. "What is it?"

The noise came again. Some one was scratching on the door. No, it was somebody tapping.

"What do you want?" he demanded in a louder voice. "Come in," he added, wondering sleepily whether he was presentable. Either the hotel was on fire or the porter was waking the wrong person for some sunrise expedition.

Nothing happened. Wide awake now, he turned the switch on, but no light flooded the room. The electricians, he remembered with a curse, were out on strike. He fumbled for the matches, and as he did so a voice in the corridor became distinctly audible. It was just outside his door.

"Aren't you ready?" he heard. "You sleep for ever."

And the voice, although never having heard it before, he could not have recognised it, belonged, he knew suddenly, to the girl who had let the olive fall. In an instant he was out of bed. He lit a candle.

"I'm coming," he called softly, as he slipped rapidly into some clothes. "I'm sorry I've kept you. I shan't be a minute."

"Be quick then!" he heard, while the candle flame slowly grew, and he found his garments. Less than three minutes later he opened the door and, candle in hand, peered into the dark passage.

"Blow it out!" came a peremptory whisper. He obeyed, but not quick enough. A pair of red lips emerged from the shadows. There was a puff, and the candle was extinguished. "I've got my reputation to consider. We mustn't be seen, of course!"

The face vanished in the darkness, but he had recognised it - the shining skin, the bright glancing eyes. The sweet breath touched his cheek. The candlestick was taken from him by a swift, deft movement. He heard it knock the wainscoting as it was set down. He went out into a pitch-black corridor, where a soft hand seized his own and led him - by a back door, it seemed - out into the open air of the hill-side immediately behind the hotel.

He saw the stars. The morning was cool and fragrant, the sharp air waked him, and the last vestiges of sleep went flying. He had been drowsy and confused, had obeyed the summons without thinking. He now realised suddenly that he was engaged in an act of madness.

The girl, dressed in some flimsy material thrown loosely about her head and body, stood a few feet away, looking, he thought, like some figure called out of dreams and slumber of a forgotten world, out of legend almost. He saw her evening shoes peep out; he divined an evening dress beneath the gauzy covering. The light wind blew it close against her figure. He thought of a nymph.

"I say - but haven't you been to bed?" he asked stupidly. He had meant to expostulate, to apologise for his foolish rashness, to scold and say they must go back at once. Instead, this sentence came. He guessed she had been sitting up all night. He stood still a second, staring in mute admiration, his eyes full of bewildered question.

"Watching the stars,' she met his thought with a happy laugh. "Orion has touched the horizon. I came for you at once. We've got just four hours!" The voice, the smile, the eyes, the reference to Orion, swept him off his feet. Something in him broke loose, and flew wildly, recklessly to the stars.

"Let us be off!" he cried, "before the Bear tilts down. Already Alcyone begins to fade. I'm ready. Come!"

She laughed. The wind blew the gauze aside to show two ivory white limbs. She caught his hand again, and they scampered together up the steep hill-side towards the woods. Soon the big hotel, the villas, the white houses of the little town where natives and visitors still lay soundly sleeping, were out of sight. The farther sky came down to meet them. The stars were paling, but no sign of actual dawn was yet visible. The freshness stung their cheeks.

Slowly, the heavens grew lighter, the east turned rose, the outline of the trees defined themselves, there was a stirring of the silvery green leaves. They were among olive groves - but the spirits of the trees were dancing. Far below them, a pool of deep colour, they saw the ancient sea. They saw the tiny specks of distant fishing-boats. The sailors were singing to the dawn, and birds among the mimosa of the hanging gardens answered them.

Pausing a moment at length beneath a gaunt old tree, whose struggle to leave the clinging earth had tortured its great writhing arms and trunk, they took their breath, gazing at one another with eyes full of happy dreams.

"You understood so quickly," said the girl, "my little message. I knew by your eyes and ears you would." And she first tweaked his ears with two slender fingers mischievously, then laid her soft palm with a momentary light pressure on both eyes.

"You're half-and-half, at any rate," she added, looking him up and down for a swift instant of appraisement, "if you're not altogether." The laughter showed her white, even little teeth.

"You know how to play, and that's something," she added. Then, as if to herself, "You'll be altogether before I've done with you."

"Shall I?" he stammered, afraid to look at her.

Puzzled, some spirit of compromise still lingering in him, he knew not what she meant; he knew only that the current of life flowed increasingly through his veins, but that her eyes confused him.

"I'm longing for it," he added. "How wonderfully you did it! They roll so awkwardly -"

"Oh, that!" She peered at him through a wisp of hair. "You've kept it, I hope."

"Rather. It's on my mantelpiece -"

"You're sure you haven't eaten it?" and she made a delicious mimicry with her red lips, so that he saw the tip of a small pointed tongue.

"I shall keep it," he swore, "as long as these arms have life in them," and he seized her just as she was crouching to escape, and covered her with kisses.

"I knew you longed to play," she panted, when he released her. "Still, it was sweet of you to pick it up before another got it."

"Another!" he exclaimed.

"The gods decide. It's a lob-sided thing, remember. It can't roll straight." She looked oddly mischievous, elusive.

He stared at her.

"If it had rolled elsewhere - and another had picked it

up -?" he began.

"I should be with that other now!" And this time she was off and away before he could prevent her, and the sound of her silvery laughter mocked him among the olive trees beyond. He was up and after her in a second, following her slim whiteness in and out of the old-world grove, as she flitted lightly, her hair flying in the wind, her figure flashing like a ray of sunlight or the race of foaming water - till at last he caught her and drew her down upon his knees, and kissed her wildly, forgetting who and where and what he was.

"Hark!" she whispered breathlessly, one arm close about his neck. "I hear their footsteps. Listen! It is the pipe!"

"The pipe -!" he repeated, conscious of a tiny but delicious shudder.

For a sudden chill ran through him as she said it. He gazed at her. The hair fell loose about her cheeks, flushed and rosy with his hot kisses. Her eyes were bright and wild for all their softness. Her face, turned sideways to him as she listened, wore an extraordinary look that for an instant made his blood run cold. He saw the parted lips, the small white teeth, the slim neck of ivory, the young bosom panting from his tempestuous embrace. Of an unearthly loveliness and brightness she seemed to him, yet with this strange, remote expression that touched his soul with sudden terror.

Her face turned slowly.

"Who *are* you?" he whispered. He sprang to his feet

without waiting for her answer.

He was young and agile; strong, too, with that quick response of muscle they have who keep their bodies well; but he was no match for her. Her speed and agility out-classed his own with ease. She leapt. Before he had moved one leg forward towards escape, she was clinging with soft, supple arms and limbs about him, so that he could not free himself, and as her weight bore him downwards to the ground, her lips found his own and kissed them into silence. She lay buried again in his embrace, her hair across his eyes, her heart against his heart, and he forgot his question, forgot his little fear, forgot the very world he knew....

"They come, they come," she cried gaily. "The Dawn is here. Are you ready?"

"I've been ready for five thousand years," he answered, leaping to his feet beside her.

"Altogether!" came upon a sparkling laugh that was like wind among the olive leaves.

Shaking her last gauzy covering from her, she snatched his hand, and they ran forward together to join the dancing throng now crowding up the slope beneath the trees. Their happy singing filled the sky. Decked with vine and ivy, and trailing silvery green branches, they poured in a flood of radiant life along the mountain side. Slowly they melted away into the blue distance of the breaking dawn, and, as the last figure disappeared, the sun came up slowly out of a purple sea.

They came to the place he knew - the deserted earthquake village - and a faint memory stirred in him.

He did not actually recall that he had visited it already, had eaten his sandwiches with "hotel friends" beneath its crumbling walls; but there was a dim troubling sense of familiarity - nothing more. The houses still stood, but pigeons lived in them, and weasels, stoats and snakes had their uncertain homes in ancient bedrooms. Not twenty years ago the peasants thronged its narrow streets, through which the dawn now peered and cool wind breathed among dew-laden brambles.

"I know the house," she cried, "the house where we would live!" and raced, a flying form of air and sunlight, into a tumbled cottage that had no roof, no floor or windows. Wild bees had hung a nest against the broken wall.

He followed her. There was sunlight in the room, and there were flowers. Upon a rude, simple table lay a bowl of cream, with eggs and honey and butter close against a home-made loaf. They sank into each other's arms upon a couch of fragrant grass and boughs against the window where wild roses bloomed ... and the bees flew in and out.

It was Bussana, the so-called earthquake village, because a sudden earthquake had fallen on it one summer morning when all the inhabitants were at church. The crashing roof killed sixty, the tumbling walls another hundred, and the rest had left it where it stood.

"The Church," he said, vaguely remembering the story. "They were at prayer -"

The girl laughed carelessly in his ear, setting his blood in a rush and quiver of delicious joy. He felt himself

Edward J. O'Brien and John Cournos

untamed, wild as the wind and animals. "The true God claimed His own," she whispered. "He came back. Ah, they were not ready - the old priests had seen to that. But he came. They heard his music. Then his tread shook the olive groves, the old ground danced, the hills leapt for joy -"

"And the houses crumbled," he laughed as he pressed her closer to his heart -

"And now we've come back!" she cried merrily. "We've come back to worship and be glad!" She nestled into him, while the sun rose higher.

"I hear them - hark!" she cried, and again leapt, dancing from his side. Again he followed her like wind. Through the broken window they saw the naked fauns and nymphs and satyrs rolling, dancing, shaking their soft hoofs amid the ferns and brambles. Towards the appalling, ruptured church they sped with feet of light and air. A roar of happy song and laughter rose.

"Come!" he cried. "We must go too."

Hand in hand they raced to join the tumbling, dancing throng. She was in his arms and on his back and flung across his shoulders, as he ran. They reached the broken building, its whole roof gone sliding years ago, its walls a-tremble still, its shattered shrines alive with nesting birds.

"Hush!" she whispered in a tone of awe, yet pleasure. "He is there!" She pointed, her bare arm outstretched above the bending heads.

There, in the empty space, where once stood sacred

Host and Cup, he sat, filling the niche sublimely and with awful power. His shaggy form, benign yet terrible, rose through the broken stone. The great eyes shone and smiled. The feet were lost in brambles.

"God!" cried a wild, frightened voice yet with deep worship in it - and the old familiar panic came with portentous swiftness. The great Figure rose.

The birds flew screaming, the animals sought holes, the worshippers, laughing and glad a moment ago, rushed tumbling over one another for the doors.

"He goes again! Who called? Who called like that? His feet shake the ground!"

"It is the earthquake!" screamed a woman's shrill accents in ghastly terror.

"Kiss me - one kiss before we forget again...!" sighed a laughing, passionate voice against his ear. "Once more your arms, your heart beating on my lips...! You recognised his power. You are now altogether! We shall remember!"

But he woke, with the heavy bed-clothes stuffed against his mouth and the wind of early morning sighing mournfully about the hotel walls.

*   *   *   *   *

"Have they left again - those ladies?" he inquired casually of the head waiter, pointing to the table. "They were here last night at dinner."

"Who do you mean?" replied the man, stupidly, gazing

at the spot indicated with a face quite blank. "Last night - at dinner?" He tried to think.

"An English lady, elderly, with - her daughter -" at which moment precisely the girl came in alone. Lunch was over, the room empty. There was a second's difficult pause. It seemed ridiculous not to speak. Their eyes met. The girl blushed furiously.

He was very quick for an Englishman. "I was allowing myself to ask after your mother," he began. "I was afraid" - he glanced at the table laid for one - "she was not well, perhaps?"

"Oh, but that's very kind of you, I'm sure." She smiled. He saw the small white even teeth....

And before three days had passed, he was so deeply in love that he simply couldn't help himself.

"I believe," he said lamely, "this is yours. You dropped it, you know. Er - may I keep it? It's only an olive."

They were, of course, in an olive grove when he asked it, and the sun was setting.

She looked at him, looked him up and down, looked at his ears, his eyes. He felt that in another second her little fingers would slip up and tweak the first, or close the second with a soft pressure -

"Tell me," he begged: "did you dream anything - that first night I saw you?"

She took a quick step backwards. "No," she said, as he followed her more quickly still, "I don't think I did.

But," she went on breathlessly as he caught her up, "I knew - from the way you picked it up -"

"Knew what?" he demanded, holding her tightly so that she could not get away again.

"That you were already half and half, but would soon be altogether."

And, as he kissed her, he felt her soft little fingers tweak his ears.

ONCE A HERO

By HAROLD BRIGHOUSE

(From *Pan*) 1922

Standing in a sheltered doorway a tramp, with a slouch hat crammed low over a notably unwashed face, watched the outside of the new works canteen of the Sir William Rumbold Ltd., Engineering Company. Perhaps because they were workers while he was a tramp, he had an air of compassionate cynicism as the audience assembled and thronged into the building, which, as prodigally advertised throughout Calderside, was to be opened that night by Sir William in person.

There being no one to observe him, the tramp could be frank with his cynicism; but inside the building, in the platform ante-room, Mr. Edward Fosdike, who was Sir William's locally resident secretary, had to discipline his private feelings to a suave concurrence in his employer's florid enthusiasm. Fosdike served Sir William well, but no man is a hero to his (male) secretary.

"I hope you will find the arrangements satisfactory," Fosdike was saying, tugging nervously at his maltreated moustache. "You speak at seven and declare the canteen open. Then there's a meal." He hesitated. "Perhaps I should have warned you to dine before you came."

Sir William was aware of being a very gallant gentleman. "Not at all," he said heroically, "not at all. I have not spared my purse over this War Memorial. Why should I spare my feelings? Well, now, you've seen about the Press?"

"Oh, yes. The reporters are coming. There'll be flash-light photographs. Everything quite as usual when you make a public appearance, sir."

Sir William wondered if this resident secretary of his were quite adequate. Busy in London, he had left all arrangements in his local factotum's hands, and he was doubting whether those hands had grasped the situation competently. "Only as usual?" he said sharply. "This War Memorial has cost me ten thousand pounds."

"The amount," Fosdike hastened to assure him, "has been circulated, with appropriate tribute to your generosity."

"Generosity," criticised Rumbold. "I hope you didn't use that word."

Mr. Fosdike referred to his notebook. "We said," he read, "'the cost, though amounting to ten thousand pounds, is entirely beside the point. Sir William felt that no expense was excessive that would result in a fitting and permanent expression of our gratitude to the glorious dead.'"

"Thank you, Fosdike. That is exactly my feeling," said the gratified Sir William, paying Fosdike the unspoken compliment of thinking him less of a fool than he looked. "It is," he went on, "from no egotistic motive that I wish the Press to be strongly represented to-night. I believe that in deciding that Calderside's War Memorial should take the form of a Works Canteen, I am setting an example of enlightenment which other employers would do well to follow. I have erected a monument, not in stone, but in goodwill, a club-house for both sexes to serve as a centre of social activities for the firm's employees, wherein the great spirit of the noble work carried out at the Front by by the Y.M.C.A. will be recaptured and adapted to peace conditions in our local organisation in the Martlow Works Canteen. What are you taking notes for?"

"I thought -" began Fosdike.

"Oh, well, perhaps you are right. Reporters have been known to miss one's point, and a little first aid, eh? By the way, I sent you some notes from town of what I intended to say in my speech. I just sent them ahead in case there was any local point I'd got wrong."

He put it as a question, but actually it was an assertion and a challenge. It asserted that by no possible chance could there be anything injudicious in the proposed speech, and it challenged Fosdike to deny that assertion if he dared.

And Fosdike had to dare; he had to accuse himself of assuming too easily that Rumbold's memory of local Calderside detail was as fresh as the memory of the man on the spot.

"I did want to suggest a modification, sir," he hazarded timidly.

"Really?" - quite below zero - "Really? I felt very contented with the speech."

"Yes, sir, it's masterly. But on the spot here -"

"Oh, agreed. Quite right, Fosdike. I am speaking to-night to the world - no; let me guard against exaggeration. The world includes the Polynesians and Esquimaux - I am speaking to the English-speaking races of the world, but first and foremost to Calderside. My own people. Yes? You have a little something to suggest? Some happy local allusion?"

"It's about Martlow," said Fosdike shortly.

Sir William took him up. "Ah, now you're talking," he approved. "Yes, indeed, anything you can add to my notes about Martlow will be most welcome. I have noted much, but too much is not enough for such an illustrious example of conspicuous gallantry, so noble a life, so great a deed, and so self-sacrificing an end. Any details you can add about Timothy Martlow will indeed -"

Fosdike coughed. "Excuse me, sir, that's just the point. If you talk like that about Martlow down here, they'll laugh at you."

"Laugh?" gasped Rumbold, his sense of propriety outraged. "My dear Fosdike, what's come to you? I celebrate a hero. Our hero. Why, I'm calling the Canteen after Martlow when I might have given it my own name. That speaks volumes." It did.

But Fosdike knew too well what would be the attitude of a Calderside audience if he allowed his chief to sing in top-notes an unreserved eulogy of Tim Martlow. Calderside knew Tim, the civilian, if it had also heard of Tim, the soldier. "Don't you remember Martlow, sir? Before the war, I mean."

"No. Ought I to?"

"Not on the bench?"

"Martlow? Yes, now I think of the name in connection with the old days, there was a drunken fellow. To be sure, an awful blackguard, continually before the bench. Dear me! Well, well, but a man is not responsible for his undesirable relations, I hope."

"No, sir. But that was Martlow. The same man. You really can't speak to Calderside of his as an ennobling life and a great example. The war changed him, but - well, in peace, Tim was absolutely the local bad man, and they all know it. I thought you did, or -"

Sir William turned a face expressive of awe-struck wonder. "Fosdike," he said with deep sincerity, "this is the most amazing thing I've heard of the war. I never connected Martlow the hero with - well, well *de mortuis*." He quoted:

"'Nothing in his life
Became him like the leaving it; he died
As one that had been studied in his death
To throw away the dearest thing he owed
As 'there a careless trifle.'

"Appropriate, I think? I shall use that."

It was, at least, a magnificent recovery from an

unexpected blow, administered by the very man whose duty it was to guard Sir William against just that sort of blow. If Fosdike was not the local watch-dog, he was nothing; and here was an occasion when the dog had omitted to bark until the last minute of the eleventh hour.

"Very apt quotation, sir, though there have never been any exact details of Martlow's death."

Sir William meditated. "Do you recall the name of the saint who was a regular rip before he got religion?" he asked.

"I think that applies to most of them," said Fosdike.

"Yes, but the one in particular. Francis. That's it." He filled his chest. "Timothy Martlow," he pronounced impressively, "is the St. Francis of the Great War, and this Canteen is his shrine. Now, I think I will go into the hall. It is early, but I shall chat with the people. Oh, one last thought. When you mentioned Martlow, I thought you were going to tell me of some undesirable connections. There are none?"

"There is his mother. A widow. You remember the Board voted her an addition to her pension."

"Oh, yes. And she?"

"Oh, most grateful. She will be with you on the platform. I have seen myself that she is - fittingly attired."

"I think I can congratulate you, Fosdike," said Sir William magnanimously. "You've managed very well.

I look forward to a pleasant evening, a widely reported speech, and - "

Then Dolly Wainwright came into the ante-room.

"If you please, sir," she said, "what's going to be done about me?"

Two gentlemen who had all but reached the smug bathos of a mutual admiration society turned astonished eyes at the intruder.

She wore a tam, and a check blanket coat, which she unbuttoned as they watched her. Beneath it, suitable to the occasion, was a white dress, and Sir William, looking at it, felt a glow of tenderness for this artless child who had blundered into the privacy of the ante-room. Something daintily virginal in Dolly's face appealed to him; he caught himself thinking that her frock was more than a miracle in bleached cotton - it was moonshine shot with alabaster; and the improbability of that combination had hardly struck him when Fosdike's voice forced itself harshly on his ears.

"How did you get in here?"

Sir William moved to defend the girl from the anger of his secretary, but when she said, with a certain challenge, "Through the door," he doubted if she were so defenceless as she seemed.

"But there's a doorkeeper at the bottom," said Fosdike. "I gave him my orders."

"I gave him my smile," said Dolly. "I won."

"Upon my word - " Fosdike began.

"Well, well," interrupted Sir William, "what can I do for you?"

The reply was indirect, but caused Sir William still further to readjust his estimate of her.

"I've got friends in the meeting to-night," she concluded. "They'll speak up for me, too, if I'm not righted. So I'm telling you."

"Don't threaten me, my girl," said Sir William without severity. "I am always ready to pay attention to any legitimate grievance, but -"

"Legitimate?" she interrupted. "Well, mine's not legitimate. So there!"

"I beg your pardon?" She puzzled Sir William. "Come now," he went on in his most patriarchal manner, "don't assume I'm not going to listen to you. I am. To-night there is no thought in my mind except the welfare of Calderside."

"Oh, well," she said apologetically, "I'm sorry if I riled you, but it's a bit awkward to speak it out to a man. Only" (the unconscious cruelty of youth - or was it conscious?) "you're both old, so perhaps I can get through. It's about Tim Martlow."

"Ah," said Sir William encouragingly, "our glorious hero."

"Yes," said Dolly. "I'm the mother of his child."

We are all balloons dancing our lives amongst pins. Therefore, be compassionate towards Sir William. He collapsed speechlessly on a hard chair.

Fosdike reacted more alertly. "This is the first I've heard of Martlow's being married," he said aggressively.

Dolly looked up at him indignantly. "You ain't heard it now, have you?" she protested. "I said it wasn't legitimate. I don't say we'd not have got married if there'd been time, but you can't do everything on short leave."

There seemed an obvious retort. Rumbold and Fosdike looked at each other, and neither made the retort. Instead, Fosdike asked: "Are you employed in the works here?"

"I was here, on munitions," she said, "and then on doles."

"And now you're on the make," he sneered.

"Oh, I dunno," she said. "All this fuss about Tim Martlow. I ought to have my bit out of it."

"Deplorable," grieved Sir William. "The crass materialism of it all. This is so sad. How old are you?"

"Twenty," said Dolly. "Twenty, with a child to keep, and his father's name up in gold lettering in that hall there. I say somebody ought to do something."

"I suppose now, Miss -" Fosdike baulked.

"Wainwright, Dolly Wainwright, though it ought to be Martlow."

"I suppose you loved Tim very dearly?"

"I liked him well enough. He was good-looking in his khaki."

"Liked him? I'm sure it was more than that."

"Oh, I dunno. Why?" asked the girl, who said she was the mother of Martlow's child.

"I am sure," said Fosdike gravely, "you would never do anything to bring a stain upon his memory."

Dolly proposed a bargain. "If I'm rightly done by," she said, "I'll do right by him."

"Anything that marred the harmony of to-night's ceremony, Miss Wainwright, would be unthinkable," said Sir William, coming to his lieutenant's support.

"Right," said Dolly cheerfully. "If you'll take steps according, I'm sure I've no desire to make a scene."

"A scene," gasped Sir William.

"Though," she pointed out, "it's a lot to ask of any one, you know. Giving up the certain chance of getting my photograph in the papers. I make a good picture, too. Some do and some don't, but I take well and when you know you've got the looks to carry off a scene, it's asking something of me to give up the idea."

"But you said you'd no desire to make a scene."

"Poor girls have often got to do what they don't wish to. I wouldn't make a scene in the usual way. Hysterics and all that. Hysterics means cold water in your face and your dress messed up and no sympathy. But with scenes, the greater the occasion the greater the reward, and there's no denying this is an occasion, is there? You're making a big to-do about Tim Martlow and the reward would be according. I don't know if you've noticed that if a girl makes a scene and she's got the looks for it, she gets offers of marriage, like they do in the police-court when they've been wronged and the magistrate passes all the men's letters on to the court missionary and the girl and the missionary go through them and choose the likeliest fellow out of the bunch?"

"But my dear young lady -" Fosdike began.

She silenced him. "Oh, it's all right. I don't know that I want to get married."

"Then you ought to," said Sir William virtuously.

"There's better things in life than getting married," Dolly said. "I've weighed up marriage, and I don't see what there is in it for a girl nowadays."

"In your case, I should have thought there was everything."

Dolly sniffed. "There isn't liberty," she said. "And we won the fight for liberty, didn't we? No; if I made that scene it 'ud be to get my photograph in the papers where the film people could see it. I've the right face for the pictures, and my romantic history will do the rest."

"Good heavens, girl," cried the scandalised Sir William, "have you no reverence at all? The pictures! You'd turn all my disinterested efforts to ridicule. You'd - oh, but there! You're not going to make a scene?"

"That's a matter of arrangement, of course," said the cool lady. "I'm only showing you what a big chance I shall miss if I oblige you. Suppose I pipe up my tale of woe just when you're on the platform with the Union Jack behind you and the reporters in front of you, and that tablet in there that says Tim is the greatest glory of Calderside -"

Sir William nearly screamed. "Be quiet, girl. Fosdike," he snarled, turning viciously on his secretary, "what the deuce do you mean by pretending to keep an eye on local affairs when you miss a thing like this?"

"'Tisn't his fault," said Dolly. "I've been saving this up for you."

"Oh," he groaned, "and I'd felt so happy about to-night." He took out a fountain pen. "Well, I suppose there's no help for it. Fosdike, what's the amount of the pension we allow Martlow's mother?"

"Double it, add a pound a week, and what's the answer, Mr. Fosdike?" asked Dolly quickly.

Sir William gasped ludicrously.

"I mean to say," said Dolly, conferring on his gasp the honour of an explanation, "she's old and didn't go on munitions, and didn't get used to wangling income tax on her wages, and never had no ambitions to go on the pictures, neither. What's compensation to her isn't compensation to me. I've got a higher standard."

"The less you say about your standards, the better, my girl," retorted Sir William. "Do you know that this is blackmail?"

"No, it isn't. Not when I ain't asked you for nothing. And if I pass the remark how that three pounds a week is my idea of a minimum wage, it isn't blackmail to state the fact."

Sir William paused in the act of tearing a page out of Fosdike's note-book. "Three pounds a week!"

"Well," said Dolly reasonably, "I didn't depreciate the currency. Three pounds a week is little enough these times for the girl who fell from grace through the chief glory of Calderside."

"But suppose you marry," suggested Mr. Fosdike.

"Then I marry well," she said, "having means of my own. And I ought to, seeing I'm kind of widow to the chief glory of -"

Sir William looked up sharply from the table. "If you use that phrase again," he said, "I'll tear this paper up."

"Widow to Tim Martlow," she amended it, defiantly. He handed her the document he had drawn up. It was an undertaking in brief, unambiguous terms to pay her three pounds a week for life. As she read it, exulting, the door was kicked open.

The tramp, whose name was Timothy Martlow, came

in and turning, spoke through the doorway to the janitor below. "Call out," he said, "and I'll come back and knock you down again." Then he locked the door.

Fosdike went courageously towards him. "What do you mean by this intrusion? Who are you?"

The tramp assured himself that his hat was well pulled down over his face. He put his hands in his pockets and looked quizzically at the advancing Mr. Fosdike. "So far," he said, "I'm the man that locked the door."

Fosdike started for the second door, which led directly to the platform. The tramp reached it first, and locked it, shouldering Fosdike from him. "Now," he said, Sir William was searching the wall, "are there no bells?" he asked desperately.

"No."

"No?" jeered the tramp. "No bell. No telephone. No nothing. You're scotched without your rifle this time."

Fosdike consulted Sir William. "I might shout for the police," he suggested.

"It's risky," commented the tramp. "They sometimes come when they're called."

"Then -" began the secretary.

"It's your risk," emphasised the tramp. "And, I don't advise it. I've gone to a lot of trouble this last week to keep out of sight of the Calderside police. They'd identify me easy, and Sir William wouldn't like that."

"I wouldn't like?" said Rumbold. "I? Who are you?"

"Wounded and missing, believed dead," quoted the tramp. "Only there's been a lot of beliefs upset in this war, and I'm one of them."

"One of what?"

"I'm telling you. One of the strayed sheep that got mislaid and come home at the awkwardest times." He snatched his hat off. "Have a good look at that face, your worship."

"Timothy Martlow," cried Sir William.

Fosdike staggered to a chair while Dolly, who had shown nothing but amusement at the tramp, now gave a quick cry and shrank back against the wall, exhibiting every symptom of the liveliest terror. Of the trio, Sir William, for whom surely this inopportune return had the most serious implications, alone stood his ground, and Martlow grimly appreciated his pluck.

"It's very near made a stretcher-case of him," he said, indicating the prostrated Fosdike. "You're cooler. Walking wounded."

"I ... really...."

"Shake hands, old cock," said Martlow, "I know you've got it writ up in there -" he jerked his head towards the hall - "that I'm the chief glory of Calderside, but damme if you're not the second best yourself, and I'll condescend to shake your hand if it's only to show you I'm not a ghost."

Sir William decided that it was politic to humour this visitor. He shook hands. "Then, if you know," he said, "if you know what this building is, it isn't accident that brings you here to-night."

"The sort of accident you set with a time-fuse," said Martlow grimly. "I told you I'd been dodging the police for a week lest any of my old pals should recognise me. I was waiting to get you to-night, and sitting tight and listening. The things I heard! Nearly made me take my hat off to myself. But not quite. Not quite. I kept my hat on and I kept my hair on. It's a mistake to act premature on information received. If I'd sprung this too soon, the wrong thing might have happened to me."

"What wrong thing, Martlow?" asked Sir William with some indignation. If the fellow meant anything, it was that he would have been spirited away by Sir William.

"Oh, anything," replied Martlow. "Anything would be wrong that made me miss this pleasure. You and me conversing affable here. Not a bit like it was in the old days before I rose to being the chief glory of Calderside. Conversation was one-sided then, and all on your side instead of mine. 'Here again, Martlow,' you'd say, and then they'd gabble the evidence, and you'd say 'fourteen days' or 'twenty-one days,' if you'd got up peevish and that's all there was to our friendly intercourse. This time, I make no doubt you'll be asking me to stay at the Towers to-night. And," he went on blandly, enjoying every wince that twisted Sir William's face in spite of his efforts to appear unmoved, "I don't know that I'll refuse. It's a levelling thing, war. I've read that war makes us all conscious we're members of one brotherhood, and I know it's true now. Consequently the chief glory of the place ain't got no right to be too high and mighty to accept your humble invitation. The best guest-room for Sergeant Martlow, you'll say. See there's a hot water-bottle in his bed, you'll say, and in case he's thirsty in the night, you'll tell them to put the whisky by his side."

After all, a man does not rise to become Sir William Rumbold by being flabby. Sir William struck the table heavily. Somehow he had to put a period to this mocking harangue. "Martlow," he said, "how many people know you're here?"

Tim gave a good imitation of Sir William's gesture. He, too, could strike a table. "Rumbold," he retorted, "what's the value of a secret when it's not a secret? You three in this room know, and not another soul in Calderside."

"Not even your mother?" queried Rumbold.

"No. I been a bad son to her in the past. I'm a good one now I'm dead. She's got a bit o' pension, and I'll not disturb that. I'll stay dead - to her," he added forcibly, dashing the hope which leapt in Rumbold.

"Why have you come here? Here - to-night?"

The easy mockery renewed itself in Martlow's voice. "People's ideas of fun vary," he stated. "The fly's idea ain't the same as the spider's. This 'ere is my idea - shaking your hand and sitting cosy with the bloke that's sent me down more times than I can think. And the fun 'ull grow furious when you and I walk arm in arm on to that platform, and you tell them all I'm resurrected."

"Like this?" The proper Mr. Fosdike interjected.

"Eh?" said Tim. "Like what?"

"You can't go on to the platform in those clothes, Martlow. Have you looked in a mirror lately? Do you know what you look like? This is a respectable occasion, man."

"Yes," said Tim drily. "It's an occasion for showing respect to me. I'll do as I am, not having had time to go to the tailor's for my dress suit yet."

"Martlow," said Sir William briskly, "time's short. I'm due on that platform."

"Right, I'm with you." Tim moved towards the platform door.

Sir William, with a serene air of triumph, played his trump card. He took out his cheque-book. "No," he said. "You're not coming. Instead -"

He shrank back hastily as a huge fist was projected vehemently towards his face. But the fist swerved and opened. The cheque-book, not Sir William's person, was its objective. "Instead be damned," said Tim Martlow, pitching the cheque-book to the floor. "To hell with your money. Thought I was after money, did you?"

Sir William met his eye. "Yes, I did," he said hardily.

"That's the sort of mean idea you would have, Sir William Rumbold. They say scum rises. You grew a handle to your name during the war, but you ain't

Edward J. O'Brien and John Cournos

grown manners to go with it. War changes them that's changeable. T'others are too set to change."

Sir William felt a strange glow of appreciation for this man who, with so easy an opportunity to grow rich, refused money. "It's changed you," he said with ungrudging admiration that had no tincture of diplomacy in it.

"Has it?" mused Tim. "From what?"

"Well -" Sir William was embarrassed. "From what you were."

"What was I?" demanded Tim. "Go on, spit it out. What sort of character would you have given me then?" "I'd have called you," said Sir William boldly, "a disreputable drunken loafer who never did an honest day's work in his life." Which had the merit of truth, and, he thought, the demerit of rashness.

To his surprise he found that Tim was looking at him with undisguised admiration. "Lummy," he said, "you've got guts. Yes, that's right. 'Disreputable drunken loafer.' And if I came back now?" he asked.

"You were magnificent in the war, Martlow."

"First thing I did when I got civvies on was to get blind and skinned. Drink and civvies go together in my mind."

"You'll get over that," said Sir William encouragingly; but he was puzzled by the curiously wistful note which had replaced Tim's hectoring.

"There's a chance," admitted Tim. "A bare chance. Not a chance I'd gamble on. Not when I've a bigger chance than that. You wouldn't say, weighing me up now, that I've got a reformed look, would you?"

Sir William couldn't. "But you'll pull yourself together. You'll remember -"

"I'll remember the taste of beer," said Tim with fierce conviction. "No, I never had a chance before, but I've got one now, and, by heaven, I'm taking it." Sir William's apprehension grew acute; if money was not the question, what outrageous demand was about to be made of him? Tim went on, "I'm nothing but a dirty, drunken tramp to-day. Yes, drunk when I can get it and craving when I can't. That's Tim Martlow when he's living. Tim Martlow dead's a different thing. He's a man with his name wrote up in letters of gold in a dry canteen. Dry! By God, that's funny! He's somebody, honoured in Calderside for ever and ever, amen. And we won't spoil a good thing by taking chances on my reformation. I'm dead. I'll stay dead." He paused in enjoying the effect he made.

Sir William stooped to pick his cheque-book from the floor. "Don't do that," said Tim sharply. "It isn't out of your mind yet that money's what I came for. Fun's one thing that brought me. Just for the treat of showing you myself and watching your quick-change faces while I did it. And I've had my fun." His voice grew menacing. "The other thing I came for isn't fun. It's this." Dolly screamed as he took her arm and jerked her to her feet from the corner where she had sought obscurity. He shook her urgently. "You've been telling tales about me. I've heard of it. You hear all the news when you lie quiet yourself and let other people do the talking. You came in here to-night to spin a yarn. I watched you in. Well, is it true?"

"No," said Dolly, gasping for breath. "I mean -" he insisted, "what you said about you and me. That isn't true?"

She repeated her denial. "No," he said, releasing her, "it 'ud have a job to be seeing this is the first time I've had the pleasure of meeting you. That'll do." He opened the platform door politely. "I hope I haven't made you late on the platform, sir," he said.

Both Sir William and the secretary stared fascinated at Dolly, the enterprising young person who had so successfully bluffed them. "I repeat, don't let me make you late," said Tim from the now wide open door.

Rumbold checked Fosdike who was, apparently, bent on doing Dolly a personal violence. "That can wait," he said. "What can't wait is this." He held out his hand to Martlow. "In all sincerity, I beg the honour."

Tim shook his hand, and Rumbold turned to the door. Fosdike ran after him with the notes of his speech. "Your speech, sir."

Sir William turned on him angrily. "Man," he said, "haven't you heard? That muck won't do now. I have to try to do Martlow justice." He went out to the platform, Fosdike after him.

Tim Martlow sat at the table and took a bottle from his pocket. He drew the cork with his teeth, then felt a light touch on his arm. "I was forgetting you," he said, replacing the bottle.

"I ain't likely to forget you," said Dolly ruefully.

He gripped her hard. "But you are going to forget me, my girl," he said. "Tim Martlow's dead, and his letters of gold ain't going to be blotted by the likes of you. You that's been putting it about Calderside I'm the father of your child, and I ain't never seen you in my life till to-night."

"Yes, but you're getting this all wrong," she blubbered. "I didn't have a baby. I was going to borrow one if they'd claimed to see it."

"What? No baby? And you put it across old Rumbold?" Laughter and sheer admiration of her audacity were mingled in his voice. With a baby it was a good bluff; without one, the girl's ingenuity seemed to him to touch genius.

"He gave me that paper," she said, pride subduing tears as she handed him her splendid trophy.

"Three pounds a week for life," he read, with profound reverence. "If you ain't a blinkin' marvel." He complimented her, giving her the paper back. Then he realised that, through him, her gains were lost.

"Gawd, I done wrong. I got no right to mess up a thing like that. I didn't know. See, I'll tell him I made you lie. I'll own the baby's mine."

"But there ain't no baby," she persisted.

"There's plenty of babies looking for a mother with three pounds a week," he said.

She tore the paper up. "Then they'll not find me," she said. "Three pounds a week's gone. And your letters of gold, Mr. Martlow, remain."

The practised voice of Sir William Rumbold, speaking on the platform, filled the ante-room, not with the rhetorician's counterfeit of sincerity, but, unmistakably, with sincerity itself. "I had prepared a speech," he was saying. "A prepared speech is useless in face of the emotion I feel at the life of Timothy Martlow. I say advisedly to you that when I think of Martlow, I know myself for a worm. He was despised and rejected. What had England done for him that he should give his life for her? We wronged him. We made an outcast of him. I personally wronged him from the magistrate's bench, and he pays us back like this, rising from an undeserved obscurity to a height where he rests secure for ever, a reproach to us, and a great example of the man who won. And against what odds he played it out to a supreme end, and -"

"You're right," said Tim Martlow, motioning the girl to close the door. He wasn't used to hearing panegyrics on himself, nor was he aware that, mechanically, he had raised the bottle to his lips.

Dolly meant to close the door discreetly; instead, she threw it from her and jumped at the bottle. Tim was conscious of a double crash, putting an emphatic stop to the sound of Sir William's eulogy - the crash of the door and the bottle which Dolly snatched from him and pitched against the wall.

"Letters of gold," she panted, "and you shan't tarnish them. I'll see to that."

He gaped for a moment at the liquor flowing from the bottle, then raised his eyes to hers. "You?" he said.

"I haven't got a baby to look after," said Dolly. "But - I've you. Where were you thinking of going now?"

His eyes went to the door behind which Sir William was, presumably, still praising him, and his head jerked resolutely. "Playing it out," he said. "I've got to vanish good, and sure after that. I'll play it out, by God. I was a hero once, I'll be a hero still." His foot crunched broken glass as he moved. "I'm going to America, my girl. It's dry."

Perhaps she distrusted the absolute dryness of America, and perhaps that had nothing to do with Dolly. She examined her hand minutely. "Going to the Isle of Man on a rough day, I wasn't a bit ill," she said casually. "I'm a good sailor."

"You put it across Sir William," he said. "You're a blinkin' marvel."

"No," she said, "but a thing that's worth doing is worth doing well. I'm not a marvel, but I might be the metal polish in those gold letters of yours if you think it worth while."

His trampish squalor seemed to him suddenly appalling. "There, don't do that," he protested - her arm had found its way into his. "My sleeve's dirty."

"Idiot!" said Dolly Wainwright, drawing him to the door.

THE PENSIONER

By WILLIAM CAINE

(From *The Graphic*) 1922

Miss Crewe was born in the year 1821. She received a sort of education, and at the age of twenty became the governess of a little girl, eight years old, called Martha Bond. She was Martha's governess for the next ten years. Then Martha came out and Miss Crewe went to be the governess of somebody else. Martha married Mr. William Harper. A year later she gave birth to a son, who was named Edward. This brings us to the year 1853.

When Edward was six, Miss Crewe came back, to be his governess. Four years later he went to school and Miss Crewe went away to be the governess of somebody else. She was now forty-two years old.

Twelve years passed and Mrs. Harper died, recommending Miss Crewe to her husband's care, for Miss Crewe had recently been smitten by an incurable disease which made it impossible for her to be a governess any longer.

Mr. Harper, who had passionately loved his wife, gave instructions to his solicitor to pay Miss Crewe the sum of one hundred and fifty pounds annually. He had some thoughts of buying her an annuity, but she seemed so ill that he didn't. Edward was now twenty-two.

In the year 1888, Mr. Harper died after a very short illness. He had expected Miss Crewe to die any day during the past thirteen years, but since she hadn't he thought it proper now to recommend her to Edward's care. This is how he did it.

"That confounded old Crewe, Eddie. You'll have to see to her. Let her have her money as before, but for the Lord's sake don't go and buy her an annuity now. If you do, she'll die on your hands in a week!" Shortly afterwards the old gentleman passed away.

Edward was now thirty-five. Miss Crewe was sixty-seven and reported to be in an almost desperate state. Edward followed his father's advice. He bought no annuity for Miss Crewe. Her one hundred and fifty pounds continued to be paid each year into her bank; but by Edward, not by his late father's solicitors.

Edward had his own ideas of managing the considerable fortune which he had inherited. These ideas were unsound. The first of them was that he should assume the entire direction of his own affairs. Accordingly he instructed his solicitors to realise all the mortgages and railway-stock and other admirable securities in which his money was invested and hand over the cash to him. He then went in for the highest rate of interest which anyone would promise him. The consequence was that, within twelve years, he was almost a poor man, his annual income having dwindled from about three thousand to about four hundred pounds.

Though he was a fool he was an honourable man, and so he continued to pay Miss Crewe her one hundred and fifty pounds each year. This left him about two hundred and fifty for himself. The capital which his so reduced income represented was invested in a Mexican brewery in which he had implicit faith. Nevertheless, he began to think that he might do well were he to try to earn a little extra money.

The only thing he could do was to paint, not at all well, in water-colours. He became the pupil, quite seriously, of a young artist whom he knew. He was now forty-seven years old, while Miss Crewe was seventy-nine. The year was 1900.

To everybody's amazement Edward soon began to make quite good progress in his painting. Yes, his pictures were not at all unpleasant little things. He sent one of them to the Academy. It was accepted. It was, as I live, sold for ten pounds. Edward was an artist.

Soon he was making between thirty and forty pounds a year. Then he was making over a hundred. Then two hundred. Then the Mexican brewery failed, General Malefico having burned it to the ground for a lark.

This happened in the spring of 1914 when Edward was sixty-one and Miss Crewe was ninety-three. Edward, after paying her money to Miss Crewe, might flatter himself on the possibility of having some fifty pounds a year for himself, that is to say, if his picture sales did not decline. A single man can, however, get along, more or less, on fifty pounds more or less.

Then the Great War broke out.

It has been said that in the autumn of 1914 the Old Men came into their kingdom. As the fields of Britain were gradually stripped bare of their valid toilers, the Fathers of each village assumed, at good wages, the burden of agriculture. From their offices the juniors departed or were torn; the senior clerks carried on desperately until the Girls were introduced. No man was any longer too old at forty. Octogenarians could command a salary. The very cinemas were glad to dress up ancient fellows in uniform and post them on their doorsteps.

Edward could do nothing but paint rather agreeable water-colours, and that was all. The market for his kind of work was shut. A patriotic nation was economising in order to get five per cent on the War Loans. People were not giving inexpensive little water-colours away to one another as wedding gifts any longer. Only the painters of high reputation, whose work was regarded as a real investment, could dispose of their wares.

Starvation stared Edward in the face, not only his own starvation, you understand, but Miss Crewe's. And Edward was a man of honour.

He hated Miss Crewe intensely, but he had undertaken to provide for her, and provide for her he must - even if he failed to provide for himself.

He wrapped some samples of his paintings in brown paper, and began to seek for a job among the wholesale stationers. He offered himself as one who was prepared to design Christmas-cards and calendars, and things of the kind.

Adversity had sharpened his wits. Even the wholesale stationers were not turning white-headed men from their portals. To Edward was accorded the privilege of displaying the rather agreeable contents of his parcel. After he had unpacked it and packed it up again some thirty times he was offered work. His pictures were really rather agreeable. It was piecework, and he was to do it off the premises, no matter where. By toiling day and night he might be able to earn as much as £4 a week. He went away and toiled. His employers were pleased with what, each Monday, he brought them. They did not offer to increase his remuneration, but they encouraged him to produce, and took practically everything he offered. Edward was very fortunate.

During the first year of the war he lived like a beast, worked like a slave, and earned exactly enough to keep his soul in his body and pay Miss Crewe her one hundred and fifty pounds. During the second year of the war he did it again. The fourth year of the war found him still alive and still punctual to his obligations towards Miss Crewe.

Miss Crewe, however, found one hundred and fifty pounds no longer what it had been. Prices were rising in every direction. She wrote to Edward pointing this out, and asking him if he couldn't see his way to increasing her allowance. She invoked the memory of his dear mother and father, added something about the happy hours that he and she had spent together in the dear old school-room, and signed herself his affectionately.

Edward petitioned for an increase of pay. He pointed out to his firm of wholesale stationers that prices were rising in every direction. The firm, who knew when they had a marketable thing cheap, granted his petition. Henceforth Edward was able to earn five pounds a week. He increased Miss Crewe's allowance by fifty pounds, and continued to live more like a beast than ever, for the price of paper and paints was soaring. He worked practically without ceasing, save to sleep (which he could not do) and to eat (which he could not afford). He was now sixty-four, while Miss Crewe was rising ninety-seven.

Edward had been ailing for a long time. On Armistice Day he struck work for an hour in order to walk about in the streets and share in the general rejoicing. He caught a severe cold, and the next day, instead of staying between his blankets (he had no sheets), he went up to the City with some designs which he had just completed. That night he was feverish. The next night he was delirious. The third night he was dead, and there was an end of him.

He had, however, managed, before he died (two days before), to send to Miss Crewe a money order for her quarter's allowance of fifty pounds. This had left him with precisely four shillings and twopence in the Post Office Savings Bank.

He was, consequently, buried by the parish.

Miss Crewe received her money. She was delighted to have it, and at once wrote to Edward her customary letter of grateful and affectionate thanks. She added in a post-script that if he *could* find it in his generous heart to let her have a still little more next quarter it would be most acceptable, because every day seemed to make it harder and harder for her to get along.

Edward was dead when this letter was delivered.

Miss Crewe sent her money order to her bank, asking that it might be placed to her deposit account. This she reminded the bank, would bring up the amount of her deposit to exactly two thousand pounds.

BROADSHEET BALLAD

By A.E. COPPARD

(From *The Dial*) 1922

At noon the tiler and the mason stepped down from the roof of the village church which they were repairing and crossed over the road to the tavern to eat their dinner. It had been a nice little morning, but there were clouds massing in the south; Sam the tiler remarked that it looked like thunder. The two men sat in the dim little tap-room eating, Bob the mason at the same time reading from a newspaper an account of a trial for murder.

"I dunno what thunder looks like," Bob said, "but I reckon this chap is going to be hung, though I can't rightly say for why. To my thinking he didn't do it at all: but murder's a bloody thing and someone ought to suffer for it."

"I don't think," spluttered Sam as he impaled a flat piece of beet-root on the point of a pocket-knife and prepared to contemplate it with patience until his stuffed mouth was ready to receive it, "he ought to be hung."

"There can be no other end for him though, with a mob

of lawyers like that, and a judge like that, and a jury too ... why the rope's half round his neck this minute; he'll be in glory within a month, they only have three Sundays, you know, between the sentence and the execution. Well, hark at that rain then!"

A shower that began as a playful sprinkle grew to a powerful steady summer downpour. It splashed in the open window and the dim room grew more dim, and cool.

"Hanging's a dreadful thing," continued Sam, "and 'tis often unjust I've no doubt, I've no doubt at all."

"Unjust! I tell you ... at majority of trials those who give their evidence mostly knows nothing at all about the matter; them as knows a lot - they stays at home and don't budge, not likely!"

"No? But why?"

"Why? They has their reasons. I know that, I knows it for truth ...hark at that rain, it's made the room feel cold."

They watched the downfall in complete silence for some moments.

"Hanging's a dreadful thing," Sam at length repeated, with almost a sigh.

"I can tell you a tale about that, Sam, in a minute," said the other. He began to fill his pipe from Sam's brass box which was labelled cough lozenges and smelled of paregoric.

"Just about ten years ago I was working over in
Cotswold country. I remember I'd been into Gloucester
one Saturday afternoon and it rained. I was jogging
along home in a carrier's van; I never seen it rain like
that afore, no, nor never afterwards, not like that. B-r-r-
r-r! it came down ... bashing! And we came to a cross-
roads where there's a public house called The Wheel of
Fortune, very lonely and onsheltered it is just there. I
see'd a young woman standing in the porch awaiting
us, but the carrier was wet and tired and angry or
something and wouldn't stop. 'No room' - he bawled
out to her - 'full up, can't take you!' and he drove on.
'For the love o' God, mate,' I says, 'pull up and take that
young creature! She's ... she's ... can't you see!' 'But I'm
all behind as 'tis' - he shouts to me - 'You knows your
gospel, don't you: time and tide wait for no man?' 'Ah,
but dammit all, they always call for a feller' - I says.
With that he turned round and we drove back for the
girl. She clumb in and sat on my knees; I squat on a
tub of vinegar, there was nowhere else and I was right
and all, she was going on for a birth. Well, the old van
rattled away for six or seven miles; whenever it
stopped you could hear the rain clattering on the
tarpaulin, or sounding outside on the grass as if it was
breathing hard, and the old horse steamed and shivered
with it. I had knowed the girl once in a friendly way, a
pretty young creature, but now she was white and
sorrowful and wouldn't say much. By and bye we came
to another cross-roads near a village, and she got out
there. 'Good day, my gal' - I says, affable like, and
'Thank you sir,' - says she, and off she popped in the
rain with her umbrella up. A rare pretty girl, quite
young, I'd met her before, a girl you could get
uncommon fond of, you know, but I didn't meet her
afterwards: she was mixed up in a bad business. It all
happened in the next six months while I was working

round those parts. Everybody knew of it. This girl's name was Edith and she had a younger sister Agnes. Their father was old Harry Mallerton, kept The British Oak at North Quainy; he stuttered. Well, this Edith had a love affair with a young chap William, and having a very loving nature she behaved foolish. Then she couldn't bring the chap up to the scratch nohow by herself, and of course she was afraid to tell her mother or father: you know how girls are after being so pesky natural, they fear, O they do fear! But soon it couldn't be hidden any longer as she was living at home with them all, so she wrote a letter to her mother. 'Dear Mother,' she wrote, and told her all about her trouble.

"By all accounts the mother was angry as an old lion, but Harry took it calm like and sent for young William, who'd not come at first. He lived close by in the village so they went down at last and fetched him.

"'Alright, yes,' he said, 'I'll do what's lawful to be done. There you are, I can't say no fairer, that I can't.'

"'No,' they said, 'you can't.'

"So he kissed the girl and off he went, promising to call in and settle affairs in a day or two. The next day Agnes, which was the younger girl, she also wrote a note to her mother telling her some more strange news:

"'God above!' the mother cried out, 'can it be true, both of you girls, my own daughters, and by the same man! Oh, whatever were you thinking on, both of ye! Whatever can be done now!'"

"What!" ejaculated Sam, "both on 'em, both on 'em!"

"As true as God's my mercy - both on 'em - same chap. Ah! Mrs. Mallerton was afraid to tell her husband at first, for old Harry was the devil born again when he were roused up, so she sent for young William herself, who'd not come again, of course, not likely. But they made him come, O yes, when they told the girl's father.

"'Well may I go to my d-d-d-damnation at once!' roared old Harry - he stuttered you know - 'at once, if that ain't a good one!' So he took off his coat, he took up a stick, he walked down street to William and cut him off his legs. Then he beat him till he howled for his mercy, but you couldn't stop old Harry once he were roused up - he was the devil born again. They do say as he beat him for a solid hour; I can't say as to that, but then old Harry picked him up and carried him off to The British Oak on his own back, and threw him down in his own kitchen between his own two girls like a dead dog. They do say that the little one Agnes flew at her father like a raging cat until he knocked her senseless with a clout over head; rough man he was."

"Well, a' called for it sure," commented Sam.

"Her did," agreed Bob, "but she was the quietest known girl for miles round those parts, very shy and quiet."

"A shady lane breeds mud," said Sam.

"What do you say? - O ah! - mud, yes. But pretty girls both, girls you could get very fond of, skin like apple bloom, and as like as two pinks they were. They had to decide which of them William was to marry."

"Of course, ah!"

"I'll marry Agnes' - says he.

"'You'll not' - says the old man - 'you'll marry Edie.'

"'No I won't' - William says - 'it's Agnes I love and I'll be married to her or I won't be married to e'er of 'em.' All the time Edith sat quiet, dumb as a shovel, never a word, crying a bit; but they do say the young one went on like a ... a young ... Jew."

"The jezebel!" commented Sam.

"You may say it; but wait, my man, just wait. Another cup of beer? We can't go back to church until this humbugging rain have stopped."

"No, that we can't."

"It's my belief the 'bugging rain won't stop this side of four."

"And if the roof don't hold it off it 'ull spoil the Lord's Commandments that's just done up on the chancel front."

"Oh, they be dry by now," spoke Bob reassuringly and then continued his tale. "'I'll marry Agnes or I won't marry nobody' - William says - and they couldn't budge him. No, old Harry cracked on, but he wouldn't have it, and at last Harry says: 'It's like this.' He pulls a half-crown out of his pocket and 'Heads it's Agnes,' he says, 'or tails it's Edith,' he says."

"Never! Ha! ha!" cried Sam.

"Heads it's Agnes, tails it's Edie, so help me God. And

it come down Agnes, yes, heads it was - Agnes - and so there they were."

"And they lived happy ever after?"

"Happy! You don't know your human nature, Sam; wherever was you brought up? 'Heads it's Agnes,' said old Harry, and at that Agnes flung her arms round William's neck and was for going off with him then and there, ha! But this is how it happened about that. William hadn't any kindred, he was a lodger in the village, and his landlady wouldn't have him in her house one mortal hour when she heard all of it; give him the right-about there and then. He couldn't get lodgings anywhere else, nobody would have anything to do with him, so of course, for safety's sake, old Harry had to take him, and there they all lived together at The British Oak - all in one happy family. But they girls couldn't bide the sight of each other, so their father cleaned up an old outhouse in his yard that was used for carts and hens and put William and his Agnes out in it. And there they had to bide. They had a couple of chairs, a sofa, and a bed and that kind of thing, and the young one made it quite snug."

"'Twas a hard thing for that other, that Edie, Bob."

"It was hard, Sam, in a way, and all this was happening just afore I met her in the carrier's van. She was very sad and solemn then; a pretty girl, one you could like. Ah, you may choke me, but there they lived together. Edie never opened her lips to either of them again, and her father sided with her, too. What was worse, it came out after the marriage that Agnes was quite free of trouble - it was only a trumped-up game between her and this William because he fancied her better than the other one. And they never had no child, them two, though when poor Edie's mischance come along I be damned if Agnes weren't fonder of it than its own mother, a jolly sight more fonder, and William - he fair worshipped it."

"You don't say!"

"I do. 'Twas a rum go, that, and Agnes worshipped it, a fact, can prove it by scores o' people to this day, scores, in them parts. William and Agnes worshipped it, and Edie - she just looked on, long of it all, in the same house with them, though she never opened her lips again to her young sister to the day of her death."

"Ah, she died? Well, it's the only way out of such a tangle, poor woman."

"You're sympathizing with the wrong party." Bob filled his pipe again from the brass box; he ignited it with deliberation; going to the open window he spat into a puddle in the road. "The wrong party, Sam; 'twas Agnes that died. She was found on the sofa one morning stone dead, dead as a adder."

"God bless me," murmured Sam.

"Poisoned," added Bob, puffing serenely.

"Poisoned!"

Bob repeated the word poisoned. "This was the way of it," he continued. "One morning the mother went out in the yard to collect her eggs, and she began calling out 'Edie, Edie, here a minute, come and look where that hen have laid her egg; I would never have believed it' -

she says. And when Edie went out her mother led her round the back of the outhouse, and there on the top of a wall this hen had laid an egg. 'I would never have believed it, Edie' - she says - 'scooped out a nest there beautiful, ain't she; I wondered where her was laying. T'other morning the dog brought an egg round in his mouth and laid it on the doormat. There now, Aggie, Aggie, here a minute, come and look where the hen have laid that egg.' And as Aggie didn't answer the mother went in and found her on the sofa in the outhouse, stone dead."

"How'd they account for it?" asked Sam, after a brief interval.

"That's what brings me to the point about this young feller that's going to be hung," said Bob, tapping the newspaper that lay upon the bench. "I don't know what would lie between two young women in a wrangle of that sort; some would get over it quick, but some would never sleep soundly any more not for a minute of their mortal lives. Edie must have been one of that sort. There's people living there now as could tell a lot if they'd a mind to it. Some knowed all about it, could tell you the very shop where Edith managed to get hold of the poison, and could describe to me or to you just how she administered it in a glass of barley water. Old Harry knew all about it, he knew all about everything, but he favoured Edith and he never budged a word. Clever old chap was Harry, and nothing came out against Edie at the inquest - nor the trial either." "Was there a trial then?"

"There was a kind of a trial. Naturally. A beautiful trial. The police came and fetched poor William, they took him away and in due course he was hanged."

136   Edward J. O'Brien and John Cournos

"William! But what had he got to do with it?"

"Nothing. It was rough on him, but he hadn't played straight and so nobody struck up for him. They made out a case against him - there was some onlucky bit of evidence which I'll take my oath old Harry knew something about - and William was done for. Ah, when things take a turn against you it's as certain as twelve o'clock, when they take a turn; you get no more chance than a rabbit from a weasel. It's like dropping your matches into a stream, you needn't waste the bending of your back to pick them out - they're no good on, they'll never strike again. And Edith, she sat in court through it all, very white and trembling and sorrowful, but when the judge put his black cap on they do say she blushed and looked across at William and gave a bit of a smile. Well, she had to suffer for his doings, so why shouldn't he suffer for hers. That's how I look at it...."

"But God-a-mighty...!"

"Yes, God-a-mighty knows. Pretty girls they were, both, and as like as two pinks."

There was quiet for some moments while the tiler and the mason emptied their cups of beer. "I think," said Sam then, "the rain's give over now."

"Ah, that it has," cried Bob. "Let's go and do a bit more on this 'bugging church or she won't be done afore Christmas."

THE CHRISTMAS PRESENT

By RICHMAL CROMPTON

(From *Truth*) 1922

Mary Clay looked out of the window of the old farmhouse. The view was dreary enough - hill and field and woodland, bare, colourless, mist-covered - with no other house in sight. She had never been a woman to crave for company. She liked sewing. She was passionately fond of reading. She was not fond of talking. Probably she could have been very happy at Cromb Farm - alone. Before her marriage she had looked forward to the long evenings with her sewing and reading. She knew that she would be busy enough in the day, for the farmhouse was old and rambling, and she was to have no help in the housework. But she looked forward to quiet, peaceful, lamplit evenings; and only lately, after ten years of married life, had she reluctantly given up the hope of them. For peace was far enough from the old farm kitchen in the evening. It was driven away by John Clay's loud voice, raised always in orders or complaints, or in the stumbling, incoherent reading aloud of his newspaper.

Mary was a silent woman herself and a lover of silence. But John liked to hear the sound of his voice; he liked to shout at her; to call for her from one room

Edward J. O'Brien and John Cournos

to another; above all, he liked to hear his voice reading the paper out loud to her in the evening. She dreaded that most of all. It had lately seemed to jar on her nerves till she felt she must scream aloud. His voice going on and on, raucous and sing-song, became unspeakably irritating. His "Mary!" summoning her from her household work to wherever he happened to be, his "Get my slippers," or "Bring me my pipe," exasperated her almost to the point of rebellion. "Get your own slippers' had trembled on her lips, but had never passed them, for she was a woman who could not bear anger. Noise of any kind appalled her.

She had borne it for ten years, so surely she could go on with it. Yet today, as she gazed hopelessly at the wintry country side, she became acutely conscious that she could not go on with it. Something must happen. Yet what was there that could happen?

It was Christmas next week. She smiled ironically at the thought. Then she noticed the figure of her husband coming up the road. He came in at the gate and round to the side-door.

"Mary!"

She went slowly in answer to the summons. He held a letter in his hand.

"Met the postman," he said. "From your aunt."

She opened the letter and read it in silence. Both of them knew quite well what it contained.

"She wants us to go over for Christmas again," said Mary.

He began to grumble.

"She's as deaf as a post. She's 'most as deaf as her mother was. She ought to know better than to ask folks over when she can't hear a word any one says."

Mary said nothing. He always grumbled about the invitation at first, but really he wanted to go. He liked to talk with her uncle. He liked the change of going down to the village for a few days and hearing all its gossip. He could quite well leave the farm to the "hands" for that time.

The Crewe deafness was proverbial. Mary's great-grandmother had gone stone deaf at the age of thirty-five; her daughter had inherited the affliction and her grand-daughter, the aunt with whom Mary had spent her childhood, had inherited it also at exactly the same age.

"All right," he said at last, grudgingly, as though in answer to her silence, "we'd better go. Write and say we'll go."

*   *   *   *   *

It was Christmas Eve. They were in the kitchen of her uncle's farmhouse. The deaf old woman sat in her chair by the fire knitting. Upon her sunken face there was a curious sardonic smile that was her habitual expression. The two men stood in the doorway. Mary sat at the table looking aimlessly out of the window. Outside, the snow fell in blinding showers. Inside, the fire gleamed on to the copper pots and pans, the crockery on the old oak dresser, the hams hanging from the ceiling.

Suddenly James turned.

"Jane!" he said.

The deaf woman never stirred.

"Jane!"

Still there was no response upon the enigmatic old face by the fireside.

"*Jane*!"

She turned slightly towards the voice.

"Get them photos from upstairs to show John," he bawled.

"What about boats?" she said.

"*Photos*!" roared her husband.

"Coats?" she quavered.

Mary looked from one to the other. The man made a gesture of irritation and went from the room.

He came back with a pile of picture postcards in his hand.

"It's quicker to do a thing oneself," he grumbled. "They're what my brother sent from Switzerland, where he's working now. It's a fine land, to judge from the views of it."

John took them from his hand. "She gets worse?" he

said nodding towards the old woman.

She was sitting gazing at the fire, her lips curved into the curious smile.

Her husband shrugged his shoulders. "Aye. She's nigh as bad as her mother was."

"And her grandmother."

"Aye. It takes longer to tell her to do something than to do it myself. And deaf folks get a bit stupid, too. Can't see what you mean. They're best let alone."

The other man nodded and lit his pipe. Then James opened the door.

"The snow's stopped," he said. "Shall we go to the end of the village and back?"

The other nodded, and took his cap from behind the door. A gust of cold air filled the room as they went out.

Mary took a paper-backed book from the table and came over to the fireplace.

"Mary!"

She started. It was not the sharp, querulous voice of the deaf old woman, it was more like the voice of the young aunt whom Mary remembered in childhood. The old woman was leaning forward, looking at her intently.

"Mary! A happy Christmas to 'ee."

And, as if in spite of herself, Mary answered in her ordinary low tones.

"The same to you, auntie."

"Thank 'ee. Thank 'ee."

Mary gasped.

"Aunt! Can you hear me speaking like this?"

The old woman laughed, silently, rocking to and fro in her chair as if with pent-up merriment of years.

"Yes, I can hear 'ee, child. I've allus heard 'ee."

Mary clasped her hand eagerly.

"Then - you're cured, Aunt - "

"Ay. I'm cured as far as there was ever anything to be cured."

"You -?"

"I was never deaf, child, nor never will be, please God. I've took you all in fine."

Mary stood up in bewilderment.

"You? Never deaf?"

The old woman chuckled again.

"No, nor my mother - nor her mother neither."

Mary shrank back from her.

"I - I don't know what you mean," she said, unsteadily. "Have you been - pretending?"

"I'll make you a Christmas present of it, dearie," said the old woman. "My mother made me a Christmas present of it when I was your age, and her mother made her one. I haven't a lass of my own to give it to, so I give it to you. It can come on quite sudden like, if you want it, and then you can hear what you choose and not hear what you choose. Do you see?" She leant nearer and whispered, "You're shut out of it all - of having to fetch and carry for 'em, answer their daft questions and run their errands like a dog. I've watched you, my lass. You don't get much peace, do you?"

Mary was trembling.

"Oh, I don't know what to think," she said. "I - I couldn't do it."

"Do what you like," said the old woman. "Take it as a present, anyways - the Crewe deafness for a Christmas present," she chuckled. "Use it or not as you like. You'll find it main amusin', anyways."

And into the old face there came again that curious smile as if she carried in her heart some jest fit for the gods on Olympus.

The door opened suddenly with another gust of cold air, and the two men came in again, covered with fine snow.

"I - I'll not do it," whispered Mary, trembling.

"We didn't get far. It's coming on again," remarked John, hanging up his cap.

The old woman rose and began to lay the supper, silently and deftly, moving from cupboard to table without looking up. Mary sat by the fire, motionless and speechless, her eyes fixed on the glowing coals.

"Any signs o' the deafness in her?" whispered James, looking towards Mary. "It come on my wife jus' when she was that age."

"Aye. So I've heered."

Then he said loudly, "Mary!"

A faint pink colour came into her cheeks, but she did not show by look or movement that she had heard. James looked significantly at her husband.

The old woman stood still for a minute with a cup in each hand and smiled her slow, subtle smile.

SEATON'S AUNT

By WALTER DE LA MARE

(From *The London Mercury*) 1922

I had heard rumours of Seaton's Aunt long before I actually encountered her. Seaton, in the hush of confidence, or at any little show of toleration on our part, would remark, "My aunt," or "My old aunt, you know," as if his relative might be a kind of cement to an *entente cordiale*.

He had an unusual quantity of pocket-money; or, at any rate, it was bestowed on him in unusually large amounts; and he spent it freely, though none of us would have described him as an "awfully generous chap." "Hullo, Seaton," he would say, "the old Begum?" At the beginning of term, too, he used to bring back surprising and exotic dainties in a box with a trick padlock that accompanied him from his first appearance at Gummidge's in a billycock hat to the rather abrupt conclusion of his school-days.

From a boy's point of view he looked distastefully foreign, with his yellow skin, and slow chocolate-coloured eyes, and lean weak figure. Merely for his looks he was treated by most of us true-blue Englishmen with condescension, hostility, or contempt. We used to call him "Pongo," but without any better excuse for the nickname than his skin. He was, that is, in one sense of the term what he assuredly was not in the other sense, a sport.

Seaton and I were never in any sense intimate at school, our orbits only intersected in class. I kept instinctively aloof from him. I felt vaguely he was a sneak, and remained quite unmollified by advances on his side, which, in a boy's barbarous fashion, unless it suited me to be magnanimous, I haughtily ignored.

We were both of us quick-footed, and at Prisoner's Base used occasionally to hide together. And so I best remember Seaton - his narrow watchful face in the dusk of summer evening; his peculiar crouch, and his inarticulate whisperings and mumblings. Otherwise he played all games slackly and limply; used to stand and feed at his locker with a crony or two until his "tuck" gave out; or waste his money on some outlandish fancy or other. He bought, for instance, a silver bangle, which he wore above his left elbow, until some of the fellows showed their masterly contempt of the practice by dropping it nearly red-hot down his neck.

It needed, therefore, a rather peculiar taste, a rather rare kind of schoolboy courage and indifference to criticism, to be much associated with him. And I had neither the taste nor the courage. None the less, he did make advances, and on one memorable occasion went to the length of bestowing on me a whole pot of some outlandish mulberry-coloured jelly that had been duplicated in his term's supplies. In the exuberance of my gratitude I promised to spend the next half-term holiday with him at his aunt's house.

I had clean forgotten my promise when, two or three days before the holiday, he came up and triumphantly reminded me of it.

"Well, to tell you the honest truth, Seaton, old chap -" I began graciously; but he cut me short.

"My aunt expects you," he said; "she is very glad you are coming. She's sure to be quite decent to *you*, Withers."

I looked at him in some astonishment; the emphasis was unexpected. It seemed to suggest an aunt not hitherto hinted at, and a friendly feeling on Seaton's side that was more disconcerting than welcome.

*　*　*　*　*

We reached his home partly by train, partly by a lift in an empty farm-cart, and partly by walking. It was a whole-day holiday, and we were to sleep the night; he lent me extraordinary night-gear, I remember. The village street was unusually wide, and was fed from a green by two converging roads, with an inn, and a high green sign at the corner. About a hundred yards down the street was a chemist's shop - Mr. Tanner's. We descended the two steps into his dusky and odorous interior to buy, I remember, some rat poison. A little beyond the chemist's was the forge. You then walked along a very narrow path, under a fairly high wall, nodding here and there with weeds and tufts of grass, and so came to the iron garden-gates, and saw the high flat house behind its huge sycamore. A coach-house stood on the left of the house, and on the right a gate led into a kind of rambling orchard. The lawn lay away over to the left again, and at the bottom (for the whole

Edward J. O'Brien and John Cournos

garden sloped gently to a sluggish and rushy pond-like stream) was a meadow.

We arrived at noon, and entered the gates out of the hot dust beneath the glitter of the dark-curtained windows. Seaton led me at once through the little garden-gate to show me his tadpole pond, swarming with what, being myself not the least bit of a naturalist, I considered the most horrible creatures - of all shapes, consistencies, and sizes, but with whom Seaton seemed to be on the most intimate of terms. I can see his absorbed face now as he sat on his heels and fished the slimy things out in his sallow palms. Wearying at last of his pets, we loitered about awhile in an aimless fashion. Seaton seemed to be listening, or at any rate waiting, for something to happen or for some one to come. But nothing did happen and no one came.

That was just like Seaton. Anyhow, the first view I got of his aunt was when, at the summons of a distant gong, we turned from the garden, very hungry and thirsty, to go into luncheon. We were approaching the house when Seaton suddenly came to a standstill. Indeed, I have always had the impression that he plucked at my sleeve. Something, at least, seemed to catch me back, as it were, as he cried, "Look out, there she is!"

She was standing in an upper window which opened wide on a hinge, and at first sight she looked an excessively tall and overwhelming figure. This, however, was mainly because the window reached all but to the floor of her bedroom. She was in reality rather an under-sized woman, in spite of her long face and big head. She must have stood, I think, unusually still, with eyes fixed on us, though this impression may be due to Seaton's sudden warning and to my consciousness of the cautious and subdued air that had fallen on him at sight of her. I know that without the least reason in the world I felt a kind of guiltiness, as if I had been "caught." There was a silvery star pattern sprinkled on her black silk dress, and even from the ground I could see the immense coils of her hair and the rings on her left hand which was held fingering the small jet buttons of her bodice. She watched our united advance without stirring, until, imperceptibly, her eyes raised and lost themselves in the distance, so that it was out of an assumed reverie that she appeared suddenly to awaken to our presence beneath her when we drew close to the house.

"So this is your friend, Mr. Smithers, I suppose?" she said, bobbing to me.

"Withers, aunt," said Seaton.

"It's much the same," she said, with eyes fixed on me. "Come in, Mr. Withers, and bring him along with you."

She continued to gaze at me - at least, I think she did so. I know that the fixity of her scrutiny and her ironical "Mr." made me feel peculiarly uncomfortable. But she was extremely kind and attentive to me, though perhaps her kindness and attention showed up more vividly against her complete neglect of Seaton. Only one remark that I have any recollection of she made to him: "When I look on my nephew, Mr. Smithers, I realise that dust we are, and dust shall become. You are hot, dirty, and incorrigible, Arthur."

She sat at the head of the table, Seaton at the foot, and

I, before a wide waste of damask tablecloth, between them. It was an old and rather close dining-room, with windows thrown wide to the green garden and a wonderful cascade of fading roses. Miss Seaton's great chair faced this window, so that its rose-reflected light shone full on her yellowish face, and on just such chocolate eyes as my schoolfellow's, except that hers were more than half-covered by unusually long and heavy lids.

There she sat, eating, with those sluggish eyes fixed for the most part on my face; above them stood the deep-lined fork between her eyebrows; and above that the wide expanse of a remarkable brow beneath its strange steep bank of hair. The lunch was copious, and consisted, I remember, of all such dishes as are generally considered mischievous and too good for the schoolboy digestion - lobster mayonnaise, cold game sausages, an immense veal and ham pie farced with eggs and numberless delicious flavours; besides sauces, kickshaws, creams, and sweetmeats. We even had wine, a half-glass of old darkish sherry each.

Miss Seaton enjoyed and indulged an enormous appetite. Her example and a natural schoolboy voracity soon overcame my nervousness of her, even to the extent of allowing me to enjoy to the best of my bent so rare a "spread." Seaton was singularly modest; the greater part of his meal consisted of almonds and raisins, which he nibbled surreptitiously and as if he found difficulty in swallowing them.

I don't mean that Miss Seaton "conversed" with me. She merely scattered trenchant remarks and now and then twinkled a baited question over my head. But her face was like a dense and involved accompaniment to her talk. She presently dropped the "Mr.," to my intense relief, and called me now Withers, or Wither, now Smithers, and even once towards the close of the meal distinctly Johnson, though how on earth my name suggested it, or whose face mine had reanimated in memory, I cannot conceive.

"And is Arthur a good boy at school, Mr. Wither?" was one of her many questions. "Does he please his masters? Is he first in his class? What does the reverend Dr. Gummidge think of him, eh?"

I knew she was jeering at him, but her face was adamant against the least flicker of sarcasm or faceti-ousness. I gazed fixedly at a blushing crescent of lobster.

"I think you're eighth, aren't you, Seaton?"

Seaton moved his small pupils towards his aunt. But she continued to gaze with a kind of concentrated detachment at me.

"Arthur will never make a brilliant scholar, I fear," she said, lifting a dexterously-burdened fork to her wide mouth....

After luncheon she preceded me up to my bedroom. It was a jolly little bedroom, with a brass fender and rugs and a polished floor, on which it was possible, I afterwards found, to play "snow-shoes." Over the washstand was a little black-framed water-colour drawing, depicting a large eye with an extremely fishlike intensity in the spark of light on the dark pupil; and in "illuminated" lettering beneath was printed very minutely, "Thou God Seest ME," followed by a long looped monogram, "S.S.," in the corner. The other pictures were all of the sea: brigs on blue water; a schooner overtopping chalk cliffs; a rocky island of prodigious steepness, with two tiny sailors dragging a monstrous boat up a shelf of beach.

"This is the room, Withers, my brother William died in when a boy. Admire the view!"

I looked out of the window across the tree-tops. It was a day hot with sunshine over the green fields, and the cattle were standing swishing their tails in the shallow water. But the view at the moment was only exaggeratedly vivid because I was horribly dreading that she would presently enquire after my luggage, and I had not brought even a toothbrush. I need have had no fear. Hers was not that highly-civilised type of mind that is stuffed with sharp material details. Nor could her ample presence be described as in the least motherly.

"I would never consent to question a schoolfellow behind my nephew's back," she said, standing in the middle of the room, 'but tell me, Smithers, why is Arthur so unpopular? You, I understand, are his only close friend." She stood in a dazzle of sun, and out of it her eyes regarded me with such leaden penetration beneath their thick lids that I doubt if my face concealed the least thought from her. "But there, there," she added very suavely, stooping her head a little, "don't trouble to answer me. I never extort an answer. Boys are queer fish. Brains might perhaps have suggested his washing his hands before luncheon; but - not my choice, Smithers. God forbid! And now, perhaps, you would like to go into the garden again. I cannot actually see from here, but I should not be surprised if Arthur is now skulking behind that hedge."

He was. I saw his head come out and take a rapid glance at the windows.

"Join him, Mr. Smithers; we shall meet again, I hope, at the tea-table. The afternoon I spend in retirement."

Whether or not, Seaton and I had not been long engaged with the aid of two green switches in riding round and round a lumbering old gray horse we found in the meadow, before a rather bunched-up figure appeared, walking along the field-path on the other side of the water, with a magenta parasol studiously lowered in our direction throughout her slow progress, as if that were the magnetic needle and we the fixed pole. Seaton at once lost all nerve in his riding. At the next lurch of the old mare's heels he toppled over into the grass, and I slid off the sleek broad back to join him where he stood, rubbing his shoulder and sourly watching the rather pompous figure till it was out of sight.

"Was that your aunt, Seaton?" I enquired; but not till then.

He nodded.

"Why didn't she take any notice of us, then?"

"She never does."

"Why not?"

"Oh, she knows all right, without; that's the dam awful part of it." Seaton was about the only fellow at

Gummidge's who ever had the ostentation to use bad language. He had suffered for it, too. But it wasn't, I think, bravado. I believe he really felt certain things more intensely than most of the other fellows, and they were generally things that fortunate and average people do not feel at all - the peculiar quality, for instance, of the British schoolboy's imagination.

"I tell you, Withers," he went on moodily, slinking across the meadow with his hands covered up in his pockets, "she sees everything. And what she doesn't see she knows without."

"But how?" I said, not because I was much interested, but because the afternoon was so hot and tiresome and purposeless, and it seemed more of a bore to remain silent. Seaton turned gloomily and spoke in a very low voice.

"Don't appear to be talking of her, if you wouldn't mind. It's - because she's in league with the devil." He nodded his head and stooped to pick up a round flat pebble. "I tell you," he said, still stooping, "you fellows don't realise what it is. I know I'm a bit close and all that. But so would you be if you had that old hag listening to every thought you think."

I looked at him, then turned and surveyed one by one the windows of the house.

"Where's your *pater*?" I said awkwardly.

"Dead, ages and ages ago, and my mother too. She's not my aunt by rights."

"What is she, then?"

"I mean she's not my mother's sister, because my grandmother married twice; and she's one of the first lot. I don't know what you call her, but anyhow she's not my real aunt."

"She gives you plenty of pocket-money."

Seaton looked steadfastly at me out of his flat eyes. "She can't give me what's mine. When I come of age half of the whole lot will be mine; and what's more" - he turned his back on the house - "I'll make her hand over every blessed shilling of it."

I put my hands in my pockets and stared at Seaton. "Is it much?"

He nodded.

"Who told you?" He got suddenly very angry; a darkish red came into his cheeks, his eyes glistened, but he made no answer, and we loitered listlessly about the garden until it was time for tea....

Seaton's aunt was wearing an extraordinary kind of lace jacket when we sidled sheepishly into the drawing-room together. She greeted me with a heavy and protracted smile, and bade me bring a chair close to the little table.

"I hope Arthur has made you feel at home," she said as she handed me my cup in her crooked hand. "He don't talk much to me; but then I'm an old woman. You must come again, Wither, and draw him out of his shell. You old snail!" She wagged her head at Seaton, who sat munching cake and watching her intently.

"And we must correspond, perhaps." She nearly shut her eyes at me. "You must write and tell me everything behind the creature's back." I confess I found her rather disquieting company. The evening drew on. Lamps were brought by a man with a nondescript face and very quiet footsteps. Seaton was told to bring out the chess-men. And we played a game, she and I, with her big chin thrust over the board at every move as she gloated over the pieces and occasionally croaked "Check!" after which she would sit back inscrutably staring at me. But the game was never finished. She simply hemmed me defencelessly in with a cloud of men that held me impotent, and yet one and all refused to administer to my poor flustered old king a merciful *coup de grâce*.

"There," she said, as the clock struck ten - "a drawn game, Withers. We are very evenly matched. A very creditable defence, Withers. You know your room. There's supper on a tray in the dining-room. Don't let the creature over-eat himself. The gong will sound three-quarters of an hour before a punctual breakfast." She held out her cheek to Seaton, and he kissed it with obvious perfunctoriness. With me she shook hands.

"An excellent game," she said cordially, "but my memory is poor, and" - she swept the pieces helter-skelter into the box - "the result will never be known." She raised her great head far back. "Eh?"

It was a kind of challenge, and I could only murmur: "Oh, I was absolutely in a hole, you know!" when she burst out laughing and waved us both out of the room.

Seaton and I stood and ate our supper, with one candlestick to light us, in a corner of the dining-room.

"Well, and how would you like it?" he said very softly, after cautiously poking his head round the doorway.

"Like what?"

"Being spied on - every blessed thing you do and think?"

"I shouldn't like it at all," I said, "if she does."

"And yet you let her smash you up at chess!"

"I didn't let her!" I said indignantly.

"Well, you funked it, then."

"And I didn't funk it either," I said; "she's so jolly clever with her knights." Seaton stared fixedly at the candle. "You wait, that's all," he said slowly. And we went upstairs to bed.

I had not been long in bed, I think, when I was cautiously awakened by a touch on my shoulder. And there was Seaton's face in the candlelight and his eyes looking into mine.

"What's up?" I said, rising quickly to my elbow.

"Don't scurry," he whispered, "or she'll hear. I'm sorry for waking you, but I didn't think you'd be asleep so soon."

"Why, what's the time, then?" Seaton wore, what was then rather unusual, a night-suit, and he hauled his big silver watch out of the pocket in his jacket.

"It's a quarter to twelve. I never get to sleep before twelve - not here."

"What do you do, then?"

"Oh, I read and listen."

"Listen?"

Seaton stared into his candle-flame as if he were listening even then. "You can't guess what it is. All you read in ghost stories, that's all rot. You can't see much, Withers, but you know all the same."

"Know what?"

"Why, that they're there."

"Who's there?" I asked fretfully, glancing at the door.

"Why, in the house. It swarms with 'em. Just you stand still and listen outside my bedroom door in the middle of the night. I have, dozens of times; they're all over the place."

"Look here, Seaton," I said, "you asked me to come here, and I didn't mind chucking up a leave just to oblige you and because I'd promised; but don't get talking a lot of rot, that's all, or you'll know the difference when we get back."

"Don't fret," he said coldly, turning away. "I shan't be at school long. And what's more, you're here now, and there isn't anybody else to talk to. I'll chance the other."

"Look here, Seaton," I said, "you may think you're going to scare me with a lot of stuff about voices and all that. But I'll just thank you to clear out; and you may please yourself about pottering about all night."

He made no answer; he was standing by the dressing-table looking across his candle into the looking-glass; he turned and stared slowly round the walls.

"Even this room's nothing more than a coffin. I suppose she told you - 'It's all exactly the same as when my brother William died' - trust her for that! And good luck to him, say I. Look at that." He raised his candle close to the little water-colour I have mentioned. "There's hundreds of eyes like that in the house; and even if God does see you, he takes precious good care you don't see Him. And it's just the same with them. I tell you what, Withers, I'm getting sick of all this. I shan't stand it much longer."

The house was silent within and without, and even in the yellowish radiance of the candle a faint silver showed through the open window on my blind. I slipped off the bedclothes, wide awake, and sat irresolute on the bedside.

"I know you're only guying me," I said angrily, "but why is the house full of - what you say? Why do you hear - what you *do* hear? Tell me that, you silly foal!"

Seaton sat down on a chair and rested his candlestick on his knee. He blinked at me calmly. "She brings them," he said, with lifted eyebrows.

"Who? Your aunt?"

He nodded.

"How?"

"I told you," he answered pettishly. "She's in league. You don't know. She as good as killed my mother; I know that. But it's not only her by a long chalk. She just sucks you dry. I know. And that's what she'll do for me; because I'm like her - like my mother, I mean. She simply hates to see me alive. I wouldn't be like that old she-wolf for a million pounds. And so" - he broke off, with a comprehensive wave of his candlestick - "they're always here. Ah, my boy, wait till she's dead! She'll hear something then, I can tell you. It's all very well now, but wait till then! I wouldn't be in her shoes when she has to clear out - for something. Don't you go and believe I care for ghosts, or whatever you like to call them. We're all in the same box. We're all under her thumb."

He was looking almost nonchalantly at the ceiling at the moment, when I saw his face change, saw his eyes suddenly drop like shot birds and fix themselves on the cranny of the door he had just left ajar. Even from where I sat I could see his colour change; he went greenish. He crouched without stirring, simply fixed. And I, scarcely daring to breathe, sat with creeping skin, simply watching him. His hands relaxed, and he gave a kind of sigh.

"Was that one?" I whispered, with a timid show of jauntiness. He looked round, opened his mouth, and nodded. "What?" I said. He jerked his thumb with meaningful eyes, and I knew that he meant that his aunt had been there listening at our door cranny.

"Look here, Seaton," I said once more, wriggling to my feet. "You may think I'm a jolly noodle; just as you please. But your aunt has been civil to me and all that, and I don't believe a word you say about her, that's all, and never did. Every fellow's a bit off his pluck at night, and you may think it a fine sport to try your rubbish on me. I heard your aunt come upstairs before I fell asleep. And I'll bet you a level tanner she's in bed now. What's more, you can keep your blessed ghosts to yourself. It's a guilty conscience, I should think."

Seaton looked at me curiously, without answering for a moment. "I'm not a liar, Withers; but I'm not going to quarrel either. You're the only chap I care a button for; or, at any rate, you're the only chap that's ever come here; and it's something to tell a fellow what you feel. I don't care a fig for fifty thousand ghosts, although I swear on my solemn oath that I know they're here. But she" - he turned deliberately - "you laid a tanner she's in bed, Withers; well, I know different. She's never in bed much of the night, and I'll prove it, too, just to show you I'm not such a nolly as you think I am. Come on!"

"Come on where?"

"Why, to see."

I hesitated. He opened a large cupboard and took out a small dark dressing-gown and a kind of shawl-jacket. He threw the jacket on the bed and put on the gown. His dusky face was colourless, and I could see by the way he fumbled at the sleeves he was shivering. But it was no good showing the white feather now. So I threw the tasselled shawl over my shoulders and, leaving our candle brightly burning on the chair, we went out together and stood in the corridor. "Now then, listen!" Seaton whispered.

We stood leaning over the staircase. It was like leaning over a well, so still and chill the air was all around us. But presently, as I suppose happens in most old houses, began to echo and answer in my ears a medley of infinite small stirrings and whisperings. Now out of the distance an old timber would relax its fibers, or a scurry die away behind the perishing wainscot. But amid and behind such sounds as these I seemed to begin to be conscious, as it were, of the lightest of footfalls, sounds as faint as the vanishing remembrance of voices in a dream. Seaton was all in obscurity except his face; out of that his eyes gleamed darkly, watching me.

"You'd hear, too, in time, my fine soldier," he muttered. "Come on!"

He descended the stairs, slipping his lean fingers lightly along the balusters. He turned to the right at the loop, and I followed him barefooted along a thickly-carpeted corridor. At the end stood a door ajar. And from here we very stealthily and in complete blackness ascended five narrow stairs. Seaton, with immense caution, slowly pushed open a door and we stood together looking into a great pool of duskiness, out of which, lit by the feeble clearness of a night-light, rose a vast bed. A heap of clothes lay on the floor; beside them two slippers dozed, with noses each to each, two yards apart. Somewhere a little clock ticked huskily. There was a rather close smell of lavender and eau de Cologne, mingled with the fragrance of ancient sachets, soap, and drugs. Yet it was a scent even more peculiarly commingled than that.

And the bed! I stared warily in; it was mounded gigantically, and it was empty.

Seaton turned a vague pale face, all shadows: "What did I say?" he muttered. "Who's - who's the fool now, I say? How are we going to get back without meeting her, I say? Answer me that! Oh, I wish to goodness you hadn't come here, Withers."

He stood visibly shivering in his skimpy gown, and could hardly speak for his teeth chattering. And very distinctly, in the hush that followed his whisper, I heard approaching a faint unhurried voluminous rustle. Seaton clutched my arm, dragged me to the right across the room to a large cupboard, and drew the door close to on us. And, presently, as with bursting lungs I peeped out into the long, low, curtained bedroom, waddled in that wonderful great head and body. I can see her now, all patched and lined with shadow, her tied-up hair (she must have had enormous quantities of it for so old a woman), her heavy lids above those flat, slow, vigilant eyes. She just passed across my ken in the vague dusk; but the bed was out of sight.

We waited on and on, listening to the clock's muffled ticking. Not the ghost of a sound rose up from the great bed. Either she lay archly listening or slept a sleep serener than an infant's. And when, it seemed, we had been hours in hiding and were cramped, chilled, and half suffocated, we crept out on all fours, with terror knocking at our ribs, and so down the five narrow stairs and back to the little candle-lit blue-and-gold bedroom.

Once there, Seaton gave in. He sat livid on a chair with closed eyes.

"Here," I said, shaking his arm, "I'm going to bed; I've had enough of this foolery; I'm going to bed." His lids quivered, but he made no answer. I poured out some water into my basin and, with that cold pictured azure eye fixed on us, bespattered Seaton's sallow face and forehead and dabbled his hair. He presently sighed and opened fish-like eyes.

"Come on!" I said. "Don't get shamming, there's a good chap. Get on my back, if you like, and I'll carry you into your bedroom."

He waved me away and stood up. So, with my candle in one hand, I took him under the arm and walked him along according to his direction down the corridor. His was a much dingier room than mine, and littered with boxes, paper, cages, and clothes. I huddled him into bed and turned to go. And suddenly, I can hardly explain it now, a kind of cold and deadly terror swept over me. I almost ran out of the room, with eyes fixed rigidly in front of me, blew out my candle, and buried my head under the bedclothes.

When I awoke, roused by a long-continued tapping at my door, sunlight was raying in on cornice and bedpost, and birds were singing in the garden. I got up, ashamed of the night's folly, dressed quickly, and went downstairs. The breakfast-room was sweet with flowers and fruit and honey. Seaton's aunt was standing in the garden beside the open French window, feeding a great flutter of birds. I watched her for a moment, unseen. Her face was set in a deep reverie beneath the shadow of a big loose sunhat. It was deeply lined, crooked, and, in a way I can't describe, fixedly vacant and strange. I coughed, and she turned at once with a prodigious smile to inquire how I had slept. And in that mysterious way by which we learn each other's secret thoughts without a sentence spoken I knew that she had followed every word and movement of the night before, and was triumphing over my affected innocence and ridiculing my friendly and too easy advances.

We returned to school, Seaton and I, lavishly laden, and by rail all the way. I made no reference to the obscure talk we had had, and resolutely refused to meet his eyes or to take up the hints he let fall. I was relieved - and yet I was sorry - to be going back, and strode on as fast as I could from the station, with Seaton almost trotting at my heels. But he insisted on buying more fruit and sweets - my share of which I accepted with a very bad grace. It was uncomfortably like a bribe; and, after all, I had no quarrel with his rum old aunt, and hadn't really believed half the stuff he had told me.

I saw as little of him as I could after that. He never referred to our visit or resumed his confidences, though in class I would sometimes catch his eye fixed on mine, full of a mute understanding, which I easily affected not to understand. He left Gummidge's, as I have said, rather abruptly, though I never heard of anything to his discredit. And I did not see him or have any news of him again till by chance we met one summer's afternoon in the Strand.

He was dressed rather oddly in a coat too large for him and a bright silky tie. But we instantly recognised one another under the awning of a cheap jeweler's shop. He immediately attached himself to me and dragged me off, not too cheerfully, to lunch with him at an Italian restaurant near by. He chattered about our old school, which he remembered only with dislike and disgust; told me cold-bloodedly of the disastrous fate of one or two of the old fellows who had been among his chief tormentors; insisted on an expensive wine and the whole gamut of the "rich" menu; and finally informed me, with a good deal of niggling, that he had come up to town to buy an engagement-ring.

And of course: "How is your aunt?" I enquired at last.

He seemed to have been awaiting the question. It fell like a stone into a deep pool, so many expressions flitted across his long un-English face.

"She's aged a good deal," he said softly, and broke off.

"She's been very decent," he continued presently after, and paused again. "In a way." He eyed me fleetingly. "I dare say you heard that she - that is, that we - had lost a good deal of money."

"No," I said.

"Oh, yes!" said Seaton, and paused again.

And somehow, poor fellow, I knew in the clink and clatter of glass and voices that he had lied to me; that he did not possess, and never had possessed, a penny beyond what his aunt had squandered on his too ample allowance of pocket-money.

"And the ghosts?" I enquired quizzically. He grew instantly solemn, and, though it may have been my fancy, slightly yellowed. But "You are making game of me, Withers," was all he said.

He asked for my address, and I rather reluctantly gave him my card.

"Look here, Withers," he said, as we stood in the sunlight on the thronging kerb, saying good-bye, "here I am, and it's all very well; I'm not perhaps as fanciful as I was. But you are practically the only friend I have on earth - except Alice.... And there - to make a clean breast of it, I'm not sure that my aunt cares much about my getting married. She doesn't say so, of course. You know her well enough for that." He looked sidelong at the rattling gaudy traffic.

"What I was going to say is this. Would you mind coming down? You needn't stay the night unless you please, though, of course, you know you would be awfully welcome. But I should like you to meet my - to meet Alice; and then, perhaps, you might tell me your honest opinion of - of the other too."

I vaguely demurred. He pressed me. And we parted with a half promise that I would come. He waved his ball-topped cane at me and ran off in his long jacket after a 'bus.

A letter arrived soon after, in his small weak handwriting, giving me full particulars regarding route and trains. And without the least curiosity, even, perhaps with some little annoyance that chance should have thrown us together again, I accepted his invitation and arrived one hazy midday at his out-of-the-way station to find him sitting on a low seat under a clump of double hollyhocks, awaiting me.

His face looked absent and singularly listless; but he seemed, none the less, pleased to see me.

We walked up the village street, past the little dingy apothecary's and the empty forge, and, as on my first visit, skirted the house together, and, instead of entering by the front door, made our way down the green path into the garden at the back. A pale haze of cloud muffled the sun; the garden lay in a grey shimmer - its old trees, its snap-dragoned faintly glittering walls. But there seemed now an air of neglect where before all had been neat and methodical. There was a patch of shallowly-dug soil and a worn-down spade leaning against a tree. There was an old broken wheelbarrow. The goddess of neglect was there.

"You ain't much of a gardener, Seaton," I said, with a sigh of ease.

"I think, do you know, I like it best like this," said Seaton. "We haven't any gardener now, of course. Can't afford it." He stood staring at his little dark square of freshly-turned earth. "And it always seems to me," he went on ruminatingly, "that, after all, we are nothing better than interlopers on the earth, disfiguring and staining wherever we go. I know it's shocking blasphemy to say so, but then it's different here, you see. We are farther away."

"To tell you the truth, Seaton, I don't quite see," I said; "but it isn't a new philosophy, is it? Anyhow, it's a precious beastly one."

"It's only what I think," he replied, with all his odd old stubborn meekness.

We wandered on together, talking little, and still with that expression of uneasy vigilance on Seaton's face. He pulled out his watch as we stood gazing idly over the green meadow and the dark motionless bulrushes.

"I think, perhaps, it's nearly time for lunch," he said. "Would you like to come in?"

We turned and walked slowly towards the house, across whose windows I confess my own eyes, too, went restlessly wandering in search of its rather disconcerting inmate. There was a pathetic look of draggledness, of want of means and care, rust and overgrowth and faded paint. Seaton's aunt, a little to my relief, did not share our meal. Seaton carved the cold meat, and dispatched a heaped-up plate by the elderly servant for his aunt's private consumption. We talked little and in half-suppressed tones, and sipped a bottle of Madeira which Seaton had rather heedfully fetched out of the great mahogany sideboard.

I played him a dull and effortless game of chess, yawning between the moves he generally made almost at haphazard, and with attention elsewhere engaged. About five o'clock came the sound of a distant ring, and Seaton jumped up, overturning the board, and so ending a game that else might have fatuously continued to this day. He effusively excused himself, and after some little while returned with a slim, dark, rather sallow girl of about nineteen, in a white gown and hat, to whom I was presented with some little nervousness as "his dear old friend and schoolfellow."

We talked on in the pale afternoon light, still, as it seemed to me, and even in spite of real effort to be clear and gay, in a half-suppressed, lack-lustre fashion. We all seemed, if it were not my fancy, to be expectant, to be rather anxiously awaiting an arrival, the appearance of someone who all but filled our collective consciousness. Seaton talked least of all, and in a restless interjectory way, as he continually fidgeted from chair to chair. At last he proposed a stroll in the garden before the sun should have quite gone down.

Alice walked between us. Her hair and eyes were conspicuously dark against the whiteness of her gown. She carried herself not ungracefully, and yet without the least movement of her arms or body, and answered us both without turning her head. There was a curious provocative reserve in that impassive and rather long face, a half-unconscious strength of character.

And yet somehow I knew - I believe we all knew - that this walk, this discussion of their future plans was a futility. I had nothing to base such a cynicism on, except only a vague sense of oppression, the fore-boding remembrance of the inert invincible power in the background, to whom optimistic plans and love-making and youth are as chaff and thistledown. We came back, silent, in the last light. Seaton's aunt was there - under an old brass lamp. Her hair was as barbarously massed and curled as ever. Her eye-lids, I think, hung even a little heavier in age over their slow-moving inscrutable pupils. We filed in softly out of the evening, and I made my bow.

"In this short interval, Mr. Withers," she remarked amiably, "you have put off youth, put on the man. Dear me, how sad it is to see the young days vanishing! Sit down. My nephew tells me you met by chance - or act of Providence, shall we call it? - and in my beloved Strand! You, I understand, are to be best man - yes, best man, or am I divulging secrets?" She surveyed Arthur and Alice with overwhelming graciousness.

They sat apart on two low chairs and smiled in return.

"And Arthur - how do you think Arthur is looking?"

"I think he looks very much in need of a change," I said deliberately.

"A change! Indeed?" She all but shut her eyes at me and with an exaggerated sentimentality shook her head. "My dear Mr. Withers! Are we not *all* in need of a change in this fleeting, fleeting world?" She mused over the remark like a connoisseur. "And you," she continued, turning abruptly to Alice, "I hope you pointed out to Mr. Withers all my pretty bits?"

"We walked round the garden," said Alice, looking out of the window. "It's a very beautiful evening."

"Is it?" said the old lady, starting up violently. "Then on this very beautiful evening we will go in to supper. Mr. Withers, your arm; Arthur, bring your bride."

I can scarcely describe with what curious ruminations I led the way into the faded, heavy-aired dining-room, with this indefinable old creature leaning weightily on my arm - the large flat bracelet on the yellow-laced wrist. She fumed a little, breathed rather heavily, as if with an effort of mind rather than of body; for she had grown much stouter and yet little more proportionate. And to talk into that great white face, so close to mine, was a queer experience in the dim light of the corridor, and even in the twinkling crystal of the candles. She was naïve - appallingly naïve; she was sudden and superficial; she was even arch; and all these in the brief, rather puffy passage from one room to the other, with these two tongue-tied children bringing up the rear. The meal was tremendous. I have never seen such a monstrous salad. But the dishes were greasy and over-spiced, and were indifferently cooked. One thing only was quite unchanged - my hostess's appetite was as Gargantuan as ever. The old solid candelabra that lighted us stood before her high-backed chair. Seaton sat a little removed, with his plate almost in darkness.

And throughout this prodigious meal his aunt talked, mainly to me, mainly at Seaton, with an occasional satirical courtesy to Alice and muttered explosions of directions to the servant. She had aged, and yet, if it be not nonsense to say so, seemed no older. I suppose to the Pyramids a decade is but as the rustling down of a handful of dust. And she reminded me of some such unshakable prehistoricism. She certainly was an amazing talker - racy, extravagant, with a delivery that was perfectly overwhelming. As for Seaton - her flashes of silence were for him. On her enormous volubility would suddenly fall a hush: acid sarcasm would be left implied; and she would sit softly moving her great head, with eyes fixed full in a dreamy smile; but with her whole attention, one could see, slowly, joyously absorbing his mute discomfiture.

She confided in us her views on a theme vaguely occupying at the moment, I suppose, all our minds. "We have barbarous institutions, and so must put up, I suppose, with a never-ending procession of fools - of fools *ad infinitum*. Marriage, Mr. Withers, was instituted in the privacy of a garden; *sub rosa*, as it were. Civilization flaunts it in the glare of day. The dull marry the poor; the rich the effete; and so our New Jerusalem is peopled with naturals, plain and coloured, at either end. I detest folly; I detest still more (if I must be frank, dear Arthur) mere cleverness. Mankind has simply become a tailless host of uninstinctive animals. We should never have taken to Evolution, Mr. Withers. 'Natural Selection!' - little gods and fishes! - the deaf for the dumb. We should have used our brains - intellectual pride, the ecclesiastics call it. And by brains I mean - what do I mean, Alice? - I mean, my dear child," and she laid two gross fingers on Alice's narrow sleeve. "I mean courage. Consider it, Arthur. I read that the scientific world is once more beginning to be afraid of spiritual agencies. Spiritual agencies that tap, and actually float, bless their hearts! I think just one more of those mulberries - thank you.

"They talk about 'blind Love,'" she ran inconsequently on as she helped herself, with eyes fixed on the dish, "but why blind? I think, do you know, from weeping over its rickets. After all, it is we plain women that triumph, Mr. Withers, beyond the mockery of time. Alice, now! Fleeting, fleeting is youth, my child! What's that you were confiding to your plate, Arthur? Satirical boy! He laughs at his old aunt: nay, but thou didst laugh. He detests all sentiment. He whispers the most acid asides. Come, my love, we will leave these cynics; we will go and commiserate with each other on our sex. The choice of two evils, Mr. Smithers!" I opened the door, and she swept out as if borne on a torrent of unintelligible indignation; and Arthur and I were left in the clear four-flamed light alone.

For a while we sat in silence. He shook his head at my cigarette-case, and I lit a cigarette. Presently he fidgeted in his chair and poked his head forward into the light. He paused to rise and shut again the shut door.

"How long will you be?" he said, standing by the table.

I laughed.

"Oh, it's not that!" he said, in some confusion. "Of course, I like to be with her. But it's not that only. The truth is, Withers, I don't care about leaving her too long with my aunt."

I hesitated. He looked at me questioningly.

"Look here, Seaton," I said, "you know well enough that I don't want to interfere in your affairs, or to offer advice where it is not wanted. But don't you think perhaps you may not treat your aunt quite in the right way? As one gets old, you know, a little give and take. I have an old godmother, or something. She talks, too.... A little allowance: it does no harm. But, hang it all, I'm no talker."

He sat down with his hands in his pockets and still with his eyes fixed almost incredulously on mine. "How?" he said.

"Well, my dear fellow, if I'm any judge - mind, I don't say that I am - but I can't help thinking she thinks you don't care for her; and perhaps takes your silence for - for bad temper. She has been very decent to you, hasn't she?"

"'Decent'? My God!" said Seaton.

I smoked on in silence; but he still continued to look at me with that peculiar concentration I remembered of old.

"I don't think, perhaps, Withers," he began presently, "I don't think you quite understand. Perhaps you are not quite our kind. You always did, just like the other fellows, guy me at school. You laughed at me that night you came to stay here - about the voices and all that. But I don't mind being laughed at - because I know."

"Know what?" It was the same old system of dull question and evasive answer.

"I mean I know that what we see and hear is only the smallest fraction of what is. I know she lives quite out of this. She *talks* to you; but it's all make-believe. It's all a 'parlour game.' She's not really with you; only pitting her outside wits against yours and enjoying the fooling. She's living on inside, on what you're rotten without. That's what it is - a cannibal feast. She's a spider. It does't much matter what you call it. It means the same kind of thing. I tell you, Withers, she hates me; and you can scarcely dream what that hatred means. I used to think I had an inkling of the reason. It's oceans deeper than that. It just lies behind: herself against myself. Why, after all, how much do we really understand of anything? We don't even know our own histories, and not a tenth, not a tenth of the reasons. What has life been to me? - nothing but a trap. And when one is set free, it only begins again. I thought you might understand; but you are on a different level: that's all."

"What on earth are you talking about?" I said, half contemptuously, in spite of myself.

"I mean what I say," he said gutturally. "All this outside's only make-believe - but there! what's the good of talking? So far as this is concerned I'm as good as done. You wait."

Seaton blew out three of the candles and, leaving the vacant room in semi-darkness, we groped our way along the corridor to the drawing-room. There a full moon stood shining in at the long garden windows. Alice sat stooping at the door, with her hands clasped, looking out, alone.

"Where is she?" Seaton asked in a low tone.

Alice looked up; their eyes met in a kind of instantaneous understanding, and the door immediately afterwards opened behind us.

"*Such* a moon!" said a voice that, once heard, remained unforgettably on the ear. "A night for lovers, Mr. Withers, if ever there was one. Get a shawl, my dear Arthur, and take Alice for a little promenade. I dare say we old cronies will manage to keep awake. Hasten, hasten, Romeo! My poor, poor Alice, how laggard a lover!"

Seaton returned with a shawl. They drifted out into the moonlight. My companion gazed after them till they were out of hearing, turned to me gravely, and suddenly twisted her white face into such a convulsion of contemptuous amusement that I could only stare blankly in reply.

"Dear innocent children!" she said, with inimitable unctuousness. "Well, well, Mr. Withers, we poor seasoned old creatures must move with the times. Do you sing?"

I scouted the idea.

"Then you must listen to my playing. Chess" - she

clasped her forehead with both cramped hands - "chess is now completely beyond my poor wits."

She sat down at the piano and ran her fingers in a flourish over the keys. "What shall it be? How shall we capture them, those passionate hearts? That first fine careless rapture? Poetry itself." She gazed softly into the garden a moment, and presently, with a shake of her body, began to play the opening bars of Beethoven's "Moonlight" Sonata. The piano was old and woolly. She played without music. The lamplight was rather dim. The moonbeams from the window lay across the keys. Her head was in shadow. And whether it was simply due to her personality or to some really occult skill in her playing I cannot say: I only know that she gravely and deliberately set herself to satirise the beautiful music. It brooded on the air, disillusioned, charged with mockery and bitterness. I stood at the window; far down the path I could see the white figure glimmering in that pool of colourless light. A few faint stars shone; and still that amazing woman behind me dragged out of the unwilling keys her wonderful grotesquerie of youth and love and beauty. It came to an end. I knew the player was watching me. "Please, please, go on!" I murmured, without turning. "Please go on playing, Miss Seaton."

No answer was returned to my rather fluttering sarcasm, but I knew in some indefinite way that I was being acutely scrutinised, when suddenly there followed a procession of quiet, plaintive chords which broke at last softly into the hymn, *A Few More Years Shall Roll*.

I confess it held me spellbound. There is a wistful strained, plangent pathos in the tune; but beneath those masterly old hands it cried softly and bitterly the solitude and desperate estrangement of the world. Arthur and his lady-love vanished from my thoughts. No one could put into a rather hackneyed old hymn-tune such an appeal who had never known the meaning of the words. Their meaning, anyhow, isn't commonplace. I turned very cautiously and glanced at the musician. She was leaning forward a little over the keys, so that at the approach of my cautious glance she had but to turn her face into the thin flood of moonlight for every feature to become distinctly visible. And so, with the tune abruptly terminated, we steadfastly regarded one another, and she broke into a chuckle of laughter.

"Not quite so seasoned as I supposed, Mr. Withers. I see you are a real lover of music. To me it is too painful. It evokes too much thought...."

I could scarcely see her little glittering eyes under their penthouse lids.

"And now," she broke off crisply, "tell me, as a man of the world, what do you think of my new niece?"

I was not a man of the world, nor was I much flattered in my stiff and dullish way of looking at things by being called one; and I could answer her without the least hesitation.

"I don't think, Miss Seaton, I'm much of a judge of character. She's very charming."

"A brunette?"

"I think I prefer dark women."

"And why? Consider, Mr. Withers; dark hair, dark eyes, dark cloud, dark night, dark vision, dark death, dark grave, dark DARK!"

Perhaps the climax would have rather thrilled Seaton, but I was too thick-skinned. "I don't know much about all that," I answered rather pompously. "Broad daylight's difficult enough for most of us."

"Ah," she said, with a sly inward burst of satirical laughter.

"And I suppose," I went on, perhaps a little nettled, "it isn't the actual darkness one admires, its the contrast of the skin, and the colour of the eyes, and - and their shining. Just as," I went blundering on, too late to turn back, "just as you only see the stars in the dark. It would be a long day without any evening. As for death and the grave, I don't suppose we shall much notice that." Arthur and his sweetheart were slowly returning along the dewy path. "I believe in making the best of things."

"How very interesting!" came the smooth answer. "I see you are a philosopher, Mr. Withers. H'm! 'As for death and the grave, I don't suppose we shall much notice that.' Very interesting.... And I'm sure," she added in a particularly suave voice, "I profoundly hope so." She rose slowly from her stool. "You will take pity on me again, I hope. You and I would get on famously - kindred spirits - elective affinities. And, of course, now that my nephew's going to leave me, now that his affections are centred on another, I shall be a very lonely old woman.... Shall I not, Arthur?"

Seaton blinked stupidly. "I didn't hear what you

said, Aunt."

"I was telling our old friend, Arthur, that when you are gone I shall be a very lonely old woman."

"Oh, I don't think so;" he said in a strange voice.

"He means, Mr. Withers, he means, my dear child," she said, sweeping her eyes over Alice, "he means that I shall have memory for company - heavenly memory - the ghosts of other days. Sentimental boy! And did you enjoy our music, Alice? Did I really stir that youthful heart?... O, O, O," continued the horrible old creature, "you billers and cooers, I have been listening to such flatteries, such confessions! Beware, beware, Arthur, there's many a slip." She rolled her little eyes at me, she shrugged her shoulders at Alice, and gazed an instant stonily into her nephew's face.

I held out my hand. "Good night, good night!" she cried. "'He that fights and runs away.' Ah, good night, Mr. Withers; come again soon!" She thrust out her cheek at Alice, and we all three filed slowly out of the room.

Black shadow darkened the porch and half the spreading sycamore. We walked without speaking up the dusty village street. Here and there a crimson window glowed. At the fork of the high-road I said good-bye. But I had taken hardly more than a dozen paces when a sudden impulse seized me.

"Seaton!" I called.

He turned in the moonlight.

"You have my address; if by any chance, you know, you should care to spend a week or two in town between this and the - the Day, we should be delighted to see you."

"Thank you, Withers, thank you," he said in a low voice.

"I dare say" - I waved my stick gallantly to Alice - "I dare say you will be doing some shopping; we could all meet," I added, laughing.

"Thank you, thank you, Withers - immensely;" he repeated.

And so we parted.

But they were out of the jog-trot of my prosaic life. And being of a stolid and incurious nature, I left Seaton and his marriage, and even his aunt, to themselves in my memory, and scarcely gave a thought to them until one day I was walking up the Strand again, and passed the flashing gloaming of the covered-in jeweller's shop where I had accidentally encountered my old schoolfellow in the summer. It was one of those still close autumnal days after a rainy night. I cannot say why, but a vivid recollection returned to my mind of our meeting and of how suppressed Seaton had seemed, and of how vainly he had endeavoured to appear assured and eager. He must be married by now, and had doubtless returned from his honeymoon. And I had clean forgotten my manners, had sent not a word of congratulation, nor - as I might very well have done, and as I knew he would have been immensely pleased at my doing - the ghost of a wedding-present.

On the other hand, I pleaded with myself, I had had no invitation. I paused at the corner of Trafalgar Square, and at the bidding of one of those caprices that seize occasionally on even an unimaginative mind, I suddenly ran after a green 'bus that was passing, and found myself bound on a visit I had not in the least foreseen.

All the colours of autumn were over the village when I arrived. A beautiful late afternoon sunlight bathed thatch and meadow. But it was close and hot. A child, two dogs, a very old woman with a heavy basket I encountered. One or two incurious tradesmen looked idly up as I passed by. It was all so rural and so still, my whimsical impulse had so much flagged, that for a while I hesitated to venture under the shadow of the sycamore-tree to enquire after the happy pair. I deliberately passed by the faint-blue gates and continued my walk under the high green and tufted wall. Hollyhocks had attained their topmost bud and seeded in the little cottage gardens beyond; the Michaelmas daisies were in flower; a sweet warm aromatic smell of fading leaves was in the air. Beyond the cottages lay a field where cattle were grazing, and beyond that I came to a little churchyard. Then the road wound on, pathless and houseless, among gorse and bracken. I turned impatiently and walked quickly back to the house and rang the bell.

The rather colourless elderly woman who answered my enquiry informed me that Miss Seaton was at home, as if only taciturnity forbade her adding, "But she doesn't want to see *you*."

"Might I, do you think, have Mr. Arthur's address?" I said.

She looked at me with quiet astonishment, as if waiting for an explanation. Not the faintest of smiles came into her thin face.

"I will tell Miss Seaton," she said after a pause. "Please walk in."

She showed me into the dingy undusted drawing-room, filled with evening sunshine and the green-dyed light that penetrated the leaves overhanging the long French windows. I sat down and waited on and on, occasionally aware of a creaking footfall overhead. At last the door opened a little, and the great face I had once known peered round at me. For it was enormously changed; mainly, I think, because the old eyes had rather suddenly failed, and so a kind of stillness and darkness lay over its calm and wrinkled pallor.

"Who is it?" she asked.

I explained myself and told her the occasion of my visit.

She came in and shut the door carefully after her and, though the fumbling was scarcely perceptible, groped her way to a chair. She had on an old dressing-gown, like a cassock, of a patterned cinnamon colour.

"What is it you want?" she said, seating herself and lifting her blank face to mine.

"Might I just have Arthur's address?" I said deferentially. "I am so sorry to have disturbed you."

"H'm. You have come to see my nephew?"

"Not necessarily to see him, only to hear how he is, and, of course, Mrs. Seaton too. I am afraid my silence must have appeared...."

"He hasn't noticed your silence," croaked the old voice out of the great mask; "besides, there isn't any Mrs. Seaton."

"Ah, then," I answered, after a momentary pause, "I have not seemed so black as I painted myself! And how is Miss Outram?"

"She's gone into Yorkshire," answered Seaton's aunt.

"And Arthur too?"

She did not reply, but simply sat blinking at me with lifted chin, as if listening, but certainly not for what I might have to say. I began to feel rather at a loss.

"You were no close friend of my nephew's, Mr. Smithers?" she said presently.

"No," I answered, welcoming the cue, "and yet, do you know, Miss Seaton, he is one of the very few of my old schoolfellows I have come across in the last few years, and I suppose as one gets older one begins to value old associations...." My voice seemed to trail off into a vacuum. "I thought Miss Outram," I hastily began again, "a particularly charming girl. I hope they are both quite well."

Still the old face solemnly blinked at me in silence.

"You must find it very lonely, Miss Seaton, with Arthur away?"

"I was never lonely in my life," she said sourly. "I don't look to flesh and blood for my company. When you've got to be my age, Mr. Smithers (which God forbid), you'll find life a very different affair from what you seem to think it is now. You won't seek company then, I'll be bound. It's thrust on you." Her face edged round into the clear green light, and her eyes, as it were, groped over my vacant, disconcerted face. "I dare say, now," she said, composing her mouth, "I dare say my nephew told you a good many tarradiddles in his time. Oh, yes, a good many, eh? He was always a liar. What, now, did he say of me? Tell me, now." She leant forward as far as she could, trembling, with an ingratiating smile.

"I think he is rather superstitious," I said coldly, "but, honestly, I have a very poor memory, Miss Seaton."

"Why?" she said. "*I* haven't."

"The engagement hasn't been broken off, I hope."

"Well, between you and me," she said, shrinking up and with an immensely confidential grimace, "it has."

"I'm sure I'm very sorry to hear it. And where is Arthur?"

"Eh?"

"Where is Arthur?"

We faced each other mutely among the dead old bygone furniture. Past all my scrutiny was that large, flat, grey, cryptic countenance. And then, suddenly, our eyes for the first time, really met. In some indescribable way out of that thick-lidded obscurity a far small something stooped and looked out at me for a mere instant of time that seemed of almost intolerable protraction. Involuntarily I blinked and shook my head. She muttered something with great rapidity, but quite inarticulately; rose and hobbled to the door. I thought I heard, mingled in broken mutterings, something about tea.

"Please, please, don't trouble," I began, but could say no more, for the door was already shut between us. I stood and looked out on the long-neglected garden. I could just see the bright greenness of Seaton's old tadpole pond. I wandered about the room. Dusk began to gather, the last birds in that dense shadowiness of trees had ceased to sing. And not a sound was to be heard in the house. I waited on and on, vainly speculating. I even attempted to ring the bell; but the wire was broken, and only jangled loosely at my efforts.

I hesitated, unwilling to call or to venture out, and yet more unwilling to linger on, waiting for a tea that promised to be an exceedingly comfortless supper. And as darkness drew down, a feeling of the utmost unease and disquietude came over me. All my talks with Seaton returned on me with a suddenly enriched meaning. I recalled again his face as we had stood hanging over the staircase, listening in the small hours to the inexplicable stirrings of the night. There were no candles in the room; every minute the autumnal darkness deepened. I cautiously opened the door and listened, and with some little dismay withdrew, for I was uncertain of my way out. I even tried the garden, but was confronted under a veritable thicket of foliage by a padlocked gate. It would be a little too ignominious to be caught scaling a friend's garden fence!

Cautiously returning into the still and musty drawing-room, I took out my watch and gave the incredible old woman ten minutes in which to reappear. And when that tedious ten minutes had ticked by I could scarcely distinguish its hands. I determined to wait no longer, drew open the door, and, trusting to my sense of direction, groped my way through the corridor that I vaguely remembered led to the front of the house.

I mounted three or four stairs and, lifting a heavy curtain, found myself facing the starry fanlight of the porch. Hence I glanced into the gloom of the dining-room. My fingers were on the latch of the outer door when I heard a faint stirring in the darkness above the hall. I looked up and became conscious of, rather than saw, the huddled old figure looking down on me.

There was an immense hushed pause. Then, "Arthur, Arthur," whispered an inexpressively peevish, rasping voice, "is that you? Is that you, Arthur?"

I can scarcely say why, but the question horribly startled me. No conceivable answer occurred to me. With head craned back, hand clenched on my umbrella, I continued to stare up into the gloom, in this fatuous confrontation.

"Oh, oh;" the voice croaked. "It is you, is it? *That* disgusting man!... Go away out. Go away out."

Hesitating no longer, I caught open the door and, slamming it behind me, ran out into the garden, under the gigantic old sycamore, and so out at the open gate.

I found myself half up the village street before I stopped running. The local butcher was sitting in his shop reading a piece of newspaper by the light of a small oil-lamp. I crossed the road and enquired the way to the station. And after he had with minute and needless care directed me, I asked casually if Mr. Arthur Seaton still lived with his aunt at the big house just beyond the village. He poked his head in at the little parlour door.

"Here's a gentleman enquiring after young Mr. Seaton, Millie," he said. "He's dead, ain't he?"

"Why, yes, bless you," replied a cheerful voice from within. "Dead and buried these three months or more - young Mr. Seaton. And just before he was to be married, don't you remember, Bob?"

I saw a fair young woman's face peer over the muslin of the little door at me.

"Thank you," I replied, "then I go straight on?"

"That's it, sir; past the pond, bear up the hill a bit to the left, and then there's the station lights before your eyes."

We looked intelligently into each other's faces in the beam of the smoky lamp. But not one of the many questions in my mind could I put into words.

And again I paused irresolutely a few paces further on. It was not, I fancy, merely a foolish apprehension of what the raw-boned butcher might "think" that prevented my going back to see if I could find Seaton's grave in the benighted churchyard. There was precious little use in pottering about in the muddy dark merely to find where he was buried. And yet I felt a little uneasy. My rather horrible thought was that, so far as I was concerned - one of his esteemed few friends - he had never been much better than "buried" in my mind.

THE REAPER

By DOROTHY EASTON

(From *The English Review*) 1922

Milgate is a rich farmer, owning his own machines; not like those poorer, smaller men who hire an engine from a neighbour. He has his reaping machine, a red and yellow "Walter Wood" Cleveland brand. Every morning now, as soon as it's dry enough, about nine o'clock, the engine starts, and from the farmer's Manor House its heavy, drowsy sounds are heard. For those on the machine the noise is harder. The only human sound that penetrates it is the old conductor's "Ohoy!" to the driver if the canvas sticks, or if weeds are making a "block." Then the young man in front slows his engine down, and wipes his forehead with his hand. Reaping goes on until nine at night.

No strange workman sits on the reaper, but one of Milgate's best men, the most trustworthy, most faithful - the waggoner; a man well over sixty, with side-whiskers, grey eyes, a long nose, and forehead and chin carved out of granite. On his head a flat "wide-awake" hat, on his bent back a white jacket. When he speaks, his mouth moves sideways first; there's always a spot of dried blood on his lip; when he smiles a tooth-stump appears like an ancient fossil. He talks slowly, stopping to spit now and then; every day of his life he gets up at half-past three. Now, mounted on the high iron seat (a crumpled sack for saddle), he rides like some old charioteer, a Hercules with great bowed back, head jutting out, chin straight; a hard, weathered look about his face, and in his heart disgust - this year, for the first time, they are using a motor engine to pull the reaper round instead of horses. He lives for his horses; he's the "Waggoner," they are his "job;" if one falls ill, he sleeps with it. He believes in horses; but, speaking of the motor, he says: "She's arlraight - when she's arlraight!" with a look which ends the sentence for him! In his youth he had reaped with a scythe.

This "Walter Wood" is a neat arrangement, you can't deny that; one bit of mechanism works as a divider, while a big, light kind of wooden windmill arrangement, continually revolving, beats the corn down into a flat pan from which it's carried, on a canvas slide, up an incline, then shot over and down the other side in one continual long, flat stream like yellow matting. And then the needle, the "threadle" as he calls it, nips in somewhere, binding the flat mass into separate, neat, round sheaves, pitched out every few moments with perfect precision by a three-pronged iron fork. Above the one big, heavy central wheel the charioteer is shaken and jolted from nine till nine. In front, on another iron seat by the boxlike engine, the driver works. Behind runs a red-faced labourer "clearing corners." The motor has to run out the full length of its cogged iron wheel bands before it can turn, and sheaves dropped on the last round get in the way; so at each corner they have to be lifted and set back. The labourer "clears," then runs after the machine - now half-way up the field - stops at the next corner, stoops once more to lift and shift three sheaves, then runs again.

This labourer was a man of forty with a face as naïve as a boy of fifteen. Though getting bald, his eyes were young; his mouth loose, untrained as a child's. He's "touched," as we say, and had never really grown up. He slept in an attic, ate in a kitchen, and worked, but was not "responsible;" he was always given "light jobs" - walking with the 'clappers," weeding, cleaning sties, "clearing." His greatest friend was a boy of twelve; on Sundays they'd laugh for an hour at nothing. Going to the coast for the first time last year, he was so taken by a Punch and Judy show that he never saw the sea. His smile was the most ridiculous thing in the world. He blushed continually, panted, grinned like some boy caught kissing, and was always apologetic. Lightning made him hide his head, and he was afraid of engines - their regularity upset him. Running behind the reaper - this quick-moving, noisy thing smelling of oil, made up of sliding chains - appalled him; there were five wheels at an angle, and all the time an oil-wet, black, flat, chain-band ran round over them! Underneath, the heavy central wheel ran round and round! To the imbecile the waggoner's courage appeared supernatural.

There should have been another man to take two corners, but all hands were wanted; so the labourer had to run all day. It was hot, no wind, no shade. If he looked up for a moment, the hills and distant elms appeared bright blue. The big field itself was ablaze with colour; wheat like brown burnt amber, poppies, small white daisies, thistles. When the engine stopped the only sounds were plaintive, anxious bird-calls from the centre of the field; sometimes a rabbit or a hare looked out, then bolted back. Once five graceful, sleek, brown pheasants ran out towards the hedge, then lost their nerve, turned and went running back. The sun shone steadily; sheaves picked up by the labourer made his hands smell oily, their string band raised a blister on his forefinger. Very often he grabbed hold of nettles and sharp thistles, and the backs of his hands were swollen and covered with stings. Blue butterflies twirled in front of his face, pale moths flew out. When his hat fell off he had no time to get it. The sweat ran down his egg-shaped forehead to his long, square, hairy chin (though he could shave himself on Sundays, he looked a little like a monkey).

When the engine stuck, the waggoner asked in his slow, flat voice:

"Woan't she speak?"

"She's not comin' out!" was the youth's reply.

Once the driver was thrown up a foot when the motor went over a hole. He yelled: "Men are often killed by the reaper." The imbecile got the startled look of a child seeing snakes at the Zoo. Each time the engine snorted, or the waggoner called out "Ohoy!" a spurt of sweat ran down his spine; the blood was beating in his head; the sun shone mercilessly on his pale, bald patch; the field began to bounce before his eyes, bloodshot from stooping. When yards of bindweed shackled the machinery, the waggoner just turned his head - a sign - for the labourer, who had to run, had to catch and tear away the long green chains full of small pink flowers.

By four o'clock they were overtaking him before he got round; the driver had to turn more sharply, the canvas stuck.

194   Edward J. O'Brien and John Cournos

"Doan you do that agen!" the old waggoner scolded with stern eye; "you'll tourn us oover!"

The engine stuck when they tried to start again; for half an hour the young driver tinkered with tools from the box, unscrewing small oily "nuts," testing "wires," feeling "levers," and in desperation wiping his black, dripping hands on his hair. Twenty times he turned the "starting handle," but "she wouldn't speak!" Then, suddenly, with a sound like a pistol-shot, the engine "fired," the machine ran backwards, upsetting the labourer, and before he could move, the central wheel ran over his ankles.

When the imbecile came to himself they were still at the corner, his feet were tied up in a jacket, he was suffering horribly, yet seemed unable to focus it; but seeing the red and yellow reaper standing close beside his head, some memory soaked his face with sweat; he fainted.

Brandy was fetched; they had lifted him on to a hurdle when he recovered again. The whole group were still at the corner. His employer stood there, stout, well-dressed, and anxious, in his grey felt hat, dark coat and trousers; the driver stood there, too, and the old waggoner. Corn was still "up" in the middle of the field. The labourer looked surprised at seeing sky before him; as a rule when he stared he saw fields. He turned his face; the men watching saw his round, boyish eyes project at sight of something red and wet and sticky (like the mess they made out sheep-killing) splashed on the stubble, while two broken boots lay oozing the same stuff in a large pool of it. Following this look, the old waggoner said slowly:

"Eh, me boy, they'm youers...." Tears were running down his stiff, dried cheeks.

"How d'you feel?" asked the farmer. His labourer blushed, then whispered to the waggoner:

"What's 'appened, Mister Collard?"

"Why, you've a-loarst your feet."

For yet another minute the imbecile lay panting, shy, self-conscious under his master's eye - until an idea struck him; once more whispering to the waggoner, he said:

"'Elp me oop. I'll get 'ome, Willy."

"You carn't walk," said the old man simply. "You carn't walk no moar."

Black hairs stiffened suddenly on the idiot's chin; he had understood that in those bleeding, mangled boots his feet were lying; he began to cry. But then, catching sight of his master, smiled as though to apologise -

THE SONG

By MAY EDGINTON

(From *Lloyd's Story Magazine*) 1922

Charlie had no true vice in him. All the same, a man may be overtaxed, over-harassed, over-routined, over-driven, over-pricked, over-preached and over-starved right up to the edge; and then the fascination of the big space below may easily pull him over.

But his wife's uncle's assertion that he must always, inwardly, have been naturally wild and bad, was as wrong as such assertions usually are, for he was no more truly vicious than his youngest baby was.

On the warm evening when he came home on that fateful autumn day, Charlie had been pushed, in the course of years, right up to the edge, and was looking into the abyss, though he was hardly aware of it, so well had he been disciplined. He emerged from a third-class carriage of the usual train without an evening paper because his wife had shown him the decency of cutting down small personal expenses, and next morning's papers would have the same news in anyway; he walked home up the suburban road for the four thousandth five hundredth and fiftieth time; entered quietly not to disturb the baby; rubbed his boots on the mat; answered his wife brightly and manfully; washed his hands in cold water - the hot water being saved for the baby's bath and the washing-up in the evenings - and sat down to about the four thousandth five hundredth and fiftieth cold supper.

His wife said she was tired and seemed proud of it.

"But never mind," she said, "one must expect to be tired." He went on eating without verbally questioning her; it was an assertion to which she always held firmly. But in his soul something stirred vaguely, as if mutinous currents fretted there.

"I have been thinking," she said, "that you really ought not to buy that new suit you were considering if Maud is to go to a better school next term. I have been looking over your pepper-and-salt, and there are those people who turn suits like new. You can have that done."

"But -" he murmured.

"We ought not to think of ourselves," she added.

"I never have," said Charlie in rather a low voice.

"We ought to give a little subscription to the Parish Magazine," she continued. "The Vicar is calling round for extra subscriptions."

Charlie nodded. He was wishing he knew the football results in the evening paper.

His wife served a rice shape. She doled out jam with a careful hand and a measuring eye. "We ought to see about the garden gate," she said.

"I'll mend it on Saturday," Charlie replied.

"I was thinking," she said presently, "that we ought to ask Uncle Henry and Aunt round soon. They will be expecting it."

Charlie put his spoon and fork together, hesitated and then replied slowly: "Life is nothing but 'ought.' 'Ought' to do this: 'Ought' to do that."

His wife looked at him, astonished. He could see that she was grieved - or rather, aggrieved - at his glimmer of anarchy.

"Of course," she explained at last. "People can't have what they like. There's one's duty to do. Life isn't for enjoyment, Charlie. It's given to us ... it is given to us...."

As she paused to crystallise an idea, Charlie cut in.

"Yes," he said, "it is given to us.... What for?"

He leaned his head on his hand. He was not looking at her. He was looking at the cloth, weaving patterns upon it. And with this question something of boyhood came upon him again, and he weaved visions upon the cloth.

"To do one's duty in," she replied gently, but rebukingly.

Charlie did not know the classic phrase, "Cui bono." He merely repeated:

"What for?"

After supper he helped her to wash up, for the daily help left early in the afternoon; and then he asked her, idle as he knew the question to be, if she would like to come for a walk - just a short walk up the road.

She shook her head. "I ought not to leave the children."

"They're in bed," he argued, "and Maud's big enough to look after the others for half-an-hour. Maud's twelve."

She shook her head. "I ought not to leave the house."

"But," he began slowly.

"I am not the kind of woman who leaves her house and children in the evenings," she said gently, but finally.

Charlie took his hat. He turned it round and round in his hands, pinching the crown in, and punching it out. He had a curious, almost uncontrollable wish to cry. For a moment it was terrible. Before it was over, she was speaking again.

"You ought not to mess your hats about like that; they don't last half as long."

Charlie went out.

He knew other men who were as puzzled about life as himself, but mostly they were of cruder stuff, and if things at home went beyond their bearing they flung out of their houses, swearing, and went to play a hundred up at the local club. Then they were

Edward J. O'Brien and John Cournos

philosophers again. But for Charlie this evening there was no philosophy big enough, for he was looking, though he did not know it, over the edge of that awful, but enchanting abyss. Its depths were obscured by rolling clouds of mist, and it was only this mist which he now saw, terrifying and confusing him. He was a little man, and knew it. He was a poor man, and knew it. He was a weary man, and knew it. He hated his wife, and knew it. He hated his children - whom she had made like herself, prim, peeking and childishly censorious - and knew it.

He had not meant it to be like this at all.

When he got married she was the starched daughter of starched parents from a starched small house - like the one he came from - but she was young, and her figure was pliant, and her hair curled rather sweetly.

He had dreamed of happy days, cosy days with laughter; little treats together - Soho restaurants, Richmond Park, something colourful, something for which he had vaguely and secretly longed all the dingy, narrow, church-parading, humbugging days of his good little boyhood. But he soon woke up to find he had married another hard holy woman like his mother.

He walked along, thinking mistily and hotly. Supposing he had a baby who roared with joy and stole the sugar ... but she wouldn't have babies like that. The first coherent thing her babies learned to say was a text.

Babies.... He hadn't wanted three, because they couldn't afford them. He tried to talk to her about it

She made him ashamed of himself, though he didn't know why; and showed him how wicked he was, though he didn't know why; and how good she was, though he didn't know why - then. But he knew now that there are still many women who are gluttons for martyrdom, who long to exalt themselves by a parrot righteousness, and who are only happy when destroying natural joy in others. And he knew there were many men like himself, married and done for; tied up to these pettifogging saints; goaded under their stupid yoke; belittled through their narrow eyes.

He thought all this mistily and hotly.

He had come to the end of the road; and the end of another road more populous; and the end of another road, more populous.

At a corner of this road stood Kitty.

She was soft and colourful, painted to a perfect peachiness, young - twenty-four and looking less; old as the world and wise. She was gay. She did not much care if it snowed; she knew enough to wriggle in somewhere, somehow, out of it. The years had not yet scared her. She was joy.

Charlie paused before he knew why. She looked at him. Then the mists rolled away from the abyss below the tottering edge on which he had been balanced for longer time than he guessed, and he saw the garden far below; lotus flowers dreaming in the sun. He launched himself simply into space towards them.

Kitty helped him. She knew how.

Charlie had, as it happened, his next week's personal allowance of seven and sixpence in his pocket - for to-day had been pay day; and his season ticket. The rest he had handed over to his wife at supper time. He had also, however, the moral support of knowing that he had in the savings bank the exact amount of his sickness and life insurance premiums due that very week. So it did not embarrass him to take Kitty straight away up to town - she, making a shrewd summary of him, did not object to third-class travelling - and to stand her coffee and a sandwich at the Monico.

"I don't happen to have much change on me, and my bank's closed," was the explanation he offered, and she tactfully accepted of this modest entertainment.

It was ten-thirty when she took him to see her tiny flat a stone's throw away. She was looking for another supporter for that flat, and explained her reason for being in Charlie's suburb that evening. She'd been trying to find the house of a man friend - a rich friend - who lived there, and might have helped her over a temporary difficulty, but when she found the house the servants told her he was away. She confided these things, leaning in Charlie's arms on a little striped divan by a gas fire. She made him a drink, and showed him the cunning and luxurious little contrivances for comfort about the flat. He loved it. She didn't try to conceal from him her real vocation, for that would have been too silly. Even Charlie might not have been such a fool as to believe her. But she invested it with glamour; she made of it romance. Once more as in boyhood he saw the world full of allurement.

So he went home, having promised her that to-morrow he would come again.

And going in quietly, so as not to disturb the baby, he undressed quietly so as not to disturb his wife, and he crept cautiously into the double bed that she decreed they must share for ever and ever, whatever their feelings towards one another, because they were married; and he hoped to fall asleep with enchantment unbroken. But she was awake, and waiting patiently to speak. "Where have you been, Charlie?"

"At the club," he whispered back. "Watching two fellows play a billiard match."

She sighed.

"Charlie," she said, "you ought to have more consideration for me. Maudie said to me when I went in to look at them before I came to bed: 'Is daddy still out?' she said. 'I do think he ought not to go out and leave you alone, mamma.' She's such a sweet child, Charlie, and I do think you ought to think more of her. Children often say little things in the innocence of their hearts that do even us grown-up people good sometimes."

So the next morning Charlie left home with a suit-case - alleged to contain the one suit for turning, but really crammed to bursting. His wife being busy with the baby, Maud saw him off with her usual air of smug reproof; and that evening he did not come back. He had written a letter to his wife, on the journey to town, telling her his decision, which she would receive by the afternoon post. But he gave her no address.

He drew out the whole amount in the savings bank, surrendered his life insurance, realising £160; and he went home after the day's work to Kitty.

Little Kitty was looking for any kind of mug, pending better developments, and she certainly had found one; but what a happy mug he was! Life was warm and light, gay and uncritical. He spent even less on his own lunches - he retained his seven and sixpence weekly personal allowance, though of course he posted the rest of his salary home - so that he might have an extra half-crown or so to buy chocolates for Kitty. It was nice to buy chocolates instead of subscribing to the Vicar's Fund. And little Kitty, who was wise, guessed he hadn't much and couldn't afford her long, so pending better things, like a sensible person, she eked him out.

She made him so happy. They laughed. She sang -

> I'm for ever blowing bubbles,
> Pretty bubbles in the air.
> They fly so high, nearly reach the sky....

She had a gramophone and she taught him to dance, and then he had to take her to the best dancing place he could afford and they danced a long evening through. He bought her a wonderful little woollen frock at one of the small French shops in Shaftesbury Avenue, and she looked exactly what she was in it; and he knew she was the most wonderful thing in the world. When he propounded the frock question to her one morning when they woke up, saying: "I would like to see you in a dress I'd bought, Kitty," she did not tell him it was wrong to consider themselves, and she would have her old black turned. She put a dear fat little arm round his neck, laid a soft selfish cheek to his, and muttered cosily, "It shall buy her a frock then. It shall."

She was sporting enough not to protest when she knew

where his weekly pay went. "Three kids must be fed," she said. In fact, according to her own codes, she was not ungenerous towards the other woman.

All the while he knew: £160 can't last. What will happen when...?

Charlie's wife thought she was sure of what must happen pretty soon. So did her Uncle Henry and Aunt, for whom she had sent a day or two after the blow had fallen.

They found her cutting down Maud's oldest dress for the second child in her tidy house.

"Charlie has left me for an immoral woman," she said, after preparing them with preliminaries.

"What!" said Uncle Henry. He was a churchwarden at the church to which Charlie, in a bowler hat, had had to take the critical Maud on Sundays.

"Fancy leaving *that*!" said Aunt, when they had digested and credited the news. She pointed at her niece sewing diligently even through this painful conversation. "Look at her scraping and economising and contriving. And he leaves her!"

"He must be naturally wild and bad," said Uncle Henry. "Shall I speak to the Vicar for you?"

"Have you written to his firm?" asked Aunt.

Charlie's wife spoke wisely, gently, and with perfection as ever. "No," she said. "I have thought it over, and I think the best thing, for the children's sake, is to say nothing. We ought not to consider ourselves. Besides, I dare say it's my duty to forgive him."

"Always thinking of your duty!" murmured Aunt admiringly.

"If I wrote to his firm about it," said Charlie's wife, "they would dismiss him."

"Ah! and he sends you his pay, you say?" said Uncle Henry, seizing the point like a business man.

"What a position for a conscientious woman like you!" mourned Aunt.

"You are quite right, my dear," said Uncle Henry. "You have three children and no other means of sustenance, and you cannot afford to do as I should otherwise advise you."

"Besides, he will come back," said Charlie's wife gently. "Men are soon sickened of these women.'

"Of course," agreed Aunt.

"Well! Well!" said Uncle Henry, "you are very magnanimous, my dear, and one day Charles will fully appreciate it. And I hope he will be duly thankful to you for your great goodness. Yes! You will soon have Master Charles creeping back, very ashamed of himself, and when he comes, I for one, intend to give him the biggest talking to he has ever had in his life. But I really think the Vicar too, should be told, in confidence, so that he may decide upon the right course of action for himself."

"Because he could not allow your husband to communicate, my love," said Aunt, "without being sure of his genuine repentance."

"I have been thinking of that too," said Charlie's wife. "It would not be right."

"I wonder what he feels about himself, when he remembers his dear little children," said Aunt. "Maud nearly old enough to understand, and all!"

So they lay for Charlie, while he basked and thrived in the abyss of the lotus-flower; and the £160 dwindled.

It was towards the end of the second month that Charlie sensed a new element in his precarious dream. All day when he was out, thinking of Kitty through the routine of his work, he had no idea of what she was doing. Sometimes he was afraid to think of what she might be doing, and for fear of shattering the dream, he never dared to ask. Always she was sweet and joyful towards him - save for petulant quarrels she raised as if to make the ensuing sweetness and joyfulness the dearer - until towards the close of the second month. Then one evening she was distrait; one evening, critical; one night, cold; then she had a dinner and dance engagement at the Savoy. Then he knew that his time had come.

He waited up for her. He had the gas fire lighted in the tiny sitting-room, and little sugary cakes and wine on the table; and the gas fire lighted in the bedroom to warm it for her, and the bed turned down, and her nightgown and slippers, so frail, warming before the fire.

But he knew.

In the early dawn her key clicked in the lock, and she came in, followed by a man. He was pale, sensual, moneyed, fashionable. Charlie got up stoutly; but he was already beaten.

The Jew looked at him, and turned to Kitty.

"I told you," she said, stammering a little, "I told you how it was. By to-morrow ... I told you...."

"I'll come again, to-morrow, then," said the man very meaningly, "fetch you out -"

"At eight," she nodded firmly.

He kissed her on the mouth, while Charlie stood looking at them with eyes that seemed to stare themselves out of his head, turned and went out.

"Nighty-night!" Kitty called after him.

After the front door clicked again there was a moment's silence. Kitty advanced, shook off her cloak, took up one of the sugary cakes, and began to munch it. She looked beautiful and careless and sorry and hard all at once.

"What are you sitting up for, Charlie?" she asked. "I didn't expect to see you. I brought that fellow in to talk."

"What about?" said Charlie in a hoarse desolate voice.

"Charlie," said Kitty, hurriedly, "you know this

arrangement of ours can't last, now, can it, dear? You haven't the cash for one thing, dear. Now, have you? And I've got to think of myself a little; a girl's got to provide. You've been awf'ly good to me. Let's part friends."

"'Part!'" he repeated.

His eyes seemed to start from his head.

"Let's part friends," wheedled Kitty. "Shall us?"

The night passed in a kind of evil vision of desolation, and Kitty was asleep long before he had stopped his futile whisperings into her ear.

Before he went to the office in the morning, he asked her from a breaking heart: "You mean it?"

"I've got to," she explained. She cried easily. "Dearie, you'll leave peaceably? You won't make a row? Now, for my sake! To oblige me! While you're out to-day I'll pack your suit-case and give it to the hall-porter for you to call for. Shall I, Charlie? Kiss me, dear. Don't take your latch-key. Good-bye. You've been awfully decent to me. We'll part friends, shall us?"

He kissed her, and went out to work, speaking no more. He had said all the things in his heart during the hours of that sleepless dawn. She knew how he loved her ... though possibly she didn't quite believe. He realised her position acutely, perhaps more acutely than his own. She had to live. And yet....

He had taken his latch-key the same as usual, and he found himself at the end of the day, going the same as usual to the tiny flat that was home if ever there was any place called home. He let himself in noiselessly. The little hall was dark. He stood in a corner against the coat cupboard. The flat was silent. He stood there a long while without moving and a clock chimed seven. He heard her singing -

"I'm for ever blowing bubbles....
Lal-la! la! la!... la! la! la!..."

She would be in her bedroom, sitting before the mirror in her diaphanous underwear, touching up her face. The pauses in the song made him see her.... Now she was using the eyebrow pencil.... The song went on and broke again; now she would be half turning from the mirror, curved on the gilt chair as he had so often seen her, hand-glass in hand, looking at the back of her head, and her eyelashes, and her profile, fining away all hard edges of rouge and lipstick. He felt quite peaceful as he imaged her.

Peace was shattered at a blast by the ringing of the front door bell. Then light streamed from the opened bedroom door, was switched off, and Kitty ran into the darkish hall. She clicked on the light by the front door, opened the door, and the big man came in.

He kissed her on the mouth.

Then Charlie stepped from beside the coat cupboard, suddenly as though some strong spring which held him there had been released, and the strong spring was in his tense body alone. For the first time in his life he felt all steel and wire and whipcord, and many fires. He threw himself on the intruder and fought for his woman.

Kitty did not scream. She knew better.

"Oh Charlie!" she panted. "For - sake go! Go! I can't have a row here. Oh, Charlie, be a good boy, do."

"He *shall* go," said the other man.

He was a big man; and still young and lithe. Kitty opened the front door, whispering: "Oh, Charlie! Oh! Charlie!" and the man pushed Charlie out. The lift was not working at the moment, the landing was quiet, there was not a soul on the stairway beside the liftshaft when the man flung Charlie headlong down the first flight and broke him on the unyielding stone.

Charlie heard his own spine crack; but as the other, scared and pale, reached him, he heard something else also; the voice of Kitty, who stood above them, looking down, sobbing: "I c-c-can't have a row here. It'd break me. Oh! Charlie! Oh Charlie! If you love me, go away!"

Charlie loved Kitty very much. "My back's broken," he whispered to the enemy bending over him. "But if you get me under the armpits, lift me down the stairs, and put me into the street, and if the hall-porter sees us go out tell him I'm dead drunk -"

The man lifted him as instructed, an arm round him, just under the shoulder-blades and armpits. Below he could feel the crumpled weight sway and sag. He tried to be merciful in his handling. "D-d-do you no g-g-good," he faltered as he lifted Charlie downstairs, "t-to get me into a mess. I'm sorry. D-d-didn't mean.... But I've got a wife and don't want hell raised.... You asked for it.... I'm sorry. I'm sorry...." When they reached the ground floor the single-handed porter was just carrying a passenger in the lift to the floor above, so they got unobserved into the street, a quietish street, a cul-de-sac.

"Take me a f-f-few d-d-doors off, and put me down," said Charlie, and the sweat of pain ran down his face, but when the man had put him down against some area railings, and laid him straight, he was comfortable.

The other man simply vanished.

A taxi-driver found Charlie by-and-by, and the police fetched an ambulance and took him to the hospital, and in a white bed he lay sleepily, revealing nothing, all that night. But they found, searching for an address in his pockets, the address of his family, and they sent a message to his wife.

His wife received it early the next morning, and first she sent Maud for Uncle Henry and Aunt, who found that all was turning out as they prophesied, save for the slight deviation of Charlie's accident.

"They don't say exactly how bad he is?" said Uncle Henry. "Ah! but he was well enough to send for you! He knows which side his bread's buttered. Yes! we shall have Master Charles creeping back again, very thankful to be in his home with every comfort, nursed by you; and I will give him the worse talking to be has ever had in his life!"

"And if he's ill he can't prevent the Vicar visiting him too," said Aunt.

So Charlie's wife set out to do her duty.

But still earlier that morning, instructed by the tremendous peace which was stealing over him that time was short, Charlie was making his first request. Would they please ring up *Shaftesbury* 84 to ask for "Kitty" and tell her "Charlie" just wanted to see her very urgently for a few minutes at once, but not to be frightened, for everything would be perfectly all right?

Pending her arrival, which in a faltering voice over the phone she promised as soon as possible, Charlie asked the kindly Sister who was hovering near to help him die:

"Sister, when a friend of mine comes in, a young lady who isn't used to - to seeing - things, if I go off suddenly as it were-what I'm afraid of is, she may be afraid if there's any kind of struggle - I saw a fellow die once and he gave a sort of rattle - well, will you just pull the bed-clothes up over me, so that she doesn't see?"

Kitty came in, wearing, perhaps incidentally, perhaps by some grace of kindness, the woollen frock, and she crept, shaking, round the screen, and stood beside Charlie, and said, "Oh Charlie! Oh Charlie!" opening his closing eyes.

"Kitty!" he smiled, "sing 'Bubbles.'"

The look Sister - who had taken her right in - gave her, pried Kitty's trembling mouth open like a crowbar, and leaning against Charlie's cot she sang -

"When shadows creep,
When I'm asleep,
To lands of hope I stray,

Then at daybreak, when I awake...."

The Sister drew the bed-clothes shadily round Charlie's face.

"... My blue bird flutters away,
I'm forever blowing bubbles....
Pretty bubbles in the air...."

Just then the good woman was brought into the ward, bearing with her messages from Maud worthy of Little Eva herself; and full of holy forgiveness; and at edge of the screen Sister met her.

"His wife?" said Sister. "A moment too late. I am sorry." The good woman was looking at the bad woman by the bed, so Sister made a vague explanation.

"He just wanted a song," she said.

A HEDONIST

By JOHN GALSWORTHY

(From *Pears' Annual* and *The Century Magazine*) 1921

Rupert K. Vaness remains freshly in my mind because he was so fine and large, and because he summed up in his person and behavior a philosophy which, budding before the war, hibernated during that distressing epoch, and is now again in bloom.

He was a New-Yorker addicted to Italy. One often puzzled over the composition of his blood. From his appearance, it was rich, and his name fortified the conclusion. What the K. stood for, however, I never learned; the three possibilities were equally intriguing. Had he a strain of Highlander with Kenneth or Keith; a drop of German or Scandinavian with Kurt or Knut; a blend of Syrian or Armenian with Kahalil or Kassim? The blue in his fine eyes seemed to preclude the last, but there was an encouraging curve in his nostrils and a raven gleam in his auburn hair, which, by the way, was beginning to grizzle and recede when I knew him. The flesh of his face, too, had sometimes a tired and pouchy appearance, and his tall body looked a trifle rebellious within his extremely well-cut clothes; but, after all, he was fifty-five. You felt that Vaness was a philosopher, yet he never bored you with his views, and was content to let you grasp his moving principle gradually through watching what he ate, drank, smoked, wore, and how he encircled himself with the beautiful things and people of this life. One presumed him rich, for one was never aware of money in his presence. Life moved round him with a certain noiseless ease or stood still at a perfect temperature, like the air in a conservatory round a choice blossom which a draught might shrivel.

This image of a flower in relation to Rupert K. Vaness pleases me, because of that little incident in Magnolia Gardens, near Charleston, South Carolina.

Vaness was the sort of a man of whom one could never say with safety whether he was revolving round a beautiful young woman or whether the beautiful young woman was revolving round him. His looks, his wealth, his taste, his reputation, invested him with a certain sun-like quality; but his age, the recession of his locks, and the advancement of his waist were beginning to dim his lustre, so that whether he was moth or candle was becoming a moot point. It was moot to me, watching him and Miss Sabine Monroy at Charleston throughout the month of March. The casual observer would have said that she was "playing him up," as a young poet of my acquaintance puts it; but I was not casual. For me Vaness had the attraction of a theorem, and I was looking rather deeply into him and Miss Monroy.

That girl had charm. She came, I think, from Baltimore, with a strain in her, they said, of old Southern French blood. Tall and what is known as willowy, with dark chestnut hair, very broad, dark eyebrows, very soft, quick eyes, and a pretty mouth, -

when she did not accentuate it with lip-salve, - she had more sheer quiet vitality than any girl I ever saw. It was delightful to watch her dance, ride, play tennis. She laughed with her eyes; she talked with a savouring vivacity. She never seemed tired or bored. She was, in one hackneyed word, attractive. And Vaness, the connoisseur, was quite obviously attracted. Of men who professionally admire beauty one can never tell offhand whether they definitely design to add a pretty woman to their collection, or whether their dalliance is just matter of habit. But he stood and sat about her, he drove and rode, listened to music, and played cards with her; he did all but dance with her, and even at times trembled on the brink of that. And his eyes, those fine, lustrous eyes of his, followed her about.

How she had remained unmarried to the age of twenty-six was a mystery till one reflected that with her power of enjoying life she could not yet have had the time. Her perfect physique was at full stretch for eighteen hours out of the twenty-four every day. Her sleep must have been like that of a baby. One figured her sinking into dreamless rest the moment her head touched the pillow, and never stirring till she sprang up into her bath.

As I say, for me Vaness, or rather his philosophy, *erat demonstrandum*. I was philosophically in some distress just then. The microbe of fatalism, already present in the brains of artists before the war, had been considerably enlarged by that depressing occurrence. Could a civilization, basing itself on the production of material advantages, do anything but insure the desire for more and more material advantages? Could it promote progress even of a material character except in countries whose resources were still much in excess of their population? The war had seemed to me to show that mankind was too combative an animal ever to recognize that the good of all was the good of one. The coarse-fibred, pugnacious, and self-seeking would, I had become sure, always carry too many guns for the refined and kindly.

The march of science appeared, on the whole, to be carrying us backward. I deeply suspected that there had been ages when the populations of this earth, though less numerous and comfortable, had been proportionately healthier than they were at present. As for religion, I had never had the least faith in Providence rewarding the pitiable by giving them a future life of bliss. The theory seemed to me illogical, for the more pitiable in this life appeared to me the thick-skinned and successful, and these, as we know, in the saying about the camel and the needle's eye, our religion consigns wholesale to hell. Success, power, wealth, those aims of profiteers and premiers, pedagogues and pandemoniacs, of all, in fact, who could not see God in a dewdrop, hear Him in distant goat-bells, and scent Him in a pepper-tree, had always appeared to me akin to dry rot. And yet every day one saw more distinctly that they were the pea in the thimblerig of life, the hub of a universe which, to the approbation of the majority they represented, they were fast making uninhabitable. It did not even seem of any use to help one's neighbors; all efforts at relief just gilded the pill and encouraged our stubbornly contentious leaders to plunge us all into fresh miseries. So I was searching right and left for something to believe in, willing to accept even Rupert K. Vaness and his basking philosophy. But could a man bask his life right out? Could just looking at fine pictures, tasting rare fruits and wines, the mere listening to good music, the scent of azaleas and the best tobacco, above all the society of pretty women, keep salt in my bread, an ideal in my brain? Could they? That's what I wanted to know.

Every one who goes to Charleston in the spring, soon or late, visits Magnolia Gardens. A painter of flowers and trees, I specialize in gardens, and freely assert that none in the world is so beautiful as this. Even before the magnolias come out, it consigns the Boboli at Florence, the Cinnamon Gardens of Colombo, Concepcion at Malaga, Versailles, Hampton Court, the Generaliffe at Granada, and La Mortola to the category of "also ran." Nothing so free and gracious, so lovely and wistful, nothing so richly coloured, yet so ghostlike, exists, planted by the sons of men. It is a kind of paradise which has wandered down, a miraculously enchanted wilderness. Brilliant with azaleas, or magnolias, it centres round a pool of dreamy water, overhung by tall trunks wanly festooned with the grey Florida moss. Beyond anything I have ever seen, it is otherworldly. And I went there day after day, drawn as one is drawn in youth by visions of the Ionian Sea, of the East, or the Pacific Isles. I used to sit paralysed by the absurdity of putting brush to canvas in front of that dream-pool. I wanted to paint of it a picture like that of the fountain, by Helleu, which hangs in the Luxembourg. But I knew I never should.

I was sitting there one sunny afternoon, with my back to a clump of azaleas, watching an old coloured gardener - so old that he had started life as an "owned" negro, they said, and certainly still retained the familiar suavity of the old-time darky - I was watching him prune the shrubs when I heard the voice of Rupert K. Vaness say, quite close:

Edward J. O'Brien and John Cournos

"There's nothing for me but beauty, Miss Monroy."

The two were evidently just behind my azalea clump, perhaps four yards away, yet as invisible as if in China.

"Beauty is a wide, wide word. Define it, Mr. Vaness."

"An ounce of fact is worth a ton of theory: it stands before me."

"Come, now, that's just a get-out. Is beauty of the flesh or of the spirit?"

"What is the spirit, as you call it? I'm a pagan."

"Oh, so am I. But the Greeks were pagans."

"Well, spirit is only the refined side of sensuous appreciations."

"I wonder!"

"I have spent my life in finding that out."

"Then the feeling this garden rouses in me is purely sensuous?"

"Of course. If you were standing there blind and deaf, without the powers of scent and touch, where would your feeling be?"

"You are very discouraging, Mr. Vaness." "No, madam; I face facts. When I was a youngster I had plenty of fluffy aspiration towards I didn't know what; I even used to write poetry."

"Oh! Mr. Vaness, was it good?"

"It was not. I very soon learned that a genuine sensation was worth all the uplift in the world."

"What is going to happen when your senses strike work?"

"I shall sit in the sun and fade out."

"I certainly do like your frankness."

"You think me a cynic, of course; I am nothing so futile, Miss Sabine. A cynic is just a posing ass proud of his attitude. I see nothing to be proud of in my attitude, just as I see nothing to be proud of in the truths of existence."

"Suppose you had been poor?"

"My senses would be lasting better than they are, and when at last they failed, I should die quicker, from want of food and warmth, that's all."

"Have you ever been in love, Mr. Vaness?"

"I am in love now."

"And your love has no element of devotion, no finer side?"

"None. It wants."

"I have never been in love. But, if I were, I think I should want to lose myself rather than to gain the other."

"Would you? Sabine, *I am in love with you.*"

"Oh! Shall we walk on?"

I heard their footsteps, and was alone again, with the old gardener lopping at his shrubs.

But what a perfect declaration of hedonism! How simple and how solid was the Vaness theory of existence! Almost Assyrian, worthy of Louis Quinze!

And just then the old negro came up.

"It's pleasant settin'," he said in his polite and hoarse half-whisper; "dar ain't no flies yet."

"It's perfect, Richard. This is the most beautiful spot in the world."

"Such," he answered, softly drawling. "In deh war-time de Yanks nearly burn deh house heah - Sherman's Yanks. Such dey did; po'ful angry wi' ol' massa dey was, 'cause he hid up deh silver plate afore he went away. My ol' fader was de factotalum den. De Yanks took 'm, suh; dey took 'm, and deh major he tell my fader to show 'm whar deh plate was. My ol' fader he look at 'm an' say: 'Wot yuh take me foh? Yuh take me foh a sneakin' nigger? No, sub, you kin du wot yuh like wid dis chile; he ain't goin' to act no Judas. No, suh!' And deh Yankee major he put 'm up ag'in' dat tall live-oak dar, an' he say: 'Yuh darn ungrateful nigger! I's come all dis way to set yuh free. Now, whar's dat silver plate, or I shoot yuh up, such!' 'No, suh,' says my fader; 'shoot away. I's neber goin' t' tell.' So dey begin to shoot, and shot all roun' 'm to skeer 'm up. I was a li'l boy den, an' I see my ol' fader wid my own eyes, suh, standin' thar's bold's Peter. No, suh, dey didn't neber git no word from him. He loved deh folk heah; such he did, suh."

The old man smiled, and in that beatific smile I saw not only his perennial pleasure in the well-known story, but the fact that he, too, would have stood there, with the bullets raining round him, sooner than betray the folk he loved.

"Fine story, Richard; but - very silly, obstinate old man, your father, wasn't he?"

He looked at me with a sort of startled anger, which slowly broadened into a grin; then broke into soft, hoarse laughter.

"Oh, yes, suh, sueh; berry silly, obstinacious ol' man. Yes, suh indeed." And he went off cackling to himself. He had only just gone when I heard footsteps again behind my azalea clump, and Miss Monroy's voice.

"Your philosophy is that of faun and nymph. Can you play the part?"

"Only let me try." Those words had such a fevered ring that in imagination I could see Vaness all flushed, his fine eyes shining, his well-kept hands trembling, his lips a little protruded.

There came a laugh, high, gay, sweet.

"Very well, then; catch me!" I heard a swish of skirts against the shrubs, the sound of flight, an astonished gasp from Vaness, and the heavy *thud, thud* of his feet following on the path through the azalea maze. I hoped fervently that they would not suddenly come running past and see me sitting there. My straining ears caught another laugh far off, a panting sound, a muttered oath, a far-away "*Cooee!*" And then, staggering, winded, pale with heat and vexation, Vaness appeared, caught sight of me, and stood a moment. Sweat was running down his face, his hand was clutching at his side, his stomach heaved - a hunter beaten and undignified. He muttered, turned abruptly on his heel, and left me staring at where his fastidious dandyism and all that it stood for had so abruptly come undone.

I know not how he and Miss Monroy got home to Charleston; not in the same car, I fancy. As for me, I travelled deep in thought, aware of having witnessed something rather tragic, not looking forward to my next encounter with Vaness.

He was not at dinner, but the girl was there, as radiant as ever, and though I was glad she had not been caught, I was almost angry at the signal triumph of her youth. She wore a black dress, with a red flower in her hair, and another at her breast, and had never looked so vital and so pretty. Instead of dallying with my cigar beside cool waters in the lounge of the hotel, I strolled out afterward on the Battery, and sat down beside the statue of a tutelary personage. A lovely evening; from some tree or shrub close by emerged an adorable faint fragrance, and in the white electric light the acacia foliage was patterned out against a thrilling, blue sky. If there were no fireflies abroad, there should have been. A night for hedonists, indeed!

And suddenly, in fancy, there came before me Vaness's well-dressed person, panting, pale, perplexed; and beside him, by a freak of vision, stood the old darky's father, bound to the live-oak, with the bullets whistling past, and his face transfigured. There they stood alongside the creed of pleasure, which depended for fulfilment on its waist measurement; and the creed of love, devoted unto death!

"Aha!" I thought, "which of the two laughs *last*?"

And just then I saw Vaness himself beneath a lamp, cigar in mouth, and cape flung back so that its silk lining shone. Pale and heavy, in the cruel white light, his face had a bitter look. And I was sorry - very sorry, at that moment for Rupert K. Vaness.

THE BAT AND BELFRY INN

By ALAN GRAHAM

(From *The Story-Teller*) 1922

It was the maddest and most picturesque hotel at which we have ever stopped. Tony and I were touring North Wales. We had left Llandudno that morning in the twoseater, lunched at Festiniog, and late in the afternoon were trundling down a charming valley with the reluctant assistance of a road whose surface, if it ever had possessed such an asset, had long since vanished. On rounding one of the innumerable hairpin bends on our road, there burst upon us the most gorgeous miniature scene that we had ever encountered. I stopped the car almost automatically.

"Oh, George, what a charming hotel!" exclaimed Tony. "Let's stop and have tea."

Tony, I should mention, is my wife. She is intensely practical.

I had not noticed the hotel, for before us the valley opened out into a perfect stage setting. From the road the land fell sharply a hundred feet to a rocky mountain stream, the rustle of whose water came up to us faintly like the music heard in a sea-shell. Beyond rose hills - hill upon hill lit patchily by the sun, so that their contours were a mingling of brilliant purple heather, red-brown bracken, and indigo shadow. Far down the valley the stream glinted, mirror-like, through a veil of trees.

And Tony spoke of tea!

I dragged my eyes from the magnet of the view and found that I had stopped the car within a few yards of a little hotel that must have been planted there originally by someone with a soul. It lay by the open roadside five miles from anywhere. It was built of the rough grey-green stone of the district, but it was rescued from the commonplace by its leaded windows, the big old beams that angled across its white plastered gables, and by the clematis and late tea roses that clung about its porch.

I could hardly blame Tony for her materialism. The hotel blended admirably with its surroundings. There was nothing about it of the beerhouse-on-the-mountain-top so dear to the German mind. It looked quiet, refined and restful, and one felt instinctively that it would be managed in a fashion in keeping with all about it.

"By Jove, Tony!" I said, as I drew up to the clematis-covered porch, "we might do worse than stop here for a day or two."

"We'll have tea anyhow, and see what we think of it." I clattered over the red-tiled floor, and when my eyes had grown accustomed to the dim light that contrasted so well with the sunshine without, found myself in a small sunshiny room, with a low ceiling, oak-rafted, some comfortable chairs, an old eight-day clock stopped at ten-thirty-five, and a man.

He was a long thin man, clean-shaven, wearing an old shooting coat and a pair of shabby grey flannel trousers. He smoked a pipe and read in a book. At my entrance he did not look up, and I set him down as a guest in the hotel.

One side of the room was built of obscured glass panes, with an open square in the middle and a ledge upon which rested several suggestive empty glasses, so I crossed to this hospitable-looking gap, and tapped upon the ledge. Several repetitions bringing no response, I turned to the only living creature who appeared to be available.

"Can you tell me, sir, if we can have tea in the hotel," I asked.

The long man started, looked up, closed his book, and jumped to his feet as if galvanized to life.

"Of course, of course, of course," he cried hastily, and added, as by an afterthought, "of course."

I may have shown a natural surprise at this almost choral response, for he pulled himself together and became something more explicit.

"I'll see to it at once," he said hurriedly. "I'm - I'm the proprietor, you know. You won't mind if we're - if we're a little upset. You see, I - I've just moved in. Left me by an uncle, you know, an uncle in Australia. I'll see to it at once. Anything you would like - specially fancy? Bread and butter now, or cake perhaps? Will you take a seat - two seats." (Tony had followed me in). "And look at yesterday's paper. Oh yes, you can have tea - of course, of course, of course. Of -"

His words petered out, as he clattered off down a like-flagged passage. I looked at Tony and raised my eyebrows.

"Seems a trifle mad," I said.

"How delightfully cool," said she, looking round the old-fashioned room appraisingly, "and so clean! I think we'll stop."

"Let's have tea before we decide," I suggested. "The proprietor is distinctly eccentric, to say the least of it."

"He looked quite a superior man. I thought," said Tony. "Not the least like a Welshman."

Tony herself comes from far north of the Tweed.

The hotel was small, and the kitchen, apparently, not far away, for we could not avoid hearing sounds of what appeared to be a heated argument coming from the direction in which mine host had vanished. We were used to heated arguments in the hotels at which we had put up, but they had invariably taken place in Welsh, whereas this one was undoubtedly in English. Snatches of it reached our ears.

"... haven't the pluck of a rabbit, Bill."

"... all very well, but -"

"I'm not afraid, I'll -"

Then our host returned.

"It's coming, it's coming, it's coming," he said, his hands thrust deep in his trousers pockets, jingling loose change in a manner that suggested agitation.

He stood looking down at us as though we were something he didn't quite know what to do with, and then an idea seemed to strike him, and be vanished for a moment to reappear almost immediately in the square gap of the bar window.

"Have a drink while you're waiting?" he asked, much more naturally.

I looked at my watch. It was half-past four. Very free-and-easy with the licensing laws, I thought.

"I thought six o'clock was opening time?" I said.

The thin man was overcome with confusion. His face flushed red, he shut the window down with a bang, and a moment after came round to us again.

"Awfully sorry," he stammered apologetically. "Might get the house a bad name. Deuced inconsiderate of - of my uncle not to leave me a book of the rules. Very bad break, that - what?"

Evidently Tony was not so much impressed by the eccentricities of our host as was I. She approved of the hotel and its situation, and had made up her mind to stop. I could tell it by her face as she addressed the proprietor.

"Have you accommodation if we should make up our

minds to stay here for a few days?" she asked.

"Stay here? You want to stay?" he repeated, consternation written large all over his face. "Good G - I mean certainly, of course, of course."

He bolted down the passage like a rabbit, and we heard hoarse whispering from the direction in which he had gone.

"Dotty?" I suggested.

"Not a bit of it," retorted Tony. "Nervous because he is new to his job, but very anxious to be obliging. We shall do splendidly here."

I shrugged my shoulders and said no more, because I know Tony. I have been married to her for years and years.

Light steps upon the tiles heralded something new - different, but equally surprising.

"Tea is served, madam, if you will step this way."

She was the apotheosis of all waitresses. Her frock was black, but it was of silk and finely cut. Her apron, of coarse white cotton, was grotesque against it. She had neat little feet encased in high-heeled shoes, and her stockings were of silk. Her common cap that she wore sat coquettishly on her dark curls, and her face was charming, though petrified in that unnatural expression of distance which, as a rule, only the very best menials can attain.

There were no other guests in the coffee-room, and this

marvel of maids devoted the whole of her attention to us, standing over us like a column of ice which thawed only to attend upon our wants. There was no getting past her veil of reticence. Tony tried her with questions, but "Yes, madam," "No, madam," and "Certainly, madam," appeared the sum of her vocabulary. Yet when we sent her to the kitchen for more hot water, we were conscious of a whispering and giggling which assured us that off the stage she could thaw.

"We must stay a day or two," said Tony. "I'm dying to paidle in that burn."

"My dear, how often have you promised me that you would never subject me to Scotch after we were married!" I protested.

"When I see a burn I e'en must juist paidle in it," retorted Tony, deliberately forswearing herself. "So we'll book that room."

At that moment the celestial waitress returned with the hot water, and Tony made known her determination. I drive the car, but Tony supplies the driving-power.

"Certainly, madam. I shall speak to Mr. Gunthorpe." Quickly she returned.

"Number ten is vacant. The boots and chambermaid are both away at a sheep-trial, but we expect them back any moment. I shall show you the room, madam, and if you will leave the car, sir, until the boots returns -"

"That will be all right. No hurry, no hurry."

While we were examining our bedroom and finding it all that could be desired, I heard a car draw up before the hotel, and the sound of voices in conversation. A few minutes later, on going downstairs, I made the acquaintance of the boots. He was obviously awaiting me by my car, and touched his forelock in a manner rarely seen off the stage. He wore khaki cord breeches with leather leggings, a striped shirt open at the neck, and chewed a straw desperately. In no other respect did he resemble the boots of an out-of-the-way hotel.

"Garage round this way, sir," he said, guiding me to my destination, which, I found, already contained a two-seater of the same make as my own.

"Ripping little car, eh?" said the boots, chewing vigorously at his straw as he stood, his hands deep in what are graphically known as "go-to-hell" pockets and his legs well straddled. "Hop over anything, what? Topping weather we're having - been like this for weeks. If you don't mind, old chap, you might wiggle her over this way a bit. Something else might blow in, eh?"

I looked at this latest manifestation with undisguised astonishment, but he was imperturbable, and merely chewed his straw with renewed energy.

"That's the stuff, old lad," he said, as I laid the car in position. "What now? Shall I give you a hand up with the trunk, or will you hump it yourself? Don't mind me a bit. I'm ready for anything."

He looked genial, but I found him familiar, so with a curt:

"Take it to number ten," I strode off to overtake Tony, whom I saw half-way down a rough path that led to her beloved "burn."

"I've seen the chambermaid," she said, when I overtook her. "Such a pretty girl, but very shy and unsophisticated. Quite a girl, but wears a wedding-ring."

I watched Tony "paidling" for some time, but as the amusement consisted mainly of getting her under-apparel wet, I grew tired of it, and climbed back to the hotel.

The bar-window was open once more in the little lounge, and Mr. Gunthorpe was behind, his arms resting upon the ledge.

"Have a drink?" he said, as I entered. "It's all right now. The balloon's gone up."

I looked at my watch. It was after six o'clock.

"I'll have a small Scotch and soda," I decided.

"This is on the house," said the eccentric landlord.

He produced two glasses and filled them, and I noticed that he took money from his pocket and placed it in the till.

"Well, success to the new management!" I said, raising my glass to his.

"Cheerio, and thank you," said he, smiling genially upon me.

He seemed to me more self-possessed and less eccentric than he had appeared upon our arrival. I determined to draw him out.

"It's funny that an Australian should have owned an hotel away up in the Welsh hills," I hazarded. "Did he die recently?"

"Australia? You must have misunderstood me," said Mr. Gunthorpe with a hunted look in his eyes. "Very likely - very likely I said Ostend."

"Ostend? Well, possibly I did," I agreed, feeling certain that I had made no mistake. "Had he a hotel there as well?"

"Yes, yes. Of course, of course, of course," agreed the landlord, largely redundant.

"And are you running that as well?"

"Heaven forbid!" he exclaimed, with a shudder. "You see ... this - this is just a small legacy. It'll be all right by and by. All right, all right. Let's have another drink."

"With me," I insisted.

"Not at all, not at all. On the house. All for the good of the house. Come along, Bob, have a drink!"

It was the boots who had now entered, and he strolled up to the bar with all the self-possession of a welcome guest.

"Just a spot of Scotch, old thing!" he said brightly. "It's

a hard life. Shaking down good and comfy, laddie?" - this last to me. "Ask for anything you fancy. It doesn't follow you'll get it, but if we have it, it's yours. Tinkle, tinkle; crash, crash!" With this unusual toast he raised his glass and drained it.

"Have another," he said. "Three Scotches, Boniface."

I protested. This was too hot and fast for me altogether. Besides, I did not fancy being indebted to this somewhat overwhelming boots. My protest was of no avail. The glasses were filled while yet the words were upon my lips. I thought of Tony, and trembled. Common decency would force me to stand still another round before I could cry a halt.

"All well in the buttery?" asked the boots, in a confidential tone of the landlord.

"The banquet is in preparation," replied the latter. "Everything is in train."

"Heaven grant that it comes out of train reasonably, laddie," said boots fervently. "But you know Molly. I wouldn't trust an ostrich to her cooking. Here's hoping for the best."

He drained his glass again, and this time I managed to get a show. "Three more whiskies, please landlord," and Tony in clear view cut up into nice squares by the little leaded panes. I got mine absorbed just in time, and was on the doorstep to meet her, draggle-skirted and untidy, but enthusiastic about her "burn." She broke her vows three times on the way up to number ten, and excused her lapses on the ground that the "burn" was the perfect image of one near a place she called "Pairth."

When she rang for hot water to wash away the traces of her ablutions in the burn, I had my first view of the chambermaid. I found her even more ravishing than the waitress downstairs, and with the additional advantage that she was not stand-offish - indeed, she was a giggler. She giggled at my slightest word, and Tony altered her first impression and dubbed her a forward hussy. Personally, I liked the girl, though she broke all precedent by attending upon us in a silk blouse and a tailor-made tweed skirt.

When I wandered downstairs before dinner I came upon her again, this time unmistakably in the arms of the ubiquitous boots. I had walked innocently into a small sitting-room where a lamp already shone, and I came upon the romantic picture unexpectedly. With a murmured word of inarticulate apology I made to retire.

"It's all right, old fruit, don't hurry away," said boots affably. "Awfully sorry, and all that. Quite forgot it was a public room, don't you know."

The chambermaid giggled once more and bolted, straightening her cap as she went.

"You don't mind, do you?" continued boots, making a clumsy show of trimming the lamp. "Warm is the greeting when seas have rolled between us. Perhaps not quite that, but you see the idea, eh?"

He would doubtless have said more, being evidently of a cheery nature, had not the waitress of the afternoon appeared in the doorway, her face as frozen as a mask of ice.

"Bob - kennel!" she said sharply, and held the door wide.

The cheeriness vanished and the boots followed it through the open doorway.

"I trust you will excuse him, sir," said the waitress deferentially. "He is just a little deranged, but quite harmless. We employ him out of charity, sir."

I may have been mistaken, but a sound uncommonly like the chambermaid's giggle came to me from the passage without.

The sound of a car stopping outside the hotel drew me to the window as the waitress left me, and I was in time to see an old gentleman with a long white beard step from the interior of a Daimler landaulette, the door of which was held open by a dignified chauffeur, whose attire seemed to consist mainly of brass buttons.

A consultation evidently took place in the smoking-room or bar between this patriarch and the proprietor, and then I heard agitated voices in the passage without.

"It's a blinking invasion," said Mr. Gunthorpe. "I tell you we can't do it. Good heavens, they threaten to stop a month if they are comfortable."

"Don't worry then, old bean. They won't stop long." This in the voice of boots.

"And they want special diet. Old girl can't eat meat. Suffers from a duodenal ulcer. I tell you, we got quick intimate! We can't do it, Molly."

"Fathead, of course we can. I'll concoct her something the like of which her what-you-may-call-it has never before tackled. Run along, Bill, and be affable."

"Shall I stand them a drink?" - Mr. Gunthorpe again.

"Do, old bean. I'll come and have one, too," said boots.

"You won't, Bob. You'll see to the chauffeur and the car, *and* the luggage."

"Hang the luggage! I'll stand the chauffeur a drink."

Then the female voice spoke warningly.

"You've had enough drinks already, both of you," it said. "You ought to bear in mind that you're not running the hotel just for your two selves."

"It's all right, old girl. There's plenty for everybody. Cellar's full of it."

The voices died away, and I strolled out into the bar once more. Mr. Gunthorpe was being affable, according to instructions, to the old gentleman, while an old lady in a bonnet looked on piercingly.

"Quite all right about the diet," the landlord was saying as I entered. "We make a specialty of special diets. In fact, our ordinary diet is a special diet. Certainly, of course. We've got mulligatawny soup, sardines, roast beef, trifle and gorgonzola cheese. Perhaps you'll have a drink while you wait?"

"Certainly not, sir," replied the old gentleman testily. "You seem to be unable to comprehend. My wife has a duodenal ulcer, sir. Had it for fourteen years in September, and you talk to me of mulligatawny soup."

"I quite understand, of course, of course," replied Mr. Gunthorpe urbanely. "Everything of a - an irritating character will be left out of the -"

"Then it won't be mulligatawny soup, you fool!" exploded the old lady, whose pressure I had seen rising for some time.

"Certainly not, madam. Of course, indubitably. We'll call it beef-tea, and it will never know."

"What will never know?" asked the old gentleman, with an air of puzzlement.

"Madam's duodenal ulcer, sir," replied the landlord, with a deferential bow, dedicated, doubtless, to that organ.

Each separate hair in the old gentleman's beard began to curl and coil with the electricity of exasperation, and at every moment I expected to see sparks fly out from it. The old lady folded her hands across her treasure, and looked daggers at the landlord.

"How far is it to the nearest hotel, John?" she demanded acidly.

"Too far to go to-night, Mary. I'm afraid we must put up with this - this sanatorium," replied her husband.

As a diversion I demanded an appetizer - a gin

and bitters.

Mr. Gunthorpe's face lit up and he bolted behind the bar.

"Certainly, of course. Have it with me!" he exclaimed eagerly, his eyes full of gratitude for the diversion.

I had the greatest difficulty in paying for our two drinks, for of course Mr. Gunthorpe would not let me drink alone, and I was equally insistent that the house had done enough for me.

"Then we must have another," he declared, as the only way out of the difficulty.

Fortunately for me, Tony appeared on the scene, clothed and in her right mind, speaking once more the English language, and I contrived to avoid further stimulation. Mr. Gunthorpe looked at me reproachfully as I moved off with my wife. I could see that he dreaded further interrogation on the subject of diets.

Nothing further of moment occurred before dinner. Tony and I went out and admired the wonderful view in the dim half-light, and just as the midges got the better of us - even my foul old pipe did not give us the victory - the gong sounded for dinner and covered our retreat.

It was the maddest dinner in which I have ever participated. Three tables were laid in the little coffee-room, and, as Tony and I were the first to put in an appearance, I had the curiosity to look at the bill of fare at the first table I came to.

"This way, sir, if you please," said the chilling voice of our exemplary waitress.

Already I had deciphered "beef-tea" and "steamed sole" on the card, and concluded that the table was reserved for the duodenal ulcer. At the table to which we were conducted I found "mulligatawny soup" figuring on the menu, and I wondered.

The old lady and gentleman were ushered to their seats by the boots, now smartly dressed in striped trousers and black coat and waistcoat. I say "smartly," because the clothes were of good material, and the wearer looked easily the best-clad man in the hotel.

The two places laid at the third table were taken by a boy and girl of such youthful appearance that both Tony and I were astonished to find them living alone in an hotel. The boy might have been fifteen and the girl twelve at the most; but that they were overwhelmingly at home in their surroundings was quickly manifest, as was the fact that they were brother and sister. This latter fact was evidenced by the manner in which the boy bullied the girl, and contradicted her at every opportunity.

There was something of a strained wait when all of us had taken our places. I saw the old gentleman, eyeglasses on the tip of his nose, studying the bill of fare intently. Then he turned to his wife.

"Minced chicken and rice - peptonized," he said suspiciously. "Did you ever hear of such a dish, Mary?"

"Never. But nothing would surprise me in this place,"

replied his wife, looking round the room with a censorious eye that even included the innocent Tony and myself.

The two children chuckled. They wore an air of expectancy such as I have noticed in my nephews and nieces when I have been inveigled into taking them to Maskelyne's show. They seemed on very intimate terms with the waitress, and the mere sight of the boots sent them into fits of suppressed chuckling. He, standing by the sideboard, napkin over arm, added to their hilarity by winking violently at regular intervals. Catching my eye upon him, he crossed to our table.

"Everything all right, eh?" he said, glancing over the lay-out of our table.

"Everything - except that so far we have had no food," I replied.

"It's the soup," he said, leaning confidentially to my ear. "The cat fell into it, and they're combing it out of her fur. Have a drink while you wait? No! All right, old thing. I dare say you know best when you've had enough. Shut up, you kids! Don't you see you're irritating the old boy."

This in a hoarse aside to the children at the next table. It made them giggle the more.

"Surely they are very young to be stopping here alone!" said Tony, with a touch of her national inquisitiveness.

"Very sad case, madam," replied the boots. "We found them here when we came. You know - wrapped in a blanket on the doorstep. Not quite, perhaps, but you see the idea. Sort of wards of the hotel."

He was interrupted by the entrance of the waitress with soup. She gave him a frozen glance and a jerk of the head, and he vanished to the kitchen, to return with more soup, and at last we got a start on our meal. The soup was good notwithstanding the story of the cat. It really was mulligatawny. There was no doubt about that.

The old couple were not so well satisfied. They sipped a little, had a whispered consultation, and beckoned the boots.

"Waiter, why do you call this beef-tea?" demanded the old gentleman.

"You can't have me there, my lad," retorted boots cheerily. "From the Latin beef, beef and tea, tea - beef-tea. Take a spoonful of tea and a lump of beef, shake well together, simmer gently till ready, and serve with a ham-frill."

The old gentleman's face showed deep purple against his white whiskers, and the waitress left our table hurriedly, hustled the boots from the room, and crossed to the old couple. I could not hear all she said, but I understood that the boots was liable to slight delusions, but quite harmless. The beef-tea was the best that could be prepared on such short notice, and so on.

It was the main course of the meal that brought the climax. It was roast beef and Yorkshire pudding, excellently cooked, and, so far as we were concerned, efficiently served. The irrepressible boots had, however, by this time drifted back to duty. I saw him bear plates to the old people's table containing a pale mess which I rightly concluded was the "minced chicken and rice - peptonized," already referred to by the old gentleman. The couple eyed it suspiciously while their attendant hovered near, apparently awaiting the congratulations which were bound to follow the consumption of the dish.

"John, it's beef!" screamed the old lady, starting to her feet and spluttering.

"Damme, so it is!" confirmed her husband, after a bare mouthful. "Hi, you - scoundrel, poisoner, assassin - send the manager here at once."

He waved his napkin in fury, and boots cocked an eye at him curiously.

"Won't you have another try?" he urged. "Be sporty about it. Hang it, it looks like chopped chicken, and it is chopped. I chopped it myself. Have another try. You'll believe it in time if you persevere. It's the first step that counts, you know. I used to be able to say that in French, but -"

He only got so far because the old gentleman had been inarticulate with rage.

"Fetch the manager, and don't dare utter another word, confound you!" he shouted.

A few moments later our friend Mr. Gunthorpe entered. His eyes were bright, and a satisfied smile rested on his lips.

"Good evening, sir," he began affably. "I believe you sent for me. I hope everything is to your taste?"

"Everything is nothing of the sort, sir!" retorted the old gentleman. "You have attempted a gross fraud upon us, sir. I find on the menu, chicken, and it is nothing more nor less than chopped beef. And 'peptonized' - peptonized be hanged, sir! It's no more peptonized than my hat!"

"Well, sir, as for your hat I can say nothing, but - "

"None of your insolence, sir. I insist on having this - filth taken away and something suitable put before us. My wife has possessed a duodenal ulcer for fourteen years come September, and - "

"Be hanged to your duodenal ulcer! As this isn't its birthday, why should it have a blinking banquet. Let it take pot-luck with the rest of us."

A sudden burst of uncontrollable laughter made me turn sharply, to find that the reserve had fallen from our chilly waitress, who was vainly endeavouring to smother her laughter in her professional napkin.

"Oh, Bill!" she cried, "you've done it now. The game's up."

The old lady and gentleman arose in outraged dignity and started to leave the room, when a diversion was caused by the entrance of a pleasant-faced lady in hat and cloak. I had been semi-conscious for some moments of a motor-engine running at the hotel door.

"Oh, Mr. Gunthorpe, what luck!" cried the newcomer.

"I've collected a full staff, and brought them all up from Dolgelly with me, look you."

"Thank heaven!" exclaimed the proprietor. "As soon as your barmaid is on her job we'll drink all their healths. I hope you won't be annoyed, Miss Jones, but I fear, I very greatly fear, you will lose a couple of likely customers at dawn or soon after. Here they are. Perhaps you can still pacify them. I can't."

Miss Jones turned to the old couple, who were waiting for the doorway to clear, with a disarming and conciliatory smile.

"I hope you will make allowances," she said, with a musical Welsh intonation. "I am the manageress, and everything is at sixes and sevens, look you. This morning I had trouble with the staff, and just to annoy me they all cleared off together. I had to leave the hotel to see what I could find in Dolgelly. Mr. Gunthorpe and the other guests in the hotel very kindly offered to see to things while I was away, and I'm sure they have done their best, indeed."

"Done their best to poison us, certainly," growled the old gentleman. "My wife has a duo -"

"That's all right, old chap," interrupted Mr. Gunthorpe. "Miss Jones is an expert in those things. She'll feed it the proper tack, believe me. Give her a chance, and don't blame her for our shortcomings."

By this time the whole mock staff had taken the stage - waitress, boots, chambermaid, and a pleasant-faced lady of matronly appearance who, I learnt, was Mrs. Gunthorpe and the mother of the two children of whom we had been told such a harrowing history.

"And just think, dear," said Tony, smiling at me across the table. "The boots and the chambermaid are on their honeymoon. He is a journalist."

"How do you know all this?" I demanded suspiciously.

"I wormed the whole thing out of the chambermaid at the very beginning," said Tony. "I didn't tell you because I thought it would be more fun."

Miss Jones succeeded in pacifying the old couple somehow - mainly, I think, by promises of a new régime - and we left them in the coffee-room looking almost cheerful.

Tony and I went out to talk in the moonlight, while I smoked an after-dinner cigar. We were gone for some time, and on our return decided to go straight upstairs to bed. I noticed that lights still burned in the coffee-room, and heard the sound of voices from that direction. Thinking that some late guests had arrived during our absence, I had the curiosity to glance round the door. The whole of our late staff sat round a table, on which were arrayed much food and several gilt-topped bottles.

"Come along. Do join us!" cried Mr. Gunthorpe, sighting us at once.

"Come and celebrate the end of this bat in the belfry sort of management," added boots, holding high a sparkling glass.

It ended in *Tony* and I being dragged into the

celebration, and *that* ended in quite a late sitting.

Tony and I lingered on for over a week at the Bat and Belfry Inn, as we all called it, and so, strange to say, did the duodenal couple, whom, indeed, we left there, special-dieting to their hearts' content.

THE LIE

By HOLLOWAY HORN

(From *The Blue Magazine* and *Harper's Bazar*) 1922

The hours had passed with the miraculous rapidity which tinctures time when one is on the river, and now overhead the moon was a gorgeous yellow lantern in a greyish purple sky.

The punt was moored at the lower end of Glover's Island on the Middlesex side, and rose and fell gently on the ebbing tide.

A girl was lying back amidst the cushions, her hands behind her head, looking up through the vague tracery of leaves to the soft moonlight. Even in the garish day she was pretty, but in that enchanting dimness she was wildly beautiful. The hint of strength around her mouth was not quite so evident perhaps. Her hair was the colour of oaten straw in autumn and her deep blue eyes were dark in the gathering night.

But despite her beauty, the man's face was averted from her. He was gazing out across the smoothly-flowing water, troubled and thoughtful. A good-looking face, but not so strong as the girl's in spite of her prettiness, and enormously less vital.

Ten minutes before he had proposed to her and had been rejected.

It was not the first time, but he had been very much more hopeful than on the other occasions.

The air was softly, embracingly warm that evening. Together they had watched the lengthening shadows creep out across the old river. And it was spring still, which makes a difference. There is something in the year's youth - the sap is rising in the plants - something there is, anyway, beyond the sentimentality of the poets. And overhead was the great yellow lantern gleaming at them through the branches with ironic approval.

But, in spite of everything, she had shaken her head and all he received was the maddening assurance that she "liked" him.

"I shall never marry," she had concluded. "Never. You know why."

"Yes, I know," the man said miserably. "Carruthers."

And so he was looking out moodily, almost savagely, across the water when the temptation came to him.

He would not have minded quite so much if Carruthers had been alive, but he was dead and slept in the now silent Salient where a little cross marked his bed. Alive one could have striven against him, striven desperately, although Carruthers had always been rather a proposition. But now it seemed hopeless - a man cannot strive with a memory. It was not fair - so the man's thoughts were running. He had shared

Carruthers' risks, although he had come back. This persistent and exclusive devotion to a man who would never return to her was morbid. Suddenly, his mind was made up.

"Olive," he said.

"Yes," she replied quietly.

"What I am going to tell you I do for both our sakes. You will probably think I'm a cad, but I'm taking the risk." He was sitting up but did not meet her eyes.

"What on earth are you talking about?" she demanded.

"You know that - apart from you - Carruthers and I were pals?"

"Yes," she said wondering. And suddenly she burst out petulantly. "What is it you want to say?"

"He was no better than other men," he replied bluntly. "It is wrong that you should sacrifice your life to a memory, wrong that you should worship an idol with feet of clay."

"I loath parables," she said coldly. "Will you tell me exactly what you mean about feet of clay?" The note in her voice was not lost on the man by her side.

"I don't like telling you - under other conditions I wouldn't. But I do it for both our sakes."

"Then, for goodness sake, do it!"

"I came across it accidentally at the Gordon Hotel at

Brighton. He stayed there, whilst he was engaged to you, with a lady whom he described as Mrs. Carruthers. It was on his last leave."

"Why do you tell me this?" she asked after a silence; her voice was low and a little husky.

"Surely, my dear, you must see. He was no better than other men. The ideal you have conjured up is no ideal. He was a brave soldier, a darned brave soldier, and - until we both fell in love with you - my pal. But it is not fair that his memory should absorb you. It's - it's unnatural."

"I suppose you think I should be indignant?" There was no emotion of any kind in her voice.

"I simply want you to see that your idol has feet of clay," he said, with the stubbornness of a man who feels he is losing.

"What has that to do with it? You know I loved him."

"Other girls have loved -" he said bitterly.

"And forgotten? Yes, I know," she interrupted him. "But I do not forget, that is all."

"But after what I have told you. Surely -"

"You see I knew," she said, even more quietly than before.

"You - knew?"

"Yes. It was I who was with him. It was his last leave,"

she added thoughtfully.

And only the faint noise of the water and the wistful wind in the trees overhead broke the silence.

A GIRL IN IT

By ROWLAND KENNEY

(From *The New Age*) 1922

I was just cooking a couple of two-eyed steaks when Black Mick walked in, and, noting the look in his eyes and being for some reason in an expansive mood, I offered him a sit down. After comparing notes on the various possibilities of the district with regard to job-getting, we turned on to a discussion of the relative moralities of begging and stealing. But in this, I found, Mick was not vitally interested - both were too deeply immoral for him to touch. For Mick was a worker. He liked work. Vagrancy to him made no appeal. To "settle down" was his one definite desire. But jobs refused to hold him, and the road gripped him in spite of himself. So the problem presented itself to him in an abstract way only; to me there was a real - but let that go.

Mick's respectability was uncanny. He could speculate on these things as if they were matters affecting none of us there. In that fourpenny doss-house he remained as aloof as a god, and in some vague way the calmness of the man in face of this infringing realism for a time repelled me.

We cleaned up my packet to the last shred and crumb, and I found a couple of fag ends in my pocket. We smoked silently. Mick's manner gradually affected me. We became somehow mentally detached from the place in which we sat. We were in a corner of the room, at the end of the longest table, and so incurious about the rest of the company that neither of us knew whether there were two or twenty men there. For a while Mick was absorbed in his smoke, and then I saw him slowly turn his head to the door. It was a languid movement. His dark eyes were half veiled as he watched for the entrance of someone who fumbled at the latch. Then, in an instant, as the face of the newcomer thrust forward, Black Mick's whole personality seemed to change. His eyelids lifted, showing great, glowing eyes staring from a cold set face. His back squared, and the table, clamped to the floor, creaked protestingly as his sprawled legs were drawn up and the knees pressed against the under part. A second only he stared, then slung himself full forward.

The newcomer was a live man, quicker than Mick. The recognition between the two was apparently mutual; for as Mick vaulted the table the other rushed forward, grabbed the poker from the grate, and got home on Mick's head with it. Before I could get near enough to grip, the door again banged and our visitor had disappeared.

"There was a girl in it," said Mick to me when we took the road together a fortnight later, and that was as far as he got in explanation. It was enough. I could read men a little. To Mick women - all women - were sacred creatures. In the scheme of nature woman was good and man was evil. Passion was a male attribute, an evil fire that scorched and burned and rendered impotent the protesting innocence of hapless femininity....

So we tramped. One public works after the other we made, always with the same result - no chance of a take-on. Often we got a lift in food, ale, or even cash from some gang where one of us was known, but that was all. Everywhere the reply to our request for a job was the same: Full Up. And then we made Liverpool.

My favourite kip in Liverpool was Bevington House in the Scotland Road district, but on this occasion I had news that Twinetoes, an old mate of mine, had taken in that night at a private doss-house, and the probability was that he would not only give us a lift but would be able to tell us pretty accurately what was the state of the labour market.

It was a rotten kip. Four men were squabbling over the frying pan when we entered, and over against the far wall sat an old crone, crooning an Irish song. The men were of the ordinary dock rat type, scraggily built, unshaven, with cunning, shifty eyes. The woman had an old browned-green kerchief round her head, and a ragged shawl drawn tightly round her breasts. One side of her face had evidently been burned some time, and the eye on that side ran continually.

"Got any money, dearie?" she said to Mick.

"No, mother," Mick replied, gently taking her hand. "Is there a fellow here called Twinetoes?"

"No blurry use t'me if no money," and she went on with her damnable singing, like a lost soul wailing for its natural hell.

The Boss came in from the kitchen. "Twinetoes? Damned funny moniker! Never 'eerd it," he said. "But there's a bloke asleep upstairs as calls 'isself Brum. Mebbe it's 'im."

It was. Twinetoes lay in his navvy clobber on a dirty bed, drunk, dead to the world. We could not rouse him.

"What a kennel!" said Mick. "There's a smell about it I don't like." There was a smell; not the common musty smell of cheap doss-houses, something much worse than that....

"You pay your fourpence and takes your choice," I said, with an intended grandiloquent sweep of my hand towards the dozen derelict beds. We selected two that lay in an alcove at the end of the room farthest from the door, and turned in. In a few minutes we were both asleep.

Suddenly I awoke. A clock outside struck one. There was no sound in the room but the now subdued snoring of Twinetoes. I was at once wide awake, but I lay quite still, breathing as naturally as possible, keeping my eyes more than half closed, for I felt some sinister presence in the room. A new pollution affected the atmosphere. Bending over me was the old crone. Downstairs she had seemed aimless, shapeless, almost helpless, an object of disgusting pitifulness. Now, dark as it was, and unexpected as was the visit, I could at once see that she was as active and alert as a monkey.

On going to bed I had put my boots under my pillow, and thrown my coat over me, keeping the cuff of one sleeve in my hand. A practised claw slipped under my head and deftly fingered the insides of my boots: Blank. The coat pockets were next examined: Blank. Still I dog-slept. The wrinkled lips were now working angrily, churning up two specks of foam that shone white in the corners of the mouth. The running eye rained tears of rage down her left cheek; and the other one glowed and dulled, a winking red spark in the gloom, as she looked quickly up and down the bed. Her left hand hung down by her side, the arm tense. Then, as she slipped her right hand under the clothes in an effort to go over the rest of me, I gave a half turn and a low sleep moan to warn her off. At once the left hand shot up over my head, the lean fingers clutching a foot of lead pipe. Again I tried to appear sound asleep. With eyes tight shut I lay still. I dared not move. One glimpse of that tortured face had shown me that I could hope for nothing; the utter folly of mercy or half measures was fully understood. Yet, effort was impossible. I was simply and completely afraid.

The lead pipe did not, however, meet my skull. Hearing a slight scuffle, I peeped out to find that there were now two figures in the gloom. The Boss had crept up, seized the hag's left arm, and was pointing to the door. She held back, and in silent pantomime showed that Mick had not been gone over yet. With her free hand she gathered her one skirt over her dirty, skinny knees and danced with rage by the side of my bed. She looked like the parody of some carrion creature seen in the nightmare of a starving man. The most terrible thing about her was her amazing silence; the mad dance of her stockinged feet on the bare boards made no sound.

The Boss loosened his hold on her wrist, but took away

the lead pipe from her, and she slipped over to Mick. Again those skinny claws went through their evolutions with uncanny silence and effect, whilst I lay, every muscle taut, ready to spring up if occasion required. My nerve had returned, and now that the piece of lead pipe was in the hands of the less fiendish partner of this strange concern, I was ready to wade in. But she found nothing, and Mick slept on. We were too poor to rob; but this only enraged her the more. Her fingers twisted themselves into the shawl at her breast, and she silently but vehemently spat at Mick's head as she moved away.

For half an hour I tried in vain to sleep, and then the Boss again appeared. This time he bore a huge bulk of patched and soiled canvas, part of an old sail, which he hung from the ceiling across the middle of the room, thus shutting off Twinetoes, Mick and myself from that part where was the door on to the stairs. He was not noisy, but he made no attempt to keep the previous death stillness of the house.

As the Boss descended the stairs, a surprising thing happened - and Mick awoke. Girlish laughter rippled up the stairs! "God Almighty," said Mick, "what's that?"

Again it came, and with it the gurgling of the old woman. It was impossible and incredible, that mingling in the fetid air of those two sounds, as if the babble of clear spring water had suddenly broken into and merged with the turgid roll of a city sewer. Mick sat up. "But this is bloody!" he said.

"Wait," was all I replied.

We waited. Mick slipped out of bed, carefully opened his knife and made a few judicious slits in the veiling canvas. My senses had become abnormally acute. I seemed to hear every shade of sound within and without the house. I could sense, I imagined, the very positions in which sat the persons in the kitchen below. Even Twinetoes was affected by the tense atmosphere. He murmured in his sleep and seemed somewhat sobered, for his limbs took more natural positions on the bed. The darkness was no longer a bar to vision. By now I could see quite clearly; and so, I believe, could Mick.

The old woman was mumbling to the girl. "'S aw ri', mi dear. 'Av' a drink o' this. W'll fix y'up aw ri'."

She had again dropped into the low uncertain voice of aimless senility. The girl remained silent. Glasses clinked. The Boss, I could hear, walked up and down the kitchen, busy with some final work of the night. A confused murmur came from another corner; but I could not distinguish the words: The dock rats were apparently discussing something.

Again that ripple of sound ascended the stairs, but this time there was an added note of apprehension. It broke very faintly but pitifully, before dying away to the sound of light footsteps. Half a dozen stairs were pressed, then came a stumble and a girlish "A-ah." She recovered herself as the hateful voice from behind said, "Aw ri', m'dear," and older, surer feet felt the stairs and pushed on behind the girl. Through the veiling canvas and the old walls I seemed to see the pair ascending. A few seconds more, and a slight farm rounded the jamb of the door. The girl's eyes blinked in the walled twilight of the room. She hesitated on the threshold, but only for a second. The touch of a following frame impelled her forward. Her uncertain foot caught against a bed leg and a white hand gripped the steadying rail. Long-nailed claws laced themselves in the fingers of her other hand and the old woman half drew, half twisted her into sitting down on the edge of the bed. They began to talk quietly. I examined them more closely....

The old crone still played the part of ancient childhood, mumbling words of little import and obscenely fingering the girl's arms, head, and waist. Some instinct led her to veil her eyes from the girl, for from those differing orbs gleamed all the wickedness of her mangled and distorted soul. Fountains rained from her left eye, whilst the right again held that sinister glow. The girl was half drunk, and, I fancied, drugged. She swayed slightly where she sat.

She wore a small hat of a dark velvety material; a white, loose blouse, and what seemed a dark blue skirt. Round her neck hung an old-fashioned link of coral beads. Her brow was low but broad, and her hair, brushed back from the forehead, was bunched large behind, but not below, the head. Her roving eyes, gradually overcoming the clinging gloom of the place, were dark brown and unnaturally bright. Half open in an empty smile, her lips disclosed white but somewhat irregular teeth. Seen plainly in such surroundings, she was - to me - a pitiable and undesirable creature. I did not like the looks of her now. The mental image formed on the sound of her laughter was infinitely preferable to the sight of her. She was, I fancied, some servant girl of a romantic nature. I was right. "I don't care," she was saying, "I'll never go back. Trust me. Had enough. Slavey for four bob a week. 'Taint good enough. They said if I couldn't be in by arf past nine I'd find the door locked. And I did! They c'n keep it locked."

"'S aw 'ri'. You go t'sleep 'ere wi' me. W'll put yo' t' ri's. Y'll 'av' a luvly dress t'morro', an' a go' time. Wait t'l y'see the young man we'll find y' t'morro'. Now go t'bed." Those twining fingers ceased toying with the girl's hair and deftly slipped a protecting hook from an all-too-easy eye in the back of the girl's blouse.

"Three years I've been a slavey for those stuck-up pigs," said the girl in a subdued mutter, and then she went on to recount, quaintly and in a half incoherent jumble, the salient facts of her life. I glanced at Mick. He was leaning forward, peering through another slit. His face had its old set look; stern, condemnatory. Twice I had had to reach out and grip his wrist. He wanted to interfere; I was waiting - I knew not for what.

As the muttering proceeded, the busy fingers of the old woman loosened the clothes of the indifferent girl, who soon stood swaying by the side of the bed in her chemise. Deftly the dirty quilt was slipped back and the girlish form rolled into the creaking bed. The muttering went on for a few minutes whilst the old woman sat watching the flushed face and the tumbled hair on the pillow. The girl's right arm was thrown carelessly abroad over the quilt, the shoulder gleaming white in the deeper shadow thrown by the old woman who sat with her back to us, looking down intently at this waiting morsel of humanity. If we had not seen her before, we could have imagined her to be praying.

Mick, for the first time since their entry into the room,

　　　　Edward J. O'Brien and John Cournos

suddenly looked over at me. The same thoughts must have flashed through both our brains. What was wrong? Was anything wrong? Surely the affair was quite simple; and the canvas screen, violated by Mick's knife, had expressed the needed attempt at decency.

The muttering died down and the room was hushed to strained silence - to be broken soon by a furtive pad on the stairs. Mick and I were again alert, staring through the canvas slits. The Boss now appeared, followed by one of the dock rats. They glanced at the bed and then looked enquiringly at the old woman.

"Ol' Soloman sh'd fork out a termer for this," she said in low but clear tones. "But it's got to be a proper job." Then, to the Boss, and pointing to the screen, indicating the position of our beds: "You lamming idiot! Didn't I tell yo'? Yo' sh'd a took their bits an' outed 'm."

The dock rat was tip-toeing about the bed, like a starved rodent outside a wire-screened piece of food. His glance shifted from that gleaming shoulder hunched up over the slim neck to the heavy face of the Boss and then to the old woman, returning quickly to the form on the bed.

"Oo's goin' t'do it?" asked the old crone of the Boss. "You or Bill?" and she drew down the clothes, exposing the limp sprawled limbs of the sleeping girl. The Boss did not reply. He simply took a half-stride back, away from the bed. The dock rat's eyes gleamed: he had noted the movement. He ceased his tip-toeing about and looked at the Boss. "What's my share?"

"Blimy! Your share?" returned the Boss in a hoarse

whisper. Then, pointing to the waiting, half-naked form: "That!"

In their contemplation of their victim they were so absorbed that they apparently forgot entirely the three of us bedded on the other side of the hanging sail. Mick and I were staggered. We looked at each other, realising at the self-same instant the whole purpose of this curious conference. By some subtle and secret processes of the mind again there seemed to be a change in the atmosphere of the room. Its sordid dinginess was no longer present to our consciousness. There was new life, heart, and vigour and, in some curious way, our mentalities seemed merged together. No longer puzzled, we were vibrant with a common purpose. I was angry and disgusted; Mick was moved to the inmost sanctuary of his Celtic being. He manifested the last degree of outrage and insult, of agonised anger. For the moment we were cleansed of all the pettiness and grossness common to manhood, inspired only with a new-born worship of the inviolable right of the individual to the disposal of its own tokens of affection and life.

And this new spirit of ours pervaded the room. The girl moaned in her drunken sleep. Twinetoes turned restlessly in bed, and the lines of his face sharpened and deepened. Something was killing the poison in both. Even the trio about the girl were momentarily moved by some new sensation.

Mick's accustomed recklessness of action was gone, he was cool and prepared to be calculating. We slipped on our boots and I moved over to Twinetoes' bed. I touched his arm. Mumbling curses he opened his eyes. "It's Mac," I whispered, leaning over and looking steadyingly into his face.

"Wot the 'ell...." he began, but I managed to silence him. Once accustomed to the gloom, his eyes took in the strangeness of the situation and, painfully swallowing the foul nausea of his drunk, he calmly and quietly pulled on his boots.

The old woman had again covered up the still sleeping girl and engaged the Boss in a wrangle about money. "You'll bloody well swing yet," said the Boss irrelevantly.

"Mebbe; but that don't alter it. I wants my full share 'n I means to 'av' it."

Dispassionately, the dock rat eyed them both and hoped for the best for himself. We had ceased to exist for them. "Goin'?" asked the dock rat as the others moved towards the stairs. They looked at him, but did not reply. So far as we were aware, though we had forgotten the entire world outside that room, there had been complete silence downstairs; but now we could hear movement. The other dock rats were evidently awake and waiting. As the foot of the Boss fell on the top stair, the spell seemed to fall from Mick. He glared fixedly at the dock rat who stood by the girl's bed. "I'll tear his guts out," said Mick with appalling certainty of tone.

The old woman heard it. The lead pipe again in her fist, like a cornered rat she whipped round. Mick did not wait; full at the canvas he sprang. His Irish impulsiveness overcame caution, and in a moment he was wrapped in the hanging sail, the old woman battering the bellying folds. The dock rat's head was knocking at the wall, Twinetoes cursing rhythmically and shutting off his breath with fingers of steel. My left eye was half closed and the Boss's knuckles were bleeding. The girl, awake and utterly confounded, blinked foolishly and silently, weakly trying to fix her eyes on some definite point in the tangled thread of palpitating life that surged about her.

"Look out! Drop him!" I shouted to Twinetoes as I swung in, furious but with some care, to the face of the Boss. Twinetoes did not heed; he staggered across the room under a blow from one of the new arrivals; but he did not loose his hold. He was a hefty man, entirely reliable, indeed almost happy in such an affair. As number two dock rat tried to follow up his blow, Twinetoes swung number one round in his way; then, changing his hold, taking both the man's shoulders in his hands, he drew back his head as a snake does and butted his man clean over one of the beds.... His face a pitiful pulp, number one was definitely out of it.

Ordinarily, the Boss would have been much too much for me; but now fate favoured me. He was considerably perturbed about the possible outcome of the row and its effect on his business; I was intent only on the fight. With a clean left-hand cut I drove him over, tore a quilt from a bed and flung it over his dazed head, then swung round to where the lead pipe was still flailing. I was concerned for Mick. Seizing the old woman's shoulders I flung her back from Mick and the sail. He would have cleared himself, but his legs were somehow mixed up with the foot of the bed, and she occupied his attention too much. The hag raised the lead and rushed, and for the only time in my life I hit a woman. Without hesitancy or compunction, only revolted at the thought of such contact with such matter, I smashed her down. The Boss and Mick freed themselves together and embraced each other willingly. Twinetoes was playing skittles with the remaining dock rats. There was surprisingly little noise. No one shouted. There was no howling hounding on of each other. All but the girl were absorbed in the immediate business of giving or warding off of blows.

"Dress, quick!" I said to the girl.

The fight had shifted to the centre, and her bed had remained unmoved, herself unmolested. In wondering silence she obeyed. "Quicker! Quicker!" I enjoined, with a new brutal note in my voice. The reaction had set in. I could cheerfully have shoved her down the stairs and flung her garments after her.

The kip was hidden away in a dark alley, the history and reputation of which were shudderingly doubtful, but there were police within dangerous hailing distance. The girl's lips began to quiver. Supposing she broke down and raised the court by hysterical howling! "Don't breathe a sound, or we'll leave you to it," I threatened. She shrank back, gave a low moan, and clutched my coat. I tore her hand loose and turned away in time to floor the Boss by an easy blow on his left ear. The fight was finished.

We wasted no time but descended the stairs and passed out through the court into the street. There were signs of life in the gloomy court, though no one spoke or molested us; the street was dead silent. Mick's arms and shoulders were a mass of bruises from the lead pipe, but his face was clear. Twinetoes was all right, he said, but craving for a wet. I alone showed evidence of the struggle; my eye was unsightly and painful, and my left wrist was slightly sprained. The girl sobbed quietly. "Oh! Oh!" she cried repeatedly, "whatever's to become of me!"

She irritated me. "Shut up!" I said at last, "*You*'ll be all right." She snuffled unceasingly. I looked across at Mick - she walked between us, Twinetoes on my right - and at once I saw the outcome of it all. "Stop it, blast you!" I shook her shoulder. "My pal is the best, biggest fool that ever raised a fist. He's silly enough for anything decent," and then, with the voice of conviction born of absolute certainty of mind: "He'll never chuck you over. He'll marry you sometime, you fool!"

And he did.

THE BACKSTAIRS OF THE MIND

By ROSAMOND LANGBRIDGE

(From *The Manchester Guardian*) 1922

Patrick Deasey described himself as a "philosopher, psychologist, and humorist." It was partly because Patrick delighted in long words, and partly to excuse himself for being full of the sour cream of an inhuman curiosity. His curiosity, however, did not extend itself to science and *belles lettres*; it concerned itself wholly with the affairs of other people. At first, when Deasey retired from the police force with a pension and an heiress with three hundred pounds, and time hung heavy on his hands, he would try to satisfy this craving through the medium of a host of small flirtations with everybody's maid. In this way he could inform himself exactly how many loaves were taken by the Sweeneys for a week's consumption, as compared with those which were devoured by all the Cassidys; for whom the bottles at the Presbytery went in by the back door; and what was the real cause of the quarrel between the twin Miss McInerneys.

But these were but blackbird-scratchings, as it were, upon the deep soil of the human heart. What Deasey cared about was what he called "the secrets of the soul."

"Never met a man," he was wont to say, "with no backstairs to his mind! And the quieter, decenter, respectabler, innocenter a man looked - like enough! - the darker those backstairs!"

It was up these stairs he craved to go. To ring at the front door of ordinary intercourse was not enough for him. When Deasey invested his wife's money in a public-house he developed a better plan. It was the plan which made him ultimately describe himself as a humorist. He would wait until the bar was deserted by all but the one lingering victim whom his trained eye had picked out. Then, rolling that same eye about him, as though to make quite sure no other living creature was in sight, he would gently close the door of the bar-parlour, pick up a tumbler, breathe on it, polish the breath, lean one elbow on the bar, look round him once again, and, setting the whisky-bottle betwixt his customer and himself, with a nod which said "Help yourself," he would lean forward, with the soft indulgent grin of the human man-of-the-world, and begin:

"Now, don't distress yourself, me dear man, but as between frien's, certain delicate little - facts - in your past life have come inadvertently to me hearing."

Sometimes he would allude to a "certain document," or "incriminating facts," or "certain letters" - he would ring the changes on these three, according to the sex and temperament with which he had to deal. But always, whatever the words, whatever the nature or sex, the shot would tell. First came the little start, the straightened figure, the pallor or flush, the shamed and suddenly-lit eyes, and then -

"Who told you, Mr. Deasey, sir?" Or "Where did you get the letter?"

"Ah, now, that would be telling!" Deasey would make reply. "But 'twas from a *certain person* whom, perhaps, we need not name!" Then the whiskey-bottle would move forward, like a pawn in chess, and the next soothing words would be, "Help yourself now - don't be shy, me dear man! And - your secret is safe with me!"

Forthwith the little skeleton in that man's cupboard would lean forward and press upon the door, until at last the door flew open and a bone or two, and sometimes the whole skeleton, would rattle out upon the floor.

He had played this game so often, that, almost at first sight he could classify his dupes under the three heads into which he had divided them: Those who demanded with violent threats - (which melted like snow before the sunshine of John Jamieson) the letter, or the name of the informant; those who asked, after a gentle sip or two how the letter had come into his hands, and those who asked immediately if the letter hadn't been destroyed. As a rule, from the type that demanded the letter back, he only caught sight of the tip of the secret's ears. From those - they were nearly always the women - who swiftly asked if he hadn't destroyed the letters, he caught shame-faced gleams of the truth.

But those who asked between pensive sips, how the facts or the letter had come his way, these were the ones who yielded Deasey the richest harvest of rattling skeleton bones.

Indeed, it was curiously instructive how John Jamieson laid down a causeway of gleaming stepping-stones, so that Deasey might cross lightly over the turgid waters of his victims' souls. At the words, accompanied by John Jamieson - "A certain dark page of your past history - help yourself, me boy! - has been inadvertently revealed to me, but is for ever sacred in me breast!" - it was strange to see how, from the underworld of the man's mind, there would trip out the company of misshapen hobgoblins and gnomes which had been locked away in darkness, maybe, this many a year.

"Well - how would I get the time to clane the childer and to wash their heads, and I working all the day at curing stinkin' hides! 'Twas Herself should have got it, and Herself alone!"...

Or -

"No, I never done it, for all me own mother sworn I did. I only give the man a little push - that way! - and he fell over on the side, and busted all his veins!"

Or -

"Well, an' wouldn't you draw two pinsions yourself, Mr. Deasey, if you'd a wife with two han's like a sieve for yellow gold!"

But there were some confessions, haltingly patchy and inadequate, but hauntingly suggestive, which Deasey could neither piece out on the spot, nor yet unravel in the small hours of the night. There was one of this nature which troubled his rest long:

"Well, the way of it was, you see, he put it up the chimbley, but when the chimbley-sweepers come he transferred it in his weskit to my place, and I dropped it down the well. They found it when they let the bucket down, but I wasn't his accomplice at all, 'twas only connivance with me!"

When he had spoken of the chimney and the well Deasey concluded at once it was a foully murdered corpse. But then, again, you could not well conceal a corpse in someone's waistcoat; and gold coins would melt or be mislaid amongst the loose bricks of a sooty chimney. Deasey had craved for corpses, but nothing so grim as that had risen to his whisky-bait until he tried the same old game on Mrs. Geraghty. What subtle instinct was it that had prompted him to add to the first unvarying words: "But all that is now past and over, and safe beneath the mouldering clay!"

At these last words, the Widow Geraghty knew well, the barrier was down that fences off one human soul from another; all the same, she shook her trembling head when Deasey drew the cork. At her refusal Deasey was struck with the most respectful compassion; until that hour he had never known one single lacerated soul decline this consolation.

"And to look at me!" she wept forthwith, "would you think I could shed a drop of ruddy gore?"

"No, ma'am," returned Deasey. "To look at you, ye'd think ma'am ye could never kill a fly!"

And respectfully he passed the peppermints.

"Sometimes," the widow muttered, "I hears it, and it

bawling in me dreams o' night. And the two bright eyes of it, and the little clay cold feet!" Deasey knew what was coming now, and he twitched in every vein. And she so white-haired and so regular at church: and the black bonnet on the head of her, an' all! "It was the only little one she had," went on the widow, bowed almost to the bar by shame, "and it always perched up on her knee, and taking food from her mouth, and she nursing it agin her face. But I had bad teeth in me head, and I couldn't get my rest, with the jaws aching, and all the whiles it screeching with the croup. 'Twould madden you!"

"All the same," Deasey whispered, "maybe it wasn't your fault: 'twas maybe your man egged you on to do the shameful deed -"

"It was so," said the widow. "'Let you get up and cut its throat,' says he, 'and then we will be shut of the domned screechin' thing.'" "Then you got the knife, ma'am," prompted Deasey. "It was the bread-knife," she answered, "with the ugly notches in the blade, - and I stole in the back way to her place in the dead hours of the night - and I had me apron handy for to quench the cries; and when I c'ot it be the throat didn't it look up at me with the two bright, innocent eyes!"

"And what'd you do with the body?" he asked.

"I dug a grave in the shine of the moon," she answered. "And I put it in by the two little cold grey feet -"

This touch of the grey feet laid a spell on Deasey's hankering morbidity.

"*What turned the feet grey?*" he whispered.

"Nature, I s'pose!" replied the white-haired widow. She drew her shawl about her shrinking form before she turned away.

"'Twas never found out, from that hour to this, who done it!" muttered the Widow Geraghty, "but, may the Divvle skelp me if I touch one drop of chucken-tea again!"

THE BIRTH OF A MASTERPIECE

By LUCAS MALET

(From The *Story-Teller*) 1922

Looking back on it from this distance of time - it began in the early and ended in the middle eighties - I see the charm of ingenuous youth stamped on the episode, the touching glamour of limitless faith and expectation. We were, the whole little band of us, so deliciously self-sufficient, so magnificently critical of established reputations in contemporary letters and art. We sniffed and snorted, noses in air, at popular idols, while ourselves weighted down with a cargo of guileless enthusiasm only asking opportunity to dump itself at an idol's feet. We ached to burn incense before the altar of some divinity; but it must be a divinity of our own discovering, our own choosing. We scorned to acclaim ready-made, second-hand goods. Then we encountered Pogson - Heber Pogson. Our fate, and even more, perhaps, his fate, was henceforth sealed.

He was a large, sleek, pink creature, slow and rare of movement, from much sitting bulky, not to say squashy, in figure, mild-eyed, slyly jovial and - for no other word, to my mind, so closely fits his attitude - resigned. A positive glutton of books, he read as instinctively, almost as unconsciously, as other men breathe. But he not only absorbed. He gave forth and that copiously, with taste, with discrimination, now and again with startlingly eloquent flights and witty sallies. His memory was prodigious. The variety and vivacity of his conversation, the immense range of subjects he brilliantly laboured, when in the vein, remain with me as simply marvellous. With us he mostly was in the vein. And, vanity apart, we must have composed a delightful audience, generously censer-swinging. No man of even average feeling but would be moved by such fresh, such spontaneous admiration! Thus, if our divinity melodiously piped, we did very radiantly dance to his piping.

Oh! Heber Pogson enjoyed it. Never tell me he didn't revel in those highly articulate evenings of monologue, gasconade, heated yet brotherly argument, lasting on to midnight and after, every bit as much as we did! Anyhow at first. Later he may have had twinges, been sensible of strain; though never, I still believe, a very severe one. In any case, Nature showed herself his friend - his saviour, if also, in some sort, his executioner. When the strain tended to become distressing, for him personally, very simply and cleverly, she found a way out.

A background of dark legend only brought the steady glow of his - and our - present felicity into richer relief. We gathered hints of, caught in passing smiling allusion to, straitened and impecunious early years. He had endured a harsh enough apprenticeship to the profession of letters in its least satisfactory, because most ephemeral, form - namely journalism, and provincial journalism at that. This must have painfully cribbed and confined his free-ranging spirit. We were filled by reverent sympathy for the trials and deprivations of his past. But at the period when the members - numbering a dozen, more or less - of our devoted band trooped up from Chelsea and down from the Hampstead heights to worship in the studio-library of the Church Street, Kensington, house, Pogson was lapped in a material well-being altogether sufficient. He treated us, his youthful friends and disciples, to very excellent food and drink; partaking of these himself, moreover, with evident readiness and relish. Those little "help-yourselves," stand-up suppers in the big, quiet, comfortably warmed and shaded room revealed in him no ascetic tendency, though, I hasten to add, no tendency to unbecoming excess. Such hospitality testified to the soundness of Pogson's existing financial position; as did his repeated assertions that now, at last - praise heaven - he had leisure to do worthy and abiding work, work through which he could freely express his personality, express in terms of art his judgments upon, and appreciations of, the human scene.

We listened breathless, nodding exuberant approval. For weren't we ourselves, each and all of us, mightily in love with art and with the human scene? And hadn't we, listening thus breathlessly to our amazing master, the enchanting assurance that we were on the track of a masterpiece? Not impossibly a whole gallery of masterpieces, since Heber Pogson had barely touched middle age as yet. For him there still was time. Fiction, we gathered to be the selected medium. He not only meant to write, but was actually now engaged in writing, a novel during those withdrawn and sacred morning hours when we were denied admittance to his presence. We previsaged something tremendous, poetic yet fearlessly modern, fixed on the bedrock of realism, a drama and a vision wide, high, deep, spectacular yet subtle as life itself. Let his confreres, French and Russian - not to mention those merely British born - look to their laurels, when Heber Pogson blossomed into print! And - preciously inspiring thought - he was our Pogson. He inalienably belonged to us; since hadn't we detected the quality of his genius when the veil was still upon its face? Oh! we knew, bless you; we knew. We'd the right to sniff and snort, noses in air, at contemporary reputations because we were snugly awaiting the disclosure of a talent which would prick them into nothingness like so many bubbles, pop them like so many inflated paper bags, knock them one and all into the proverbial cocked hat!

Unfortunately youth, with a fine illogic, though having all the time there is before it, easily waxes impatient. In our eagerness for his public recognition, his apotheosis, we did, I am afraid, hustle our great man a little. Instead of being satisfied with his nocturnal coruscations - they brilliant as ever, let it be noted - we just a fraction resented the slowness of his progress, began ever so gently to shove that honoured bulky form behind and pull at it in front. We wanted the tangible result of those many sacred and secret morning hours during which his novel was in process of being formed and fashioned, gloriously built up. Wouldn't he tell us the title, enlighten us as to the theme, the scheme, thus allaying the hunger pangs of our pious curiosity by crumbs - ever so small and few - dropped from his richly furnished table? With exquisite good-humour, he fenced and feinted. Almost roguishly he would laugh us off and launch the conversation into other channels, holding us - after the first few vexatiously outwitted seconds - at once enthralled and delicately rebuked.

But at last - in the late spring, as far as I remember, of the second year of our devotion - there came a meeting at which things got pressed somehow to a head. Contrary to custom feminine influence made itself felt.

And here I pause and blush. For it strikes me as so intimately characteristic of our whole relation - in that earlier stage, at least - that I should have written all this on the subject of Heber Pogson without making one solitary mention of his wife. She existed. Was permanently in evidences - or wasn't it, rather, in eclipse? - as a shadowy parasitic entity perambulating the hinterland of his domestic life. She must have been by some years his junior - a tall, thin, flat-chested woman, having heavy, yellowish brown hair, a complexion to match, and pale, nervous eyes. Her clothes hung on her as on a clothes-peg. She affected vivid greens - as was the mistaken habit of Victorian ladies possessing the colouring falsely called "auburn" - but clouded their excessive verdure to neutrality by semi-transparent over-draperies of black. Harry Lessingham, in a crudely unchivalrous mood, once described her as "without form and void," adding that she "had a mouth like a fish." These statements I considered unduly harsh, yet admitted her almost miraculously negative. She mattered less, when one was in the room with her, than anything human and feminine which I, so far, had ever run across. And I was at least normally susceptible, I'm very sure of that.

As a matter of course, on our arrival at the blest house in Church Street, we one and all respectfully greeted her, passed, to put it vulgarly, the time of day with her. But there intercourse ceased. At some subsequent instant she faded out - whether into space or into some adjacent connubial chamber, I had no notion. I only realized, when the act was accomplished, that we now were without her, that she had vanished, leaving behind her no faintest moral or emotional trace.

But, on the occasion in question, she did not vanish. We fed her at supper. And still she remained - in the interests of social propriety, as we imagined, since for once the Pogson symposium included a stranger, an eminently attractive lady guest.

Harry Lessingham had begged to bring his sister with him. He told me of this beforehand, and I rejoiced. Lessingham had long been dear to me as a brother; while that Arabella should only be dear to me as a sister was, just then, I own, among the things I wished least. I craved, therefore, to have her share our happy worship. She had a pretty turn for literature herself. I coveted to see her dazzled, exalted, impressed - it would be a fascinating spectacle. Before I slept that night, or rather next morning, I recognized her coming as a disastrous mistake. For she had received insufficient instruction in ritual, in the suitable forms of approach to so august a presence as that of our host. She played round him, flickering, darting, like lightning round a cathedral tower, metal tipped. Where we, in our young male modesty, had but gently drawn or furtively shoved, she tickled the soft, sedentary creature's ribs as with a rapier point. And - to us agitated watchers - the amazing thing was, that Pogson didn't seem to mind. He neither rebuked her nor laughed her off; but purred, veritably purred, under her alternate teasing and petting like some big, sleek cat.

At last, with a cajoling but really alarming audacity, she went for him straight.

"Of course, dear Mr. Pogson, Harry has told me all about your wonderful novel," she said. "I am so interested, so thrilled - and so grateful to you for letting me join your audience to-night. But I want quite frightfully to know more. Speaking not only for myself, but for all who are present, may I implore a further revelation? Pray don't send us empty away in respect of the wonderful book. It would be so lovely while we sit here at your feet."...

She, in fact, sat by his side, her chair placed decidedly close to his.

"If you would read us a chapter.... A chapter is impossible?"...

Her charming, pliant mouth; her charming dancing eyes; her caressing voice - I won't swear even her caressing hands didn't, for a brief space, take part - all wooed him to surrender.

"Well, a page then, a paragraph? Ah! don't be obdurate. The merest sentence? Surely we may claim as much as that? Picture our pride, our happiness."

She enclosed us all in a circular and sympathetic glance, which ended, as it had started, by meeting his mild eyes, lingering appealingly upon his large, pink countenance.

Pogson succumbed. No, he wouldn't read; but, since she so amiably desired it....

"More than anything in all my life!" with the most convincing and virginal sincerity.

... He thought he might rehearse a passage, which wasn't - as he gladly believed - altogether devoid of merit. He did rehearse it. And we broke into applause the more tempestuous because suspicion of a chill queerly lay upon us. A chill insidious as it was vague, disturbing as it was - wasn't it? we silently, quite violently, hoped so - ridiculously uncalled for.

"After all, that passage is thundering good, you know," Harry Lessingham announced, as though arguing with himself, arguing himself out of that same invidious chill, an hour later.

Arabella had refused a hansom, declaring herself excited, still under the spell, and so wanting to walk. Leaving the Church Street house, the three of us crossed into Campden Grove, with a view to turning down Campden House Road, thus reaching Kensington High Street.

"It was out of sight of the average - packed with epigram; worthy of all we've ever believed or asked of him. It takes a master of technique, of style, to write like that."

"Beloved brother, which of us ever said it didn't?" Arabella took him up sweetly.

Slender, light-footed, the train of her evening gown switched over her arm, beneath her flowing orange and white-flowered satin cloak, she walked between us.

"Why, it was good to the point of being inevitable. One seemed - I certainly did - to know every phrase, every word which was coming. None could have been other, or been placed otherwise than it was - and that's the highest praise one can give to anybody's prose, isn't it? One jumped to the perfect rightness of the whole - a rightness so perfect as to make the sentences sound quite extraordinarily familiar."

This last assertion dropped as a bomb between Lessingham and myself.

"By the way," the girl presently said, as our awkward silence continued, "has either of you happened to read, or re-read, Meredith's 'Egoist' just lately?"

Lessingham stopped short, and in the light of a neighbouring gas-lamp I saw his handsome, boyish face look troubled to the point of physical pain.

"What on earth are you driving at? What do you mean, Arabella - that Pogson is a plagiarist?"

"Don't eat me, Harry dearest, if I incline to use a shorter, commoner expression."

"A thief?"

"An unconscious one, no doubt," she threw off quickly, fearful of explosions, possibly, in her turn. "He may have been betrayed by his own extraordinary memory."

"But this is horrible, horrible," Lessingham cried. "All the names, though, were different."

Arabella appeared to have overcome her fear of explosions. Her charming eyes again danced.

"Exactly," she said. "That was the peculiar part of it,

the thing which riveted my attention. He had - I mean the names of the characters and places were different - were altered, changed."

Lessingham stood bare-headed in the light of a gas-lamp. He ran the fingers of his left hand through his crisp fair hair, rumpling it up into a distracted crest. I could see, could almost hear, the travail of his honest soul. Loyalty, faith and honour worked at high pressure to hit on a satisfactory explanation.

Suddenly he threw back his head and laughed.

"Why, of course," he cried, "it's as clear as mud. Pogson wasn't betrayed by anything. He did it on purpose. Don't you understand, you dear goose, you very-much-too-clever-by-half dear goose? It was simply his kindly joke, his good-natured little game. And we, like the pack of idiots which - compared with him - we are, never scented it. You pestered - yes, Arabella, most unconscionably pestered him to read an excerpt from his novel; and to pacify you he quoted a page from Meredith instead."

Harry Lessingham tucked his hand under the folds of the orange and white-flowered cloak, and taking the girl affectionately by the elbow, trotted her down the sloping pavement towards Kensington High Street.

"All the honours of war rest with Pogson," he joyfully assured her. "You made an importunate, impertinent demand for bread. He didn't mean to be drawn; but was too civil, too tender-hearted to put you off with a stone, so slyly cut you a slice from another man's loaf. Does it occur to you, my sweet sister, you've been had - very neatly had?"

"If it comes to that, Miss Lessingham by no means stands alone," I interrupted. "We've all been had, as you so gracefully put it, very neatly and very extensively had."

For though I trusted Lessingham's view was the correct one - trusted so most devoutly - I could not but regret the discomfiture of Arabella. Her approach to our chosen idol may have slightly lacked in reverence; she may, indeed, in plain English, have cheeked him. But she had done so in the prettiest, airiest manner. Pogson's punishment of her indiscretion, if highly ingenious, still struck me as not in the best taste. For was it not at once rather mean and rather cheap to make so charming a person the subject, and that before witnesses, of a practical joke?

If, after all, it really was a joke. That insidious, odious chill which earlier prompted my tempestuous applause, as I woefully registered, hung about me yet. Unquestionably Arabella Lessingham's visit to Church Street showed more and more, when I considered it, as a radical mistake! From it I date the waning of the moon of my delight in respect of both Pogson and herself. I had bowed in worship, equally sincere, though diverse in sentiment, before each; and to each had pledged my allegiance. To have them thus discredit one another represented the most trying turn of events.

For a full month I cold-shouldered the band, abjured the shrine, and avoided the lady. Then, while still morose and brooding, my trouble at its height, a cousin - in the third degree - rich, middle-aged, and conveniently restless, invited me to be his travelling companion. We had taken trips together before. This one promised fields of wider adventure - nothing less than the quartering of southern Europe, along with nibblings at African and Asiatic Mediterranean coasts. It was the chance of a life-time. I embraced it. I also called at the house in Church Street to make my farewells. I could do no less.

I have used the word "resigned" in describing Pogson. To-day that word notably covered him. Our friend appeared depressed; yet bland in his depression, anxious to mollify and placate rather than reproach. His attitude touched me. I hardly deserved it after my neglect - to which, by the way, he made no smallest reference. But as I unfolded my plans, he increasingly threw off his depression and generously entered into them. Would have me fetch an atlas and trace out my proposed itinerary upon the map. It included names to conjure with. These set wide the flood-gates of his speech. He at once enchanted and confounded me by his knowledge of the literature, art, history, of Syria, Egypt, Italy, Greece, and the Levant.

For the next three-quarters of an hour I had Pogson at his best. And oh! how vastly good that same best was! Under the flashing, multi-coloured light of it, he routed my suspicions; put my annoyance and distrust to flight. As he leaned back in the roomy library chair, filled to veritable overflowing by his big, squashy, brown-velvet jacketted person - Pogson had put on flesh of late; put it on sensibly, as I remarked, even during the few weeks of my absence - he reconquered all my admiration and belief.

As I rose to depart:

"Ah! you fortunate youth," he thus genially addressed

me; "thrice fortunate youth, in your freedom, your enterprise, your happy elasticity of flesh and spirit! What won't you have to tell me of things actually seen, of lands, cities, civilizations, past and present, and the storied wonder of them, when you come back!"

"And what won't you have to read to me in return, dear Master," I echoed, eager to testify to my recovered faith. "By then the book will be finished on which all our hopes and affections are set. Ten times more precious, more illuminating than anything I have seen, will be what I hear from you when I come back!"

But, as I spoke, surely I wasn't mistaken in thinking that for an agitating minute the pinkness of Pogson's large countenance sickly ebbed and blanched. And while my attention was still engaged by this disquieting phenomenon, I became aware that Mrs. Pogson had joined us. Silently, mysteriously, she faded - the term holds good - into evidence, as on so many former occasions she had silently, mysteriously faded out.

Dressed in one of those verdant gowns, so dolorously veiled in semi-transparent black, she stood behind her husband's chair. Her eyes met mine. They were no longer nervous or in expression vague; but oddly aggressive, challenging, defiantly alight.

"Oh, yes," she declared, "by then Heber will have completed his great novel, without doubt."

When uttering his name, she laid a thin, long-fingered hand upon his rounded shoulder, and to my - little short of - stupefaction, I saw Pogson's fat, pink hand move up to seek and clasp it.

Edward J. O'Brien and John Cournos

On me this action - hers soothing, protective; his appealing, welcoming - produced the most bewildering effect. I felt embarrassed and abashed; an indecently impertinent intruder upon the secret places of two human hearts. That any such intimate and tender correspondence existed between this so strangely ill-assorted couple I never dreamed.

I uttered what must have sounded wildly incoherent farewells and fled.

Of the ensuing eighteen months of foreign travel it is irrelevant here to speak. Suffice it that on my return to England and to Chelsea, the earliest news which greeted me was that Arabella Lessingham had been now five weeks married and Heber Pogson a fortnight dead. Lessingham, dear, good fellow, was my informant, and minded acquainting me, so I fancied, only a degree less with the first item than with the second.

For some considerable time, he told me, Pogson had been ailing. He grew inordinately stout, unwieldy to the extent of all exertion, all movement causing him distress. Suffocation threatened if he attempted to lie down; so that, latterly, he spent not only all day, but all night sitting in the big library chair we knew so well. If not actually in pain, he must still have suffered intolerable discomfort. But he never complained, and to the last his passion for books never failed.

"We took him any new ones we happened to run across, as you'd take a sick woman flowers. To the end he read."

"And wrote?" I asked.

"That I can't say," Lessingham replied. "There were things I could not make out. And I couldn't question him. It didn't seem to be my place, though I had an idea he'd something on his mind to speak of which would be a relief. It worried me badly. I felt sure he wanted to tell us, but couldn't bring himself to the point. He talked of you. He cared for you more than for any of us; yet - I may be all wrong - it seemed to me he was glad you weren't here. Once or twice, I thought, he felt almost afraid you might come back before - before it was all over, you know. It sounds rather horrible, but I had a feeling he longed to slink off quietly out of sight - for he did not dread death, I'm certain of that. What he dreaded was that life had some trick up her sleeve which, if he delayed too long, might give him away; put him to shame somehow at the last."

"And Mrs. Pogson?"

Lessingham looked at me absently.

"Oh! Mrs. Pogson? She's never interested me. She's too invertebrate; but I believe she took care of Pogson all right."

Next day I called at the house in Church Street. After some parley I was admitted into the studio-library. Neither in Mrs. Pogson nor in the familiar room did I find any alteration, save that the green had disappeared from her dress. She wore hanging, trailing, unrelieved black. And that a piece of red woollen cord was tied across, from arm to arm, of Pogson's large library chair, forbidding occupation of it. This pleased me. It struck the positive, the, in a way, aggressive note, which Mrs. Pogson had once before so strangely, unexpectedly, sounded in my presence.

I said the things common to such occasions as that of our present meeting; said them with more than merely conventional feeling and emphasis. I praised her husband's great gifts, his amazing learning, his eloquence, the magnetic charm by which he captivated and held us.

Finally I dared the question I had come here to ask, which had burned upon my tongue, indeed, from the moment I heard of Pogson's death.

"What about the novel? Might we hope for speedy, though posthumous, publication? We were greedy; the world should know how great a literary genius it had lost. Was it ready for press, as - did she remember? - she'd assured me it would certainly be by the time I came back?"

Mrs. Pogson did not betray any sign of emotion. Her thin hands remained perfectly still in her crape-covered lap.

"There is no novel," she calmly told me. "There never has been any novel. Heber did not finish it because he never began it. He did not possess the creative faculty. You were not content with what he gave. You asked of him that which he could not give. At first he played with you - it amused him. You were so gullible, so absurdly ignorant. Then he hesitated to undeceive you - in that, I admit, he was weak. But he suffered for his weakness. It made him unhappy. Oh I how I have hated - how I still hate you! - for I saved him from poverty, from hard work. I secured him a peaceful, beautiful life, till you came and spoilt it.... All the money was mine," she said.

GENIUS

By ELINOR MORDAUNT

(From *Hutchinson's Magazine* and
The Century Magazine) 1921, 1922

I have written before of Ben Cohen, with his eternal
poring and humming over the scores of great masters;
of the timber-yard at Canning Town, for ever changing
and for ever the same, devouring forests with the
eternal wind-like rush of saws, slide of gigantic planes;
practical and chill; wrapped in river-fogs, and yet
exotic with the dust of cedar, camphor, paregoric.

In those days Ben Cohen was wont to read music as
other boys read their penny-dreadfuls, avidly, with the
imagined sounds like great waves for ever a-rush
through his soul.

In the very beginning it was any music, just music.
Then for a while Wagner held him. Any Wagnerian
concert, any mixed entertainment which included
Wagner - it seemed as though he sniffed them upon the
breeze - and he would tramp for miles, wait for hours;
biting cold, sleet, snow, mud, rain, all alike disregarded
by that persistence which the very poor must bring to
the pursuit of pleasure, the capture of cheap seats.

Once ensconced, regardless of hard, narrow seats, heights, crowds, his passion of adoration and excitement took him, shook him, tore him so that it was wonder his frail body did not split in two, render up the soul coming forth as Lazarus from the sepulchre. It was indeed, if you knew little Ben Cohen, him, *himself*, difficult to realise that his body had anything more to do with him than the yellow-drab water-proof which is a sort of uniform - a species of charity, covering a multitude of sins of poverty, shabbiness, thread-bareness - had to do with the real Jenny Bligh.

And yet, Ben Cohen's body was more completely his than one might have imagined. Jenny could, and indeed did, slough off her disguise on Sundays or rare summer days; but Ben and that self which was apart from music - that wildly-beating heart, pulsing blood, flooding warmth, grateful as the watchman's fire in the fog-sodden yard, that little fire over which he used to hang, warming his stiffened hands - were, after all, amazingly one.

The thing surprised him even more than it surprised any one else; above all, when it refused to be separated from his holy of holies, crept, danced, smiled its way through the most portentous scores - a thrilling sense of Jenny Bligh, all crotchets and quavers, smiles and thrills, quaint homeliness, sudden dignity.

By the time he first met Jenny he was clear of Wagner, had glanced a little patronisingly at Beethoven, turned aside and enwrapped himself in the sombre splendour of Bach, right away from the world; then, harking back, with a fresh vision, a sudden sense of the inevitable, had anchored himself in the solemn, wide-stretching harbourage of Beethoven.

It was like a return from a long voyage, tearing round a world full of beauty and interest, and yet, at the same time, full of pettiness, fuss, annoyance: a home-coming beyond words. There was a sense of eternity, a harmony which drew everything to itself, smoothing out the pattern of life, the present life and the life to come, so crumpled that, up to this time, he had had no real idea of the meaning of it.

All at once everything was immensely right, with Jenny as an essential and inevitable part of the rightness. He felt this so strongly that he never stopped to wonder if other people felt it as plainly as he did.

Apart from all this, he was bound by the inarticulateness of his class. His Jewish blood lent him a wider and more picturesque vocabulary than most, and yet it stopped at any discussion of his feelings.

We have an idea that what we call the "common people" are more communicative on such subjects than we are; but this is not so. They talk of their physical ailments and sensations, but they are deeply shy upon the subject of their feelings. Ben's mother would discuss the state of her inside, the deaths of her relations and friends; his own birth, down to the smallest detail. But she would never have dreamt of telling her son that she loved him, desired his love, hungered for his coming, grieved at his going.

Ben himself put none of his feeling for Beethoven into words, above all to his mother; she would not have understood him if he had. He said nothing of Jenny, either, save as a girl he'd met, a girl he was going to bring home to tea; but she understood that without any words; that was courting, part of the business of human nature; much like the preparation of meals.

It was odd, coming to think of it - might have been ridiculous, save that ridicule was the sort of thing which could find no possible lodgment with Ben - that his determination to devote his whole musical life to Beethoven, to interpret him as no Englishman had ever done before, should have been synonymous with his sacred, heady, and yet absolute determination to marry Jenny Bligh.

Jenny worked in the jam-factory, and there was something of the aroma of ripe fruit about her: ripe strawberries, raspberries, plums, damsons. She was plumpish and fresh: very red lips and very bright eyes, reddish-brown, the colour of blackberry leaves in autumn, with hair to match. Her little figure was neat; her small hands, with their square-tipped fingers, deft and quick in their movements; there was something at once rounded and clear-cut about everything she did.

A sea-faring admirer used to say that she was "a bit short in the beam, but a daisy fur carryin' sail"; and that was the idea she gave: so well-balanced, so trim, going off to work in her wide white apron on those rare mornings when she shook off the yellow mackintosh.

Ben saw her like that for the first time crossing the Lee just below the timber-yard with its cranes like black notes zigzagging out over the river, which had for once discarded its fog. It was a day of bright blue sky, immense, rounded, silvery clouds, fresh and clean; with a wind which caught up the white apron and billowed it out for the sheer fun of the thing: showing trim ankles, the turn of a plump calf, such as Ben Cohen had never even thought of before, the realisation of which was like wine: freshly tasted, red, fruity, running through his veins, mounting to his head. He had known that women had legs; his mother, the laundress, suffered from hers - complainingly, devoted woman as she was - swollen with much standing, and "them there dratted veins": stocky legs, with loose folds of stocking.

As to thinking any more of a woman's legs than of the legs of a table, the idea had never even occurred to him. But there you are! It is the unexpected that happens: the sort of thing which we could never have imagined ourselves as doing, thinking, feeling. The temptations we have recognised, struggled against, are nothing; but there comes a sort of wild, whistling wind from nowhere - much the same as that wind about jenny's skirts, white apron - and our life is like a kaleidoscope, suddenly shaken up and showing a completely fresh pattern.

Who could have thought it - who? - that Ben Cohen, dreamer, idealist, passionate, pure, the devotee of art, would have fallen in love with Jenny Bligh's legs - or, rather, a pair of ankles, and a little more at that side where the wind caught her skirt - before he had so much as a glimpse of her face?

Just over the bridge she stopped to speak with another girl who worked in his own counting-house. As Ben hurried up to pass them before they separated, really see her, this other girl recognised him, flung him a friendly "Hullo!" and was answered in the same fashion.

As he moved on he heard her - was meant to hear, knew that he was meant to hear, from the pitch of the voice - "Clever ain't no word fur it! There ain't no tune as -"

The end of the sentence was lost; but he knew the sort of thing, knew it by heart, had spent his time running away from it. Now, however, he was grateful: more grateful still when he met Miss Ankles again, and she herself, regarding Florry Hines' eulogy as a sort of introduction, smiled, moved on a step, and herself tossed a "Hullo" over one shoulder.

Ben's thin olive-tinted face was flushed as he drew forward to her side with his odd stoop, his way of ducking his head and raising his eyes, dark and glowing. He took jenny's dinner-basket, and she noticed his hands, large and well-shaped, with long fingers, widened at the tips. Florry had said that he was a "Sheeny," but there was nothing of the Jew about him apart from his colouring, his brilliant dark eyes; unless it were a sort of inner glow, an ardour, curbed by his almost childlike shyness, lack of self-confidence in everything apart from his music: that something, at once finer and more cruelly persistent, vital, than is to be found in the purely Anglo-Saxon race.

Though Jenny liked what she called "a pretty tune," she knew nothing whatever of music, understood less. And yet, almost from that first moment, she understood Ben Cohen, realising him as lover and child: understood him better, maybe, then than she did later on: losing her sureness for a while, shaken and bewildered; everything blurred by her own immensity of love, longing; of fearing that she did not understand - feeling out of it.

But that was not for sometime to come: in the

meanwhile she was like a dear little bantam hen with one chick; while Ben himself was content to shelter under her wing, until it grew upon him that, loving her as he did, loving his mother - realising what it meant to be a mother, in thinking of jenny herself with a child - his child - in her arms - it was "up to" him to prove himself for their sakes, to make them proud of him and his music, without the faintest idea of how proud they were already, lift the whole weight of care from their shoulders.

The worst of it was, he told them nothing whatever about it. The better sort of men are given to these crablike ways of appearing to move away from what they intend to move towards. It simply seemed as though he were forgetting them a little - then, more and more; elbowing them aside to clear the way for his beloved music.

He was no longer deprecating, appealing, leaning upon them: each woman thought of him as "her child," and when his love made a man of him, they realised the hurt, nothing more.

He overdid it, too, as genius does overdo things; was brusque, entirely immersed in his great scheme. Sometimes he even laughed to himself over this. "They don't know what I'm up to!" he would declare to himself, with a sense of triumph.

He had never even thought of his music in the money sense before, but as his love and ambition for the two women grew upon him, he was like a child with a new toy. He would not only make a great name, he would make an immense fortune: his mind blinked, dazzled at the very thought. He moved with a new pride, and also

Edward J. O'Brien and John Cournos

- alas! - a new remoteness.

His health had broken when he was about seventeen - his bent shoulders still showed that old drag upon the chest - and he was away in a sanatorium for a year. When he came back he was cured. It was young Saere, the junior partner in the timber business, who had sent him away; and it was he who, when Ben returned, paid for lessons for him, so that he learnt to play as well as read music.

From that time onward he had always stuck to the firm, working in the tally sheds; paid, out of his earnings, for the use of a room and a piano for practising upon so many hours each week, completely happy and contented.

He had never even thought of leaving the business until he realised his immense love for Jenny, and, through her, for his mother; the necessity for doing something big. What did sacrifice matter? What did it matter being poor, hungry, shabby? - What did anything matter just for a while? There was so little he wanted; meals were a nuisance; his eyes were so dazzled by the brilliance of the future, set upon a far horizon, that he forgot the path of the present, still beneath his feet.

If his mother had not set food before him he would scarcely have thought of it. But, all the same, he ate it, and money had to be earned by some one or other.

His mother had never let him know the actual pinch of poverty; she wore that shoe upon her own foot. He had no more idea than a child of the cost of mere daily necessities; and during the last few years, between his work and hers, they had been comfortable enough.

"We can hang on for a bit," he said, when he spoke of leaving the wood-yard; and she answered, almost with triumph, that she had "hung on" well enough before he'd earned "aught but a licking."

At first she was proud of reshouldering the entire burden; it made him more entirely hers. He could not do without her; even with Jenny he could not do without her. But she had not been a young woman when Ben was born; she was old now, and tired, with that sort of tiredness which accumulates, heaps up, and which no single night's rest can ever cure; the tiredness which is ready, more than ready, for a narrower bed - eternal sleep.

" - Hold on until after the concert?"

"Sorry fur meself if I couldn't."

The concert! That was the goal. There was a public hall at Clapton where Ben had chanced on some really good music - just one night of it, and quite by chance - and this, to his mind, ennobled the Claptonites; there was the place in which to start the revolutionising of the musical world. Besides - and here he thought himself very canny, by no means a Jew for nothing - there were fine old houses at Clapton, and where there were such houses there must be rich people.

When the date was actually arranged, he practised for the best part of the day. While he was at home he read music; he lived in a maze of music. He never thought of advertising, collecting his public; he even avoided his old friends, his patrons at the timber-yard, overcome by agonies of shyness at the very thought of so much as mentioning his concert. Quite simply, in a way he did not even attempt to explain to himself, he felt that the world of London would scent it from afar off. As to paid *claques*, presentation-tickets, patrons, advance agents, all the booming and flattery, the jam of the powder for an English audience, he had no idea of the existence of such things. Beethoven was wonderful, and he had found out wonderful things about him: that was enough.

When the Angel Gabriel blew the last trump, there would be no need to invite the dead to rise. Neither was there any need to invite the really elect to his concert. Not to hear him, Ben Cohen, but to hear Beethoven as he ought to be heard; that's how he felt.

During those weeks of preparation for the concert, his mother worked desperately hard to keep their home together without his earnings, while Jenny helped. At first that had been enough for her, too: to help. But later -

Throughout those long evenings when, already tired from her work in the factory, she had stood sorting, sprinkling, folding, ironing, the two women got to a state where they scarcely dared to look at each other: just a passing glance, a hardish stare, but no *looking into*.

If he had but once said, "I can't bear you to work so hard for me," everything would have been different, the fatigue wiped out. But he didn't; he didn't even know they were working for him, working beyond the limit of an ordinary working-woman's working-day, hard enough, in all conscience.

"Men can't not be expected to notice things the way we do." That's what they told themselves - they did not say even this much to each other. But far, far away, out of sight, out of all actual knowledge, was the fear which neither of them would have dared to realise, a vague horror, a sort of ghost....

"He don't care - he's changed."

And, indeed, this is how it appeared. All through that time he wore an odd look of excitement, triumph, pleasure, which lifted him away from himself. There was a sort of lilt in his very step; his eyes shone, his cheeks were flushed. When he cleared a pile of freshly-ironed, starched things from the end of a table, so as to spread out a score upon it, laid them on the floor where the cat padded them over with dirty feet, and his mother railed at him, as she still did rail - on any subject apart from this of not caring - he glanced up at her with bright, amused eyes, his finger still following the black-and-white tangle of notes, looked at Jenny, and laughed - actually laughed.

"You great oaf!" cried Mrs. Cohen, and could have killed him. Up at four o'clock next morning, rewashing, starching, ironing, she retched with sick fatigue and something more - that sense of giddiness, of being hit on the head which had oppressed her of late. It was as though that laugh of Ben's had stuck like a bone in her chest, so sharp that she could scarcely draw breath; driven all the blood to her head.

And yet it had been full of nothing but triumph, a sort of tender triumph, almost childish delight. He was going to do wonders - wonders! - open a new world to them! He was so dazzled by his own work, dreams, by

all he had in store for them, that he did not even see
them, themselves, worn with toil, realise the meaning
of it, the reason for it. In any case he would have
laughed, because they had no idea how near it was to
an end.

That concert! It would be like nothing so much as
opening a door into a new world, where they need
never so much as soil a finger: floating around, dressed
in silk, feeding from off the finest china, sleeping upon
down.

Man-like, his eyes were fixed upon the future. No two
women had ever been loved as they were loved. All
this work, this washing and ironing, it resembled
nothing more than the opening scene in an opera: a sort
of prelude, for the sake of contrast. They would see -
O-o-oh, yes, they would see!

It was like that old childish "Shut your eyes and open
your mouth."

But they - they were bound in the close-meshed strait-
waistcoat of endless toil, petty anxiety. The days and
hours heaped in front of them obliterated all possible
view of the future.

In the beginning they had been as excited as he was
over the thought of the concert. He must wear a rosette
- no, a flower in his button-hole; and white kid gloves;
as he moved forward upon the platform, he must bow
right and left, and draw them off as he bowed.

This was Jenny's idea. It was Jenny who made him
practise his bows, and it was Jenny who borrowed a
dress-suit from a waiter-friend; while it was his mother

who "got up" the borrowed shirt to go with it, stiff and shining; who polished his best boots until they looked "near as near like patent."

All this had been done close upon a fortnight before. Jenny was a good girl, but if she was not there to see to things, Jenny might fail with a bubble on the shirt-front. No amount of meaning well was of any use in getting up a stiff shirt as it ought to be got up.

"Better 'ave it all ready, 'a-case o' anything happening." That was what Mrs. Cohen said to herself, with a dull dread at the back of her mind: a feeling as though every next day were a Friday.

Her face had been oddly flushed of late, with a rather fixed and glassy look about the eyes. Jenny thought of this, on her way to the concert; alone, for by some ill fate, his nearer vision blurred in that golden maze of the future, Ben had fixed his concert for a Friday.

This Friday! Always a bad day, bad in itself, bad for every one, like an east wind; worst of all for a laundress: not so depressing as a Monday, but so hurried, so overcrowded, with all the ironing and folding, the packing of the lots, all small, into their separate newspaper parcels; the accumulated fatigue of a whole week. Some demon seemed to possess her clients that week: they had come in with a collar here, a shirt there, an odd pillow-slip, tablecloth, right over Thursday. She was working until after twelve o'clock that night - so was Jenny - up before dawn next morning, though no one save herself knew of this.

"Whatever they do, they shan't not keep me from my Ben's concert!" That was what she said, with a vision of motors blocking the road in front of the little hall. But she had been a laundress best part of a lifetime - before she discovered herself as the mother of a genius - and it had bit into her bone: she could not get finished, and she could not leave the work undone.

"Some one's got to earn a living!" - that was what she said, embittered by fatigue, the sweat pouring down her face, beaten to every sensibility, apart from her swollen feet, by the time that Jenny called in for her, soon after six. She had longed to go, had never even thought of not going; but by now, apart from her physical pain and weariness, she was alive to but one point, her whole being drawn out to a sort of cone with an eye at the end of it; and far, far away at the back of her brain, struggling with impenetrable mists, but one thought - if she scorched anything, she would have to replace it.

When Jenny found that it was impossible to move her, she made her own way up to Clapton alone. For Ben had to be at the hall early; there were certain matters to arrange, and he would try over the piano.

Her efforts with Mrs. Cohen had delayed her; she was driven desperate by that cruel malice of inanimate things: every 'bus and tram was against her, whisking out of sight just as she wanted them, or blocked by slow crawling carts and lorries. There was a tight, hard pain in her heart, like toothache, round which her whole body gathered, pressing, impaled upon it; a sense of desperation, and yet at the heart of this, like a nerve, the wonder if anything really mattered.

Ben had promised to reserve seats for his mother and herself; but had he? - Had he? Would she find the place blocked by swells with their hard stare, duchesses and such-like, glistening in diamonds? In her mind's eye she saw billows of silk, slabs of black cloth and shining white shirt-fronts - hundreds and hundreds of them. And Ben bowing, bowing to them as she had taught him to do.

For some time past he had been so far away, so detached that she was haunted by the fear that if she put out a finger to touch him it might go through him, as though he were a ghost. At times she had caught him, held him to her in a passion of love and longing. But even then, with his head against her heart, his lips, or some pulse or nerve, had moved in a wordless tune, the beat of time.

If only he had still seemed to need her, nothing, nothing would have mattered. But he didn't: he needed no one - no one. He seemed so frail, she had made sure that he wanted looking after; but he didn't. A drunkard might have fallen down in the street, needed fetching, supporting, exhorting; a bully come home with a broken head. But it seemed as though Ben were, in reality, for all his air of appeal, sufficient to himself, moving like a steady light through the darkness; unstirred by so much as a breath of wind.

Overcome by anxiety, she got out of the tram too soon. It had begun to rain, a dull, dark night, and there was a blur of misty light flooding the pavement a little way ahead. That must be the hall. She was afraid of over-shooting the mark. Those trams had such a way of getting going just as one wanted to be out of them!

But the light was nothing more than a cinema, and she she had a good quarter of a mile to walk in the wet.

The cruel wet! - just like it to be wet on this night of all nights! Even her optimism was gone. She kept on thinking of Mrs. Cohen, her flushed face and oddly-glazed eyes; the queer stiff way in which she moved, held her head. For once she was angry with Ben.

"'Im and his crowds,' 'Im an' 'is fine lydies! 'Im an' 'is *motor-cars!*"

After all, she did overshoot her mark; on inquiry for the hall, she was told that she had passed it, and was obliged to retrace her steps.

No wonder she had passed it; with all she had expected at the back of her mind! The strip of pavement outside was dark, with not so much as a single taxi in sight; the door half-shut, the dreary vestibule badly-lighted, empty, smelling of damp. The sodden-looking sketch of a man in the pay-box seemed half asleep; stretched, yawned when she spoke, pushing a strip of pink paper towards her as she gave her name.

"For two." He poked out a long neck and peered round the edge of the box, like a tortoise from its shell.

"The other lydy wasn't not able ter come ter-night," answered Jenny with dignity, and the beast grinned, displaying a wreckage of broken teeth.

"Ain't not what you might call a crowd, anyway," he remarked.

She could have killed him for that! She realised the white face of a clock, but she would not look at it. She was early, that was it. Look how she had hurried. No wonder that she was early. And great ladies were always late: she had learnt that from the *Daily Mail* stories.

"Two an' two make four - them too late an' me too early!" she said to herself, with a gallant effort after her own brisk way of taking things, a surer tap of heels on the stone floor as she turned towards a swing-door to her left; pushed it open, and was hit in the face by what seemed like a thick black curtain.

A dim white-gloved hand was thrust through it and took her ticket.

"Mind you don't fall - no good wasting the lights until they come - if ever they does come," exhorted and explained a voice out of the darkness; for, after all, it was not a curtain, but just darkness.

At first Jenny could see nothing. Then, little by little, it seemed as though different objects crept forward, one by one, like wild animals from their lair.

Those white patches, the hands of two white-gloved men, holding sheaves of programmes - she realised one between her own fingers - whispering together.

There was the platform, the great piano sprawling over it; and in front of this, rows and rows and rows - and rows upon rows - of empty seats.

She looked behind her - they had argued long over the question of places for herself and his mother. "The very best," that's what Ben had said; but they fought against this, fought and conquered, for the best seats meant money. "What's a seat more or less, I'd like to know?"

"Money, all money." Old Mrs. Cohen had been firm upon this point.

Still, there were a great many seats yet further back - and all empty: a little raised, seeming to push themselves forward with the staring vacuity of an idiot: more seats overhead in a curving balcony, rising above each other as though proud of their emptiness. It would have been impossible to believe that mere vacant places could wear so sinister, as well as foolish, an aspect. An idiot, but a cruel idiot, too: the whole thing one cruel idiot, of the sort that likes to pull legs from flies.

There was a clock there, also. For a long while Jenny would not allow herself to look at it. But something drew her, until it became an unbearable effort to keep her eyes away from it, to look anywhere else; and at last she turned her head, stared, sharply, defiantly, as though daring it.

It was five-and-twenty minutes to nine. Five-and-twenty minutes to nine, and the concert was to have begun at eight! - Five-and-twenty minutes to nine, and there was no one there - no one whatever!

The clock hands dragged themselves on for another five-minutes; then one of the men disappeared behind the scene; came back, speaking excitedly, gesticulating with white hands:

"We're to turn on the light. 'E swears as 'e won't give it up - 'e's goin' ter play."

"Goin' ter play? Well, I'll be blowed! - Goin' ter play! An' with nothing 'ere but *That*"

Jenny saw how he jerked his head in her direction. So she was "That" - she, Jenny Bligh! - and so far gone that she did not even care.

As the lights went up the hall seemed to swim in a sort of mist: the terra-cotta walls, the heavy curtains at either side of the platform, those awful empty seats!

Jenny spread her skirt wide, catching at the chair to either side of her, stretching out her arms along the backs of them. She had a wild feeling as though it were up to her to spread herself sufficiently to cover them all. She half rose. Perhaps she could hide more of that emptiness if she moved nearer to the front: that was her thought.

But no; she mustn't do that: this was the place Ben had chosen for her; she must stay where she was. He might look there, miss her, and imagine that there was nobody, nobody at all; that even she had failed him.

If only she could spread herself - spread herself indefinitely - multiply herself: anything, anything to cover those beastly chairs: sticking out there, grinning, shaming her man!

Then she had a sudden idea of running into the street, entreating the people to come in; was upon her feet for the second time, when Ben walked on to the platform.

For once he was not ducking or moving sideways; he came straight forward, bowed to the front of him, right and left; drew off his gloves and bowed again. Mingling with her agony of pity, a thrill, ran through Jenny Bligh at this. He remembered her teaching; he was hers - hers - hers - after all, hers - more than ever hers!

The borrowed coat, far too big for him, rose in a sort of hood at the back of his neck; as he bowed something happened to the centre stud of his shirt, and it disappeared into an aperture shaped like a dark gourd in the whiteness.

But, for all that, Jenny felt herself overawed by his dignity, as any one would have been: there was something in the man so much greater than his clothes, greater than his conscious, half-childish self.

Jenny's hands were raised to clap; but they dropped into her lap, lay there, as, with a face set like marble, Ben turned and seated himself at the piano. There was a moment's pause, while he stared straight in front of him - such a pause that a feeling of goose-flesh ran down the back of her arms - then he began to play.

Jenny had not even glanced at her programme; she would have understood nothing of it if she had; but it gave the Sonata, Op. III, as the opening piece.

Ben, however, took no notice of this; but, for some reason he could not have explained, flung himself straight-way into the third item, the tremendous "Hammerclavier."

The sounds flooded the hall; swept through it as if it were not there, obliterating time and space. It was as though the Heavenly Host had descended upon the earth, sweet, wonderful, and yet terrible, with a sweep of pinions, deep-drawn breath - Tubal Cain and his kind, deified and yet human in their immense masculinity and strength.

Jenny Bligh was neither imaginative nor susceptible to

sound, but it drew her out of herself. It was like bathing in a sea whose waves overpower one so that, try as one may to cling to the earth, it slips off from beneath one's feet - shamed, beaten. She had a feeling that if it did not stop soon she would die; and would yet die when it did stop. Her heart beat thickly and heavily, her eyes were dim; she was bewildered, lost, and yet exhilarated. It was worse than an air raid, she thought - more exciting, more wonderful.

The end left her almost as much exhausted as Ben himself. The sweat was running down his face as he got up from his seat, came forward to the front of the platform, and bowed right and left. Jenny had not clapped - she would as soon have thought of clapping God with His last trump - but Ben bowed as though a whole multitude had applauded him.

By some chance, the only direction in which he did not turn his eyes was the gallery: even then, he might not have seen a single figure seated a little to one side - a man with a dark overcoat buttoned up to his chin, who clapped his two thumbs noiselessly together, drawing in his breath with a sort of whistle.

"That's the stuff!" he said. "That's the stuff to give 'em!"

After a moment's pause, Ben turned again to the piano. This time he played the Sonata Pathétique in C Minor, Op. XIII; then the Sonata Walstein in C Major. Between each, he got up, moved forward to the edge of the platform, and bowed.

At the end of the Sonata, Op. III - by rights the first on the programme - during the short interval which followed it he straightened his shoulders with a sort of swagger, utterly unlike himself, swung round to the piano again, and slammed out "God Save the King."

He played it through to the very end, then rose, bowed from where he stood, stared round at the empty hall - a dreadful, strained, defiant smile stiffening upon his face - and sinking back upon his stool, laid his arms across the keyboard with a crash of notes, burying his head upon them.

In a moment Jenny was out of her seat. There were chairs in her way, and she kicked them aside; raked one forward with her foot, and scrambled on to the platform; then, catching a sideways glimpse of the empty seats, bent forward and shook her fist at them.

"Beasts! Pigs! A-a-a-ah! - You!"

The attendants had disappeared, the stranger was lost in shadows. There was nobody there but themselves: it would not have mattered if there had been: all the lords and ladies, all the swells in the world, would not have mattered. The great empty hall, suddenly friendly, closed, curving, around them.

Jenny dropped upon her knees at Ben's side, and flung her arms about him, with little moans of love and pity; slid one hand beneath his cheek, with a muffled roll of notes, raised his head and pressed it against her heart.

"There, my dear! There, my love - there - there - there!"

She laid her lips to his thick dark hair, in a passion of adoration, loving every lock of it; and then, woman-like, picked a white thread from off his black coat; clasped him afresh, with joy and sorrow like runnels of living water pouring through and through her.

"There, there, there, there!"

He was too much of a child to fight against her: all his pride was gone. "Oh, Jenny, Jenny, Jenny!" he cried; then, in an extremity of innocent anguish, amazement -

"They didn't come! They don't care - they don't want it! Jenny, they don't want it!"

"Don't you worry about them there blighters, my darling. Selfish pigs! they ain't not worth a thought. Don't you worry about them."

"But - Beethoven...."

"Don't you worry about Beethoven, neifer - ain't no better nor he oughter be, taeke my word fur it. Lettin' you in like this 'ere! There - there - there, my dear!"

They clung together, weeping, rocking to and fro. "Well," said the man in the gallery, "I'm jiggered!" and crept out very softly, stumbling a little because of the damp air which seemed to have got into his eyes and made them smart.

As the lovers came out into the little vestibule, clinging to each other, they did not so much as see the stranger, who stood talking to the man in the box-office, but went straight on out into the rain, with their umbrellas unopened in their hands.

"A good thing as the 'all people insists upon payment

in advance," remarked the man in the box-office.

The other gave him a curious, half-contemptuous glance. "I'd like to hear you say that in a year's time."

"Why?"

"Because that chap will be able to buy and sell a place like this a hundred times over by then - Queen's Hall - Albert Hall - I know. It's my business to know. There's something about his playing. That *something different* they're all out for."

It took a long time to get back to Canning Town. Even Jenny had lost her certainty: her grasp of the ways of 'buses and such things. She felt oddly clear and empty: like a room swept and garnished, with the sense of a ghost in some dim corner of it; physically sapped out.

Ben clung to her. He said very little, but he clung to her, with an odd, lost air: the look of a child who has been slapped in the face, and cannot understand why.

She was so much smaller than he, like a diminutive, sturdy steam-tug; and yet if she could have carried him, she would have done so.

As it was, she threw her whole heart and soul into guiding, comforting; thinking of a hundred things at once, her soft mouth folded tight with anxiety. - How to prevent him from feeling shamed before his mother: how to keep the trouble away from her: though at the back of her own mind was a feeling - and she had an idea that it would be at the back of old Mrs. Cohen's also - of immense relief, of some load gone: almost as though her child had been through a bad attack of scarlet-fever, or something which one does not take twice.

With all this, there was the thought of what she would step out and buy for their supper, if the fried-fish shop were still open; all she would do and say to cheer them.

As for Ben, the "Hammerclavier" was surging through his brain, carrying the empty hall with it, those rows upon rows of empty seats - swinging them to and fro so that he felt physically sick, as though he were at sea.

Quite suddenly, as they got out of the last tram, the rain ceased. At the worst it had been a mild night of velvety darkness and soft airs, the reflection from the lamps swimming in a haze of gold across the wet pavement; but now, just as they reached the end of his own street, the black sky opened upon a wide sea of pinkish-amber and a full moon sailed into sight. At the same moment, Ben's sense of anguished bewilderment cleared away, leaving in its place a feeling of incalculable weariness.

To be back in his own home again - that was all he asked. "You'll stay the night at our place, Jenny?" "Yes; I promised your mother." Her brow knitted, and then cleared again. Ah, well; that was all over: Ben would go back to his regular job again; they would get married; then there would be her money, too: no need for old Mrs. Cohen to do another hand's turn. Plenty of time for her to rest now: all her life for resting in.

"Your mother." As she spoke Ben remembered, for the first time, actively remembered, for of course it was his mother that he meant when he thought of home.

"She wasn't there, Jenny! She wasn't there!"

"She was very busy, 'adn't not finished 'er work."
Something beyond Jenny's will stiffened within her. So
he had only just realised it! She tried not to remember,
but she could not help it - the flushed face, the glassy
eyes: the whole look of a woman beaten, with her back
against a wall; condemning Ben by her very silence,
desperate courage.

"Work?"

"Yes, work." Jenny snapped it: hating herself for it,
drawing him closer, and yet unable to help it. "Why -"
began Ben, and then stopped - horrified. At last he
realised it: perhaps it ran to him through Jenny's arm;
perhaps it was just that he was down on earth again,
humble, ductile, seeing other people's lives as they
were, not as he meant to make them.

"Ter-night - workin'"

"All night; one the saeme as another."

"But why -" he began again; stopped dead, loosed his
own arm and caught hers. "All this while workin' like
that! She works too hard. Jenny, look here: she works
too hard. And I - this damned music! Look here, Jenny,
it's got to stop! I'll never play a note again; she shall
never do a hard stroke of work again; never, never -
not so long as I'm here to work for her. All my life -
ever since I can remember - washing and ironing, like -
like - the very devil!"

He pulled the girl along with him. "That was what I
was thinking all the time: to make a fortune so that

you'd both have everything you wanted, a big house, servants, motors, silk dresses - And all the time letting you both work yourselves to death! But this is the end; no more of that. To be happy - that's all that matters - sort of everyday happiness.

"No more of that beastly washing, ironing - it's the end of that, anyhow. When I'm back at the timber-yard -"

He was like a child again, planning; they almost ran down the street. "No more o' that damned washin' and ironin' - no more work -"

True! How true! The street door opened straight into the little kitchen. She was not in bed, for the light was still burning; they could see it at either side of the blind, shrunk crooked with steam. There was one step down into the kitchen; but for all that, the door would not open when they raised the latch and pushed it, stuck against something.

"Some of those beastly old clothes!" Ben shoved it, hailing his mother. "Mother! Mother, you've got something stuck against the door." Odd that she did not come to his help, quick as she always was.

After all, it gave way too suddenly for him to altogether realise the oddness; and he stumbled forward right across the kitchen, seeing nothing until he turned and faced Jenny still standing upon the step, staring downward, with an ashy-white face, wide eyes fixed upon old Mrs. Cohen, who lay there at her feet, resting - incomprehensibly resting.

They need not have been so emphatic about it all - "No more beastly washing, no more work" - for the whole thing was out of their hands once and for all.

She had fallen across the doorway, a flat-iron still in her hand - the weapon with which she had fought the world, kept the wolf from that same door - all the strain gone out of her face, a little twisted to the left side, and oddly smiling. One child's pinafore was still unironed; the rest were folded, finished.

They raised her between them, laid her upon her bed. It was Jenny who washed her, wrapped her in clean linen - no one else should touch her; Ben who sat by her, with hardly a break, until the day that she was buried, wiped out with self-reproach, grief; desolate as any child, sodden with tears.

He collected all his music into a pile, the day before the funeral, gave it to Jenny to put under the copper - a burnt-offering.

"If it hadn't been for that, she might be here now. I don't want ever to see it again - ever to hear a note of it!" That was what he said.

Jenny went back to the house with him after the funeral: she was going to give him his tea, and then return to her own room. In a week they were to be married, and she would be with him for good, looking after him. That evening, before she left, she would set his breakfast, cut his lunch ready for the morrow. By Saturday week they would be settled down to their regular life together. She would not think about his music; pushed it away at the back of her mind - over and done with - would not even allow herself the disloyalty of being glad. And yet was glad, deeply glad, relieved, despite her pride in it, in him: as though it were something unknown, alien, dangerous, like things forbidden.

Two men were waiting at the door of the narrow slip of a house: the tall, thin one with his overcoat still buttoned up to his chin, and another fat and shining, with a top-hat, black frock-coat, and white spats.

"About that concert -" said the first man.

"We were thinking that if we could persuade you to play -" put in the other.

"There was no one there," interrupted Ben roughly. His shoulders were bent, his head dropped forward on his chest, poking sideways, his eyes sullen as a child's.

"I was there," put in the first man, "and I must say, impressed -"

"Very deeply impressed," added the other; but once again Ben brushed him aside.

"You were there - at my concert!" Jenny, standing a little back - for they were all three crowded upon the tiny door-step - saw him glance up at the speaker with something luminous shining through the darkness of his face. "At my concert - ! And you liked it? You liked it?"

"'Like' is scarcely the word."

"We feel that if you could be persuaded to give another concert," put in the stout man, blandly, "and would allow -"

"I shall never play again - never - never!" cried Ben, harshly; but this time the other went on imperturbably: "- allow us to make all arrangements, take all responsibility: boom you; see to the advertising and all that - we thought if we were to let practically all the seats for the first concert go in complimentary tickets; get a few good names on the committee - perhaps a princess or something of that sort as a patroness - a strong claque"

"Of course, playing Beethoven - playing him as you played him the other night. Grand-magnificent!" put in the first man realising the weariness, the drop to blank indifference in the musician's face. "The 'Hammer-clavier' for instance -"

It was magical. - "Oh, yes, yes - that - that!" Ben's eyes widened, his face glowed. He hummed a bar or so. "Was there ever anything like it? My God! was there ever anything like it!'

Jenny, who had the key, squeezed past them at this, and ran through the kitchen to the scullery, where she filled the kettle and put it upon the gas-ring to boil; looked round her for a moment, with quick, darting eyes - like a small wild animal at bay in a strange place - then drew a bucketful of water, turned up her sleeves, the skirt of her new black frock, tied on an old hessian apron of Mrs. Cohen's, with a savage jerk of the strings, and dropping upon her knees, started to scrub the floor, the rough stone floor.

"Men! - trapsin' in an' out, muckin' up a place!"

She could hear the murmur of men's voices in the kitchen, and through it that "trapsin'" of other men struggling with a long coffin on the steep narrow stairs.

On and on it went - the agonised remembrance of all that banging, trampling; the swish of her own scrubbing-brush; the voices round the table where old Mrs. Cohen had stood ironing for hours and hours upon end.

Then the door into the scullery was opened. For a moment or so she kept her head obstinately lowered, determined that she *would* not look up. Then, feeling her own unkindness, she raised it and smiled upon Ben, who stood there, flushed, glowing, and yet too shame-faced to speak - smiled involuntarily, as one must smile at a child.

"Well?"

"That - that - music stuff - I suppose it's burnt?" he began, fidgeting from one foot to another, his head bent, ducking sideways, his shoulder to his ear.

Her glance enwrapped him - smiling, loving, bitter-sweet. Things were not going to be as she had thought; none of that going out regularly to work, coming home to tea like other men; none of that safe sameness of life. At the back of her calm was a fierce battle; then she rose to her feet, wiped her hands upon her apron, stooped to the lowest shelf of the cupboard, and drew out a pile of music.

"There you are, my dear. I didn't not burn it, a'cause Well, I suppose as I sorter knowed all the time as you'd be wantin' it."

Children! Well, one knew where one was with children

- real children. But men, that was a different pair of shoes altogether - something you could never be sure of - unless you remembered, always remembered, to treat them as though they were grown-up, think of them as children.

"Now you taeke that an' get along back to yer friends an' yer playin', and let me get on with my work. It'll be dark an' tea-time on us afore ever I've time ter so much as turn round."

"That woman," said the fat, shining man, as they moved away down the street, greasy with river-mist. - "Hang it all! where in the world are we to get a taxi? - Common-place little thing; a bit of a drag on him, I should think."

"Don't you believe it, my friend - that's the sort to give 'em - some'un who will sort of dry-nurse 'em - feed em - mind 'em. That's the wife for a genius. The only sort of wife - mark my word for it."

THE DEVIL TO PAY

By MAX PEMBERTON

(From *The Story-Teller*) 1922

To say that the usually amiable Ambrose Cleaver was in the devil of a temper would be merely to echo the words of his confidential clerk, John, who, looking through the glass partition between their offices, confessed to James, the office boy, that he had not seen such goings on since old Ambrose, the founder of the firm, was gathered to his fathers.

"There won't be a bit of furniture in the place presently," said he, "and I wouldn't give twopence for the cat when he's finished kicking her. This comes of the women, my boy. Never have nothing to say to a woman until you've finished your dinner and lighted your cigar. Many a good business have I seen go into the Bankruptcy Court because of a petticoat before lunch. You keep away from 'em if you want to be Lord Mayor of London, same as Dick Whittington was."

James did not desire particularly to become Lord Mayor of London, but he was greatly amused by his employer's temper.

"Never heard such language," said he - "and him about

to marry her. Why, he almost threw them jewels at her 'ead; and when she told him he must have let the devil in by accident, he says as he was always glad to see her friends. They'll make a happy couple, surely."

John shook his old dense head, and would express no opinion upon the point.

"Misfortunes never come singly," said he. "Here's that Count Florian waiting for him in the ante-room. Now that's a man I can't abide. If anybody told me he was the devil, I'd believe him soon enough. A bad 'un, James, or I don't know the breed. An evil man who seems to pollute the very air you breathe."

James was not so sure of it.

"He give me half a crown for fetching of a cab yesterday, and told me to go to the music-hall with it. He must have a lot of money, for he never smokes his cigars more than half-way through, and he wears a different scarf-pin every day. That's wot comes of observation, Mr. John. I could tell you all the different pairs of trousers he's worn for the last three weeks, and so I'm going to make my fortune as the advertisements say."

Mr. John would not argue about that. The bell of the inner office now tinkled, and that was an intimation that the Count Nicholas Florian was to be admitted to the Holy of Holies. So the old man hurried away and, opening the sacred door with circumspection, narrowly escaped being knocked down by an enraged and hasty cat - glad to escape that inferno at any cost.

"You rang, sir?"

Ambrose Cleaver, thirty-three years of age, square-jawed, fair-haired, a florid complexion and with a wonderful pair of clear blue eyes, admitted that he did ring.

"And don't be so d -d slow next time," he snapped. "I'll see the Count Florian at once."

The old man withdrew timidly, while his master mopped up the ink from the pot he had broken in his anger.

"Enough to try the devil himself," was the sop that argument offered to his heated imagination. "She knows I hate Deauville like poison, and of course it's to Deauville she must go for the honeymoon. And she looks so confoundedly pretty when she's in a temper - what wonderful eyes she's got! And when she's angry the curls get all round her ears, and it's as much as a man can do not to kiss her on the spot. Of course, I didn't really want her to have opals if she thinks they're unlucky, but she needn't have insisted that I knew about it and bought them on purpose to annoy her. Good God! I wish there were no women in the world sometimes. What a splendid place it would be to live in, and what a fine time the men would have - for, of course, they are all the daughters of the devil really, and that's why they make life too hot for us."

Mr. John entered at this moment showing in the Count, and so a very cheerful argument was thus cut short. Ambrose pulled himself together and suppressing, as best he could, any appearance of aversion from the caller who now presented himself, he sat back in his chair and prepared to hear "the tale."

Count Florian was at that time some fifty-nine years of age, dark as an Italian and not without trace of an Eastern origin. Though it was early in the month of May, he still wore a light Inverness cape of an ancient fashion, while his patent-leather boots and his silk hat shone with the polish of a well-kept mirror. When he laughed, however, he showed ferocious teeth, some capped with gold, and in his eyes was a fiery light not always pleasant to behold.

"A chilly morning," he began. "You have no fire, I see."

"You find it so?" queried Ambrose. "Well, I thought it quite warm."

"Ah," said the count, "you were born, of course, in this detestable country. Do not forget that where I live there are people who call the climate hell," and he laughed sardonically, with a laugh quite unpleasant to hear.

Ambrose did not like such talk, and showed his displeasure plainly.

"The climate is good enough for me," he said. "Personally, I don't want to live in the particular locality you name. Have a cigar and tell me why you called - the old business, I suppose? Well, you know my opinion about that. I want none of it. I don't believe it is honest business, and I think that if we did it, we might all end in the dock. So you know my mind before we begin."

The Count heard him patiently, but did not seem in any way disturbed.

"There is very little business that is honest," he said; "practically none at all. Look at politics, the Church, art, the sciences - those who flourish are the imposters, while your honest men are foolish enough to starve in garrets. If a man will undertake nothing that is open to the suspicion of self-interest, he should abandon all his affairs at once and retire to a monastery, where possibly he will discover that the prior is cheating the abbot and the cellarer cheating them both. You have a great business opportunity, and if anybody suffers it is only the Government, which you must admit is a pure abstraction - suggesting chiefly a company of undiscovered rascals. The deal which I have to propose to you concerns a sum of half a million sterling, and that is not to be passed by lightly. I suggest, therefore, that at least you read the documents I have brought with me, and that we leave the matter of honesty to be discussed by the lawyers."

He laid upon the table a bundle of papers as he spoke, and lighted a cigarette by lightly rubbing a match against the tip of the fourth finger of his left hand. Ambrose felt strangely uneasy. A most uncanny suspicion had come upon him while the man was speaking. He felt that no ordinary human being faced him, and that he might in very truth be talking with the devil. Nor would this idea quit him despite its apparent absurdity.

"You must have great influence, Count," he remarked presently - "great influence to get such a valuable commission as this!"

The Count was flattered.

"I have servants in every country," he said; "the rich

are always my friends - the poor often come to me because they are not rich. Few who know me can do without me; indeed, I may say that but for such men as I am the world would not go on. I am the mainspring of its endeavour."

"And yet when I met you it was on the links above La Turbie."

The count laughed, showing his glittering teeth as any carnivorous animal might have done.

"Ah, I remember. You met me when I was playing golf with a very saintly lady. Latterly, I hear, she has ceased to go to church and taken to bobbed hair. Women are strange creatures, Mr. Cleaver, but difficult, very difficult sometimes. I have had many disappointments with women."

"You find men easier?"

"Indeed, there are few men who are not willing to go to the devil if the consideration be large enough. A woman, on the other hand, is too often the victim of her emotions. She will suffer eternal torment for the man she loves, and she will cheat for him. But for the rest of us - nothing, positively nothing at all; she is neither honest nor dishonest, she merely passes us by."

"Ah," exclaimed Ambrose, a little wearily, "I wish I could think that about my *fiancée*. She's just been up - that's why you find me upset. I bought her opals, and, of course, she wants diamonds. You see, I forgot she wasn't born in October."

The Count nodded his head in sympathy.

"I must have a little talk to her. I am sure we shall be good friends. Miss Kitty Palmer, is it not? Forgive me, I read it in the newspapers - a charming face but a little temper, I think. Well, well, there is no harm in that. What a dull place the world would be but for a little temper! You have much to be thankful for, Mr. Cleaver - very, very much. And now this concession, by which you will make two hundred thousand pounds at a very moderate estimate. There will be very little temper when you take home that news. No woman is angry with a man who makes money, but she has a great contempt for him who does not."

"Even if he made it dishonestly?"

"She does not care a snap of the fingers how he makes it, believe me."

"And afterwards, when he goes to prison -"

"Pshaw - only fools go to prison. If your foolish principles were made the test, there would hardly be a free man in Mincing Lane. We should have to lock up the whole City. Come, let me have your signature, and I will do the rest. To refuse is madness. You are offered the chance of a lifetime."

Ambrose did not reply to him immediately. It had come to him suddenly that this was the hour of a great temptation, and he sat very still, conscious that his heart beat fast because of the evil that was near him. The Count watched him, meanwhile, as a wild beast may watch its prey. The man's eyes appeared to have turned to coals of fire; his fingers twitched; his teeth were on edge - he had even ceased to smoke.

"Well?" he said at last, unable to suffer the silence any longer.

Ambrose rose from his chair and went over slowly to the great safe, which stood in the corner of his office; he unlocked it and took some documents from a shelf upon the right-hand side. The Count stood at his elbow while he did so, and he could feel the man's breath warm upon his shoulder.

Suddenly a violent impulse overcame him. He swung round and seized the fellow by the collar, and in an instant, endowed as it were with superhuman strength, he hurled the man into the safe and turned the key upon him.

"By heaven!" he cried, "but I have locked up the devil."

II

Ambrose dismissed John, the man, and James, the boy, and told them he would have no need of their services for some days.

"I am going away for a little holiday," he said. "The letters can await my return. You may both go down to Brighton for a week, and I will pay your expenses. It is right that you should have a little change of air more than once a year, so away with you both, and don't let me hear of you until Monday next."

James looked at John and John looked at James. Was their excellent employer demented, then, or had they understood him incorrectly?

"Not," said John, when they were alone together, "that I particularly wished to go to Brighton just now, but there you are. Half the pleasure in life, my boy, is wanting to do things, and when you have to do them without wanting it, even though they are pleasant things, somehow all the savour has gone out of the salt, so to speak. But, of course, we shall have to go, seeing that we couldn't tell Mr. Cleaver a lie."

James was a little astonished at that, for he had told thousands of lies in his brief life, though now he really had no desire to tell one at all.

"I shall be glad to get away from here for a few days, any'ow," he said; "it's so 'ot and close, and when you go near the safe in the other horfice it's just as though you stood by a roaring fire. Good thing, Mr. John, that the thing is fire-proof, or we might have the whole show burned down, as Mr. Ambrose hisself was saying. 'Very 'ot for the time of year, James,' says he, and 'burnin, 'ot,' says I. We'll find it cooler at Brighton, Mr. John, and perhaps we can go to the pictures, though I'm fed up with all them rotten stories about crooks and such like, and so are you, I'm sure."

Mr. John said that he was, though he was surprised at such an opinion emanating from James. When they locked up the inner office - their master being gone home - they discovered in the fire-grate the ashes of what had been a formidable-looking document, and it really did seem as though the concrete upon which the great safe stood had become quite hot, but there was no visible sign of fire, and so they went off, wondering and contented, but by no means in a mood of exhilaration, as properly they should have been.

Ambrose had taken a cab at his own door, and his first visit was to the Bond Street jeweller who had sold him the opals.

He was quite sure that he had shut up the devil in his office safe, and as he drove it seemed to him that he became conscious of a new world round about him, though just how it was new he could not have told you.

Everybody wore a look of great content - there was subdued laughter but no real merriment - nor did any hasten as though he had real business to do; while the very taxi-cabs drove with circumspection, and actually waited for old ladies to cross the street before them. When his own cab stopped he gave the man half a crown as usual; but the driver called him back and pointed out his error.

"Excuse me, sir, eighteenpence is the fare with three-pence for my gratuity, that makes one and ninepence. So I have to give you ninepence back, although I thank you all the same."

Ambrose pocketed the money, quite insensible of anything but the man's civility, and entered immediately into the sanctum of the great jeweller. He found that worthy a little distrait and far from any desire to do big business. In fact, his first words told of his coming retirement from an occupation which had enriched him during a good forty years of profit and rarely of loss.

"The fact is, Mr. Cleaver, that I foresee the day coming when women will wear no jewellery. Already the spirit of competition has passed, and it is by competition and the pride of competition that this trade has flourished. A woman buys a rope of pearls because another woman wears one. Lady A cannot allow Lady B to have more valuable diamonds than she possesses. Very few really admire the gems for their own sake, and when you think of the crimes that have been committed because of them, the envious passions they arouse, and the swindles to which they give birth, then, indeed, we may wish that every precious stone lay deep at the bottom of the sea."

"But, my dear sir, are you not thus banishing much beauty from the world - did not the Almighty create precious stones for pretty women to wear?"

The jeweller shrugged his shoulders, sweeping aside carelessly some priceless pearls that lay on the table before him.

"The Almighty created them to lie securely in their shells, or deep in the caverns of the earth; for the rivers to wash them with sweet waters or the lurid fire to shape them in the bowls of the mountains. The beauties given us to enjoy are those upon which our eyes may light in the woodlands or from the heights - the glory of the sunset, the stillness of the sea, the thousand hues of a garden of flowers, or the cascade as it falls from the mountain top. These things are common to all, but the precious stone is too often for the neck or the fingers of the harlot and the adventuress. No, sir, I shall retire from this business and seek out some quiet spot where I can await with composure the solemn moment of dissolution we all must face."

Ambrose was almost too astonished to speak.

"I admire your philosophy," he said at length, "but the fact is, that I want a diamond ring and a rope of pearls and if -"

"Ah," said the old man interrupting him, "it is odd that you should speak of pearls, for I have just been telling my partner here that whatever he may do in the future, he will find pearls of little profit to him. What with imitations and the 'cultured' article, women are coming already to despise them. But even if you take your *fiancée* a diamond ring, will she not merely say to herself: 'an excellent beginning, now what is the next thing I can get out of him?' Be wise and cultivate no such spirit of cupidity, foreign to a good woman's nature but encouraged by the men, who, for vanity's sake, heap presents upon her. Take rather this little cross, set with pure amethysts, the emblem of faith and so discover, my dear sir, whether she loves the man or the jewel, for indeed but few women love both, as all their story teaches us."

Ambrose took the cross and thanked the old man for his words of wisdom. Another cab carried him on his way to Upper Gloucester Place where Kitty Palmer then lived with her saintly mother - and as he went, he reflected upon the jeweller's words.

"I'll put her to the proof," he said to himself, "if she likes this twopenny halfpenny cross, she is a miracle among women. But, of course, she won't like it and there'll be another scene. What a devil of a temper she was in this morning and how she made the fur fly! If she's like that now, I shall just take her into my arms and kiss her until she's done fighting. After all, I wouldn't give sixpence for a woman who had no spirit. It's their moods that make them so fascinating - little devils that they are at their best!"

The arrival at the house cut short his ruminations and he hastened into the well-known drawing-room and there waited impatiently while the maid summoned Kitty from her bedroom. She came down immediately to his great surprise - for usually she kept him waiting at least half an hour - and her mood was strangely changed, he thought. A pretty, flaxen-haired, blue-eyed, cream and white English type she was, but her chin spoke also of determination and the eyes which could "look love to eyes that looked again," upon occasion could also speak of anger which resented all control. This afternoon, however, Kitty was as meek as a lamb. She had become so utterly changed in an hour that Ambrose hardly knew her.

"My dear girl," he began, "I am so sorry that I lost my temper this morning - "

"Oh, no - not you, Ambrose dear. It was I - of course it was awfully silly and we won't go to Deauville if you don't want to. Let it be Fontainebleau by all means - though really, it does not seem important whether we do get married or don't while you love me. Love after all is what matters, isn't it, Ambrose dearest?"

He had to say that it was, though he did not like her argument. When, with some hesitation and not a little fear he showed her the little gold cross, she admitted to his astonishment that it was one of the prettiest things she had ever seen.

"Somehow," she said, "I do not seem to care much for jewellery now. It has become so vulgar - the commoner the people, the more diamonds they wear. I shall treasure this, darling - I'll wear it now at lunch. Of course you are going to take me to lunch, aren't you? Suppose we go to the Ritz grill-room, the restaurants are so noisy, and I know that you like grill-rooms, don't you, dear?"

Ambrose said "yes" and they started off. Somehow he felt rather depressed and he had to confess that Kitty - usually so smart - looked quite shabby. She wore one of her oldest dresses and obviously had neither powder on her face nor the lightest touch of the rouge which became her so well. Moreover, she was listless beyond experience, and when he asked her if she would go to the Savoy and dance that night, she answered that she thought she would give up dancing altogether. It quite took his breath away.

"Give up dancing - but, Kitty, you're mad about it!"

"No, dear, I was mad to be mad about it: but what good

does it do to anybody, just going up and down and round and round with a man you may never see again. Surely we were not sent into the world to do that! Ask the vicar of the parish what he thinks, or Doctor Lanfry, who is doing such splendid work at the hospitals. I think we have to make good in life, and dancing, surely, will not help us. So I mean to give it up, and smoking and all horrid things. I'm sure you'll like me better for that, dear; you know how jealous my dancing used to make you, but now you'll never have any cause to be jealous again."

Ambrose did not know what to say. This seemed to him quite the flattest lunch he had ever sat out with her, while, as for the people round about, he thought he had never seen a duller lot. Perhaps, after all, he had been a little hasty in shutting up the devil so unceremoniously, but it made him laugh to think that the fellow would get no lunch anyway and that his stock of cigars would hardly last him through the day. "And at any rate," he argued, "the rascal will do no mischief to-day."

He drove Kitty to the King's New Hospital when the stupid meal was over - she was visiting some old people there - and while he waited for her, he met Dr. Lanfry himself and had a little chat with that bene-volent old gentleman. Naturally their talk concerned the hospital and he was not a little surprised to find the worthy doctor altogether in an optimistic mood.

"Yes," he said, "we shall have no need of these costly places. Disease is disappearing rapidly from our midst. I see the day coming when men and women will go untroubled by any ailment from the cradle to the grave. In some ways, I confess the world will be poorer.

Think of all the human sympathy which human suffering awakens - the profound love of the mother for the ailing child, the sacrifice of those who wait and watch by the beds of the sick, the agony of parting leading to the eternal hope in the justice of God. All these things, the world will miss when we conquer disease, and the spirit will be the poorer for them. Indeed, I foresee the day when men will forget the existence of God just because they have no need to pray for those who suffer; the devil will have no work to do in that day; but, who knows, humanity may be worse and not better because of his idleness."

Ambrose agreed with him, though he would never have expressed such sentiments to Kitty. He found her a little sad when she came out of the ward, and it seemed that all the patients were so very much better that they cared but little for her kindly attentions, and when she tried to read to them, most of them fell asleep. So she went back to Ambrose and asked him to drive to the vicarage where she hoped to see Canon Kenny, her good pastor, and find out if he could tell her of some work of mercy to be done.

"I feel," she said, "that I must find out the sorrow in the world, I must help it."

"But suppose, my dear, that there isn't any sorrow -"

"Oh, then the world would not be worth living in, I should go out to the islands of the Pacific and become a missionary. Do you know, Ambrose dear, I've often thought of putting on boys' clothes and going to live in the wilderness. A boy seems so much more active than a girl, and what does it matter since sex no longer counts?"

He looked at her aghast.

"Sex no longer counts!"

"No," she said in the simplest way, "people will become too spiritual for that. You will have to love me as though I were your sister, Ambrose -"

Ambrose gulped down a "d - n" and was quite relieved to find himself presently in the study of the venerable canon, who was just leaving England for a Continental holiday. He said that he was not tired, but really there was very little work to do - and he added, with a laugh: "It would almost appear, my children, as though some one had locked up the devil and there was no more work left for us parsons."

"But that surely would be a great, good thing," exclaimed Ambrose, astonished.

"In a way, yes," the canon rejoined, "but consider, all life depends upon that impulse which comes of strife - strife of the body, strife of the soul. I worship God believing He has called upon me to take my share in fighting the evil which is in the world. Remove that evil, and what is my inspiration? Beyond the grave, yes, there may be that sphere of holiness to which the human condition contributes nothing - a sphere in which all happiness, all goodness centres about the presence of the Eternal - but here we know that man must strive or perish, must fight or be conquered - must school his immortal soul in the fire of temptation and of suffering. So, I say, it may even be a bad day for the world could the devil be chained in bonds which even he could not burst. It might even be the loss of the knowledge of the God by whom evil is permitted to live that good may come."

This and much more he said, always in the tone of one who bared his head to destiny and had a faith unconquerable. When they left him, Kitty appeared to have made up her mind, and she spoke so earnestly that even her lover could not argue with her.

"Ambrose, dear," she said, "I must see you no more, I shall devote my life to good works. To-night I shall enter the Convent of the Little Sisters at Kensington. It is a long, long good-bye, my dearest."

He did not answer her, but calling a taxi, he ordered the man to drive to Throgmorton Street like the deuce.

III

He had told James and John to go home, but to his annoyance he found them still in the office and busy as though nothing extraordinary had happened. Brushing by them, he dashed into the inner room and turned the key in the lock of his safe.

"Come out!" he cried, but nobody answered him.

It was odd, but when he looked inside that massive room of steel, nobody was to be discerned there. At the same instant, however, he heard the Count's voice immediately behind him, and turning he discovered the man at his elbow.

"Well?" asked the fellow.

So there he stood, exactly in the same attitude as Ambrose had left him when he crossed the room to find the document. Indeed, the very same cigarette was held by his evil-looking fingers, and it was clear that he waited for the word which would signify acceptance of his contract.

"Good heavens," thought Ambrose, "I must have imagined it all."

He returned to his chair and tossed the paper across the table.

"I refuse to sign it," he said curtly, "you had better call on Alderman Karlbard; he's a church-warden, a justice of the peace and a philanthropist. He's your man and he's pretty sure to end in prison anyway."

"Thank you for your introduction," said the Count quietly, and, bowing, he withdrew with the same nonchalant air as he had entered. Trust the devil to know when he is beaten.

Ambrose watched him go and then calling John, he asked what time it was.

"A quarter to one, sir," said that worthy.

"Just in time to lunch with Kitty," Ambrose thought. And then jumping up as a man who comes by a joyous idea, he cried: "By Gad, what a row I mean to have with her - the darling!"

EMPTY ARMS

By ROLAND PERTWEE

(From *The Ladies' Home Journal*) 1922

There was a maroon wall paper in the dining-room, abundantly decorated with sweeping curves unlike any known kind of vegetation. There were amber silk sashes to the Nottingham lace curtains at the huge bow window and an amber winding sheet was wrapped about the terra cotta pot in which a tired aspidistra bore forth a yearly leaf. Upon the Brussels carpet was a massive mahogany dining table, and facing the window a Georgian chiffonier, brass railed and surmounted by a convex mirror. The mantlepiece was draped in red serge, ball fringed. There were bronzes upon it and a marble clock, while above was an over-mantel, columned and bemirrored, upon the shelves of which reposed sorrowful examples of Doulton ware and a pair of wrought-iron candlesticks. It was a room divorced from all sense of youth and live beings, sunless, grave, unlovely; an arid room that bore to the nostrils the taint and humour of the tomb.

From somewhere near the Edgware Road came the clot-clot of a late four-wheeler and the shake and rumble of an underground train. The curtains had been discreetly drawn, the gas turned off at the metre and an

Edward J. O'Brien and John Cournos

hour had passed since the creaking of the old lady's shoes and the jingle of the plate basket ascending the stairs had died away. A dim light from the street lamp outside percolated through the blinds and faintly illuminated the frame and canvas of a large picture hanging opposite the mantlepiece.

It was a beautiful picture, a piece of perfect painting - three figures in a simple curve of rocks, lit as it were by an afterglow of sunset. In the centre was a little Madonna draped in blue and gold. Her elbows were tight to her sides and her upturned palms with their tender curving fingers were empty. It seemed almost as though they cradled some one who was not there. Her mouth was pulled down at the corners, as is a child's at the edge of tears, and in her eyes was a questing and bewildered look. To her right, leaning upon a slender staff, was the figure of St. John the Baptist, and upon his face also perplexity was written. A trick brushwork had given to his eyes a changing direction whereby at a certain angle you would say he was looking at the Madonna, and again that he was following the direction of her gaze out into unknown places. His lips were shaped to the utterance of such a word as "why" or "where." It seemed as though the two were in a partnership of sorrow or of search.

The third figure was of Saint Anne, standing a little behind and looking upward. A strange composition, oddly incomplete, giving an impression of sadness, of unrest and of loss irredeemable.

A clock was chiming the parts of an hour when the little Madonna stepped from the frame and tiptoed across the room. To her own reflection in the mirror opposite she shook her head in a sorrowful negative

She peeped into a cupboard and behind the draperies of the mantlepiece, but there was nothing there. She paused before an engraving of Raphael's Holy Family, murmured "Happy Lady" and passed on.

On a small davenport table next to one of the two inexorable armchairs she found the old lady's work-basket. That was a great piece of good fortune, since nightly it was locked away with the tea, the stamps and other temptations that might persuade a soul to steal should opportunity allow.

In the many years of her dwelling in the house, but three times only had she found it unguarded. There are glorious possibilities in a workbasket. Once she had found wool there, not carded, but a hank of it, soft, white and most delicate to touch. To handle it had given her the queerest sensation. She had shut her eyes, and it had seemed to weave itself into the daintiest garments - very small, you understand, and with sleeves no longer than a middle finger. But it was a silly imagining, for not many days afterward, looking down from the canvas, she had seen the old lady, with her clicking ivory needles, knit the wool into an ugly pair of bed socks.

Quite a while she played in the basket that night. She liked the little pearl buttons in the pill box, and the safety pins were nice too. Kind and trustworthy pins they were to hide their points beneath smooth round shields. She felt it would be good to take some of them back in one of her empty hands and hide them in that little crevice of rock under the juniper tree.

It was the banging of a front door opposite and the sound of running footsteps that moved her to the window. She drew back the curtain and peeped out across the way. There were lights in an upstairs window and a shadow kept crossing and recrossing the blind. It was a nice shadow and wore a head-dress like her own except that it was more sticky out.

The hall, too, showed a light, and, looking up the street, she saw a maidservant, running very fast, disappear round the corner. After that there was silence for a long time. In the street no one moved; it was deserted, empty as the little Madonna's arms, and dark. A fine rain was falling, and there were no stars. The sound of distant traffic had died away. The last underground train had drilled its way through sulphurous tunnels to the sheds where engines sleep.

She could not tell what kept her waiting at the window; perhaps it was the moving shadow on the blind, perhaps a prescience, a sense of happenings near at hand, wonderful yet frightening. A thousand other times she had looked across the street in the dead of night, only to shake her head and steal back sorrowfully to her canvas. But to-night it was different; there was a feeling of promise, as though the question that she ever asked with her eyes might at last be given an answer.

The front door opened a second time, and a man came out and, though he was quite young, he looked older than the world. He was shaking and very white; his hair was disordered and straggled across his brow. He wore no collar, but held the lapels of his coat across his throat with trembling fingers. Fearfully he looked up the street where the maid had gone, then stamped his foot on the paving stones and with his free hand rubbed his forehead and beat it with his knuckles.

"Oh, will he never come!" she heard him cry, and the words echoed through her as though they had been her own. If it was a prayer he had uttered it was swiftly answered; for at the moment the maid and a bearded man came round the corner at a fast walk. The bearded man had a kind face and broad shoulders.

She did not hear what passed between them; but the bearded man seemed confident and comfortable and compelling, and presently he and the maid went into the house, while the other man leaned against the railings and stared out before him at a tiny star which had appeared in a crack between the driven clouds. Lonely and afraid he looked, and strangely like herself. The misery of him drew her irresistibly. Always before, she had shunned the people of every day, having no understanding of their pleasures or sorrows, seeing little meaning in their lives or deaths. But here was a mortal who was different, who was magnetic, and, almost without realising, she passed out of the house, crossed the road and stood before him, the corners of her cloak draped across her arms.

He did not seem aware of her at once, and even when she spoke to him in Italian of the Renaissance he did not hear. So she spoke again and this time in English: "What is it?"

He started, rubbed his eyes, blinked at her and answered: "Hullo, who are you?"

"What is it?" she repeated. "Have you lost something?"

"Don't - don't!" he pleaded. "Don't even suggest such a thing, little lady."

"I won't. I only thought - and you looked so sad."

"Be all right directly. It's the waiting. Kind of you to stop and speak to me." His eyes strayed over the gold and blue of her cloak. "Been to a theatre?" he asked.

She shook her head and looked up at him with a child's perplexity.

"A play?" he amended.

"I've no one to play with," she answered simply. "See!" And she held out her empty arms.

"What's wrong then?"

"I don't know." She seemed to dwell on the last word. "I only thought - perhaps you could tell me."

"Tell you what?"

"Help me to find it perhaps. It seemed as if you were looking, too; that's why I came."

"Looking?" he repeated. "I'm waiting; that's all."

"Me too. But it's such a long time, and I get no nearer."

"Nearer to what?"

"Finding."

"Something you lost?"

"I think so. Must be. I'll go back now."

He put out a hand to stop her. "Listen," he said. "It'll be hours before I shall know. I'm frightened to spend them alone. Be a friend, little lady, and bear me company. 'Tisn't fair to ask, but if you could stay a little."

"I'll stay," she said.

"And will you talk to me?"

"Yes."

"Tell me a story then - just as if I were a kid, a child. A man isn't much more these times."

At the word "child" her arms went out to him, but dropped to her sides again as he said "a man."

"Come under the porch, where the rain won't spoil your pretty silk. That's better. Now tell away."

They sat side by side, and she began to talk. He must have been listening for other sounds, or surely he would have been bewildered at the very beginning of what she told.

"It's hard to remember when one was alive, but I used to be - yes, hundreds of years ago. I lived - can't remember very well; there was a high wall all around, and a tower and a bell that rang for prayers - and long, long passages where we walked up and down to tell our beads. Outside were mountains with snow caps like the heads of the sisters, and it was cold as snow within, cold and pure as snow. I was sixteen years old and very unhappy. We did not know how to smile; that I learnt later and have forgotten since. There was the skull of a dead man upon the table where we sat to eat, that we might never forget to what favour we must come. There were no pretty rooms in that house."

"What would you call a pretty room?" he asked, for the last sentence was the first of which he was aware.

"I don't know," she answered. "I think a room with little beds, and wooden bars across the window, and a high fender would be a pretty room."

"We have been busy making such a room as that," he said. "There's a wall paper with pigs and chickens and huntsmen on it. But go on."

"There were iron bars to the window of my cell. He was very strong and tore them out with his hands as he stood up on the saddle of his horse. We rode into Florence as dawn broke, and the sun was an angry red; while we rode his arm was around me and my head upon his shoulder. He spoke in my ear and his voice trembled for love of me. We had thrown away the raiment of the sisterhood to which I had belonged, and as I lay across the saddle I was wrapped in a cloak as crimson as the sun."

"Been reading Tennyson, little lady?" asked the man.

She did not understand, and went on: "It was a palace to which he brought me, bright with gold, mosaic and fine hangings that dazzled my eyes after the grey they had been used to look upon. There were many servants and richly clad friends, who frightened me with their laughter and the boldness of their looks. On his shoulder he bore me into the great dining hall, where they sat awaiting us, and one and all they rose to their feet, leaping upon stools and tables with uplifted goblets and shouting toasts.

"The noise was greater than any I had heard before and set my heart a-beating like the clapper of the convent bell. But one only stayed in his chair, and his looks were heavy with anger. At him the rest pointed fingers and called on him derisively to pay the wager and be glad. Whereat he tugged from his belt a bag of gold which he flung at us as though with the will to injure. But he who held me caught the bag in his free hand, broke the sealed cord at the neck of it and scattered the coins in a golden rain among the servants.

"After this, he set me by his side at the board, gave me drink from a brimming goblet and quails cooked in honey from wild bees and silver dishes of nectarines and passion fruit. And presently by twos and threes the guests departed, singing and reeling as they went, and he and I were left alone. Alone," she repeated shuddering.

"Did you hear anything?" said the young man, raising his head. "A cry, a little cry? No? I can hear footsteps moving up and down. Doctors' boots always creak. There! Listen! It was nothing. What were you saying?"

"Twice in the months that followed I tried to run away, to return to the convent; but the servants whom I had counted my friends deceived me, and I was brought back to a beating, brought back strapped to his stirrup iron as I might have been a Nubian slave. Long since he had ceased loving me; that lasted such a little while. He called me Madonna, as though it were a term of shame, and cursed me for coldness and my nunnery ways. He was only happy when he read in my face the fear I held him in. And I was always afraid!"

"Afraid!" echoed the man. "Until to-night I was never afraid."

"And then my baby came, and I was not afraid any more, but contented all through. I carried him always in my arms by day and night. So pink and little and with a smile that warmed like sunshine." She paused and added plaintively: "It's hard to remember when one was alive. My hands, my arms have forgotten the feel of him."

"I wish," said the man, "I'd had a second opinion. It might have frightened her though. Oh, heaven, how much longer! Don't mind me, little lady. You're helping no end. You were speaking of baby. Yes!"

"He killed my baby," said the little Madonna, "because he had killed my fear of him. Then being done with me, he threw me out in the streets alone. I thought to end it that night, because my arms were empty and nothing could be good again. But I could not believe the baby was indeed gone; I thought if I searched I would find him in the course of time. Therefore I searched the city from end to end and spoke with mothers and peeped into nurseries and knocked at many doors. And one day a door was opened by a man with great eyes and bronze hair swept back from his brow - a good man. He wore a loose smock over his doublet, smeared with many colours, and in his left hand he held a palette and brushes. When he saw me he fell back a pace and his mouth opened. 'Mother of mercy!' he breathed. 'A real Madonna at last!' His name was Andrea del Sarto, and he was a painter."

"I am a painter, too," said the young man, forgetting his absorption at the mention of a great name.

"He brought me into his room, which was bright with windows and a fire. He bade me tell my story, and while I spoke never once did his eyes desert me. When I had ended he rose and walked up and down. Then he took from a chest a cloak of blue and gold and draped it round me. 'Stand upon that throne, Madonna,' said he, 'and I will put an infant in your arms that shall live down all the ages.' And he painted me. So with the child at my breast, I myself had passed into the picture and found contentment there.

"When it was finished the great ones of many cities came to look upon it, and the story of how I came to be painted went from mouth to mouth. Among those who were there was he who had taken me from the nunnery, and, seeing me in perfect happiness, a fury was born in him.

"I was hidden behind a hanging and watched the black anger rising up and knotting his brow into ugly lines. He bought the canvas, and his servants carried it away. But since the child was in my arms for all time it mattered little to me.

"Then one night two men came to my lodging and without question took me across the city and led me into the palace where I had lived with him. And he came forward to meet me in the great hall. There was a mocking smile on his lips and he pointed to a wall upon which a curtain was hanging.

"'I took away that child,' he said, 'because you valued it higher than the love of man. Look now.' At a gesture a servant threw back the hanging and revealed the picture. The babe was gone and my arms crooked to cradle him were empty with the palms upturned.

"I died then - to the sound of his laughter I died, and, looking down from the canvas, I watched them carry me away. And long into the night the man who twice had robbed me of my child sat at the long table staring out before him, drinking great draughts and sometimes beating the boards with his bare fists. As dawn broke he clapped his hands and a servant entered. He pointed at me with a shaking hand. 'Take it away,' he cried. 'To a cellar, and let masons brick up the door.' He was weeping as they carried me down to the dark beneath the house."

"What a strange being you are!" said the young man. "You speak as though these were real memories. What happened to the picture then?"

"I lay in the dark for so long - hundreds of years, I think - and there was nowhere I might look. Afterward I was found and packed in a box and presently put upon the wall in the sad room, where everything is so old that I shall not find him there. This is the furthest I have dared to look. Help me find him, please! Won't you help me find him?"

"Why, little lady," he answered soothingly, "how shall I help? That's a woman's burden that heaven isn't merciful enough to let a man share." He stopped abruptly and threw up his head. "Did you hear that - there?"

Through the still, early morning air came a faint, reedy cry.

The young man was upon his feet, fiercely fitting a key into the lock.

The little Madonna had risen, too, and her eyes were luminous, like glowworms in the dark.

"He's calling me," she cried. "He's calling."

"Mine," said the young man.

She turned to follow, but the door closed between them.

*   *   *   *   *

To the firm of Messrs. Ridgewell, Ridgewell, Hitchcock and Plum was given the task of disposing of the furniture and effects of the late Sabina Prestwich, spinster, of 22a Cambridge Avenue, Hyde Park, W.

As Mr. Ridgewell, junior, remarked to Mr. Plum while engaged in compiling the sale list and supplying appropriate encomiums to describe an upright grand by Rubenthal, Berlin: "Victorian muck! Lucky if we clean up two-fifty on the lot."

Mr. Plum was disposed to agree. "Though I must say," he added, "it wouldn't surprise me if that picture was worth a bit. Half a mind to let old Kineagie have a squint at it."

"Please yourself," responded Mr. Ridgewell, junior, "but to my mind it's ten guineas for nix."

It was the chance discovery of an old document amongst a litter of receipts and papers that persuaded them to engage an expert opinion. The document stated that the picture had been discovered bricked up in a Florentine cellar some fifty years before and had been successfully smuggled out of Italy. But the man who found it died, and it passed with a few other unvalued possessions to Sabina Prestwich, now deceased.

The result of Eden Kineagie's visit to the house in Cambridge Avenue was the immediate transference of the canvas to Sotheby's Sale Rooms, a concerted rush on the part of every European and American connoisseur, a threatening letter from the Italian Foreign Office, some extravagant bidding and the ultimate purchase of the picture for the nation, after a heated debate on the part of twenty-two Royal Academicians and five painters of the new school, who would have accepted death rather than the letters; R.A., after their names. Extensive correspondence appeared in the leading papers; persons wrote expressing the opinion that the picture had never been painted by Del Sarto, that it was the finest example of his work, that the price paid was a further example of government waste, and that the money would have been better employed repairing the main road between Croydon Town Hall and Sydenham High Street, the condition of which constituted a menace to motor-cyclists.

For nearly ten days scarcely a single publication appeared that failed to reproduce a comment or criticism upon the subject; but, strangely enough, no single leader, writer or casual contributor remarked upon the oddness of the composition or the absence of the Infant from the Madonna's arms. In the course of time - that is to say, on the eleventh day - the matter passed from the public mind, a circumstance explainable perhaps by the decent interment of the canvas in the National Gallery, where it affected no one save those mysterious folk who look at pictures for their pleasure and the umbrellaless refugee who is driven to take shelter from the fierceness of storms.

The little Madonna was placed upon a south wall, whence she could look out upon a brave company. And sometimes people would pause to gaze at her and then shake their heads. And once a girl said, "How sad she looks! I wonder why." And once a little old lady with industrious hands set up an easel before her and squeezed little twists of colour upon a palette, then thought a long time and pursed her lips, and puzzled her brow and finally murmured, "I could never copy it. It's so - so changing." And she, too, went away.

The little Madonna did not dare to step from her frame at night, for other mothers were at hand cradling their babes and the sound of her footfalls might have wakened them. But it was hard to stay still and alone in that happy nursery. She could see through an archway to the right a picture Rubens had painted, and it was all aglow with babies like roses clustered at a porch - fat, dimpled babies who rolled and laughed in aërial garlands. It would have been nice to pick one and carry it back with her. Yet perhaps they were not really mothers' children, but sprites and joys that had not learned the way to nestle. Had it been otherwise surely the very call of her spirit must have brought one leaping to her arms.

And then one day came a man and girl, who stopped before her. The girl was half child, half woman, and the man grey and bearded, but with brave blue eyes. It was seventeen years since the night she had stolen across the way and talked with this man in his hour of

Edward J. O'Brien and John Cournos

terror, but time did not cloud the little Madonna's memory with the dust of forgetfulness.

"That's the new Del Sarto," said the girl, who was reading from a small blue book. "See, daddy?"

Then the man turned and looked at her, fell back a step, came forward again, passed a hand across his mouth and gasped. "What is it?" asked the girl.

He did not answer at once, then: "The night you were born -" he said. "I'm certain.... It's - it's Del Sarto too! And the poor empty arms.
Just how she looked, and I closed the door on her."

"Daddy, what are you saying?" There was a frightened tone in the girl's voice.

"It's all right, dear, don't mind me. I must find the keeper of the gallery. Poor little lady! Run back home, tell your mother I may be late."

"But, daddy -"

"There are more things in heaven and earth," he began, but did not finish. It seemed as though the Madonna's eyes were pleading to him, and it seemed as if he could still hear her say, "Help me find him, please!"

He told his story to the Committee of the National Gallery and, to do them credit, it was received with the utmost courtesy.

They did not require him to leave them while their decision was made. This was arrived at by a mere exchange of glances, a nod answered by a tilt of the head, a wave of the hand, a kindly smile; and the thing was done.

As the chairman remarked: "We must not forget that this gentleman was living at the time opposite to the house in which the picture was hanging, and it is possible that a light had been left burning in the room that contained it.

"Those of us who are fathers - and I regret for my own part that I cannot claim the distinction - will bear me out that the condition of a man's mind during the painful period of waiting for news as to his wife's progress is apt to depart from the normal and make room for imaginings that in saner moments he must dismiss as absurd. There has been a great deal of discussion and not a little criticism on the part of the public as to the committee's wisdom in purchasing this picture, and I am confident you will all agree with me that we could be responsible for no greater folly than to work upon the canvas with various removers on the bare hypothesis, unsupported by surface suggestion, that the Madonna's arms actually contain a child painted in the first intention. For my own part, I am well assured that at no period of its being has the picture been tampered with, and it is a matter of no small surprise to me, sir, that an artist of your undoubted quality and achievement should hold a contrary opinion. We are, greatly obliged for the courtesy of your visit and trust that you will feel after this liberal discussion that your conscience is free from further responsibility in the matter. Good-day."

That was the end of the interview. Once again the door was slammed in the little Madonna's face.

That night the man told his wife all about it. "So you see," he concluded, "there is nothing more I can do."

But she lay awake and puzzled and yearned long after he had fallen asleep. And once she rose and peeped into the room that used to be the nursery. It was a changed room now, for the child had grown up, and where once pigs and chickens and huntsmen had jostled in happy, farmyard disorder upon the walls, now there were likenesses of Owen Nares and Henry Ainley, obligingly autographed.

But for her the spirit prevailed, the kindly bars still ribbed the windows and the sense of sleeping children still haunted the air.

And she it was who told the man what he must do; and although it scared him a great deal he agreed, for in the end all good husbands obey their wives.

It felt very eerie to be alone in the National Gallery in the dead of the night with a tiny electric lamp in one's buttonhole and a sponge of alcohol and turpentine in one's hand. While he worked the little Madonna's eyes rested upon him and it could hardly have been mere fancy that made him believe they were full of gratitude and trust. At the end of an hour the outline of a child, faint and misty, appeared in her arms, its head, circled by a tiny white halo, snuggling against the curve of her little breast.

Then the man stepped back and gave a shout of joy and, remembering the words the painter had used, he cried out, "I will put an infant in your arms that shall live down all the ages."

He had thought perhaps there would come an answering gladness from the Madonna herself and looked into her face to find it. And truly enough it was there. Her eyes, which for centuries had looked questingly forth from the canvas, now drooped and rested upon the baby. Her mouth, so sadly downturned at the corners, had sweetened to a smile of perfect and serene content.

But the men will not believe he washed away the sadness of her looks with alcohol and turpentine. "I did not touch the head. I am certain I did not," he repeated.

"Then how can you explain -"

"Oh, heaven!" he answered. "Put a child in any woman's arms."

LENA WRACE

By MAY SINCLAIR

(From *The Dial*) 1921, 1922

She arranged herself there, on that divan, and I knew she'd come to tell me all about it. It was wonderful, how, at forty-seven, she could still give that effect of triumph and excess, of something rich and ruinous and beautiful spread out on the brocades. The attitude showed me that her affair with Norman Hippisley was prospering; otherwise she couldn't have afforded the extravagance of it.

"I know what you want," I said. "You want me to congratulate you."

"Yes. I do."

"I congratulate you on your courage."

"Oh, you don't like him," she said placably.

"No, I don't like him at all."

"He likes you," she said. "He thinks no end of your painting."

"I'm not denying he's a judge of painting. I'm not even denying he can paint a little himself."

"Better than you, Roly."

"If you allow for the singular, obscene ugliness of his imagination, yes."

"It's beautiful enough when he gets it into paint," she said. "He makes beauty. His own beauty."

"Oh, very much his own."

"Well, *you* just go on imitating other people's - God's or somebody's."

She continued with her air of perfect reasonableness. "I know he isn't good-looking. Not half so good-looking as you are. But I like him. I like his slender little body and his clever, faded face. There's a quality about him, a distinction. And look at his eyes. *Your* mind doesn't come rushing and blazing out of your eyes, my dear."

"No. No. I'm afraid it doesn't rush. And for all the blaze -"

"Well, that's what I'm in love with, the rush, Roly, and the blaze. And I'm in love, *for the first time*" (she underlined it) "with a man."

"Come," I said, "come."

"Oh, *I* know. I know you're thinking of Lawson Young and Dickey Harper."

I was.

"Well, but they don't count. I wasn't in love with Lawson. It was his career. If he hadn't been a Cabinet Minister; if he hadn't been so desperately gone on me; if he hadn't said it all depended on me -"

"Yes," I said. "I can see how it would go to your head."

"It didn't. It went to my heart." She was quite serious and solemn. "I held him in my hands, Roly. And he held England. I couldn't let him drop, could I? I had to think of England."

It was wonderful - Lena Wrace thinking that she thought of England.

I said "Of course. But for your political foresight and your virtuous action we should never have had Tariff Reform."

"We should never have had anything," she said. "And look at him now. Lock how he's crumpled up since he left me. It's pitiful."

"It is. I'm afraid Mrs. Withers doesn't care about Tariff Reform."

"Poor thing. No. Don't imagine I'm jealous of her, Roly. She hasn't got him. I mean she hasn't got what I had."

"All the same he left you. And you weren't ecstatically happy with him the last year or two."

"I daresay I'd have done better to have married you, if that's what you mean."

It wasn't what I meant. But she'd always entertained the illusion that she could marry me any minute if she wanted to; and I hadn't the heart to take it from her since it seemed to console her for the way, the really very infamous way, he had left her.

So I said, "Much better."

"It would have been so nice, so safe," she said. "But I never played for safety." Then she made one of her quick turns.

"Frances Archdale ought to marry you. Why doesn't she?"

"How should I know? Frances's reasons would be exquisite. I suppose I didn't appeal to her sense of fitness."

"Sense of fiddlesticks. She just hasn't got any temperament, that girl."

"Any temperament for me, you mean."

"I mean pure cussedness," said Lena.

"Perhaps. But, you see, if I were unfortunate enough she probably *would* marry me. If I lost my eyesight or a leg or an arm, if I couldn't sell any more pictures -"

"If you can understand Frances, you can understand me. That's how I felt about Dickey. I wasn't in love with him. I was sorry for him. I knew he'd go to pieces if I wasn't there to keep him together. Perhaps it's the maternal instinct."

"Perhaps," I said. Lena's reasons for her behaviour amused me; they were never exquisite, like Frances's, but she was anxious that you should think they were.

"So you see," she said, "they don't count, and Norry really *is* the first."

I reflected that he would be also, probably, the last. She had, no doubt, to make the most of him. But it was preposterous that she should waste so much good passion; preposterous that she should imagine for one moment she could keep the fellow. I had to warn her.

"Of course, if you care to take the risk of him - " I said. "He won't stick to you, Lena."

"Why shouldn't he?"

I couldn't tell her. I couldn't say, "Because you're thirteen ears older than he is." That would have been cruel. And it would have been absurd, too, when she could so easily look not a year older than his desiccated thirty-four.

It only took a little success like this, her actual triumph in securing him.

So I said, "Because it isn't in him. He's a bounder and a rotter." Which was true.

"Not a bounder, Roly dear. His father's Sir Gilbert Hippisley. Hippisleys of Leicestershire."

"A moral bounder, Lena. A slimy eel. Slips and wriggles out of things. You'll never hold him. You're not his first affair, you know."

"I don't care," she said, "as long as I'm his last."

I could only stand and stare at that; her monstrous assumption of his fidelity. Why, he couldn't even be faithful to one art. He wrote as well as he painted, and he acted as well as he wrote, and he was never really happy with a talent till he had debauched it.

"The others," she said, "don't bother me a bit. He's slipped and wriggled out of their clutches, if you like.... Yet there was something about all of them. Distinguished. That's it. He's so awfully fine and fastidious about the women he takes up with. It flatters you, makes you feel so sure of yourself. You know he wouldn't take up with *you* if you weren't fine and fastidious, too - one of his great ladies.... You think I'm a snob, Roly?"

"I think you don't mind coming *after* Lady Willersey."

"Well," she said, "if you *have* to come after some-body -"

"True." I asked her if she was giving me her reasons.

"Yes, if you want them. *I* don't. I'm content to love out of all reason."

And she did. She loved extravagantly, unintelligibly, out of all reason; yet irrefutably. To the end. There's a sort of reason in that, isn't there? She had the sad logic of her passions.

She got up and gathered herself together in her sombre, violent beauty and in its glittering sheath, her red fox skins, all her savage splendour, leaving a scent of crushed orris root in the warmth of her lair.

Well, she managed to hold him, tight, for a year, fairly
intact. I can't for the life of me imagine how she could
have cared for the fellow, with his face all dried and
frayed with make-up. There was something lithe and
sinuous about him that may, of course, have appealed
to her. And I can understand his infatuation. He was
decadent, exhausted; and there would be moments
when he found her primitive violence stimulating,
before it wore him out.

They kept up the *ménage* for two astounding years.

Well, not so very astounding, if you come to think of
it. There was Lena's money, left her by old
Weinberger, her maternal uncle. You've got to reckon
with Lena's money. Not that she, poor soul, ever
reckoned with it; she was absolutely free from that
taint, and she couldn't conceive other people recko-
ning. Only, instinctively, she knew. She knew how to
hold Hippisley. She knew there were things he couldn't
resist, things like wines and motor cars he could be
faithful to. From the very beginning she built for
permanence, for eternity. She took a house in Avenue
Road with a studio for Hippisley in the garden; she
bought a motor car and engaged an inestimable cook.
Lena's dinners, in those years, were exquisite affairs,
and she took care to ask the right people, people who
would be useful to Hippisley, dealers whom old
Weinberger had known, and journalists and editors and
publishers. And all his friends and her own; even
friends' friends. Her hospitality was boundless and
eccentric, and Hippisley liked that sort of thing. He
thrived in a liberal air, an air of gorgeous spending,
though he sported a supercilious smile at the *fioritura*,

the luscious excess of it. He had never had too much, poor devil, of his own. I've seen the little fellow swaggering about at her parties, with his sharp, frayed face, looking fine and fastidious, safeguarding himself with twinklings and gestures that gave the dear woman away. I've seen him, in goggles and a magnificent fur-lined coat, shouting to her chauffeur, giving counter orders to her own, while she sat snuggling up in the corner of the car, smiling at his mastery.

It went on till poor Lena was forty-nine. Then, as she said, she began to "shake in her shoes." I told her it didn't matter so long as she didn't let him see her shaking. That depressed her, because she knew she couldn't hide it; there was nothing secret in her nature; she had always let "them" see. And they were bothering her - "the others" - more than "a bit." She was jealous of every one of them, of any woman he said more than five words to. Jealous of the models, first of all, before she found out that they didn't matter; he was so used to them. She would stick there, in his studio, while they sat, until one day he got furious and turned her out of it. But she'd seen enough to set her mind at rest. He was fine and fastidious, and the models were all "common."

"And their figures, Roly, you should have seen them when they were undressed. Of course, you *have* seen them. Well, there isn't - is there?"

And there wasn't. Hippisley had grown out of models just as he had grown out of cheap Burgundy. And he'd left the stage, because he was tired of it, so there was, mercifully, no danger from that quarter. What she dreaded was the moment when he'd "take" to writing again, for then he'd have to have a secretary. Also she was jealous of his writing because it absorbed more of his attention than his painting, and exhausted him more, left her less of him

And that year, their third year, he flung up his painting and was, as she expressed it, "at it" again. Worse than ever. And he wanted a secretary.

She took care to find him one. One who wouldn't be dangerous. "You should just see her, Roly." She brought her in to tea one day for me to look at and say whether she would "do."

I wasn't sure - what can you be sure of? - but I could see why Lena thought she would. She was a little unhealthy thing, dark and sallow and sulky, with thin lips that showed a lack of temperament, and she had a stiffness and preciseness, like a Board School teacher - just that touch of "commonness" which Lena relied on to put him off. She wore a shabby brown skirt and a yellowish blouse. Her name was Ethel Reeves.

Lena had secured safety, she said, in the house. But what was the good of that, when outside it he was going about everywhere with Sybil Fermor? She came and told me all about it, with a sort of hope that I'd say something either consoling or revealing, something that she could go on.

"*You* know him, Roly," she said.

I reminded her that she hadn't always given me that credit.

"*I* know how he spends his time," she said. "How do you know?"

"Well, for one thing, Ethel tells me."

"How does she know?"

"She - she posts the letters."

"Does she read them?"

"She needn't. He's too transparent."

"Lena, do you use her to spy on him?" I said.

"Well," she retorted, "if he uses her -"

I asked her if it hadn't struck her that Sybil Fermor might be using him?

"Do you mean - as a *paravent*? Or," she revised it, "a parachute?"

"For Bertie Granville," I elucidated. "A parachute, by all means."

She considered it. "It won't work," she said. "If it's her reputation she's thinking of, wouldn't Norry be worse?"

I said that was the beauty of him, if Letty Granville's attention was to be diverted.

"Oh, Roly," she said, "do you really think it's that?" I said I did, and she powdered her nose and said I was a dear and I'd bucked her up no end, and went away quite happy.

Letty Granville's divorce suit proved to her that I was right.

The next time I saw her she told me she'd been mistaken about Sybil Fermor. It was Lady Hermione Nevin. Norry had been using Sybil as a "*paravent*" for *her*. I said she was wrong again. Didn't she know that Hermione was engaged to Billy Craven? They were head over ears in love with each other. I asked her what on earth had made her think of her? And she said Lady Hermione had paid him thirty guineas for a picture. That looked, she said, as if she was pretty far gone on him. (She tended to disparage Hippisley's talents. Jealousy again.)

I said it looked as if he had the iciest reasons for cultivating Lady Hermione. And again she told me I was a dear. "You don't know, Roly, what a comfort you are to me."

Then Barbara Vining turned up out of nowhere, and from the first minute Lena gave herself up for lost.

"I'm done for," she said. "I'd fight her if it was any good fighting. But what chance have I? At forty-nine against nineteen, and that face?"

The face was adorable if you adore a child's face on a woman's body. Small and pink; a soft, innocent forehead; fawn skin hair, a fawn's nose, a fawn's mouth, a fawn's eyes. You saw her at Lena's garden parties, staring at Hippisley over the rim of her plate while she browsed on Lena's cakes and ices, or bounding about Lena's tennis court with the sash ribbons flying from her little butt end.

Oh, yes; she had her there. As much as he wanted. And there would be Ethel Reeves, in a new blouse, looking on from a back seat, subtle and sullen, or handing round cups and plates without speaking to anybody, like a servant. I used to think she spied on them for Lena. They were always mouthing about the garden together or sitting secretly in corners; Lena even had her to stay with them, let him take her for long drives in her car. She knew when she was beaten.

I said, "Why do you let him do it, Lena? Why don't you turn them both neck and crop out of the house?" "Because I want him in it. I want him at any cost. And I want him to have what he wants, too, even if it's Barbara. I want him to be happy.... I'm making a virtue of necessity. It can be done, Roly, if you give up beautifully."

I put it to her it wasn't giving up beautifully to fret herself into an unbecoming illness, to carry her disaster on her face. She would come to me looking more ruined than ruinous, haggard and ashy, her eyes all shrunk and hot with crying, and stand before the glass, looking at herself and dabbing on powder in an utter abandonment to misery.

"I know," she moaned. "As if losing him wasn't enough I must go and lose my looks. I know crying's simply suicidal at my age, yet I keep on at it. I'm doing for myself. I'm digging my own grave, Roly. A little deeper every day."

Then she said suddenly, "Do you know, you're the only man in London I could come to looking like this."

I said, "Isn't that a bit unkind of you? It sounds as though you thought I didn't matter."

She broke down on that. "Can't you see it's because I

know I don't any more? Nobody cares whether my nose is red or not. But you're not a brute. You don't let me feel I don't matter. I know I never did matter to you, Roly, but the effect's soothing, all the same.... Ethel says if she were me she wouldn't stand it. To have it going on under my nose. Ethel is so high-minded. I suppose it's easy to be high-minded if you've always looked like that. And if you've never *had* anybody. She doesn't know what it is. I tell you, I'd rather have Norry there with Barbara than not have him at all."

I thought and said that would just about suit Hippisley's book. He'd rather be there than anywhere else, since he had to be somewhere. To be sure she irritated him with her perpetual clinging, and wore him out. I've seen him wince at the sound of her voice in the room. He'd say things to her; not often, but just enough to see how far he could go. He was afraid of going too far. He wasn't prepared to give up the comfort of Lena's house, the opulence and peace. There wasn't one of Lena's wines he could have turned his back on. After all, when she worried him he could keep himself locked up in the studio away from her.

There was Ethel Reeves; but Lena didn't worry about his being locked up with *her*. She was very kind to Hippisley's secretary. Since she wasn't dangerous, she liked to see her there, well housed, eating rich food, and getting stronger and stronger every day.

I must say my heart bled for Lena when I thought of young Barbara. It was still bleeding when one afternoon she walked in with her old triumphant look; she wore her hat with an *air crâne*, and the powder on her face was even and intact, like the first pure fall of snow. She looked ten years younger and I judged that Hippisley's affair with Barbara was at an end.

Well - it had never had a beginning; nor the ghost of a beginning. It had never happened at all. She had come to tell me that: that there was nothing in it; nothing but her jealousy; the miserable, damnable jealousy that made her think things. She said it would be a lesson to her to trust him in the future not to go falling in love. For, she argued, if he hadn't done it this time with Barbara, he'd never do it.

I asked her how she knew he hadn't, this time, when appearances all pointed that way? And she said that Barbara had come and told her. Somebody, it seemed, had been telling Barbara it was known that she'd taken Hippisley from Lena, and that Lena was crying herself into a nervous break-down. And the child had gone straight to Lena and told her it was a beastly lie. She hadn't taken Hippisley. She liked ragging with him and all that, and being seen about with him at parties, because he was a celebrity and it made the other women, the women he wouldn't talk to, furious. But as for taking him, why, she wouldn't take him from anybody as a gift. She didn't want him, a scrubby old thing like that. She didn't *like* that dragged look about his mouth and the way the skin wrinkled on his eyelids. There was a sincerity about Barbara that would have blasted Hippisley if he'd known.

Besides, she wouldn't have hurt Lena for the world. She wouldn't have spoken to Norry if she'd dreamed that Lena minded. But Lena had seemed so remarkably not to mind. When she came to that part of it she cried.

Lena said that was all very well, and it didn't matter

whether Barbara was in love with Norry or not; but
how did she know Norry wasn't in love with *her*? And
Barbara replied amazingly that of course she knew.
They'd been alone together.

When I remarked that it was precisely *that*, Lena said,
No. That was nothing in itself; but it would prove one
way or another; and it seemed that when Norry found
himself alone with Barbara, he used to yawn.

After that Lena settled down to a period of felicity.
She'd come to me, excited and exulting, bringing her
poor little happiness with her like a new toy. She'd sit
there looking at it, turning it over and over, and
holding it up to me to show how beautiful it was.

She pointed out to me that I had been wrong and she
right about him, from the beginning. She knew him.
"And to think what a fool, what a damned silly fool I
was, with my jealousy. When all those years there was
never anybody but me. Do you remember Sybil
Fermor, and Lady Hermione - and Barbara? To think I
should have so clean forgotten what he was like....
Don't you think, Roly, there must be something in me,
after all, to have kept him all those years?"

I said there must indeed have been, to have inspired so
remarkable a passion. For Hippisley was making love
to her all over again. Their happy relations were
proclaimed, not only by her own engaging frankness,
but still more by the marvellous renaissance of her
beauty. She had given up her habit of jealousy as she
had given up eating sweets, because both were
murderous to her complexion. Not that Hippisley gave
her any cause. He had ceased to cultivate the society of
young and pretty ladies, and devoted himself with

almost ostentatious fidelity to Lena. Their affair had become irreproachable with time; it had the permanence of a successful marriage without the unflattering element of legal obligation. And he had kept his secretary. Lena had left off being afraid either that Ethel would leave or that Hippisley would put some dangerous woman in her place.

There was no change in Ethel, except that she looked rather more subtle and less sullen. Lena ignored her subtlety as she had ignored her sulks. She had no more use for her as a confidant and spy, and Ethel lived in a back den off Hippisley's study with her Remington, and displayed a convenient apathy in allowing herself to be ignored.

"Really," Lena would say in the unusual moments when she thought of her, "if it wasn't for the clicking, you wouldn't know she was there."

And as a secretary she maintained, up to the last, an admirable efficiency.

Up to the last.

It was Hippisley's death that ended it. You know how it happened - suddenly, of heart failure, in Paris. He'd gone there with Furnival to get material for that book they were doing together. Lena was literally "prostrated" with the shock; and Ethel Reeves had to go over to Paris to bring back his papers and his body.

It was the day after the funeral that it all came out. Lena and Ethel were sitting up together over the papers and the letters, turning out his bureau. I suppose that, in the grand immunity his death conferred on her, poor

Lena had become provokingly possessive. I can hear her saying to Ethel that there had never been anybody but her, all those years. Praising his faithfulness; holding out her dead happiness, and apologizing to Ethel for talking about it when Ethel didn't understand, never having had any.

She must have said something like that, to bring it on herself, just then, of all moments.

And I can see Ethel Reeves, sitting at his table, stolidly sorting out his papers, wishing that Lena'd go away and leave her to her work. And her sullen eyes firing out questions, asking her what she wanted, what she had to do with Norman Hippisley's papers, what she was there for, fussing about, when it was all over?

What she wanted - what she had come for - was her letters. They were locked up in his bureau in the secret drawer.

She told me what had happened then. Ethel lifted her sullen, subtle eyes and said, "You think he kept them?"

She said she knew he'd kept them. They were in that drawer.

And Ethel said, "Well then, he didn't. They aren't. He burnt them. *We* burnt them.... We could, at least, get rid of *them*!"

Then she threw it at her. She had been Hippisley's mistress for three years.

When Lena asked for proofs of the incredible assertion she had *her* letters to show.

Oh, it was her moment. She must have been looking out for it, saving up for it, all those years; gloating over her exquisite secret, her return for all the slighting and ignoring. That was what had made her poisonous, the fact that Lena hadn't reckoned with her, hadn't thought her dangerous, hadn't been afraid to leave Hippisley with her, the rich, arrogant contempt in her assumption that Ethel would "do" and her comfortable confidences. It made her amorous and malignant. It stimulated her to the attempt.

I think she must have hated Lena more vehemently than she loved Hippisley. She couldn't, *then*, have had much reliance on her power to capture; but her hatred was a perpetual suggestion.

Supposing - supposing she were to try and take him?

Then she had tried.

I daresay she hadn't much difficulty. Hippisley wasn't quite so fine and fastidious as Lena thought him. I've no doubt he liked Ethel's unwholesomeness, just as he had liked the touch of morbidity in Lena.

And the spying? That had been all part of the game; his and Ethel's. *They* played for safety, if you like. They had *had* to throw Lena off the scent. They used Sybil Fermor and Lady Hermione and Barbara Vining, one after the other, as their *paravents*. Finally they had used Lena. That was their cleverest stroke. It brought them a permanent security. For, you see, Hippisley wasn't going to give up his free quarters, his studio, the dinners and the motor car, if he could help it. Not for Ethel. And Ethel knew it. They insured her, too.

Can't you see her, letting herself go in an ecstasy of revenge, winding up with a hysterical youp? "You? You thought it was you? It was me - *me* - ME.... You thought what we meant you to think."

Lena still comes and talks to me. To hear her you would suppose that Lawson Young and Dickey Harper never existed, that her passion for Norman Hippisley was the unique, solitary manifestation of her soul. It certainly burnt with the intensest flame. It certainly consumed her. What's left of her's all shrivelled, warped, as she writhed in her fire.

Yesterday she said to me, "Roly, I'm *glad* he's dead. Safe from her clutches."

She'll cling for a little while to this last illusion: that he had been reluctant; but I doubt if she really believes it now.

For you see, Ethel flourishes. In passion, you know, nothing succeeds like success; and her affair with Norman Hippisley advertised her, so that very soon it ranked as the first of a series of successes. She goes about dressed in stained-glass futurist muslins, and contrives provocative effects out of a tilted nose, and sulky eyes, and sallowness set off by a black velvet band on the forehead, and a black scarf of hair dragged tight from a raking backward peak.

I saw her the other night sketching a frivolous gesture -

THE DICE THROWER

By SIDNEY SOUTHGATE

(Thomas Moult)

(From *Colour*) 1922

Hunger is the most poignant when it has forced physical suffering to the highest point without impairing the mental functions. Thus it was with Silas Carringer, a young man of uncommonly high spirit, when he found himself a total stranger in a ramshackle Mexican city one rainy night in November. In his possession remained not a single article that he might have pawned for a morsel of food. And he had already stripped his body of every shred of clothing except the few garments he was compelled by an inborn sense of the fitness of things to retain. Bodily starvation, as a consequence, was added to hunger, and his misery was complete.

It chanced that an extraordinary happening awaited Silas Carringer that night in Mexico; otherwise he would either have drowned himself in the river within twenty-four hours or died of pneumonia within three days. He had been without food for seventy hours, and his mental desperation had driven him far in its race with his physical needs to consume the remaining strength of his emaciated body. Pale, weak, and tottering, he took what comfort he could find in the savoury odours which came streaming up from the basement kitchens of the restaurants in the main streets. He lacked the courage to beg or steal. For he had been reared as a gentleman, and was accordingly out of place in the world.

His teeth chattered, his eyes had dark, ugly lines under them, he shambled, stooped, and gasped. He was too desperate to curse his fate - he could only long for food. He could not reason. He could not reflect. He could not understand that there were pitying hands somewhere that might gladly have succoured him. He could think only of the hunger which consumed him, of the food that could give him warmth and comparative happiness.

Staggering along the streets, he came at last to a restaurant a little way from the main thoroughfares. Stopping before the window, he stared greedily at the steaks within, thick and juicy and lined with big, fat oysters lying on ice; at the slices of ham as large as his hat; at the roasted chickens, brown and ready for the table; and he ground his teeth, groaned, and staggered on.

A few steps onward was a drinking saloon. At one side of it was a private door with the words "Family entrance" painted thereon. And in the recess of the door (which was closed) there stood the dark figure of a man.

In spite of his own agony, Carringer saw something which appalled him in the stranger's face as the street light fell upon it; and yet at the same time he was fascinated. Perhaps it was the unspeakable anguish of those features that appealed to the starving man's sympathy, and he came to an uncertain halt at the doorway and stared rudely upon the stranger. At first the man did not notice him, seeming to look straight out into the street with a curious fixity of expression, and the death-like pallor of his face sent a chill through Carringer's limbs, chilled nigh to stone though they were already.

The stranger caught sight of him at last. "Ah," he said slowly, and with peculiar clearness, "the rain has caught you too, without overcoat or umbrella. Stand in this doorway - there is room for two."

The voice was not unkind, though it sounded strangely harsh. It was the first word that had been addressed to Carringer since hunger possessed him, and to be spoken to at all gave him cheer. So he took his place in the doorway beside the mysterious stranger, who at once relapsed into his fixed gaze at nothingness across the street.

"It may rain for a long time," he said presently, stirring himself. "I am cold, and I can feel you trembling and shivering. Let us step inside and drink."

He turned and opened the door. Carringer followed, hope slowly warming his chilled heart. The pale stranger led the way into one of the little private compartments with which the place was fitted. Before sitting down he drew from his pocket a roll of bank bills.

"You are younger than I," he said to Carringer. "Will you go to the bar and buy a bottle of absinthe, and bring also a pitcher of water and some glasses? I don't like the waiters hanging round. Here is a twenty-dollar bill."

Carringer took the money and started down the corridor towards the bar. He clutched the sudden wealth in his hand tightly. It felt warm and comfortable, sending a delicious tingling sensation through his arm. How many glorious meals did not the money represent? He could smell an imaginary steak, broiled, with fat mushrooms and melted butter in the steaming dish. Then he paused and looked stealthily backward to where he had left the stranger. Why not slip away while he had the opportunity - away from the drinking saloon with the money, to the restaurant he had passed half-an-hour ago, and buy something to eat? It was risky, but.... He hesitated, and the coward in him (there are other names than this) triumphed. He went straight to the bar as the stranger had requested, and ordered the liquor.

His step was weaker as he returned to the compartment. The stranger was sitting at the little table, staring at the opposite wall just as he had stared across the street. He wore a wide-brimmed slouch hat, pulled well over his eyes. Carringer could only vaguely take the measure of the man's face.

It was only after Carringer had set the bottle and the glasses on the table and seated himself opposite that the stranger noticed his return. "Oh, you have brought it!" he exclaimed without raising his voice. "How kind of you. Now please close the door."

Carringer was counting out the change from his pocket when the stranger interrupted him. "Keep that," he said. "You will need it, for I am going to win it back in a way that may interest you. Let us drink first, though, and I will explain."

He mixed two drinks of absinthe and water, and the two men lifted their glasses. Carringer had never tasted the liquor before, and it offended his palate at first; but no sooner had it passed down his throat than he began to feel warm again, and the most delicious thrills. He had heard of the absinthe drinkers of Paris, and he wondered no longer at the deadly fascination of the liquor - not realising that his extreme weakness and the emptiness of his stomach made him peculiarly susceptible to its effects.

"This will do us good," murmured the stranger, setting down his glass. "Presently we shall have more. Meanwhile, tell me if you know how to play with the dice."

Carringer replied that he did not.

"I was afraid that you might not," said the stranger. "All the same, please go to the bar and bring a dice-box. I would ring for it," he explained, seeing Carringer glance towards the bell, "but I don't want the waiters coming in and out."

Carringer brought the dice-box, closed the door carefully again, and the play began. It was not one of the simpler games, but had complications in which judgment as well as chance played a part. After a game or two without stakes, the stranger said:

"You have picked it up very quickly. All the same, I will show you that you don't understand it. We will throw for a dollar a game, and in that way I shall win the money that you received in change. Otherwise I would be robbing you, and I imagine that you cannot afford to lose. I mean no offence. I am a plain-spoken man, but I believe in honesty before politeness." Here his face relaxed into a most fearful grin...."I merely want a little recreation, and you are so good-natured that I am sure you will not object."

"On the contrary," replied Carringer politely, "I shall enjoy it."

"Very well; but let us drink again before we start. I believe I am growing colder."

They drank again. Carringer took the liquor now with relish, for it was something in his stomach at least, and it warmed and soothed him. Then the play commenced. He won.

The pale stranger smiled quietly and opened another game. Again Carringer won.

Then the stranger pushed back his hat, and fixed his quiet gaze upon his opponent, smiling yet. Carringer obtained a full view of the man's face for the first time, and it appalled him. He had begun to acquire a certain self-possession and ease, and the novelty of the adventure was beginning to pall before the new advances of his terrible hunger, when this revelation of the man's face threw him back into confusion.

It was the extraordinary expression of the face that alarmed him. Never upon the face of a living being had he beheld a pallor so chilling, so death-like. The features were more than pale. They were ghastly as sunless frost. Carringer's powers of observation had been sharpened by the absinthe, and after having detected the stranger in an absent-minded effort on several occasions to stroke a beard which had no existence, he reflected that some of the whiteness of the face might be due to the recent shaving and removal of a full beard. The eyes were black, and his lower lip was purple. The hands were fine, white and thin, and black veins bulged out upon them.

After gazing for a few moments at Carringer, the stranger pulled his hat down over his eyes again. "You are lucky," he said, referring to the success of his opponent. "Suppose we try another drink. There is nothing to sharpen a man's wits like absinthe, and I see that you and I are going to have a delightful game."

After the drink the play proceeded. Carringer won from the first, rarely losing a game. He became greatly excited. Colour flooded his cheeks, and he forgot his hunger. The stranger exhausted the little roll of bills which he had first produced and drew forth another, much larger in amount. There were several thousand dollars in the roll.

At Carringer's right hand were his winnings - something like two hundred dollars. The stakes were raised, and the game went on. Another drink was taken and then fortune turned to the stranger. He began to win easily. Carringer was stung by these reverses, and began to play with all the skill and judgment at his command. He took the lead again. Only once did it occur to him to wonder what he should do with the money if he continued to win. But a sense of honour decided for him that it belonged to the stranger.

As the play went on Carringer's physical suffering

returned with increased aggressiveness. Sharp pains darted through him viciously, and he writhed within him and ground his teeth in agony. Could he not order a supper with his winnings, he wondered? No; it was, of course, out of the question.

The stranger did not observe his suffering, for he was now completely absorbed in the game. He seemed puzzled and disconcerted. He played with great care, studying each throw minutely. Not a word escaped him. The two men drank occasionally, and the dice continued to rattle. And the money kept piling up at Carringer's hand.

The pale stranger suddenly began to behave strangely. At moments he would start and throw back his head, listening intently. His eyes would sharpen and flash as he did so; then they sank back into heaviness once more. Carringer saw a strange expression sweep over the man's face on several occasions - an expression of ghastly frightfulness, and the features would become fixed in a peculiar grimace.

He noticed also that his companion was steadily sinking deeper and deeper into a condition of apathy. Occasionally, none the less, he would raise his eyes to Carringer's face after some lucky throw, and he would fix them upon him with a steadiness that made the starving man grow chiller than ever he had been before.

Then came the time when the stranger produced another roll of bills, and braced himself for a bigger effort. With speech somewhat thick, but still deliberate and very quiet, he addressed his young opponent.

"You have won seventy-four thousand dollars, and that is the exact amount I have remaining. We have been playing for several hours, and I am very tired, and so are you. Let us hasten the finish. You have seventy-four thousand dollars, I have seventy-four thousand dollars. Nether of us has a cent beside. Each will now stake his all and throw a final game for it."

Without hesitation Carringer agreed. The bills made a considerable pile upon the table. Carringer threw, and his starving heart beat violently as the pale stranger took up the dice-box with exasperating deliberation. Hours seemed to pass before he threw, but at last the dice rattled on to the table, and the pale stranger had won. The winner sat staring at the dice, and then he leaned slowly back in his chair, settled himself with seeming comfort, raised his eyes to Carringer's and fixed that unearthly stare upon him.

He did not speak. His face showed not a trace of emotion or even of intelligence. He simply stared. One cannot keep one's eyes open very long without winking, but the stranger never winked at all. He sat so motionless that Carringer became filled with a vague dread.

"I will go now," he said, standing back from the table. As he spoke he recollected his position and found himself swaying like a drunken man.

The stranger made no reply, nor did he relax his gaze. Under that gaze the younger man shrank back into his chair, terrified and faint. A deathly silence filled the compartment.... Suddenly he became aware that two men were talking in the next room, and he listened curiously. The walls were of wood, and he heard every

Edward J. O'Brien and John Cournos

word distinctly.

"Yes," said a voice, "he was seen to turn into this street about three hours ago."

"And he must have shaved?"

"He must have shaved. To remove a full beard would naturally make a great change in the man. His extreme pallor attracted attention. As you know, he has been seriously troubled with heart disease lately, and it has greatly altered him."

"Yes, but his old skill remains. Why, this is the most daring bank-robbery we have ever had! A hundred and forty-eight thousand dollars - think of it! How long is it since he came out of prison after that New York affair?"

"Eight years. In that time he has grown a beard, and lived by throwing dice. No human being can come out winner in a game with him."

The two men clinked glasses and a silence fell between them. Then Carringer heard the shuffling of their feet as they passed out, and he sat on, suffering terrible mental and bodily pain.

The silence remained unbroken, save for the sounds of voices far off, and the clink of glasses. The dice-players - the pale man and the starving one - sat gazing at each other, with a hundred and forty-eight thousand dollars piled upon the table between them. The winner made no attempt to gather up the money. He merely sat and stared at Carringer, wholly unmoved by the conversation in the adjoining compartment.

Carringer began to shake with an ague. The cold, unwavering gaze of the stranger sent ice into his veins. Unable to bear it longer, he moved to one side, and was amazed to discover that the eyes of the pale man, instead of following him, remained fixed upon the spot where he had sat.

A great fear came over him. He poured out absinthe for himself with shaking fingers, staring back at his companion all the while, watching him, watching him as he drank alone and unnoticed. He drained the glass, and the poison had a peculiar effect upon him; he felt his heart bounding with alarming force and rapidity, and his breathing came in great, pumping spasms. His hunger was now become a deadly thing, for the absinthe was destroying his vitals. In terror he leaned forward to beg the hospitality of the stranger, but his whisper had no effect. One of the man's hands lay on the table. Carringer placed his own upon it, and drew back quickly, for the hand was as cold as stone!

Then there came into the starving man's face a crafty expression, and he turned eagerly to the money. Silently he grasped the pile of bills with his skeleton fingers, looking stealthily every moment at the stark figure of his companion, mortally dreading lest he should stir.

And yet, instead of hastening from the room with the stolen fortune, he sank back into his chair again. A deadly fascination forced him there, and he sat rigid, staring back into the wide stare of the other man. He felt his breath coming heavier and his heart-beats growing weaker, but he was comforted because his hunger was no longer causing him that acute pain. He felt easier, and actually yawned. If he had dared he would have gone to sleep. The pale stranger still stared at him without ceasing. And Carringer had no inclination for anything but simply to stare back.

* * * * *

The two detectives who had traced the notorious bank robber to the drink saloon moved slowly through the compartments, searching in every nook and cranny of the building. At last they reached a compartment from which no answer came when they knocked.

They pushed the door open with a stereotyped apology on their lips. They beheld two men before them, one of middle age and the other very young, sitting perfectly still, and in the queerest manner imaginable staring at each other across the table. Between the two was a pile of money, and near at hand an empty absinthe bottle, a water pitcher, two glasses, and a dice-box. The dice lay before the elder man as though he had just thrown them.

With a quick movement one of the detectives covered the older man with a revolver and commanded him to put up his hands. But the dice-thrower paid not the slightest heed.

The detectives exchanged startled glances. They stepped nearer, looked closely into the gamesters' faces, and knew in the same instant that they were dead.

THE STRANGER WOMAN

By G.B. STERN

(From *John o'London's Weekly*) 1922

After Hal Burnham had banged himself with his usual vigour out of the house, Dickie sat quite inconsolably staring in front of him at a favourite picture on his wall; a dim, sombre effect of quays and masts and intent hurrying men; his neat little brows were pulled down in a worried frown, his childish mouth was puckered.

Was it accurate and just, what Hal had said? Or, simpler still, was it true?

"What you damn well need, Dickie, old son, is life in the raw. You're living in a lady's work-box here."

It was a bludgeoning return for the courteous attention with which Dickie had that evening listened to his friend's experiences of travel, for Hal was not even a good raconteur; he started an anecdote by its point, and roughly slapped in the scenery afterwards; he had likewise a habit of disconnecting his impressions from any sequence of time; also he exaggerated, and forgot names and dates; and even occasionally lapsed into odd silence just when Dickie was offering himself

Edward J. O'Brien and John Cournos

receptively for a climax.

And then the inevitable: "Well - and what have *you* been doing meanwhile?"

Dickie was not in the least at a loss; he had refurnished his rooms, to begin with; and that involved a diligent search in antique shops and at sale rooms, and one or two trips across country in order not to miss a real gem. And they had to be ready for comfortable habitation before the arrival of M. and Mlle. St. André for their annual stay with him - a delightful old pair, brother and sister, with peppery manners and hypercritical appreciation of a good cuisine - but so poor, so really painfully poor, that, as Dickie delicately put it: "I could not help knowing that it might make a difference to them if I postponed their visit, of less trivial annoyance, but more vital in quality, than with other of my friends for whom I should therefore have hurried my preparations rather less - this is in confidence, of course, my dear Hal!" He had set himself to complete his collection of Watts's Literary Souvenirs - "I have the whole eleven volumes now -" And he had been a guest at two charming house-parties in the country, and at one of them had been given the full responsibility of rehearsing a comic opera in the late eighteenth-century style. "Amateurs, of course. But I was so bent on realizing the flavour of the period, that I'm indeed afraid that I did not draw a clear enough line between the deliciously robust and the obnoxiously coarse -"

"Coarse - *you*!" Hal guffawed. And then - out came the accusation which was so disturbing little Dickie.

Life in the raw! Why did the phrase make him want to

clear his throat? Raw - yes, that was the association - when you opened your mouth and the fog swirled in. Newsboys scampering along a foggy street that was neither elegant nor squalid, but just a street of mixed shops and mixed traffic and barrows lit with a row of flapping lights, and men and women with faces that showed they worked hard to earn a little less than they needed.... Public-houses.... Butchers' shops with great slabs of red meat.... Yes, and a queue outside the picture palace - and a station; people bought the evening papers as they hurried in and out of the station. "'Ere yer are, sir," and on the sheets were headlines that blared out all the most sordid crimes of the past twenty-four hours, ignored during a sober morning of politics and commerce, but dragged into bold view for the people's more leisured reading.

Newsboys in a foggy street on a Saturday night - thus was Dickie's first instinct to define "life in the raw...." Then he discovered that this was only the archway, and that the crimes themselves were life in the raw - and the criminals.

But one must get nearer by slow degrees.

If at all.

Hal had said that he was living in a lady's work-box. Dickie was sensitive, and not at all stupid. His penetration was quite aware that Burnham's remark was not applied to the harmonizing shades of the walls between which he dwelt, nor to the soft, mellow pattern of his silky Persian rugs, nor to his collections - heavens, *how* he collected! - of glowing Sèvres china, of Second Empire miniatures, of quaint old musical instruments with names that in themselves were a tender tinkle of song, and of the shoes that had been worn by queens.

All these things were merely accessories: his soul making neat, tiny gestures, shrugging its shoulders, pointing a toe. What Hal meant was that Dickie dared not live dangerously.

"What am I to do?"

He raised wistful, light brown eyes to the picture which was the one incongruous touch to the dainty perfection of his octagonal sitting-room. He had bought it at a rummage sale; it was unsigned, and the canvas, overcrowded with figures, had grown sombre and blurred; yet queerly Dickie liked the suggestion of powerful, half-naked men; the foreign quay-side street, with a slatternly woman silent against a doorway, and the clumsy ship straining to swing out to a menacing sea beyond.

All these things that he would never do: strip and carry bales on his back; linger in strange doorways and love hotly an animal woman who was unaccomplished and without grace and breeding; and then embark on an evil-smelling hulk that would have no human sympathy with his human ills.

He had done a little yachting, of course; with the Ansteys the year before last.

His lips bent to a small ironical smile as he reflected on the difference between "a little yachting" and the sinister fascination of that ugly, uninspired painting....

Slowly he got up and went out; that is to say, he very

precisely selected the hat, gloves, coat, and silk muffler suitable to wear, and as precisely put them on. Then he blew up the fire with an old-fashioned pair of worked brass bellows; turned out the lamp; told Mrs. Derrick - who would have died in his service every day from eight to eight o'clock, but would not crook a finger for him a minute before she entered the house nor five seconds after she left it - that he was going for a walk and would certainly be back at a quarter to seven, but probably before; and then went out.

For this was the natural way for Dickie Maybury to behave.

At twenty to seven he returned, with a sheaf of newspapers - raucous, badly-printed papers with smudged lines and a sort of speckled film over the illustrations, and startlingly intimate headlines to every item of news.

Dickie was trying to get into touch with "life in the raw."

At first he was merely bewildered. He had read his daily newspaper, of course - though not with the stolid regularity with which the average man does so. And besides, it was pre-eminently a journal of dignity and good form, with an art column, and a curio column, and a literary page, and a chess problem, and rather a delicately witty causerie by "Rapier"; it is to be feared that Dickie absorbed himself in these items first, and altogether left out most of the topical and sensational news.

Now, however, he read it. And out of it, the horror of the underworld swayed up at him. A twilit world, where cisterns dripped, and where homely, familiar things like gas-brackets and braces and coal-shovels were turned to dreadful weapons of death. The coroner and the broker's man and the undertaker sidled in and out of this world, dispassionately playing their frequent parts.... Stunted boys and girls died for love, like Romeo and Juliet, leaving behind them badly-punctuated cries of passion and despair that made Dickie wince as he read them....

Pale but fascinated, Dickie turned over a page, and came to the great sensation of the moment. "Is Ruth Oliver Guilty?" "Dramatic Developments." "I Wish You Were Dead, Lucas!"

The account of the first day of the trial filled the entire page, and dribbled excitedly over on to the next. There was a photograph of Ruth Oliver, accused of murdering her husband. You could see that she had gay eyes in a small oval face, and a child's wistful mouth. This must have been taken while she was very happy.

Dickie had never read through a murder trial before. But he did so now, every line of it ... and the next day, and the next. Until the woman who had pleaded "Not guilty" was acquitted. And then he wrote to her, and asked her to marry him.

And who would dare say of him now that he had feared to meet life in the raw?

He did not know, of course, that his offer was one among fifty; did not know that the curious state of mind he was in, between trance and hysteria, was a very common one to the public after a trial in which the elements are dramatic or the central figure in any way picturesque. He did not even know how Ruth Oliver was being noisily besieged by Pressmen and Editors anxious for her biography; by music-hall and theatrical managers willing to star her; by old friends curiously proud of association with her notoriety; by religious fanatics with their proofs of a strictly localized Deity - "whose Hand has clearly been outstretched to save you!"; by unhealthy flappers who had Believed in her all along - (autograph, please).

But not knowing, yet his letter, chivalrous, without ardour, promised her a cool, quiet retreat from the plague of insects which was buzzing and stinging in the hot air all about her.... "My house is in a little square with trees all around it; it is shady and you cannot hear the traffic. I wonder if you are interested in old china and Japanese water-colours?..." Finally: "I shall be very proud and happy if you can trust me to understand how deeply you must be longing for sanctuary after the sorrowful time you have been through...."

"Sanctuary." She saw it open for her like a cloistered aisle between cold pillars. He offered her, not the emotional variations, intolerable to her weariness just then, of a new devotion; but green shaded rooms, and the beauty of old things, and a little old-fashioned gentleman's courtesy.... So, ignoring the fifty other offers of marriage which had assailed her, she wrote to Dickie Maybury and asked him to come and see her.

He went, still in a strangely exultant mood, in which his will acted as easily and yet as fantastically as though it were on a slippery surface. And if he had met Hal Burnham on his way back from his visit to Ruth

Oliver he would undoubtedly have swaggered a little. Nevertheless, he was thinking of Ruth, too, as well as of his own dare-devilry in thus seizing reality with both hands. Ruth's face, much older and more tormented than it had been in the photograph, had still that elusive quality which had from the beginning and through all the period of her trial haunted him. It outraged his refinement that any woman with the high looks and the breeding of his own class should have been for any space of time the property of a coarse public. As *his* wife, the insult should be tenderly rectified.... "The poor child! the poor sweet child!" He felt almost godlike with this new power upon him of acting, on impulse.

As for the peril of death which for a short while had threatened her, that was a fact too stark and hideous for contemplation: even with Dickie's altered appetite for primitive adventure....

They did not leave town after their quiet, matter-of-fact wedding at the registrar's. A journey, in Dickie's eyes, would have seemed too blatant an interruption to his everyday existence, as though he were tactlessly emphasising to his wife the necessity of a break and a complete change; she might even think - and again "poor child!" that events should have rubbed into such super-sensitiveness - that he was slightly ashamed of his act, and was therefore hustling her and himself out of sight. So they went straight home. And Mrs. Derrick said: "Indeed, sir," when informed that her new mistress was the Ruth Oliver who had recently been acquitted of the charge of murdering her husband; she neither proffered a motherly bosom to Ruth, nor did she tender a haughty resignation from Mr. Maybury's service; but said she hoped it wouldn't be expected of her, under the new circumstances, to arrive earlier, nor to leave later, because she couldn't do it. As for Dickie's friends, most of them were of the country-house variety whom he visited once a year; next autumn would show whether Ruth would be included in those week and week-end invitations. Meanwhile, those few dwelling in London marvelled in a detached sort of way at Dickie's feat, liked Ruth, and pronounced it a shame that she should have been accused. Hal Burnham, the indirect promoter of the match, had returned to China.

Nobody was unkind; no word jarred; life was padded in dim brocade - Ruth drew a long breath, and was at peace. She was perfectly happy, watching Dickie. And Dickie was at play again, enjoying his collection and his *objets d'art*, and even his daily habits, with the added appreciation of a gambler who had staked, but miraculously, not lost them. Because, after all, anything might have resulted from his tempestuous decision at all costs to get into contact with naked actuality; all that *had* resulted was the presence in his house of a slim, grave woman who dressed her hair like a very skilful and not at all unconscious Madonna; whose taste was as fastidious as his own, and whose radiantly human smile had survived in vivid contrast to something quenched from her voice and shadowed in her eyes. A woman who, with a "May I?" of half-laughing reverence, discovered that she could slip on to her exquisite feet one pair after another from his collection of the shoes of dead queens - "It sounds like a ballade - Austin Dobson, I think - except that they're not all powder-and-patch queens."

For she had an excellent feel of period - the texture of it, the fine shades of language, the outlook; Dickie hated people who had a blunt sense of period and in a jumbled fashion referred to old Venetian lace, and the Early Spanish School, and Louise de la Vallière, and a play by Wycherley indiscriminately as "historical."

Yes, Dickie had certainly been lucky, and, like a wise man, he did not strain his star to another effort. The big thing - well, he had squared up to it - and, truth to say, he had been fearfully shaky and uncertain about his capacity to do so when Hal had first roused his pride in the matter. Now the little things again, the little beautiful things - he had earned them.

Anyway, he could not have a newspaper in the house nowadays, for Ruth's sake - he owed it to Ruth to shut out for ever those cries of horror and fear and violence from the battering underworld.

"What I love about the way we live, Dickie, is that the just-rightness of it all flows on evenly the whole time; one can be certain of it. Most people get it set aside for them in stray lumps - picture galleries and churches and a holiday on the Continent. And all the rest of their time is just-wrongness."

Dickie wondered how much of her existence with Lucas Oliver had been "just-wrongness" - or indeed "all-wrongness." But he never disturbed her surface of creamy serenity by referring to the husband who had been murdered by "some person or persons unknown."

He and Ruth were the most harmonious of comrades, but never, so far, confidential. Perhaps Dickie overdid tact and non-intrusiveness; or perhaps Ruth, in her very passion of gratitude to him, was yet checked for ever from passionate expression by the memory that her innermost love and her innermost hate, wrung into words, had once, and not so long ago, been read aloud and commented upon in public court and in half the homes of England.

One evening, sitting together in front of the fire, they drifted into talk of their separate childhoods.

"There was a garden in mine," said Ruth.

"And in mine - a Casino garden!" His eyes twinkled. "Palm trees like giant pineapples, and flower beds in a pattern, and a fountain -"

"Oh, you poor little Continental kiddie!"

He shrugged his shoulders. "The ways of the Lord are thoughtful and orderly. Why should He have wasted a heavenly wilderness of gnarled old apple-trees on a small boy who hated climbing?"

"You can't have hated climbing - if you hang that on your wall." She nodded towards the quayside picture. "Surely you must have played 'pirates and South Seas' with your brothers."

"I had none. A sister, that's all - who carried a sunshade." "I had no sisters; but there was a girl next door - and her brother."

"I note in jealous anguish of spirit," remarked Dickie. "that you do not simply say 'a girl and boy next door.'"

Ruth's mischievous laugh affirmed his accusation. "The wall was not very high - I kicked a foothold into it half-way up, and Tommy gave me a pull from the top."

"Tommy was ungallant enough to leave the wall to you?"

"There were cherries in his garden - sweet black cherries. And only crab-apples in ours."

"He might have filled his pockets with cherries, and then climbed. No - I reject Tommy, he was unworthy of you. I may have been a horrid little Casino brat, I may even have worn a white satin sailor-suit with trousers down to my ankles -"

"Oh!" Ruth winced.

"I may have danced too well, and I understood too early the art of complimenting ladies whose hats were too big and whose eyes were too bright.... But once, after Annunciata Maddalena's nose had bled over this same sailor-suit, I said it was my own nose, because I knew how bitterly she was ashamed of her one bourgeois lapse...."

"Tommy would have disowned her, instead of owning the nose. Oh, I grant you the nobler nature ... but it breaks my heart that you didn't have the wild English garden and the cherries and the grubby old dark-blue jersey."

"If we have a kiddie - " Dickie began softly, his mouth puckered to its special elvish little smile. Then he met her eyes lapping him round with such velvet tenderness - that Dickie suddenly knew he was loved, knew that impulsively she was going to tell him so, and breathlessly happier than he had ever been before, waited for it -

"I *did* kill my husband. They acquitted me, but I was guilty. It was an accident. I was so afraid. They would never have believed it could be an accident. But I had to, in self-defence."

And now she had told him she loved him.

Only Dickie was too numb to recognise the form her confession of love had taken; love, as always, was clamouring to be clearly seen - naked, if need be, blood-guilty, if need be - but *seen* ... and then swept up, sin and all, by another love big enough to accept this truth, also, as essentially part of her.

Ruth waited several seconds for Dickie to speak. Then she got up, and strolled over to the picture, and said, examining intently, as though for the first time, the woman in the doorway: "I'm not sorry, Dickie. That is to say, I'm sorry, of course, if I've shattered an illusion of yours, but - I can't be melodramatic, you know, not even to the extent of using the word 'murderess' on myself. If I hadn't killed Lucas -"

"He would have killed you?" So he was able to utter quite natural and coherent sounds! Dickie was surprised.

"Yes - " But Ruth found that, after all, she could not tell Dickie much about Lucas. Lucas had not been a pleasant gentleman to live with - and there were things that Dickie was too fine himself, and too innocent, to realise. The only comprehension in this thoroughly well-groomed atmosphere of soft carpets and dim silken panels and miniatures and rare frail china might have come from the woman in the doorway of that incongruous picture ... a woman sullenly patient, brutalised, but - yes, her man might quite easily have been another Lucas.

For that which Dickie had always thought of as mysterious, elusive, was, to Ruth's eyes, only sorrowful wisdom.

"Come here, Ruth."

She dragged her eyes away from the picture; crossed the room; broke down completely, her head on his knees, her shuddering body crouched closely to the floor: "When you've - been frightened - and have to live with it - and it doesn't even stop at night - for weeks and months and years - one's nerves aren't quite reliable.... They've no right to call that murder, have they? have they, Dickie? When you've been afraid for a long time - and there's no one you can tell about it except the person who *makes* the *fear*...."

But Dickie was all that she had perilously dared to hope he would be at this crisis. He soothed her and healed her by his loyalty; promised, without her extorting it, that he would never tell a soul what she had just told him; pixie-shy, yet he spoke of his personal need of her - and more than anything else she had desired to hear this. He mentioned some trivial intimate plans for their unbroken, unchanged future together, so as to reassure her of its continuance. He even made her laugh.

In fact, for a last appearance in the *rôle* of a gallant little gentleman, Dickie did not do so badly.

He woke in the night from a bad dream - with terror clinging thickly about his senses. But it did not slowly dissolve and release him, as nightmare is wont to do. It remained - so that he lay still as a man in his winding-sheet, afraid to move - remembering -

"I *did* kill my husband."

Yes - that was it. In the room with him was a strange woman who had killed her husband.

Not Ruth - but a strange woman. How had she got into the room with him?

She had killed her husband. And now, *he* was her husband.

He lay motionless, but his imagination began to crawl.... What might happen to a man shut up alone in a house with a woman who - murdered?

His imagination began to race - and he lost control of it. Murder ...with dry, sandy throat and a kicking heart, Dickie had to pay for his audacity in imagining he was big enough to claim life in the raw.

"Not big enough! Not big enough!" - the goblins of the underworld croaked at him in triumphant chorus.... They capered ... they snapped their fingers at him ... they spun him down to where fear was ... he had delivered himself to them, by not being big enough.

"Mrs. Bigger had a baby - which was bigger, Mrs. Bigger or the baby?"

The silly conundrum sprang at him from goodness

knows what void - and over and over again he repeated it to himself, trying to remember the answer, trying to forget fear....

"Mrs. Bigger had a baby -"

He dared not fall asleep ... with the woman who had killed her husband, alone in the room with him ... alone in the house with him.

A stir from the other bed, and one arm flung out in sleep. Dickie's knees jerked violently - his skin went cold and sticky with sweat. "You fool - it's only Ruth!"

But she *did* it - she did it once. There are people who can't kill, and a few, just a very few, who can. And because they can, they are different, and have to be shut away from the herd.

But - but this woman. They've made a ghastly mistake - they've let her go free - and I can't tell anyone ... nobody knows, except me and Ruth - Ah, yes - a quivering sigh of relief here - Ruth knows, too - Ruth, my wife - ruth means pity....

There is no Ruth ... there never was ... quite alone except for a strange, strange woman - the kind that gets shut away and kept by herself....

* * * * *

To this bondage had Dickie's nerves delivered him. The custom of punctilious courtesy, so deeply ingrained as to mean in his case the impossibility of wounding another, decreed that some pretence must be kept up before Ruth. But with one shock she divined the next morning the significant change in him, and bowed her head to it. What could she do? She loved him, but she had overrated the capacity of his spirit. There had never been any courage, only kindness and sweetness and chivalry - all no good to him, now that courage was wanted. She had made a mistake in telling him the truth.

Suffering - she thought she had suffered fiercely with Lucas, she thought she had suffered while she was being ignominiously tried for her life - but what were either of these phases compared with the helpless bitterness of seeing Dickie, whom she loved, afraid of her?

Even her periodic fits of wild arrogant passion, which usually, when they surged past restraint, wrecked and altered whatever situation was hemming her in, and left gaps for a passage through to something else - even these had now to be curbed. Useful in hate, they were impotent in love. So Ruth recognised in her new humility. But when one day, seized by panic at having spoken irritably to her, Dickie hastily tried to propitiate her, to ingratiate himself so that she might spare him, might let him live a little longer, then Ruth felt she must cry aloud under the strain of this subtle torture. Why, he was her lover, her man, her child.... In thought, her arm shaped itself into a crook for his head to lie there; her fingers smoothed out the drawn perplexity of his brows; her kisses were cool as snow on his hot, twitching little mouth; her voice, hushed to a lullaby croon, promised him that nobody should hurt him, nobody, while she was there to heal and protect -

"Sleep, baby, sleep,
The hills are white with sheep -"

412   Edward J. O'Brien and John Cournos

Over and over again she lulled herself with the old rhyme, for comfort's sake. But Dickie she could not comfort, since, irony of ironies, she was the cause of his pitiful breakdown. Why, if she spoke, he started; if she moved towards him, he shrank. Yet still Ruth dreamt that if he would only let her touch him, she could bring him reassurance. But meanwhile his appetite was meagre, the rare half-hours he slept were broken with evil dreams, from which he awoke whimpering. He did not care any more about the little beautiful things he had collected and grouped about him, but sat for hours listless and blank; his appearance a grotesque parody of the trim and dapper Dickie Maybury of the past - what could it matter how he looked with death slicing so close to him?

"The master seems poorly of late, don't he, ma'am? His digestion ain't strong. P'r'aps something 'as disagreed with 'im." Thus Mrs. Derrick, taking her part in the drama, as the simple character who makes speeches of more significant portent than she is aware of.

Something had, indeed, disagreed with Dickie. In the slang phrase: "He had bitten off more than he could chew."

And the goblins were hunting him; whispering how she would creep up to him stealthily from behind, this woman who killed ... and put her arms round him, and put her fingers to his throat - that was one way.

Other ways there were, of course. He must learn about them all, so as to be watchful and prepared. Self-defence ... accident. Of course, they always said it was accident. He knew that now, for the evening crime-sheets began to appear in the flat again, and Dickie studied them, in place of the *villanelles*, the graceful essays, the *belles-lettres* of his former choice. Ruth saw him, with his delicate shaking hands clutching the newspapers, his mild eyes bright with sordid fascination. He was ill, certainly; and brain-sick and oppressed; and she yearned for his illness to show itself a tangible, serious matter; a matter of bed and doctor and complete prostration and unwearied effort on the part of his nurse. "My darling - my darling....He did everything for me, when I most needed it. And now, I can do nothing.... It isn't fair!"

She stood by one of the open windows of the pretty Watteau sitting-room. The lamps had just sprung to fiery stars in the blue glamorous twilight of the square; the fragrance of wet lilac blew up to her, and a blackbird among the bushes began to sing like mad ... the fist which was cruelly squeezing Ruth's spirit seemed slowly to unclench ... and suddenly it struck her that things might be made worth while again for her and Dickie.

After all, how insane it was for him to be huddling miserably, as she knew he would be, in the arm-chair of his study, gazing with forlorn eyes at the squalid columns, which it had grown too dark for him to decipher. She had a vision of what this very evening might yet hold of recovered magic, if only she had the courage to carry out her simple cure of his head drawn down on to her left breast, just where her heart was beating. "Dickie, it's *all right*, you know - it's only Ruth I You've been sitting with your bogies all the time the white lilac has been coming out -"

A faint smile lay at last on Ruth's mouth, and in the curve of her tired eyelids. She went softly into the study. The door was open....

Dickie sprang to his feet with a yell of terror as her hands came round his neck from behind. He clutched at the revolver in his pocket and fired, at random, backwards.... In the wall behind them was the round dark mark of a merciful bullet. And -

"Dickie - oh, Dickie - when you've been frightened - and have to live with it - and it doesn't even stop at nights - do you understand, now, how it happens? They've no right to call *that* murder, have they, Dickie?"

And now, indeed, understanding that the awful act of killing could be, in a rare once or twice, a human accident for the frightened little human to commit - understanding, Dickie was shocked back to sanity.

"Dear, dear Ruth -" Why, this stranger woman was no stranger, after all, but Ruth, his own sweet wife. Dickie was tired, and he knew he need not explain things to her. He laid his head down on her left breast, just where the heart was beating.

THE WOMAN WHO SAT STILL

By PARRY TRUSCOTT

(From *Colour*) 1922

When he went, when he had to go, he took with him the memory of her that had become crystallised, set for him in his own frequent words to her, standing at her side, looking down at her with his keen, restless eyes - such words as: "It puzzles me how on earth you manage to sit so still...."

Then, enlarging: "It is wonderful to me how you can keep so happy doing nothing - make of enforced idleness a positive pleasure! I suppose it is a gift, and I haven't got it - not a bit. It doesn't matter how tired I am, I have to keep going - people call it industry, but its real name is nervous energy, run riot. I can't even take a holiday peacefully. I must be actively playing if I cannot work. I'm just the direct descendant of the girl in the red shoes - they were red, weren't they? - who had to dance on and on until she dropped. I shall go on and on until I drop, and then I shall attempt a few more useless yards on all fours...."

"Come now," in answer to the way she shook her head at him, smiled at him from her sofa, "you know very well how I envy you your gift, your power of sitting still - happily still - your power of contemplation...."

And one day, more intimately still, with a sigh and a look (Oh, a look she understood!), "To me you are the most restful person in the world...."

*   *   *   *   *

Why he went, except that he had to go; why he stayed away so long, so very long, are not really relevant to this story; the facts, stripped of conjecture, were simply these: she was married, and he was not, and there came the time, as it always comes in such relationships as theirs, when he had to choose between staying without honour and going quickly. He went. But even the bare facts concerning his protracted absence are less easily stated because his absence dragged on long after the period when he might, with impeccable honour, have returned.

The likeliest solution was that setting her aside when he had to, served so to cut in two his life, so wrenched at his heartstrings, so burnt and bruised his spirit, that when, in his active fashion he had lived some of the hurt down, he could not bring himself easily to reopen the old subject - fresh wounds for him might still lurk in it - how could he tell? Although it had been at the call, the insistence of honour, still hadn't he left her - deserted her? Does any woman, even his own appointed woman, forgive a man who goes speechless away? Useless, useless speculation! For some reason, some man's reason, when another's death made her a free woman, yet he lingered and did not come.

He knew, afterwards, that it was from the first his intention to claim her. He wanted her - deep down he wanted her as he had always wanted her; meant to come - some time. Knew all the time that he could not always keep away. And then, responding to a sudden whim, some turn of his quickly moving mind - a mind that could forcibly bury a subject and as forcibly resurrect it - hot-foot and eager he came.

* * * * *

He had left her recovering slowly and surely from a long illness; an illness that must have proved fatal but for her gift of tranquillity, her great gift of keeping absolutely, restfully still in body, while retaining a happily occupied mind. Her books, and her big quiet room, and the glimpse of the flower-decked garden from her window, with just these things to help her, she had dug herself into the deep heart of life where the wells of contentment spring. Bird's song in the early morn and the long, still day before her in which to find herself - to take a new, firmer hold on the hidden strength of the world. And, just to keep her in touch with the surface of things, visits from her friends. Then later, more tightly gripping actuality, with a new, keen, sharp, growing pleasure - the visits of a friend.

While those lasted there was nothing she would have changed for her quiet room, her sofa: the room that he lit with his coming; where she rested and rested, shut in with the memory of all he said, looked, thought in her presence - until again he came.

While they lasted! She had been content, never strong, never able to do very much, with seclusion before. During the time of his visits she revelled, rejoiced in it, asking nothing further. While they lasted, sitting still

Edward J. O'Brien and John Cournos

(Oh, so still), hugging her joy, she didn't think, wouldn't think, how it might end.

Sometimes, just sometimes, by a merciful providence, things do not end. She lived for months on the bare chance of its not ending.

Yet, as we know, the end came.

At first while the world called her widowed she sat with her unwidowed heart waiting for him in the old room, in the old way. Surely now he would come? She had given good measure of fondness and duty and friendship - that was only that under another name - to the one who until now had stood between her and her heart's desire, and parting with him, and all the associations that went with him, had surprisingly hurt her. Always frail, she was ill - torn with sorrow and pity - and then, very slowly again, she recovered. And while she recovered, lying still in the old way, she gave her heart wings - wild, surging wings - at last, at last. Sped it forth, forth to bring her joy - to compel it.

While she waited in this fashion a sweet, recaptured sense of familiarity made his coming seem imminent. She had only to wait and he would be here. She couldn't have mistaken the looks that had never been translated into words - that hadn't needed words. Though she had longed and ached for a word - then - she was quite content now. He had wanted her just as she was, unashamed and untainted. And to preserve her as she was he had gone away. And now for the very first time she was truly glad he had gone in that abrupt, speechless fashion - in spite of the heartache and the long years between them, really and truly glad. Nothing had been spoilt; they had snatched at no stolen joys. And the rapture, (what rapture!) of meeting would blot out all that they had suffered in silence - the separation - all of it!

As she waited, getting well for him, she had no regrets, growing more and more sure of his coming.

It was not until she was well again, not until the months had piled themselves on each other, that, growing more frightened than she knew, she began her new work of preparation.

*　*　*　*　*

Suddenly, impulsively, when she had reached the stage of giving him up for days at a time, when hope had nearly abandoned her, then he came.

He had left a woman so hopeful in outlook, so young and peaceful in spirit, that with her the advancing years would not matter. On his journey back to her, visualising her afresh, touching up his memory of her, he pictured her going a little grey. That would suit her - grey was her colour - blending to lavender in the clothes she always wore for him. A little grey, but her clear, pale skin unfaded, her large eyes full of pure, guarded secrets - secrets soon to unfold for him alone.

A haven - a haven! So he thought of her, and now, ready for her, coming to her, he craved the rest she would give him - rest more than anything in all the world. She, with her sweet white hands, when he held them, kissed them, would unlock the doors of peace for him, drawing him into her life, letting him potter and linger - linger at her side. Even when long ago he had insisted to her that for him there was no way of rest, he had known that she, just she, meant rest for him, when he could claim her for his own. Other women, other pursuits, offered him excitement, stimulation - and then a weariness too profound for words. But rest, bodily, spiritually, was her unique gift for him. She - he smiled as he thought it - would teach him to sit still.

And tired, so tired, he hurried to her across the world as fast as he could go.

Waiting at her door, the door opened, crossing the threshold - Oh, he had never thought his luck would be so great as to be taken direct to the well remembered room upstairs! Yet with only a few short inquiries he was taken there - she for whom he asked, the mistress of the house, would be in her sitting-room, he was told, and if he was an old friend...? He explained that he was a very old friend, following the maid upstairs. But the maid was mistaken; her mistress was not in her private sitting-room; not in the house at all - she had gone out, and it proved on investigation that she had left no word. The maid, returning, suggested however, that she would not be long. Her mistress had a meeting this evening; she was expecting some one before dinner; no, she would certainly not be long, so - so if he would like to wait?

He elected to wait - a little impatiently. He knew it was absurd that coming, without warning - after how many years was it? - he should yet have made so sure of finding her at home. Absurd, unreasonable - and yet he was disappointed. He ought to have written, but he had not waited to write. He had pictured the meeting - how many times? Times without number - and always pictured her waiting at home. And then the room?

Left alone in it he paced the room. But the room enshrined in his heart of hearts was not this room. Was there, surely there was some mistake?

There could be no mistake. There could not be two upstairs rooms in this comparatively small house, of this size and with this aspect; westward, and overlooking with two large windows the little walled garden into which he had so often gazed, standing and talking to her, saying over his shoulders the things he dare not say face to face - that would have meant so much more, helped out with look and gesture, face to face.

The garden, as far as he could see, was the same except that he fancied it less trim, less perfect in order: in the old days it would be for months at a time all the outside world she saw - there had been object enough in keeping it trim. Now it looked, to his fancy, like a woman whose beauty was fading a little because she had lost incentive to be beautiful. He turned from the garden, his heart amazed, fearful, back to the room.

The room of the old days - with closed eyes he reproduced it; its white walls, its few good pictures, its curtains and carpet of deep blue. Her sofa by the window, the wide armchair on which he always sat, the table where, in and out of season, roses, his roses, stood. The little old gilt clock on the mantlepiece that so quickly, cruelly ticked away their hour. Books, books everywhere, the most important journals and a medley of the lighter magazines; those, with her work-basket, proving her feminine and the range of her interests, her inconsistency. A woman's room, revealing at a glance her individuality, her spirit.

But this room -! He looked for the familiar things - the sofa, the bookshelves, the little table dedicated to flowers. Yes, the sofa was there, but pushed away as though seldom used; on the bookshelves new, strange books were crowding out the old; on the little table drooped a few faded flowers in an awkward vase. On the mantlepiece, where she would never have more than one or two good ornaments, and the old gilt clock, were now stacks of papers, a rack bulging with packing materials - something like that - an ink-bottle, a candlestick, the candle trailed over with sealing-wax, and an untidy ball of string. And right in the centre of the room a great clumsy writing-table, an office table, piled with papers again, ledgers, a portable typewriter, and - a litter of cigarette ends.

Like a Mistress on the track of a much-doubted maid he ran his finger along the edge of a bookcase and then the mantlepiece. He looked at his fingers; there was no denying the dust he had wiped away.

She must have changed her room - why had she done it? But the maid had said - in her sitting-room -

He waited now frightened, now fuming. Still she did not come. Should he not wait - should he go - if this was her room? But he had come so far, and he needed her so - he must stay. For some dear, foolish woman's reason she must have lent her room for the use of a feminine busy-body; a political, higher-thought, pseudo-spiritualistic friend. (He must weed out her friends!) The trend of the work done in this room now his quick mind had seized upon - titles of books, papers, it was enough. Notices stuck in the Venetian Mirror (the desecration!) for meetings of this and that society, and all of them, so he judged, just excuses for putting unwanted fingers into unwanted, dangerous pies. He thought of it like that - he could not help it; he saw too far into motive and internal action; was too impatient of the little storms, the paltry, tea-cup things. She, with her unique gift of serenity - her place was not among the busybodies grinding axes that were better blunt; interfering with the slow, slow working of the Mills of God. Her gift was example - rare and delicate; her light the silver light of a soul, that through 'suffering and patience and contemplation, knows itself and is unafraid.

For such fussing, unstable work as it was used for now she ought not even to have lent her room - the room he had looked on as a temple of quietness; the shrine of a priceless temperament.

He smiled his first smile - she should not lend it again.

Then the door opened. Suddenly, almost noisily, she came in.

She had heard, downstairs, his name. So far she was prepared with her greeting. She came with hands outstretched - he took her hands and dropped them.

When he could interrupt her greeting he said - forcing the words - "So now you are quite strong - and busy?"

She told him how busy. She told him how, (but not why) she had awakened from her long, selfish dream. She said she had found so late - but surely not too late? - the joy of action; constant, unremitting work for the world's sake. *"Do you remember how you used to complain you couldn't sit still? I am like that now -"*

And he listened, listened, each word a deeper stab straight at his defenceless heart.

Of all the many things he had done since they met he had nothing to say.

Having just let her talk (how she talked!) as soon as he decently could he went. Of all he had come to tell her he said not a word. Tired, so bitterly tired, he had come seeking rest, and now there was no more a place of rest for him - anywhere.

Yes, he had come across the world to find himself overdue; to find himself too late. He went out again - as soon as he decently could - taking only a picture of her that in sixty over-charged minutes had wiped out the treasured picture of years.

Sixty minutes! After waiting for years she had kept him an hour, desperately, by sheer force of will keeping a man too stunned at first to resist, to break free. (Then at last he broke free of that room and that woman, and went!) For years he had pictured her sitting still as no other woman sat still, tranquil and graceful, her hair going a little grey above her clear, pale skin, her eyes of a dream-ridden saint. And now he must picture her forced into life, vivaciously, restlessly eager; full of plans, (futile plans, how he knew those plans!) for the world's upheaval, adding unrest to unrest. And now he must picture her with the grey hair outwitted by art, with paint on her beautiful ravaged face.

At first he had wanted to take her in his arms; with his strength to still her, with his tears to wash the paint off.

But he couldn't - he couldn't. He knew that his had been a dream of such supreme sweetness that to awaken was an agony he could never hide; knew that you can't re-enter dreamland once you wake.

So he went.

He never knew, with the door shut on him, how she fell on her sofa - her vivacity quenched, her soul spent. He never knew that having failed, (as she thought) to draw him to her with what she was, she had vainly, foolishly tried a new model - himself.

He did not know how inartistic love can be when love is desperate.

MAJOR WILBRAHAM

By HUGH WALPOLE

(From *The Chicago Tribune*) 1921

I am quite aware that in giving you this story just as I was told it I shall incur the charge of downright and deliberate lying.

Especially I shall be told this by any one who knew Wilbraham personally. Wilbraham was not, of course, his real name, but I think that there are certain people who will recognize him from this description of him. I do not know that it matters very much if they do. Wilbraham himself would certainly not mind did he know. (Does he know?) It was the thing above all that he wanted those last hours before he died - that I should pass on my conviction of the truth of what he told me to others. What he did not know was that I was not convinced. How could I be? But when the whole comfort of his last hours hung on the simple fact that I was, of course I pretended to the best of my poor ability. I would have done more than that to make him happy.

It is precisely the people who knew him well who will declare at once that my little story is impossible. But did they know him well? Does any one know any one else well? Aren't we all as lonely and removed from one another as mariners on separate desert islands? In any case I did not know him well and perhaps for that very reason was not so greatly surprised at his amazing revelations - surprised at the revelations themselves, of course, but not at his telling them. There was always in him - and I have known him here and there, loosely, in club and London fashion, for nearly twenty years - something romantic and something sentimental. I knew that because it was precisely those two attributes that he drew out of me.

Most men are conscious at some time in their lives of having felt for a member of their own sex an emotion that is something more than simple companionship. It is a queer feeling quite unlike any other in life, distinctly romantic and the more that perhaps for having no sex feeling in it.

Like the love of women, it is felt generally at sight, but, unlike that love, it is, I think, a supremely unselfish emotion. It is not acquisitive, nor possessive, nor jealous, and exists best perhaps when it is not urged too severely, but is allowed to linger in the background of life, giving real happiness and security and trust, standing out, indeed, as something curiously reliable just because it is so little passionate. This emotion has an odd place in our English life because the men who feel it, if they have been to public school and university, have served a long training in repressing every sign or expression of sentiment towards any other man; nevertheless it persists, romantically and deeply persists, and the war of 1914 offered many curious examples of it.

Wilbraham roused just that feeling in me. I remember

with the utmost distinctness my first meeting with him. It was just after the Boer war and old Johnny Beaminster gave a dinner party to some men pals of his at the Phoenix. Johnny was not so old then - none of us were; it was a short time after the death of that old harpy, the Duchess of Wrexe, and some wag said that the dinner was in celebration of that happy occasion. Johnny was not so ungracious as that, but he gave us a very merry evening and he did undoubtedly feel a kind of lightness in the general air.

There were about fifteen of us and Wilbraham was the only man present I'd never seen before. He was only a captain then and neither so red faced nor so stout as he afterwards became. He was pretty bulky, though, even then, and with his sandy hair cropped close, his staring blue eyes, his toothbrush moustache and sharp, alert movements, looked the typical traditional British officer.

There was nothing at all to distinguish him from a thousand other officers of his kind, and yet from the moment I saw him I had some especial and personal feeling about him. He was not in type at all the man to whom at that time I should have felt drawn. My first book had just been published and, although as I now perceive, its publication had not caused the slightest ripple upon any water, the congratulations of my friends and relations, who felt compelled, poor things, to say something, because "they had received copies from the author," had made me feel that the literary world was all buzzing at my ears. I could see at a glance that Kipling was probably the only "decent" author about whom Wilbraham knew anything, and the fragments of his conversation that I caught did not promise anything intellectually exciting from his acquaintanceship.

The fact remains that I wanted to know him more than any other man in the room, and although I only exchanged a few words with him that night, I thought of him for quite a long time afterwards.

It did not follow from this as it ought to have done that we became great friends. That we never were, although it was myself whom he sent for three days before his death to tell me his queer little story. It was then at the very last that he confided to me that he, too, had felt something at our first meeting "different" to what one generally feels, that he had always wanted to turn our acquaintance into friendship and had been too shy. I also was shy - and so we missed one another, as I suppose in this funny, constrained, traditional country of ours thousands of people miss one another every day.

But although I did not see him very often and was in no way intimate with him, I kept my ears open for any account of his doings. From one point of view, the Club Window outlook, he was a very usual figure, one of those stout, rubicund, jolly men, a good polo player, a good man in a house party, genial-natured, and none too brilliantly brained, whom every one liked and no one thought about. All this he was on one side of the report, but, on the other, there were certain stories that were something more than the ordinary.

Wilbraham was obviously a sentimentalist and an enthusiast; there was the extraordinary case shortly after I first met him of his championship of X, a man who had been caught in an especially bestial kind of crime and received a year's imprisonment for it. On X leaving prison Wilbraham championed and defended him, put him up for months in his rooms in Duke Street, walked as often as possible in his company down Piccadilly, and took him over to Paris. It says a great deal for Wilbraham's accepted normality and his general popularity that this championship of X did him no harm. It was so obvious that he himself was the last man in the world to be afflicted with X's peculiar habits. Some men, it is true, did murmur something about "birds of a feather"; one or two kind friends warned Wilbraham in the way kind friends have, and to them he simply said: "If a feller's a pal he's a pal."

All this might in the end have done Wilbraham harm had not X most happily committed suicide in Paris in 1905. There followed a year or two later the much more celebrated business of Lady C. I need not go into all that now, but here again Wilbraham constituted himself her defender, although she robbed, cheated, and maligned him as she robbed, cheated, and maligned every one who was good to her. It was quite obvious that he was not in love with her; the obviousness of it was one of the things in him that annoyed her.

He simply felt apparently that she had been badly treated (the very last thing that she had been), gave her any money he had, put his rooms at the disposal of herself and her friends, and, as I have said, championed her everywhere. This affair did very nearly finish him socially, and in his regiment. It was not so much that they minded his caring for Lady C - (after all, any man can be fooled by any woman) - but it was Lady C's friends who made the whole thing so impossible. Such a crew! Such a horrible crew! And it was a queer thing to see Wilbraham with his straight blue eyes and innocent mouth and general air of amiable simplicity in the company of men like Colonel B and young Kenneth Parr. (There is no harm, considering the later publicity of his case, in mentioning his name.) Well, that affair luckily came to an end just in time. Lady C disappeared to Berlin and was no more seen.

There were other cases into which I need not go when Wilbraham was seen in strange company, always championing somebody who was not worth the championing. He had no "social tact," and for them at any rate no moral sense. In himself he was the ordinary normal man about town, no prude, but straight as a man can be in his debts, his love affairs, his friendships, and his sport. Then came the war. He did brilliantly at Mons, was wounded twice, went out to Gallipoli, had a touch of Palestine, and returned to France again to share in Foch's final triumph.

No man can possibly have had more of the war than he had, and it is my own belief that he had just a little too much of it.

He had been always perhaps a little "queer," as we are most of us "queer" somewhere, and the horrors of that horrible war undoubtedly affected him. Finally he lost, just a week before the armistice, one of his best friends, Ross McLean, a loss from which he certainly never recovered.

I have now, I think, brought together all the incidents that can throw any kind of light upon the final scene. In the middle of 1919 he retired from the army, and it was from this time to his death that I saw something of him. He went back to his old home at Horton's in Duke street, and as I was living at that time in Marlborough Chambers in Jermyn street we were in easy reach of one another. The early part of 1920 was a "queer time." People had become, I imagine, pretty well accustomed to realizing that those two wonderful hours of Armistice day had not ushered in the millennium any more than those first marvellous moments of the Russian revolution produced it.

Every one has always hoped for the millennium, but the trouble since the days of Adam and Eve has always been that people have such different ideas as to what exactly that millennium shall be. The plain facts of the matter simply were that during 1919 and 1920 the world changed from a war of nations to a war of classes, that inevitable change that history has always shown follows on great wars.

As no one ever reads history, it was natural enough that there should be a great deal of disappointment and a great deal of astonishment. Men at the head of affairs who ought to have known better cried aloud, "How ungrateful these people are, after all we've done for them!" and the people underneath shouted that everything had been muddled and spoiled and that they would have done much better had they been at the head of affairs, an assertion for which there was no sort of justification.

Wilbraham, being a sentimentalist and an idealist, suffered more from this general disappointment than most people. He had had wonderful relations with the men under him throughout the war. He had never tired of recounting how marvelously they had behaved, what heroes they were, and that it was they who would pull the country together.

At the same time he had a naive horror of bolshevism and anything unconstitutional, and he watched the transformation of his "brave lads" into discontented and idle workmen with dismay and deep distress. He used sometimes to come around to my rooms and talk to me; he had the bewildered air of a man walking in his sleep.

He made the fatal mistake of reading all the papers, and he took in the Daily Herald in order that he might see "what it was these fellows had to say for themselves."

The Herald upset him terribly. Its bland assumption that Russians and Sein Feiners could do no wrong, but that the slightest sign of assertion of authority on the part of any government was "wicked tyranny," shocked his very soul. I remember that he wrote a long, most earnest letter to Lansbury, pointing out to him that if he subverted all authority and constitutional government his own party would in its turn be subverted when it came to govern. Of course, he received no answer.

During these months I came to love the man. The attraction that I had felt for him from the very first deeply underlay all my relation to him, but as I saw more of him I found many very positive reasons for my liking. He was the simplest, bravest, purest, most loyal, and most unselfish soul alive. He seemed to me to have no faults at all unless it were a certain softness towards the wishes of those whom he loved. He could not bear to hurt anybody, but he never hesitated if some principle in which he believed was called in question.

He had not, of course, a subtle mind - he was no

analyst of character - but that did not make him uninteresting. I never heard any one call him dull company, although men laughed at him for his good nature and unselfishness and traded on him all the time. He was the best human being I have ever known or am ever likely to know.

Well, the crisis arrived with astonishing suddenness. About the second or third of August I went down to stay with some friends at the little fishing village of Rafiel in Glebeshire.

I saw him just before I left London, and he told me that he was going to stay in London for the first half of August, that he liked London in August, even though his club would be closed and Horton's delivered over to the painters.

I heard nothing about him for a fortnight, and then I received a most extraordinary letter from Box Hamilton, a fellow clubman of mine and Wilbraham's. Had I heard, he said, that poor old Wilbraham had gone right off his "knocker"? Nobody knew exactly what had happened, but suddenly one day at lunch time Wilbraham had turned up at Grey's (the club to which our own club was a visitor during its cleaning), had harangued every one about religion in the most extraordinary way, had burst out from there and started shouting in Piccadilly, had, after collecting a crowd, disappeared and not been seen until the next morning, when he had been found, nearly killed, after a hand-to-hand fight with the market men in Covent Garden.

It may be imagined how deeply this disturbed me, especially as I felt that I was myself to blame. I had noticed that Wilbraham was ill when I had seen him in

London, and I should either have persuaded him to come with me to Glebeshire or stayed with him in London. I was just about to pack up and go to town when I received a letter from a doctor in a nursing home in South Audley street saying that a certain Major Wilbraham was in the home dying and asking persistently for myself. I took a motor to Drymouth and was in London by five o'clock.

I found the South Audley Street nursing home and was at once surrounded with the hush, the shaded rooms, the scents of medicine and flowers, and some undefinable cleanliness that belongs to those places.

I waited in a little room, the walls decorated with sporting prints, the green baize table gloomily laden with volumes of Punch and the Tatler. Wilbraham's doctor came in to see me, a dapper, smart little man, efficient and impersonal. He told me that Wilbraham had at most only twenty-four hours to live, that his brain was quite clear, and that he was suffering very little pain, that he had been brutally kicked in the stomach by some man in the Covent Garden crowd and had there received the internal injuries from which he was now dying.

"His brain is quite clear," the doctor said. "Let him talk. It can do him no harm. Nothing can save him. His head is full of queer fancies; he wants every one to listen to him. He's worrying because there's some message he wants to send... he wants to give it to you."

When I saw Wilbraham he was so little changed that I felt no shock. Indeed, the most striking change in him was the almost exultant happiness in his voice and eyes.

It is true that after talking to him a little I knew that he was dying. He had that strange peace and tranquillity of mind that one saw so often with dying men in the war.

I will try to give an exact account of Wilbraham's narrative; nothing else is of importance in this little story but that narrative; I can make no comment. I have no wish to do so. I only want to pass it on as he begged me to do.

"If you don't believe me," he said, "give other people the chance of doing so. I know that I am dying. I want as many men and women to have a chance of judging this as is humanly possible. I swear to you that I am telling the truth and the exact truth in every detail."

I began my account by saying that I was not convinced. How could I be convinced?

At the same time I have none of those explanations with which people are so generously forthcoming on these occasions. I can only say that I do not think Wilbraham was insane, nor drunk, nor asleep. Nor do I believe that some one played a practical joke....

Whether Wilbraham was insane between the hours when his visitor left him and his entrance into the nursing home I must leave to my readers. I myself think he was not.

After all, everything depends upon the relative importance that we place upon ambitions, possessions, emotions, - ideas.

Something suddenly became of so desperate an

importance to Wilbraham that nothing else at all mattered. He wanted every one else to see the importance of it as he did. That is all....

It had been a hot and oppressive day; London had seemed torrid and uncomfortable. The mere fact that Oxford street was "up" annoyed him. After a slight meal in his flat he went to the Promenade Concert at Queen's Hall. It was the second night of the season - Monday night, Wagner night.

He bought himself a five shilling ticket and sat in the middle of the balcony overlooking the floor. He was annoyed again when he discovered that he had been given a ticket for the "non-smoking" section of the balcony.

He had heard no Wagner since August, 1914, and was anxious to discover the effect that hearing it again would have upon him. The effect was disappointing. The music neither caught nor held him.

"The Meistersinger" had always been a great opera for him. The third act music that Sir Henry Wood gave to him didn't touch him anywhere. He also discovered that six years' abstinence had not enraptured him any more deeply with the rushing fiddles in the "Tannhäuser" Overture nor with the spinning music in the "Flying Dutchman." Then came suddenly the prelude to the third act of "Tristan." That caught him; the peace and tranquillity that he needed lapped him round; he was fully satisfied and could have listened for another hour.

He walked home down Regent Street, the quiet melancholy of the shepherd's pipe accompanying him, pleasing him and tranquillizing him. As he reached his flat ten o'clock struck from St. James' Church. He asked the porter whether any one had wanted him during his absence - whether any one was waiting for him now - (some friend had told him that he might come up and use his spare room one night that week). No, no one had been. There was no one there waiting.

Great was his surprise, therefore, when opening the door of his flat he found some one standing there, one hand resting on the table, his face turned towards the open door. Stronger, however, than Wilbraham's surprise was his immediate conviction that he knew his visitor well, and this was curious because the face was, undoubtedly strange to him.

"I beg your pardon," Wilbraham said to him, hesitating.

"I wanted to see you," the Stranger said, smiling.

When Wilbraham was telling me this part of his story he seemed to be enveloped - "enveloped" is the word that best conveys my own experience of him - by some quite radiant happiness. He smiled at me confidentially as though he were telling me something that I had experienced with him and that must give me the same happiness that it gave to him.

"Ought I to have expected? Ought I to have known -" he stammered.

"No, you couldn't have known," the Stranger answered. "You're not late. I knew when you would come."

Wilbraham told me that during these moments he was surrendering himself to an emotion and intimacy and companionship that was the most wonderful thing that he had ever known. It was that intimacy and companionship, he told me, for which all his days he had been searching. It was the one thing that life never seemed to give; even in the greatest love, the deepest friendship, there was that seed of loneliness hidden. He had never found it in man or woman.

Now it was so wonderful that the first thing he said was: "And now you're going to stay, aren't you? You won't go away at once...?"

"Of course, I'll stay," he answered. "If you want me."

His Visitor was dressed in some dark suit; there was nothing about Him in any way odd or unusual. His Face was thin and pale, His smile kindly.

His English was without accent. His voice was soft and very melodious.

But Wilbraham could notice nothing but His Eyes; they were the most beautiful, tender, gentle Eyes that he had ever seen in any human being.

They sat down. Wilbraham's overwhelming fear was lest his Guest should leave him. They began to talk and Wilbraham took it at once as accepted that his Friend knew all about him - everything.

He found himself eagerly plunging into details of scenes, episodes that he had long put behind him - put behind him for shame perhaps or for regret or for sorrow. He knew at once that there was nothing that he

Edward J. O'Brien and John Cournos

need veil nor hide - nothing. He had no sense that he must consider susceptibilities nor avoid self-confession that was humiliating.

But he did find, as he talked on, a sense of shame from another side creep towards him and begin to enclose him. Shame at the smallness, meanness, emptiness of the things that he declared.

He had had always behind his mistakes and sins a sense that he was a rather unusually interesting person; if only his friends knew everything about him they would be surprised at the remarkable man that he really was. Now it was exactly the opposite sense that came over him. In the gold-rimmed mirror that was over his mantlepiece he saw himself diminishing, diminishing, diminishing ... First himself, large, red-faced, smiling, rotund, lying back in his chair; then the face shrivelling, the limbs shortening, then the face small and peaked, the hands and legs little and mean, then the chair enormous about and around the little trembling animal cowering against the cushion.

He sprang up.

"No, no ... I can't tell you any more - and you've known it all so long. I am mean, small, nothing - I have not even great ambition ... nothing."

His Guest stood up and put His Hand on his shoulder.

They talked, standing side by side, and He said some things that belonged to Wilbraham alone, that he would not tell me.

Wilbraham asked Him why He had come - and to him.

"I will come now to a few of My friends," He said. "First one and then another. Many people have forgotten Me behind My words. They have built up such a mountain over Me with the doctrines they have attributed to Me, the things that they say that I did. I am not really," He said laughing, His Hand on Wilbraham's shoulder, "so dull and gloomy and melancholy as they have made Me. I loved Life - I loved men; I loved laughter and games and the open air - I liked jokes and good food and exercise. All things that they have forgotten. So from now I shall come back to one or two.... I am lonely when they see Me so solemnly."

Another thing He said. "They are making life complicated now. To lead a good life, to be happy, to manage the world only the simplest things are needed - Love, Unselfishness, Tolerance."

"Can I go with You and be with You always?" Wilbraham asked.

"Do you really want that?" He said.

"Yes," said Wilbraham, bowing his head.

"Then you shall come and never leave Me again. In three days from now."

Then he kissed Wilbraham on the forehead and went away.

I think that Wilbraham himself became conscious as he told me this part of his story of the difference between the seen and remembered Figure and the foolish, inadequate reported words. Even now as I repeat a little of what Wilbraham said I feel the virtue and power slipping away.

And so it goes on! As the Figure recedes the words become colder and colder and the air that surrounds them has in it less and less of power. But on that day when I sat beside Wilbraham's bed the conviction in his voice and eyes held me so that although my reason kept me back my heart told me that he had been in contact with some power that was a stronger force than anything that I myself had ever known.

But I have determined to make no personal comment on this story. I am here simply as a narrator of fact....

Wilbraham told me that after his Visitor left him he sat there for some time in a dream. Then he sat up, startled, as though some voice, calling, had wakened him, with an impulse that was like a fire suddenly blazing up and lighting the dark places of his brain. I imagine that all Wilbraham's impulses in the past, chivalric, idealistic, foolish, had been of that kind - sudden, of an almost ferocious energy and determination, blind to all consequences. He must go out at once and tell every one of what had happened to him.

I once read a story somewhere about some town that was expecting a great visitor. Everything was ready, the banners hanging, the music prepared, the crowds waiting in the street.

A man who had once been for some years at the court of the expected visitor saw him enter the city, sombrely clad, on foot. Meanwhile his Chamberlain entered the town in full panoply with the trumpets blowing and many riders in attendance. The man who knew the real thing ran to every one telling the truth, but they laughed at him and refused to listen. And the real king departed quietly as he had come.

It was, I suppose, an influence of this kind that drove Wilbraham now. Suddenly something was of so great an importance to him that nothing else, mockery, hostility, scorn, counted. After all, simply a supreme example of the other impulses that had swayed him throughout his life.

What followed might I think have been to some extent averted had his appearance been different. London is a home of madmen and casually permits any lunacy so that public peace is not endangered; had poor Wilbraham looked a fanatic with pale face, long hair, ragged clothes, much would have been forgiven him, but for a stout, middle-aged gentleman, well dressed, well groomed.... What could be supposed but insanity and insanity of a very ludicrous kind?

He put on his coat and went out. From this moment his account was confused. His mind, as he spoke to me, kept returning to that Visitor... What happened after his Friend's departure was vague and uncertain to him, largely because it was unimportant. He does not know what time it was when he went out, but I gather that it must have been about midnight. There were still people in Piccadilly.

Somewhere near the Berkeley Hotel he stopped a gentleman and a lady. He spoke, I am sure, so politely that the man he addressed must have supposed that he was asking for a match, or an address, or something of the kind. Wilbraham told me that very quietly he asked the gentleman whether he might speak to him for a moment, that he had something very important to say.

That he would not, as a rule, dream of interfering in any man's private affairs, but that the importance of his communication outweighed all ordinary conventions; that he expected that the gentleman had hitherto, as had been his own case, felt much doubt about religious questions, but that now all doubt was, once and forever, over, that...

I expect that at that fatal word "Religion" the gentleman started as though he had been stung by a snake, felt that this mild-looking man was a dangerous lunatic and tried to move away. It was the lady with him, so far as I can discover, who cried out:

"Oh, poor man, he's ill," and wanted at once to do something for him. By this time a crowd was beginning to collect and as the crowd closed around the central figures more people gathered upon the outskirts and, peering through, wondered what had happened, whether there was an accident, whether it were a "drunk," whether there had been a quarrel, and so on.

Wilbraham, I fancy, began to address them all, telling them his great news, begging them with desperate urgency to believe him. Some laughed, some stared in wide-eyed wonder, the crowd was increasing and then, of course, the inevitable policeman with his "move on, please," appeared.

How deeply I regret that Wilbraham was not, there and then, arrested. He would be alive and with us now if that had been done. But the policeman hesitated, I suppose, to arrest any one as obviously a gentleman as Wilbraham, a man, too, as he soon perceived, who was perfectly sober, even though he was not in his right mind.

Wilbraham was surprised at the policeman's interference. He said that the last thing that he wished to do was to create any disturbance, but that he could not bear to let all these people go to their beds without giving them a chance of realizing first that everything was now altered, that he had the most wonderful news..

The crowd was dispersed and Wilbraham found himself walking alone with the policeman beside the Green Park.

He must have been a very nice policeman because before Wilbraham's death he called at the Nursing Home and was very anxious to know how the poor gentleman was getting on.

He allowed Wilbraham to talk to him and then did all he could to persuade him to walk home and go to bed. He offered to get him a taxi. Wilbraham thanked him, said he would do so, and bade him good night, and the policeman, seeing that Wilbraham was perfectly composed and sober, left him.

After that the narrative is more confused. Wilbraham apparently walked down Knightsbridge and arrived at last somewhere near the Albert Hall. He must have spoken to a number of different people. One man, a politician apparently, was with him for a considerable time, but only because he was so anxious to emphasise his own views about the Coalition Government and the wickedness of Lloyd George. Another was a journalist, who continued with him for a while because he scented a story for his newspaper. Some people may remember that there was a garbled paragraph about a "Religious Army Officer" in the *Daily Record*. One lady thought that Wilbraham wanted to go home with her and was both angry and relieved when she found that it was not so.

He stayed at a cabman's shelter for a time and drank a cup of coffee and told the little gathering there his news. They took it very calmly. They had met so many queer things in their time that nothing seemed odd to them.

His account becomes clearer again when he found himself a little before dawn in the park and in the company of a woman and a broken down pugilist. I saw both these persons afterwards and had some talk with them. The pugilist had only the vaguest sense of what had happened. Wilbraham was a "proper old bird" and had given him half a crown to get his breakfast with. They had all slept together under a tree and he had made some rather voluble protests because the other two would talk so continuously and prevented his sleeping. It was a warm night and the sun had come up behind the trees "surprisin' quick." He had liked the old boy, especially as he had given him half a crown.

The woman was another story. She was quiet and reserved, dressed in black, with a neat little black hat with a green feather in it. She had yellow fluffy hair and bright childish blue eyes and a simple, innocent expression. She spoke very softly and almost in a whisper. So far as I could discover she could see nothing odd in Wilbraham nor in anything that he had said. She was the one person in all the world who had understood him completely and found nothing out of the way in his talk.

She had liked him at once, she said. "I could see that he was kind," she added earnestly, as though to her that was the most important thing in all the world. No, his talk had not seemed odd to her. She had believed every word that he had said. Why not? You could not look at him and not believe what he said.

Of course it was true. And why not? What was there against it? It had been a great help for her what the gentleman had told her... Yes, and he had gone to sleep with his head in her lap... and she had stayed awake all night thinking... and he had waked up just in time to see the sun rise. Some sunrise that was, too.

That was a curious little fact that all three of them, even the battered pugilist, should have been so deeply struck by that sunrise. Wilbraham on the last day of his life, when he hovered between consciousness and unconsciousness, kept recalling it as though it had been a vision.

"The sun - and the trees suddenly green and bright like glittering swords. All shapes - swords, plowshares, elephants, and camels - and the sky pale like ivory. See, now the sun is rushing up, faster than ever, to take us with him, up, up, leaving the trees like green clouds beneath us - far, far beneath us -"

The woman said that it was the finest sunrise she had ever seen. He talked to her all the time about his plans. He was looking disheveled now and unshaven and dirty. She suggested that he should go back to his flat. No, he wished to waste no time. Who knew how long he had got? It might be only a day or two ... He would

Edward J. O'Brien and John Cournos

go to Covent Garden and talk to the men there.

She was confused as to what happened after that. When they got to the market the carts were coming in and men were very busy.

She saw the gentleman speak to one of them very earnestly, but he was busy and pushed him aside. He spoke to another, who told him to clear out.

Then he jumped on to a box, and almost the last sight she had of him was his standing there in his soiled clothes, a streak of mud on his face, his arms outstretched and crying: "It's true! Stop just a moment - you *must* hear me!"

Some one pushed him off the box. The pugilist rushed in then, cursing them and saying that the man was a gentleman and had given him half a crown, and then some hulking great fellow fought the pugilist and there was a regular mêlée. Wilbraham was in the middle of them, was knocked down and trampled upon. No one meant to hurt him, I think. They all seemed very sorry afterwards....

He died two days after being brought into the Nursing Home. He was very happy just before he died, pressed my hand and asked me to look after the girl....

"Isn't it wonderful," were his last words to me, "that it should be true after all?"

As to Truth, who knows? Truth is a large order. This *is* true as far as Wilbraham goes, every word of it. Beyond that? Well, it must be jolly to be so happy as Wilbraham was.

This will seem a lying story to some, a silly and pointless story to others.

I wonder....

Edward J. O'Brien and John Cournos

www.ingramcontent.com/pod-product-compliance
Lightning Source LLC
Chambersburg PA
CBHW020828030726
47496CB00001B/143